An Intergalactic Christmas

EJT

Written By: -

Emma Jayne Taylor

(EJT)

Disclaimer

This is a work of fiction. All names, characters, locations, events, businesses, incidents, are either the products of the author's imagination or used in a fictitious manner. Any resemblance to actual persons, living or dead or actual events is purely coincidental.

Any public agencies, institutions or historical figures or locations mentioned in the story serve as a backdrop to the characters and their actions, which are completely imaginary.

This book or parts thereof may not be reproduced in any form, stored in any retrieval system or transmitted in any form by any means – electronic, mechanical, photocopying, recording, digital or otherwise – without prior written permission of the publisher, author, or agent.

All copyrights belong to the author, Emma Jayne Taylor (EJT).

All rights reserved.

ISBN: 9798346141372

Copyright © 2024 Emma Jayne Taylor

Cover Illustration Copyright © Fiverr

Was it worth it?
                The discovery?
                                The experimentation?
                                                        The rush?

I guess, in many ways, it *was*!

Here I was, on the ground, knowing that the blood was creeping out faster than there was any time for any last word or action.

At first, I didn't want to let things fall into the wrong hands, but a bigger picture was unfolding. The mind was fading, and a new view of light was forming in front of my eyes. Was this the afterlife? I guess I was about to find out. I could still hear, but everything otherwise felt paralysed. It was time to accept the final curtain. It seemed a peaceful process despite the cause. Thoughts were still churning through my mind – those such as how this death would appear in the newspapers, and who would miss me the most. The secret may be released, and the world *might* change forever. It's a shame I wouldn't get to see the next chapter. Or would I? Knowing what I know? Either way, I played my part... I had an amazing time. My final thoughts weren't as bad as people may have expected.

I could tell the body was literally drained of everything. I thought I heard somebody call my name, almost in a whisper, and then... nothingness... at least for now.

Present Time

Ethan Taylor was trying to unload the boxes quickly at his new home in Wiltshire, England. His brother, Tom, was at hand, trying to aid with additional speed. It was the eighth time within four years that Ethan had moved into rented property - this time stating that it was in the right location to settle into, with his partner, Rachel. They were trialling this big move before deciding on a potential marriage in the not-too-distant future. Tom always thought that Ethan was the scatter-brained, unsettled type, which was evident in the multiple house-moves that *appeared* unnecessary. Tom was always there to aid despite his opinion – always out to help his brother. Besides, Rachel always caught his eye, making him soft and pliable when his help was needed.

The three of them managed to empty the van-load and erect the all-important bed, sofa, and television, all in good time for an evening meal.
Agreeably, they all settled to a well-earnt rest on the sofa with an ordered pizza and spot of entertainment. Tom secretly hoped for a swift escape to his own home, but patiently enjoyed his food until the appropriate time.
They all sat with weary bodies and heavy eyelids, feeling successful with their accomplishments.
Rachel was the first to fall into a nodding head and light sleep.
Tom fought the fatigue and told them that he needed to get back to his own bed. He stood politely with a mild stretch.
"Stay the night." Rachel added as she woke to his decisive words.
If only Rachel knew of his secret admiration - or perhaps it was better that she didn't!
"Oh, and where would I sleep exactly?"

Ethan looked on with a cheeky smile and patted the sofa as a gesture.
Rachel realised it wasn't the most rewarding offer after his laboured efforts.
"Thanks, but I really don't think my back would appreciate such soft furnishings." He grinned.
Ethan stood to offer a kind goodbye wish, and a slow, joint walk to the front door. Boxes were stacked kindly against the walls, leaving a nice walk-way.
The brothers gave a hardy, patty-hug, underlyingly appreciating one another.

Tom knew he was blurry-eyed, but he felt focussed enough to take the fifteen-minute drive back to his humble abode which sat back from some quiet country roads. He was grateful for his tucked-away home when he needed to retreat for a good rest.

On his journey, the road seemed extra dark, which he blamed on his weary eyes.
He approached a tight corner and decided to slow down more than usual, holding more caution.
The roads were otherwise empty, much to his preference at this time.
As he approached a familiar, straight stretch, his eyes were suddenly hit by an immense light! He questioned this within the milli-second of time that he had to think about it. The light was a huge, unexplainable ball, that instantly blinded him! He hit the brakes as hard as he could, knowing that he was still headed in a straight direction, having taken this road so many times before.
As the light hit him, time appeared to stand still. He folded an arm over his eyes, feeling that the car should have stopped moving at this point. Thoughts of activating the hazard lights came to him, but when he allowed his eyes to refocus, he noticed that his car

had blended in with this immense light! Everything felt as if it had lifted, as we would assume lack of gravity to feel.
Consumed by this intense light and lack of gravity, he slowly caught view of everything, including himself, floating in what felt like a timeless state. He captured the moment to be like floating in a huge white ball, staring into vague images, like a huge television screen before him. It didn't make sense, but his instant assumption was that he had passed away somehow. This didn't *feel* like any kind of *heaven*ly place to Tom, but there was no other explanation with this event. He *thought* he heard the name of his brother whispered into the back of his head, but he couldn't confirm this, given the confused state. Gripping the driver's seat with both hands and looking in all directions – he literally felt out of this world!

Before he had time to comprehend what had occurred, he was suddenly thrown back into the force of his own bodyweight, the normal construction of the car, and dark road ahead. Everything returned to normality, with his two usual headlights holding focus on the familiar images.
He couldn't explain it... It wasn't normal!
He caught his breath, looking around, feeling calmer than he *should* have felt, considering. He looked outward, followed by a brief study of the car internals. Everything seemed fine, other than a small glimmer of blue light shining on the passenger carpet that he couldn't quite make out. He reached out to attempt to pick up whatever was there. It appeared to be solid initially. Tom realised he was touching a shiny, blue and white stone. The stone glimmered, and he swore he heard the whisper of his brother's name fall into the back of his head - again! He dropped the stone in a slight panic, but as it fell, it dispersed, disappearing into thin air!
Tom was now wishing for these unusual events to end so that he could find a moment to catch-up with his mind. He sat in the same

spot for several minutes, realising he *truly* needed to switch the hazard lights on for anyone approaching. There was a moment where he bravely walked out onto the road to check around for logical reasoning, but everything was exactly as it always was on this "patch." He had spent much time cycling, driving, and walking through the same road for years without any event.

After a long wait with observations, he confirmed normality. He felt brave enough to drive home, trying to comprehend what had just happened.

October 15, 1860

Edward was writing in his diary, occasionally struggling for a smooth ink-run. He needed to keep daily track of his sales. The table had scattered pieces of silver, thread, and small gemstones.

His regular customer, Mrs Phelps, came in through the front door of the shop, forcing a jingle of the homemade door chime for Edward's attention.

"Good morning Mrs Phelps!" His tone was professionally welcoming, with a personalised feel.

"Hello young Edward," was her usually predictable reply, "How is one doing this fine morning?"

Edward found that the end of the ink wasn't running smoothly again, allowing a wasted scraping of his valuable paper.

"Well, it's a beautiful morning, so I need to be chirping with the birds."

Mrs. Phelps didn't *always* care for small talk but retained some form of polite "opening" to her visit. Edward always recognised her change of behaviour when she found an item of her desire. He watched her intentions, waiting for her keen eye to fall on one of his latest creations.

The door chime noise fell upon his ears again, much to his surprise. An unknown visitor steadily walked in. His eyes fell on a wonderful flowing dress with an elegant walk guiding the material forward. He moved his eyes upward to notice a bottle-glass figure and glossy brown hair that seemed to blend in with the style of dress. This lady was elegant and extremely eye-catching.

"Perhaps *you* are the one shopping at this very time young Edward!" Mrs. Phelps couldn't help but comment on his gawping expression, perhaps demonstrating a small amount of jealousy.

Edward felt his cheeks warming with embarrassment, noting Mrs. Phelps slowly walking back to the front door empty-handed, but holding a knowing smile.
He returned his eyes to the captivating stranger who was now walking up and down the short isles, admiring his hand-made jewellery. Thankfully, this new guest hadn't paid attention to Mrs Phelp's embarrassing comments!
"Is there anything I can help you with, particularly ma'am?" His voice felt ridiculously shaky.
Her face turned to expose her extraordinary features. Glimmering eyes and porcelain skin portrayed a healthy life before him. When she parted her lips to speak, the tone felt like velvet to his ears.
"I am certain that I am fine, thank you."
In his peripherals, Edward noticed a figure at the front door. He turned his head to notice an older man waiting – assumingly her father – at least he *hoped* it was!
This elegant lady began her route to departure, disappointingly paying no attention to Edward on the way out. She left the shop, but as the door closed behind her, he felt an immense sense of loss. He wanted to approach her, but felt it was impossible with the waiting gentleman turning to ensure of her safe return to him.
Well, that was a huge boost of unexpected emotion first thing in the morning, he thought!
He looked down to notice some ink had dribbled onto the paper, ruining a couple of potential lines of useful listing. He moaned under his breath, just as the door opened to chime yet *another* visitor inward. Before he had chance to look up, he recognised the arm slap and cheeky behaviour of his greatest friend, William.
"Damn it, Edward, why do you get the most eye-popping dames visit your fancy jewels?"
Edward grinned, knowing that it didn't make any difference, since all he could ever do was look.
"Why aren't you at work yourself?"

"Ah, well you see, I have plenty of stock at the moment, so I can take it easy for a while. Fancy doing something fun when you shut the shop later today?"

"I've never known anyone successfully escape work quite like you. What idea did you have for later, may I ask?"

William leant on the desk, making himself comfortable in the surroundings.

"You know I have greater plans than simply collecting wood. Perhaps you could come and have a look at the trade I managed to pull together in the last few weeks."

Edward looked at William with a knowing smile, "I suppose it has been a while since our last deal. Do you have any plans this evening?"

William grinned broadly. "You mean you haven't made any plans with that beautiful lady?"

"I'm not like you. I can't speak to someone just like *that*."

Edward could see William plotting something in his mind.

"Well, how about one of your special *sales* to encourage her back? At the same time, we could let her know about this little event." William pointed to one of the posters in Edward's shop window, advertising a local ball.

"I don't even know how to approach that particular subject." Edward doubted in an instant.

"Oh, young gentleman! You do need to learn to become a little more confident within the lady department. Perhaps you could have a one-day sale event which I could be involved in, then in such case I could have a conversation with her and gently introduce you. Would that be agreeable with you?"

Edward grinned with a slight displeasure. "Your plan is cunning, but it may help. She is perhaps the most beautiful lady I have ever set eyes upon. The embarrassment I may endure however…"

"You do need to relax more my good friend!" William gathered himself together, preparing for an exit, "Shall I see you at my place

this evening in the meantime then? I have also prepared an amazing beverage that I am certain you will approve of."
Edward was very familiar with William's beverage preparations. This would involve the standard preparing of fruits in order to make and store an alcoholic beverage over a period of time. Sometimes William experimented with various options, which would taste disgusting, but they would suffer the consequences in order to entertain themselves with the slight intoxication. William was always creative with his ideas, but not always completely successful with the results. This brought immensely humorous moments to their already-strong friendship.

William departed the shop scene with pleasant goodbyes, leaving Edward to a slightly dulled day of an occasional shopper of minor items.
Edward sat for hours, creating new shop-product ideas, dreaming about finding a luxurious item of great value to sell in excess, allowing him the potential ability to purchase the most amazing home, only to fill it with loved ones.
He was known for his beautiful creations of jewellery pieces that came in the form of rings, necklaces, brooches, earrings, buttons, cufflinks, and then designs that sat on top of fancy-looking lanterns. His supply of gems allowed him the sale of engagement rings, wedding rings and then some simple dressy jewellery. His designs were respected locally, and quite often he would speak to someone who praised his work. Whenever he had the opportunity to attend a local party or gathering of any kind, there would be at least one person wearing something of his creation. He would usually spot it from a distance anyway. It was satisfactory to see, but he was never fully contented with his work role. He had a sporty side that needed satisfying, so he would often team up with the local young men for a game of football in the local fields. He was also quite a good boxer and trained in a spit-n-sawdust gymnasium only a short walk away from home. William

occasionally popped in to watch him after work, picking up a few tips without getting physically involved.

Edward decided to shut the shop early and head over to William's after the offer of a beverage and a view of his latest business deals. Both Edward and William enjoyed their single lives, but in this day and age, they were pressed for time to settle into a courtship that would typically turn to a partnership in marriage. They both felt the pressure but enjoyed their youth together. They often discussed their vow to retain their friendship even when both of them found their life partners.

It was a beautiful October day, so Edward walked with his tie undone and shirt unbuttoned at the top. William's house could be seen in the distance, ending a long, cobbled road.
As he approached, the front door was already opening with William's observational eyes.
"Why, hello! It's good to see you!"
Their usual back-slapping hug occurred before William stepped back to allow entry.
They both walked to a back room, which was where William's items of interest always sat on an old solid table. The table always looked cluttered and disorganised.
William threw Edward an apple, which landed well into his palm with instantly-gripping fingers.
"So, take a view at these beautiful items." William had a few gems and crystals collected on his table. He shuffled them around, spreading them across a wider space. There were so many different colours available to their eyes. Edward wanted every single one of them.
"What do you think?" William enticed.
"Well, they are *all* so amazing to look at."
"You know I'll do you a good deal, so tell me how many you wish to take."

Edward thought for a few moments, weighing up what items he could use and sell well.

"How much for *all* of them?"

"Well," William wasn't surprised, "I was going to make an unusual deal with you this time."

"Go on..." Edward's tone was curious.

"I wish to have a gentleman and lady wedding ring made with your finest silver created for me."

"Are you...? Edward didn't finish his sentence.

"Not yet. I just wish to prepare for the future, and it seems a good time with all of the parties we're getting invited to. I have a wonderful feeling. I have my mother's engagement ring that I plan to use on the right lady."

Edward raised his eyebrows, surprised at the words he heard.

"Well, it seems a very good deal to *me*. I have a good amount of purchased silver at the moment, so with these gems I could create my greatest works." He brushed his hand over the colourful mixture of shapes and sizes.

William seemed excited, picking up a heavy sack to place them in.

"When do you receive your next trade then?" Edward was supplied for many months already with this regular agreement but couldn't help but ask.

"They've given me a date that I have written down somewhere, but I cannot remember off hand. I shall check and let you know when I think of it."

William cleared the table of the glimmering items and handed the heavy bag to his friend.

Edward grew excited with the prospects of creative profit.

William poured two glasses of his latest creation of drink for them to enjoy.

They moved, with the bag of gems, to a seating area, and gave off relaxed sighs, predicting a calm evening of one another's company. Edward took a sip of the drink and nearly gagged with the strong taste. William laughed with such mischievousness, but they both continued to drink it, knowing it would bring the merriness they craved.

William was always able to acquire the mass of gems in exchange for a generous payment from Edward, feeding one another with a comfortable income.
William supplied his gem provider with wood, which the supplier always seemed to be in desperate need of. It wasn't William's interest as to why they wanted wood. He was always extremely happy to make the easy trade.

William lit a large candle for the two of them to relax to, enjoying the feeling of the drink.

Present Time

Tom woke to a sudden start, recalling the recent event that simply couldn't be explained.

He slowly picked himself up after the night of deep sleep, to get himself showered and dressed.

He decided to head over to his brother's new home to see if he could aid with setting some of the furniture up. He wanted to feel useful with a good distraction and an innocent glance at Rachel's natural beauty to brighten up his day.

Tom had a non-eventful drive over to Ethan's, but the energy appeared to feel manic once he had arrived. Rachel was throwing cushions together rapidly, and Ethan had heavy music on, trying to fix some cupboards in the kitchen. One of their friends had arrived to help too. Her task seemed to be cleaning up the work surfaces with her young daughter.

Tom wasn't sure his appearance was useful, despite knowing many hands make light work.

His brother spotted him however, with a very appreciative expression, "Tom!"

He smiled and felt better about his decision to help.

Ethan handed a screwdriver to his hand. "I just can't undo this one."

The friend asked if anyone wanted a drink. Tom looked over to notice that she was actually very attractive to his eyes. He tried to hide his observations.

Divorced at the tender age of twenty eight, he knew he had plenty of time but felt keen to settle down again. Two years of being single felt like a lifetime already.

"Oh, sorry!" Rachel suddenly spoke up, "I didn't introduce you to Megan. Megan, this is Tom, and Tom, this is Megan and her little lady, Sky."
Rachel gestured kindly with an interesting look in her eyes. Tom attempted to read her expression - perhaps incorrectly. It was easy for him to assume a deliberate participation for a "coincidental" arrangement. He decided to ignore the possibility in order to avoid the likelihood of awkwardness. He reached toward Megan for the offer a gentle handshake, which was reciprocated, thankfully. He then followed with a gentle wave to the young Sky, who stood slightly behind Megan's legs in shyness.

"Do you have any beers hanging around?" Tom assumed not, despite the question.
Rachel lifted a surprise box of cans from one end of the kitchen to sit in Tom's eyeline.
"Are you serious?" Tom smiled.
"Help yourself. Self-control if you're driving though!"
"Wow! Just one." He felt in to pull one free.
"Already?" Ethan was surprised, "What's with you?"
Tom smiled, opening a can for a swift sip, then switched focus to the screwdriver for the intentional assistance.

The men worked on fixing up the kitchen cupboards and re-attaching some hefty wooden legs to a very large dining-room table. Working together gave them comfortable bonding time.
"I love this area Tom. There's a lot to investigate. It's not too far from some amazing hills and interesting history." Ethan sounded unusually mature. Perhaps some caution for what the ladies may catch the sound of.
"Yeah, it's like that around here. You're making me realise I don't venture out much in my own zone."

"I never thought I'd like looking at historical stuff, but I started noticing things and wondering what they were. When you start delving it seems to open up more and more questions."
"Wow, you're starting to sound like our parents."
"Shit, don't say that." He punched Tom on the arm in jest.
"I must admit, I'm glad you moved more this way. Maybe we could investigate things together a lot more."
"It's gotta be done now. Let's promise ourselves."

The men worked merrily on putting the various furniture parts together, whilst the ladies worked on the cleaning and emptying of some boxes. Rachel took the initiative to entertain Sky with a small chair in front of the television. Once the right channel caught her eyes, she was hooked.
The day was a pleasing, sociable adventure. It was amazing to see the home take shape with success, based around fun.

Tom didn't particularly want to leave once the sunlight began to fade and the hunger of the pending evening meal began to kick in. There were no offers of food ideas however, and Megan began to speak words of departure. The abrupt memory of his previous drive home triggered his mind. He realised that he must've been stood still in thought when Rachel called his name more than twice.
"Earth to Tom!"
He spun to eyes boring into the side of his head.
"Ah, there *is* life in the spaceman."
Tom smiled, apologising for being deep in thought, then began collecting his movements for departure.
"I'd better go." Tom collected his keys, phone, and wallet, and turned his attention initially to Megan, "It was nice to meet you and Sky. Thanks for helping the crazy bunch."

"I hope we get to see you again." Megan gave him a good view of wide, sparkly eyes. Her personality appeared strong and confident.

In the meantime, everyone gave very thankful goodbye messages, both verbally and in the form of hugs. Tom found himself walking towards his car with Megan, and Sky only a footstep behind. He noted their large family car and questioned her marital status, in his mind. Megan gave a kind smile as she aided Sky into the back seat. He realised that he could easily be miss-reading a naturally friendly disposition, so decided to forget that any creative, deliberate set-up was designed by Ethan or Rachel. His feelings on relationships were still tender, and he needed to focus on a safe drive home at this time.

Tom managed to get home event-free much to his relief. He fell into his sofa to relax fully for the night.

October 16, 1860

The morning came to find William and Edward in a deep sleep not too far from one another in the sitting room. The furniture wasn't particularly comfortable, but they wouldn't have noticed in their intoxicated state.
Edward was always the first to rise from the deep sleep state that they occasionally found themselves in. He sat up into a slumped position and slowly pushed himself up into a standing position. It didn't take much effort to get his legs working, finding himself rinsing his face in the kitchen basin, slurping some water from his cupped hands.
William's voice gave him a huge fright.
"I do have cups you know."
Edward spun his head, "I know, it just felt nice to do."
They noticed one another's heavy eyelids and knew it was well deserved.
"Let me put some food together." William encouraged as he gradually pulled *himself* together.
Edward was encouraged to move over to the kitchen table with a gentle nudge on the shoulder.
"I think I am quite on form this fine morning, considering."
William's words didn't match his appearance, leaving Edward less convinced of his optimism.
William appeared to be quite swift in producing them both the most delicious display of breakfast options. Edward was left impressed. They both devoured the entirety in a relaxed and gradual time, and sat back in their chairs, feeling extremely satisfied. Edward admitted the food had pretty much cured him of a sluggish hangover feeling. After some gentle chats, Edward stood to prepare for departure, giving gratitude to his friend, and exchanging hugs.

In his recovery state he almost forgot to collect his big bag of gems on the way out. He looked out to the corner of the room in which it was left, and he needed to take a double glance for something that was glimmering so brightly. William noticed his altered expression, so looked in the same direction.
"Can you see that light coming from the bag Will? Or am I still in a drunken state?"
They both stood with an ongoing stare.
"I surely can. Shall I take a look inside?"
William walked over to the bag to investigate, crouching down, unfolding the material to note one of the larger gems shining immensely. He looked over at the light from the window to attempt to make sense of it.
"Can you see what it is Will?" Edward simply didn't want to crowd him.
He tilted his head, "I can see that it's one of the gems but wondering if it is normal for it to shine in the way that it is."
Edward decided that he needed to join in on the view.
They both stared for a few moments, trying to make logical sense of it.
William reached in and took hold of the shiny stone which was big enough to sit in most of the palm of his hand. It still shone too brightly to make sense. A small piece of it broke away, so he placed that small part on the side of the table for the meantime and focussed on the large part which continued to shine immensely.
"What is this all about?" His face was that of complete confusion. Edward was just as close, frowning with similar thoughts.
William turned the stone to look at it from different directions, as Edward looked on with equal curiosity for answers.
"It is brighter than the brightest candle." Edward said with excitement, "Shall we place it on the table for a while and see if it remains the same?"

William didn't reply, but instantly responded with the suggested action.

They both sat, staring at the light on the table, not knowing what their next course of action *should* be.

"Where do your men get hold of these gems from William?"

"I'm not entirely sure. I think I need to ask these questions during our next trade."

"I wonder why that one shines, and the others do not. I can see that it is a beautiful crystal. Should we be staring into such a bright light? It truly is too bright for our eyes."

"Perhaps there is something rather unique about it. Perhaps we could make a lot of money from this somehow."

They continued to stare.

"I don't know how we could possibly make money from it."

"Perhaps if we smash it into smaller particles, they may all illuminate in the same way. We could tell the people that it is brighter than candlelight. Each item could sell for a significant amount."

"We know nothing of this item Will. Perhaps we may study the item over a period of time to monitor the purpose. That small piece that came away from it does not shine in the same way. Perhaps smashing it into pieces might ruin it."

William looked up to meet Edward's eyes for the first time since their new discovery. They both then realised how the brightness had impacted their eyes.

"We have been staring continually at this bright light. It may not be best to do that."

Edward agreed but wondered what their next plan *should* be.

"How do we put it out do you think?" Will began to stare yet again whilst asking the question.

"I don't think there is a putting-out option." Edward began to see the humour of it all and erupted with laughter. "What is this all about? Did you perhaps make the drink unusually strong?"

William laughed in return, always picking up on his best friend's feelings.

"Do you think we are in some terrible state?"

They both laughed hard for a while, releasing all feelings of stress and shock.

William wiped the happy tears from his eyes, standing to prepare for an alternative scene.

"Why don't we leave it there for a day and night, and just see if the brightness calms?"

"Not a bad idea." Edward was grateful for the suggestion and stood with intention to revert to his plan of departure. "I should really be making my merry way."

"Oh, my goodness, we are both meant to be leaving for work shortly. What have we been thinking?"

"Well, I would say that our minds were well and truly shaken!"

They both walked towards William's front door, with Edward collecting his bag.

"I shall return at the end of the day then, unless of course you find reason to visit me in the shop once again."

"Okay Ed. Either way, I shall see you later." He gave Edward a pat on his shoulder.

The day had moved on...

Edward drank a lot of fluid that day, hoping to see the beautiful lady, even if he did sense a bit of extra ruggedness in his own appearance. He was beginning to desire less of William's drinking nights so that he could feel more functional at work. It seemed to affect his natural creativities.

As the day slowly and painfully came to a quiet ending, he looked at the posters on his door and window, considering William's cunning sale idea.

Just as Edward was locking up, William came running, almost slamming into the front door.
"Ed!" He was breathless, "you wouldn't believe what this stone is doing!"
Edward looked his friend up and down, trying to wake up to his startled behaviour after such a dreary day for himself.
"Come back to take a look. I don't even know if it is at all safe!"
Edward placed a reassuring hand on William's arm, "I'm sure it will be fine, but I just need to turn this key."

They were able to walk hurriedly back to William's home, already able to see some star-like rays shining through parts of the home as they approached.
Both of them were gazing with a startled expression.

When William opened his front door, the light was almost too intense to witness. They both lifted their hands to cover their eyes.
"I don't think we will even be able to approach this stone if it's too bright to get near." Edward had uncertainty in his voice.
"I believe we should try." William was determined to understand the occurrence.
As they grew near, William reached out to touch the stone.
"No don't!"
As soon as one of his little fingers touched the outer edge, the light instantly faded to leave the original appearance of a simple, yet interesting looking stone.
They both stood, dumbfounded.
Silence hit the room – both of them in their own confused thoughts.
Edward was the first to speak.

"You switched it off with your touch!"
William stood, staring at the stone, assuming another pending occurrence.
Edward was able to retain a calm mind, but William appeared slightly anxious.
"It's okay Will, look!"
Edward reached to pick the stone up in order to solidify his statement, but without a second's notice, Edward felt the most overwhelming tug, leaving William extremely shocked at what he witnessed!
An intense vacuum pulled him into the stone's size, as if separating every cell into individual particles. To William's eyes, he witnessed Edward transpiring into colourful, miniscule dust particles. The stone dropped with a heavy clang, almost instantly. William stood, shocked, noting the disappearance of his best friend!
He picked the stone up and shook it intensely, panicking and calling to Edward.
"Ed! What? Ed! Ed!"
The shock was intense, with no initial thought. He paced up and down the room, trying to make sense of what had just happened, waving his arms around to see if he could feel anything in the air.

After a few minutes of pacing with a numb mind, thoughts began to flood William: *What just happened?... Is Edward dead?... How could he explain his disappearance?... Why hasn't he, himself been sucked into the little stone?... What is this stone doing?... Where is Ed? Is this a dream?... What about the shop?... What about their joint life venture?*

William didn't know who to turn to for help. This wasn't an ordinary event to report to a doctor, and he needed to protect himself against any accusations of insanity.

He sat on one of his dining room chairs, holding his head in his hands, beginning to feel a rush of emotion. Tears flooded his palms. His friend had suddenly gone!
He wanted to figure out the puzzle. He wanted the people who traded these gems to appear right at this moment to answer some serious questions.
His feeling of being upset turned to anger and frustration. He held the gem in his hand, shaking it and begging it to release his friend. Those short few minutes of confusion and distress felt too long to comprehend. His mind raced; his emotions peaked and troughed. He decided that he needed to accept this situation and placed the gem on his dining room table. His thoughts felt cruel but necessary. There was nothing he could do to logically help. He knew that he needed to hide his grief and attempt to move on with ignorance but knew it would be hard – hard to move forward without his best friend.
He placed the gem back on the table, admitting defeat.
The stone made a heavy magnetic noise as he placed it on the table. The noise was enough to make him look at the stone with last hopes, but nothing appeared to occur.
As he looked away, he heard crackling noises of a static energy kind. This time he chose to ignore what he was hearing and stood to walk towards a large mirror that hung on his wall. He needed to check that his cheeks were clear of tears, with the intention to head outdoors for a head-clearing stroll. This was the only action he could think of. The brief time of shock seemed very long in his head.
Just as he thought he looked relatively okay in the mirror he noticed an unusual movement in the background. He jumped with a fresh fear inside, to note a figure appear from a bent-over position, rising to a full standing pose, gradually revealing the features of his friend! He spun to view a vague image forming, which progressively became clearer to appear more of a solid

form. Some particles were still magnifying back to the body from the stone.

"Edward!" William was beyond joy.

Relief, and a sense of calm filled his body at the sight of his returning friend.

Edward stood emotionless, not looking his usual character generally. His entire behaviour appeared to be completely different.

"Edward? Are you in there?"

William looked on, walking closer, meeting eyes.

"Ed! It looks as if you are switched off. Can you come back?"

He didn't know what to say otherwise as he observed his friend staring forward in a very straight-standing position.

Edward's eyes suddenly moved to the left corner, followed by the turning of his neck. He looked about, slightly dazed, landing his focus on William.

"Will, did I disappear from here?"

"Oh, thank goodness!" William's body fell into a greater sense of calm. He moved to sit on the nearest chair, feeling tears of relief welling up.

"I went somewhere Will! It was so different!" He looked down at his friend with concern, "but I was safe! I felt so safe!"

"I was so worried Ed! What the heck is going on here?" He looked at the stone and then returned his stares to Ed.

"Are you sure you are in a well state? Perhaps we should bury this stone somewhere. We should not take notice of it ever again!"

"Oh, no, no, no! Will, this could be something of an adventure. I think we were meant to find it. It fell into the right hands."

William studied Edward's face to notice a confident smile.

"So, so, please tell me exactly what you just experienced so that I may understand and feel the same way in which you *appear* to feel. All I could see was you disappearing into the stone somehow and then returning a few minutes later. It terrified me! Did it not terrify you? I thought you had left my world forever and I had no

idea how to cope. I tried to force a way to move on, but it was not true to our friendship."
Edward smiled broadly and knelt near his friend.
"Will, I feel amazing! It's all coming back to me swiftly! I went to this wonderful place and spent time getting to know some interesting characters and events."
"Getting to know some characters?" William looked at his large Grandfather Clock, "but you were only gone for about twenty minutes!"
"Twenty minutes, and you already left me for dead! The experience is very difficult to explain, but it felt very good. Let me sit with you for a moment to help you to relax."
"I had no idea how to cope my good friend. I realise how important you are to me." William studied his actions, hoping that his friend was truly okay.
Edward looked hard at the gem, noting its beauty. This stone was of a reasonable size – large enough to fill a closed palm and stood comfortably to form a tall structure with a solid foundation. This stone had the transparency of a clear Quartz but had a beautiful *blue* section of stone that wrapped comfortably around the main structure.
William noticed Edward's stare.
"You see Will, there is something extremely powerful about what has just occurred! This is a crystal that holds a lot of power that I do not fully understand. All that I know so far is that it can transform me and transport me. That is the only way I can describe what happened." He stared on, "I was just getting to know some of the parts when I felt a pull to return to this time."
"Transformed? This... time?" Will frowned.
"I went somewhere *else* Will. This place was most certainly ahead of our time. I feel I have picked up some information that I would not usually understand. It is difficult to explain to you, but I shall try."

"Well, how is it that you came to go to this place through a stone? And why would it be that you went to another time? Why would *you* be the one to disappear into another place?"

Edward looked extremely bright in his eyes. Excitement and adventure appeared to be in his mind.

William continued to study his friend, noting his new stare toward the stone.

"You are transfixed on the stone Ed. Is there a way in that *I* may travel to this place ahead of time? If it is as wonderful as you appear to describe."

"This is no ordinary stone. I do not know if many of us can use it in the same way. I was told that we both have a responsibility for it, but my memory of our purpose is unclear."

There was a pause for William to digest some of Edward's words. "Has your mind forgotten some of the experience? What kind of responsibility do you think we need for a *stone*? How do we know how to use this so-called crystal?" William reached out to touch Edward's forearm to feel for anything unusual, noting the temperature of his arm. "I was going to ask for more detail, but your arm has phased me. It feels hotter than I am sure it should be! Tell me where you went to, and what it was like, please, for my best understanding."

"I do not fully understand it Will. It is incredibly difficult to put to words."

"Well then allow me to do the same, somehow."

Edward stood, preparing to leave. "Allow me some time to digest the occurrences. I need to make some notes to make sense of it all."

"Okay, but I feel we are meddling with something particularly dangerous. Perhaps I need to discard this stone. Something doesn't seem right."

"Perhaps you are correct William. This may be some mixed-up magic."

William was concerned, as they mostly used one another's abbreviated names, which confirmed some altered or confused state of mind.

Edward walked towards the front door, almost robotically.
William observed his structure and actions, noting his slightly cold departure.
Their usual hug had been forgotten, leaving William feeling uncertain and slightly unnerved.
Did the same Edward return? Or was he altered in some way?

Present Time

Tom and Ethan had arranged to do some hill running local to the new home. They both felt invigorated on this relatively warm, sunny morning, so wanted to investigate the rolling green hills that had partly influenced Tom's choice of home relocation.

There was a slight mist running over the hills, almost as majestic as the appearance of some mountainous regions. They were running intermittently up the slight incline before approaching some steeper parts. Tom had the advantage of slightly longer legs, but Ethan had been running more frequently as of late. They had friendly competition with one another, pushing their limits with deep breaths and heavy leg muscles.
The occasional bird of prey flew overhead, allowing them both some visual admiration for nature.
Tom was the first to beg for a longer break in order to recover slightly.
In the distance they could see a couple of mountain bikers riding bumpily and swiftly over vast space.
"Maybe a go at *that* next time?" Tom said under his strained breath.
"Yeah!" Ethan struggled to say more.
They both strained up the steep incline.
"It's probably easier to run up this part to get it out the way." Ethan was keen to move along.
"Gimme just a few more breaths if you wanna help me live."
Ethan laughed slightly, trying to keep his breathing steadier.

They slowly, as if telepathically, began jogging again, picking up a relatively equal pace. Reaching the highest point, they plateaued for a while, allowing a more consistent jog.
Tom looked up, noting a structure.

"What's that up there?"
"Oh, that's a monument to mark the memory of someone I think."
"I guess we also need to start understanding them chalky white horses." Tom was referring to a historical white horse that had been marked out on the local hill.
"That's what I want to learn more about. Apparently there's a few of them white horses, all marked out. Can you see why I find the place interesting? I plan to find out a lot more about them."
"I guess I haven't paid too much attention to local history with work and my divorce."
"You gotta let all of that divorce crap go. Open your eyes to fun and living a bit more again."
"You're right. I am trying!"
Their breath grew slightly laboured again as they came to another slight incline. Tom slowed to a fast walking pace.
"Sorry man, I need to practice this hill stuff. Phew!" He couldn't speak any further for the heavy breathing.
"I'm with ya!" Ethan partly laughed as he grew deep breaths.
They both attempted to rebalance their breathing for the rest of the incline, walking with much effort. The aim appeared to be reaching the large, popular, structural monument that sat just before the turning hills that held the beautiful, chalk white horse feature.
As soon as they found their feet touching the circumference of the monument, they stood to gain their full recovery.
They looked out at the tremendous view, noting the mist settling enough to bring more clarity. The green hills rolled and folded into beautiful shapes.
Tom began looking closely at the monument itself, reading a sign that explained the structure.
"Hey, look at this," Tom pointed. "Interesting how this was built in memory of Sir William Petty. We should check out who this guy was."
Ethan smiled. "Ah, look at you getting all interested!"

Tom smiled, taking a good look at the surrounding parts.
"Hey! This is you!" Tom pointed to an inscription. "Is this E.Taylor, or E. Tayler?"
Ethan held his breath, noting the interesting coincidence. He looked, noting the same markings.
"E.Tayler, I think. Eighteen sixty one. Interesting."
Tom appeared to hold *more* interest, however, "We should definitely look into it."
"Do you think it's a genuine marking?"
Tom looked at Ethan's expression, noting his lesser interest. He observed his vision moving to other markings, not holding too much attention to the initial one.
Tom took a closer look at the marking again, still trying to detect whether the surname was written with an "e" or an "o."
Ethan noted his behaviour, wondering if he was building a slight obsession.
"I guess we can assume it's an interesting coincidence, hey. Fun though, since it's our first run together near my new place."
Tom was still interested in the inscription and decided to run his fingers along the words. He thought he noticed a swirl of gold colour moving under his finger.
"Ooh." He pulled away, still staring.
Ethan looked at Tom, "Maybe take a photo bro." Tom appeared to be transfixed.
Tom ran his fingers over the lettering again, just to see if he was imagining things, but just as he did it, a run of gold glittering-type of "whirl" followed his hand!
"What? That's so weird!...Can you see that Ethan?"
Ethan was growing bored. "I've already seen it. I think we should run up to that set of trees over there, then turn to head back. What do you reckon?"
"Hold on!" Tom began to run his fingers over the inscription yet again.

"What are you doing? Can we let it go now? As interesting as it is, it would be nice to get back for our nosh-up meal we've planned." Tom wanted to look at things a little more but realised Ethan wasn't experiencing the same thing. He looked at his brother, noting his slight frustration.
"Ah sorry. Let's stick to the plan." He closed the experience for now, looking back as he walked away. "Let's go!"
Tom decided he'd return in his own time, since this was so intriguing to him. He needed to understand the strange golden haze, particularly with the coincidental name.

Meanwhile, Rachel had promised her reputable breakfast to the two brothers, also including herself in on the indulgence. She expected their planned return at around ten A.M.
Some baked beans were the last offer to the plates on the side, already filled with fried eggs, tomatoes, hash browns and perfectly crunchy toast. It was slightly risky dishing the food up before she spotted their approach, but she could guarantee Ethan's clockwork accuracy when promised, since his loyalty to this *feast* was always perfect!
"Aha!" She proudly expressed as she spotted the two familiar figures approaching at the end of the small road.
The baked beans were positively slapped on the plates whilst she admired her loved ones grow nearer.
As she looked on, she admired the two handsomely tall, toned figures with their dark features. Her taste had always been for the sharp, dark brown hair and deep brown eyes. With the two brothers always taking part in physical activities, their chiselled cheekbones and jawlines said it all. She had picked some wonderful genes for her own eye candy.
Without going into detail of their abilities and features, she would summarise to her friends that the brothers always made her feel *protected*. Ethan and Tom had a great loyalty to one another,

which was also always greatly received by Rachel. There was always plenty of time every day for her private relationship routines.
She always felt confident about herself, and this was always enhanced by the regular compliments received from Ethan. She always felt something special when Tom was around too. She assumed it was an enhancement of energy, but he never had-to make any kind of effort for her to feel that they had some kind of special connection.

The two figures grew close, and she assumed from their pace that they had cooled down sufficiently enough to sit and eat just as soon as they entered the home.
Tom was the first to speak as the door opened.
"Oh, my word! That smells so delicious!"
"Why thank you." Rachel played innocent with a humorous twirl of her waist and a finger touching her lips.
Tom laughed and rushed to give her the first hug of gratitude. Ethan smiled and followed suit, adding a mutually received kiss.
They all followed one another to the dining room table as Rachel offered them their plates.
"Are your bodies relaxed enough to consume all of this now?"
"Of course!" Ethan exclaimed extremely wilfully. "My turn tomorrow. I'll make you proud."
Tom felt the slight jealousy he always held when noting their genuine love and respect for one another.
They devoured their meals relatively swiftly, allowing the tantalising flavours to touch the *happy* receptors of the brain.
As they were captivated by their taste buds, an unexpected knock appeared at the door!
They all jumped at the surprise as they licked their lips, disgusted at the disruption to their long awaited pleasure.
"I'll get it." Rachel attempted to retain their relaxed treat.

She stood with a hurried walk to the door and opened it with a deliberate plan to end this disruption swiftly.

The door opened to a hand pushed directly in front of her face! It was just as if someone was actioning her to "stop" before she could even begin to welcome *any* visitor.

"What?" She shouted, allowing the two men inside to stand automatically in protective urgency.

The hand touched her face with a slight force, just enough to push her back enough to allow illegal entry to their home.

Rachel was too surprised to respond verbally in any shape or form, feeling the adrenaline pump through her body instantly!

In the meantime, the two men rushed to the scene only to note an extremely tall figure forcing their way in!

Tom ran in first, shouting to the person to leave whilst gaining distance to push the person away from Rachel. He successfully caused the tall person to shuffle back.

"Get the hell out!" Ethan added as he grew just as close.

Their adrenaline pumped swiftly into their bodies, with Rachel's response to stand as stiffly as a statue.

The figure moved back slightly further, allowing the features to settle into Tom and Ethan's observations. This person appeared to be a very tall, powerful lady, with very short hair and an extremely determined expression. Her eyes were deep and quite striking in the colour of emerald-green. Her cheek bones were high, with eyebrows falling to convey her seriousness.

Neither of the three victims of this disturbance could make sense of the sudden event.

"What do you want?" Tom shouted automatically, recognising the severity of their appearance, and considering the potential consequences of this circumstance.

The person spoke with a neutral voice, neither feminine nor masculine.

"I believe you have something of mine that needs returning this very second."

The three of them turned hurriedly at one another, looking for hopeful answers to this person's request.

All of them appeared perplexed and concerned.

Ethan spoke with a wobbly voice. "We truly have no idea what you are looking for. You obviously have the wrong place. Please leave! You're not welcome here with this kind of behaviour!"

Tom stepped back to begin the process of contacting the police. His hand reached into his pocket to remove his phone. During this movement he wondered how someone of this stature could be so overpowering and threatening.

"You have something of mine. I have sensed it; it has pulled me in! This is the exact location!" The overpowering voice expressed.

"What?" Rachel grew some anger now, allowing confidence to move to the forefront. "How dare you force your way into my home and push my fucking face! I don't know *what* the hell you think we have, but we don't have whatever the hell you think you can bloody-well sense! Who the fuck do you think you are? Get out, you rude bitch!"

Rachel attempted to push the body backwards to force movement, but this body was stronger than anyone she'd ever made literal contact with. Her confidence dropped again, knowing that the two strong men would even struggle. This caused her mouth to drop with new concern. She stepped back, causing her body language to communicate persuasively to the two men by her side.

Tom stepped forward, "I'm calling the police, so I suggest you leave now!"

The tall person looked down at the mobile phone Tom was holding, noting the light on the screen confirming the threat.

"Police can do nothing." The confident voice bellowed.

The three of them stood with new worry, not knowing what further action to take.

A fresh voice sounded in the distance.

"Are you guys okay? I heard some disturbance!"
They all looked to notice a broad man and partner of a similar stature walking towards the house.
The tall person spun to respond.
"They are fine. I am about to leave now."
Tom, Ethan, and Rachel felt a huge sense of relief fill them, knowing that they were no longer alone in this frightful situation. The tall figure moved backwards, steadily, allowing a brief spin to face the opposite way in order to begin a long, deliberate walk away from the home.
The two broad men walked past the departing person to approach the three shocked-looking figures ahead.
Tom watched on past the men to ensure the figure continued on without reconsideration of return.
He looked down at his phone, hitting the button to end the threatening call. He wanted to confer with the other two before pursuing an official report.

One of the kind, helpful men grew close to the three of them.
"Are you guys okay? We thought you were in some kind of trouble. You sounded distressed."
"We're fine thanks." Ethan assured, "I'm not sure who the heck that was, but they certainly felt like a different, threatening breed!"
"What do you mean?"
The broad man could be noted to have depicting tattoos on every patch of his body other than his face. He gave off the demeanour of a kind, gentle, yet strong giant type.
"This is my buddy, Geoff." The kind man introduced his companion.
"Hi, we just heard some threatening words and assumed trouble."
"You're life savers man!" Ethan moved forward and offered an emotional handshake which was very enthusiastically reciprocated. "Thank you so much!"

They stood, looking at one another for a moment.
"So, what did you mean by the threatening *breed*?"
Tom stepped forward, "It was just odd! She seemed almost *un-human*… if that's a word."
They all frowned in thought.
The two tough-looking men seemed content that all appeared to be resolved.
"Well, it looks as if you're all fine now, so we'll leave you in peace." They turned to walk away, one slapping the side of his thigh in a gesture that all was complete."
"Okay, but thanks again! Thanks so much!" Ethan shouted with strong demonstration of appreciation.

Rachel closed the door firmly, breathing a huge sigh of relief. They all moved in for a group hug.
"We need an intercom system Ethan! And some cameras!" Rachel sounded rigidly serious.
They all hugged on with silence following the statement.
"Do you still feel like having breakfast?" Tom asked with slight humour in his tone.
"Well, I'm not going to let some crazy person ruin my fun!" Ethan sounded determined to put the event behind him, thankfully, encouraging everyone else to do the same.

October 27, 1860

Finally! The two young men had managed to get into a local, popular, arranged Ball! They had almost two weeks to recover from the strange occurrences that left them feeling peculiar about life itself. Edward had no recollection of any unusual behaviour, and the two of them decided not to return to the subject. It was now time to literally relax and live out the evening with fun!
A mutual friend, Albert, invited himself to join their arrangement for company in confidence. Albert frequently joined in on social events, as he too, was a single young man, seeking a partnership of some kind, although he mostly enjoyed the social interaction for heavy *intoxication*.
The three of them initially met at William's home to soak up some of the homemade alcohol. They all found it disgustingly sour on this occasion, but they felt their nerves calm in a short space of time.

The three of them found their place in the huge hall, sharing the smartest appearance that they could muster up from their wardrobes.
They admired the beautiful ladies of all shapes and sizes passing their eyes, equally receiving admiration in return.
It was clear that this was more of a marketplace for partner-seeking.

The music was respectfully played in the background; people were walking fairly between the guests, carrying trays of an assortment of finger food.
"We are so fortunate." Edward recognised his abundant life.
"We certainly are." Albert said with a slight slur.
"Pull yourselves together." William offered, "This is what we work for. We deserve our efforts. This kind of event does not arrive too

frequently... Speaking of which..." William reached into his pocket, "You know the two rings I requested Ed?"
"Indeed, I do." Edward's tone expressed curiosity, wondering if he'd spotted someone he already had a keen interest in, with instant assumptions.
"I wondered if you'd mind using *this* piece for them." William handed a small piece of crystal to Edward.
As he accepted this bit of crystal, he remembered that it had fallen off the main crystal that held the *mystical* events. This piece was so small that he worried about losing it in his pocket.
William noted his thoughts and pulled a handkerchief from his top pocket, handing it over to Edward.
"Good idea. Is this the piece that fell off the bigger piece?"
"It is indeed. I noticed it has a piece of clear and a piece of blue. They would go well in two separate rings."
Edward stared at the beauty and gave an expression of agreement.
"About the right size too I would say."
"I am pleased you agree."
Edward placed the items within the handkerchief into the inside pocket of his jacket.

The young men looked on with pleasure, noting the dancing that began to grow in numbers.
William admired a lady with an amazing, curvy figure who captured his eyes so intensely that it almost drew him over to her like an overpowering magnet. She danced with such heartiness, like a sexual empress, captivated by her own imagination that drove her movements.
Seemingly within her own thoughts, it took a while for her to open her eyes to the staring man just before her. She stopped in her tracks, observing his glaring behaviour.
"Are you just going to stand there and stare?" She offered with a firm voice that completely matched her dancing personality.

"Shall we dance?" William asked in his slightly merry trance.
"What else are we here for?" She seemed strong and cheeky.
"My name is Will." He offered whilst taking her hand gently.
"I am Eleanor." She accepted the respected hand.

Edward distantly observed the gradual incline of dance movement that William and his new acquaintance had manifested between them.
"Look at them two. I sense a new partnership." Edward spoke awkwardly to his friend beside him.
"It could be one down and two to go my good friend."
"William holds such confidence with the ladies."
"I suppose one must simply do as the heart tells us."
They both smiled, looking on, hoping for their golden invitation.

A tray passed, giving a moment to Albert and Edward to eat for comfort. Time without drinking allowed a reduction in merriness from the pre-drinking efforts. This was much to Edward's disappointment, knowing he needed some crutch of confidence. Despite this, he held his awareness, watching on with joy.
There grew a time of arrangement where the ladies were lined up on one side of the room, and the gentlemen were advised to stand on the opposite side, facing one another. Any already-formed partnerships were planned to stand opposite, but a new sense of dis-ease stood before those who were falling in afresh.
Edward and Albert needed to face their challenge and appear confident to the lady stood opposite them in this party game. Albert's eyes grew wide in recognition of his need for alertness. Edward noted a serious-looking lady opposite himself, as if dragged to the event in disapproval. *Great! A miserable partner* (he presumed).
A fresh set of music began, and they all skipped to the centre to meet their partners arm-in-arm, for a gentle spin and dance of adventure, before un-clinging and returning to their starting point.

Thankfully, one side would shuffle up, allowing a fresh sight of partners, giving fair chance of dance partners – much to Edward's relief!
As the third partner of arm-clinging and spinning attachments arrived before them, Edward noted the most stunning figure opposite. Reminiscent of the recognisable feature in front of him, brought a strong combination of nervousness and excitement! He was absolutely certain that this was the lady he had encountered and observed in the shop who so powerfully caught his eyes!
He felt the sweat build on his forehead and on the palms of his hands. *This isn't going to go well!*
Already filling with self-doubt, he began to shake slightly.

This was now happening!
The approach was good; the arm-clinging connected well; the spinning spun proudly; and the detachment and return to the opposite sides went amazingly smoothly!
Edward breathed a huge sigh of relief!

The dance went on, until some partners moved forward and gradually brought the usual view of arranged courtships, leaving Albert and Edward feeling awkward about being *single* in the centre of all of this action.
Edward took a huge gulp of air and walked with a slight mist of fear, over to the lady he so much needed to approach.
As he grew nearer, she spun to note his stern face.
He offered an open palm and held his lips tightly shut, knowing that any of his words would only make a fool of him.
The lady looked at his face, followed by his open palm and calmly reciprocated with a gentle hand to meet his.
Her hand felt so delicate and small as he clasped the two together, gently guiding her into a friendly dance.
As they moved glidingly, Edward suddenly realised the success he was presently recognising.

Oh my, oh my!
His palms began to sweat again, his heart racing.
The lady didn't seem phased by the approach or the kind gesture of the dance, as if she had received such offers regularly. Edward had a feeling the competition for her may be fierce.
The song ended, and after these few minutes of intensity, they mutually lost the connection of their hands, and they gently moved away from one another.

Edward slowly moved back to his friend, Albert, who was leaning on a side wall, attempting to look relaxed.
"You did it!" Albert praised the brave actions.
"I did! I did!"
"You walked away. Do you not wish to hold an initial conversation?"
"I do not know what to say." Edward was slowly regaining his normal breath and attempting to look as relaxed as Albert was managing to look.
"Get back in there before someone else does! I have heard many-a story of lost opportunity."
Edward knew he was absolutely right! He looked outward to note the lady's body language. She was walking away, looking about, as if rejected. This gave him some confidence to head back towards her. He noted another man paying attention to her singularity. Edward panicked, observing the height and width of his possible competition. Swift thoughts of his lightweight and speed possibly making him a quicker candidate for another connection, encouraged him to pick up his pace.
He arrived beside his dream lady and hastily touched her shoulder. The lady looked toward him in shock, giving Edward the fear of an error movement. He removed his hand swiftly.
"Oh, I am terribly sorry m-lady. I just wanted to re-engage connection and ask if I may take your hand again for a less formal dance."

Her face dropped to a more relaxed expression, bringing about a friendly smile.

As there wasn't sign of a verbal response, he was about to ask her if the smile was a positive confirmation.

Thankfully, the lady raised her nearest arm and welcomely cupped her hand into Edward's.

The other, larger man noted the approach and pretended his aim was to track towards a drink table.

Edward breathed a sigh of relief with his observations, along with a new elated gasp of acceptance! This person *appeared* to be the lady of his dreams!

For a split second he wondered if *he* was the man of *her* dreams. He looked directly into the lady's eyes and noted the fluttering eyelashes. He remembered the perfect porcelain skin that he recalled on his first inspection.

Words finally left her lips, "Dear Sir, you are staring."

Edward realised his slight trance and spoke to save the vital second-impression of himself.

"Oh, I am so sorry my dear lady, I am just so transfixed on your beauty."

She smiled with a slight blush, "Well, let us dance again, and see."

Edward wondered what the lady meant by the word "see."

Was she going to test his dancing skills out? Was she going to see if they fit well in movement somehow?

Either way, he felt the gentle pull towards the dance floor, and with instant compliance, he found this person blending some smooth movements that made it easy for him to reflect in return. They danced comfortably together to uplifting music, making them both feel very compatible. Edward occasionally stamped the floor with one foot to see if the scene before him was real or if he had fallen into a trance. This was so magical for him.

Once he felt confident about himself, he looked about the hall to clock William's figure moving in musical joy in the near distance. His friend was dancing non-stop with the beautiful lady, who seemed to hold the character he suited. Edward wondered if this night held a new chapter in life for the two of them. He caught sight of Albert talking politely to a gentleman, both leaning against the same wall in what seemed like a mirror image of one another. It was good to see them laughing joyfully.

Edward and William continued to dance with their partners for what felt like an amazing few hours, when the music suddenly stopped, and a clear announcement was made to conclude the party.

The entire crowd paused collectively, appearing to comply just the same as a set of soldiers under strict instruction.

Edward spoke to break the harsh ending.

"I truly hope that we may exchange names. Mine is Edward, and what might yours be?"

"Ann."

"A pleasure to meet your acquaintance Ann." He politely bowed with slight humour.

"And yours, Edward." She bowed with an equal jest in mind.

"You may find me in the jewellery shop whenever you please, if you recall our initial encounter."

Ann looked surprised, "Oh, I thought I noted some similarity somehow."

Edward felt slightly disappointed that he wasn't greatly noticed or remembered.

Perhaps *this* was actually the first impression then?

"I am sorry if I did not recognise you from the shop." She appeared slightly sympathetic.

He smiled swiftly. "Oh, that is okay. I would prefer that you notice me at my finest."

Ann smiled with an impressed set of eyes.

Edward's mind began working on the next opportunity.

"I shall see you again then perhaps? Should I walk you home?"

"Actually, my father is collecting me at the front door, at closure."

Oh, the gentleman who waited for her at the shop initially. He may be a challenge to overcome.
Edward worried slightly at the prospect of asking permissions.
"My father is rather protective of me."
As predicted. I must retain a good attitude.
"I can understand that." Edward wanted to gain or retain favour. With that, a twirl of Ann's dress filled his view, followed by a slow walk to the main hall door for departure. She seemed to hold a strong confidence about herself.
Edward looked over at William who was still conversing with his new-found dance partner.
Albert appeared to be in a continual, deep conversation with his new acquaintance, leaving Edward deciding to gain eye contact with his friends so that he could *signal* for his decision to escape. William caught his eyes first, allowing an exchange of polite waves goodbye.
Albert was too busily engaged, so Edward decided that he would allow William the opportunity to explain that he'd left.
Edward didn't like heading to bed too late on a Saturday as he played football on Sundays and preferred to be in relatively good form.
After the night's events however, he was worried that the excitement may not aid a good night sleep. Ann was already a whirlwind dream!

Present Time

Tom sat, working in the office with one other person, waiting for the rest of the team to arrive for the day. It was a typical start to his working week.
Everyone seemed their usual lethargic selves after the events of the weekend, whatever they may have been. It was always clear that a team member, Craig had overdone his party life with his red eyes and heavy wrinkles, that looked out of place on a young, twenty three year old.
He barely spoke on a Monday morning, bringing in some occasional sympathetic looks from the long-term team.
Tom always found him funny to observe - but then Tom was a bit of a people-watcher anyway, observing the typical habits of everyone.
Jenny was another who appeared to over-do the weekends, coming in with straggled hair, trying to hold it together. Patricia was a clear partner of hers, heading over to offer shoulder hugs and kisses to the cheek before the zombie-land of office workers grew fully distracted by the bright screens.
Tom felt slightly different since his marriage collapse and isolated himself to his brother and Rachel's company most weekends.
He thought about the recent events that created some ripples in the usual routine, however, such as the new change of location for Ethan; the very strange vision for himself during the car journey; the aggressive lady's actions, frightening all three of them; and the unusual golden mist over the inscription they had found at the monument.
Thankfully, the last few days had calmed their hearts and minds into the more usual life circumstances, leaving slight curiosities, however.

As it was early in the office, Tom had the thought to look-up the details of the monument with the inscription on it, to see if any information was a simple find.
People were settling in, so to stare at his screen was a crafty way of looking proactively busy.
A few keywords thrown into his laptop still didn't seem to locate the meaning of the inscription, annoyingly for him.
He then took a look at any Census list that was openly available, as well as the old obituaries through churches in the area. He was getting quite focussed on the subject.

"Good weekend?" The loud voice startled Tom, panicking him to throw a work-relevant page back into full-screen view.
He looked up to see his supervisor momentarily glancing at his screen, leaving Tom uncertain as to whether he was caught out on his internet snooping.
"Hi, yes, it was a great weekend thanks Carla." He quickly offered, hoping for the disguise.
"You didn't go to the same party as Craig and Jenny did you? Have you seen the state of them today?"
"I did note their bedraggled look." Tom wanted to sound as observant as he actually *was*, "I assumed it was a separate event though. What did they get up to then?"
"Apparently, they did some dodgy drinking game that got too competitive. They'd better do a darn good job today. Their appraisals are going to look shoddy if they keep doing this. It makes me look bad. We have some auditors in today."
Tom was initially grateful for the fact that Carla hadn't noticed his own lack of work that morning!
"I'm sure they'll pick up as the day goes along." Tom pointed to a big mug of coffee being carried by Jenny.
Both Carla and Tom noted the originally-frazzled appearance of Jenny beginning to improve as if she'd been to the bathroom to straighten out her curly blonde hair and add some fresh make-up.

Carla placed a hand on Tom's shoulder and moved away, expressing compliments, obviously hoping for others to hear, "So long as I have *you* coherent, Tom!"

He cringed, hoping for ignorant ears, waiting for Carla's movements to take her back to her private office.

The moment he knew he was once-again safe, he continued with the search history. He read about the available information of Lansdown Monument, which he found quite interesting, but he was beginning to realise the finer detail wasn't going to be found with ease.

Tom noticed a few emails piling through, so he gave up on the idea of research for now.

As soon as he picked up his first work related message, a can of worms opened, leaving him full of conscious effort.

Lunch time arrived very swiftly, much to Tom's relief. Taking deep breaths, he decided to head outdoors for a walk towards his car. A nap was calling, and he visualised the comfort of a declined car seat.

He slipped comfortably into the passenger side and lifted the handle to release the seat into an almost-flat position.

Before he knew it, he slipped into a deep sleep.

Tom had slipped into a journey of adventure.

His mind appeared to be taking him somewhere very futuristic. This event seemed to be so realistic that he was certain he *was* actually there!

He stood vividly in a *huge* globe that he could only visually perceive to be in the form of a large, gridded ball, perhaps similar to the image that represents the "World Wide Web." This globe was large enough inside to fit a significant, futuristic village of people!

As he stood, observing the globe from his internal location, he noticed some of the layout. His feet were planted comfortably on a smooth, shiny, plastic-like pathway, that curved into the far distance, leading to a semi-circle of shape, which encompassed a sitting area. He noticed a small proportion of people sitting calmly and sociably.

In another direction, the pathway curved *again*, just like a mirror image of the first noticed curve (he recognised he was stood in the centre of an "S-shaped" pathway. This other semi-circle created yet another area that people were gathered in. This particular assembly of people appeared to be stood, working on something behind a perfect, white glass-shielded desk, like a well-designed reception area.

He looked in another direction to note a crowd of people *booking* themselves into this reception of interesting design. A small amount of people were standing behind a large, clear screen, a bit like receptionists, accepting the details gradually from many individuals.

As he stood, observing these zones so clearly, he wondered if this was a vivid dream or if he had stepped into an alternative reality. He noticed a couple of unusually shaped flight vehicles above him, moving through the globe, from one side to the other, exiting the globe via a hole that automatically opened up, and sealed itself once the vehicle had departed. The hole opened and closed so naturally, as if the shell of the globe was *alive*!

He observed the flying vehicles to be that of cubes with convex tops to them. One of the shapes was more of a rectangular prism with a slim joining item like a rod, that held a dome shaped part on top to it. These vehicles moved as if they were live bodies with minds of their own. As he observed, he wondered how mechanical items could *seem* so alive.

He heard a voice shouting his name in the distance as he stood on this very shiny, clinical pathway. *How would anyone know my name here?*

Tom spun his head in all directions to respond. He couldn't calculate the direction the voice was coming from. The voice came again, this time much louder.
Something was about to consume him, but it didn't feel like a human presence.
"Tom!" The voice hit at the loudest peak!
He rushed into a spin and woke in his car seat, finding Jenny tapping on his car window.
Dazed, he rolled his window down and wearily looked to see her vibrant expression looking very attentive - her eyes staring directly into his. He thought this situation was now a weird turn of events. Jenny was the one looking vague and hung over when he last saw her, and here she stood, hovering over his guessingly-tired looking expression.
"Tom, I don't know if you realise this, but you've been in your car for quite a while. Carla wanted me to check on you with concern."
He sat upright, adjusting his seat to a vertical position.
"Well, I'm entitled to have a snooze in my lunch break. I've done it quite a few times."
Jenny gave a strange, demeaning grin. "Well, maybe next time you should set your alarm - you wally."
Tom rubbed his eyes and ran a hand through his hair, pulling the mirror down above his eyeline to confirm improvement of form.
Jenny didn't seem to move from her invasive posture. He looked at her with a questioning frown.
"Tom, you do realise it's almost the end of the day, don't you? If it was freezing outdoors..."
He stopped her mid-sentence. "What? End of the day?"
Looking at his watch, he realised it was shortly after 4pm!
He opened the car door, not watching for Jenny's legs, forcing a quick movement backwards for her.
"Am I in big shit?" He worried for his employment.
"I doubt it Tom. Maybe just a little wrist slapping."
Jenny had the look of half humour, and half concern.

Tom walked now, aiming for his supervisor, imagining the worst case scenario. Jenny was obviously trailing behind, perhaps enjoying the drama of potentials.
He walked back into the office space, catching the slight glance and mutter of others.
Carla sat in her office, looking up, not attempting to move towards him. He knew he'd need to go through the whole motion of respectful action.
He knocked on her door despite knowing that she had seen his approach.
"Come in." Her tone slightly disappointed.
"I know, Carla, but it was a genuine error on my part. It was meant to be a lunchtime snooze!"
"Tom, of all the days you could've picked. You know this afternoon had a bunch of auditors knocking around. I've had it already with people walking in half-cut after stupid behaviour at the weekend. Nobody seems to think of consequences around here!"
Tom knew he was a final trigger of frustration for his supervisor.
"Look, Carla, I intend to make it up to you. Sometimes you just can't help nature. I genuinely didn't mean to fall into a deep sleep. I take good care of myself. I'm not like the others. I rarely drink, and when I do, it's only a small amount! This hasn't ever happened in my entire life! I've even shocked myself!" He realised he was blabbing with over-explanation.
Carla looked up from a low brow and sighed.
"You've just made my day really crap, Tom. I can usually depend on you. The others slop about and I'm kind of used to the way they are, but I thought I was used to the way *you* are."
"Honestly, Carla, I am so stunned *myself*. When have I ever let you down before? Be honest. I've never taken time off other than holiday, and I've been as loyal as hell."
Carla softened and looked up at his face to check for genuine word. As she did, Tom caught glance of her features. Her eyes

were slightly glazed as if she'd shed a tear or two in private. With more observation he noted the colour of her eyes. They were a beautiful, glimmering blue. Her hair shades of various browns and blondes were highlighting her eyes more than he had ever noticed.

Am I starting to fancy my own bloody supervisor now?

Tom was aware of his thoughts and unusual stare, so quickly pulled his eyes back to face her desk. It was too late however, as Carla's body-language observation had clocked his behaviour. There was a moment of silence before Tom felt an intense fuse of sympathy for her.

"Carla, I am so, so sorry. Please let me make it up to you, even if I work late into the evening. I mean, come on, I've had plenty of rest. Who needs a good night sleep now, right?" He grinned, hoping she would connect with his humoured gesture of peace. He noticed an uneven smile, which drew his attention to the curves of her lips.

What am I doing? He realised Carla's beauty had been unrecognised for the entirety of his career so far!

Carla broke the awkwardness again with a final resolve.

"Okay Tom, I tell you what – you work until security closes up tonight, which isn't as late as I'd ideally like, and we'll put this to bed."

"To bed? I can sleep in a car seat." Tom was pushing his humour. Carla grinned equally now.

Stop it Tom, stop it! He was disappointing himself with his nervousness.

Carla looked at him with a better expression, causing Tom to offer a final apology.

"I'm sorry. I was just trying to bring more humour, but that was totally out of line."

"Okay Tom, I think it's time to head back to your desk, while the rest of us prepare for home. Make the most of the quiet time. I expect you to get a lot done."

Phew! She decided to move along.
Tom walked slowly back to his desk, feeling weird about beginning work for his second half at this much later time.
A huge sigh and flump into his chair attracted the attention of his nearest work colleague, Steve.
"Tough time huh?"
Tom looked over at Steve, who was slowly gathering his items together for departure. Steve was very much into routine. He was always in and out promptly. Obviously a family man, he wanted to return to his household promptly.
Tom had met his beautiful family in previous social work events. Steve used-to work as a farmer, changing his career to office administration which he seemed to adapt quickly to.
Tom helped him with his initial training and built quite a swift work relationship with him. Steve helped Tom with the difficult time of his divorce, advising him of his advantages of youth and second chances.
Their friendship was relatively strong.
With work colleague connections, Tom generally felt comfortable in his environment.

Steve walked out now. "I'll leave you to it buddy." He patted him heavily on the back.
Tom looked up to note that most, if not all colleagues were packing up and heading out, sharing their words of departure. This felt strange to him!
Jenny looked up from her desk, appearing slightly disappointed. He realised he hadn't acted gratefully for her concern.
Ah shit. He stood again, approaching her desk.
"Hey, thanks for coming to wake me. I'm sorry for just walking off."
Jenny grinned with his realisation. "That's okay. You were probably confused."
"Oh heck, I sure was. I still am. Ha!"

"Late one tonight then?"
"Yup. I guess I'll see you tomorrow."
Jenny smiled in agreement and walked off, tapping him on his shoulder. He felt he had the support from his work colleagues at this point, hoping to make final amendments with Carla.

An hour had passed, and Tom was the only person in the office space other than Carla (in her private office), who seemed to be on a long telephone conversation.
He longed for her to leave so that he could at least get the daily *expectancy* completed swiftly, and then have a look around the internet, for appearances sakes. Cameras hovered over the huge work plan, just for security reasons, but it was enough to prove his presence. If security staff needed to confirm his attendance, then simply looking at his screen would suffice.

Moments later, Carla appeared to be filling her work documents into her satchel in preparation to leave, at last.
He kept his focus despite his occasional glance at her actions.
She walked by casually, actually thanking him for staying on late. He noticed her different glance, holding an air of confidence. She obviously knew his new attraction to her. No words were needed. He just had to tidy his thoughts up and continue with his professionalism from now on. Tom couldn't understand his new observations but needed to keep them under control for work's sake.

Now that he had his own space, he sat back in his chair, sighing a private breath of relief. The very real dream came back to his mind, making him bolt upright for a moment. How could he have forgotten about the *dream*?
The foreign spaceships felt normal to him during that time. The globe felt like a place of home. In-fact the entire event felt so real that his current position was only confirmed as real by him

deciding to touch his skin, and then his desk. He ran his fingers gently over the sensitive keyboard in front of him. *This is reality, surely?*

Tom started to pinpoint the moment in time where things began to get rather strange. He recalled the trip home from helping his brother move and realised that his reality was questioned from that point.

Different dimensions? Surely not. He tried to put a label on the latest events.

He questioned his mental health status.

Holiday... I need a holiday.

The sleep in the car could justify and strengthen his need! And with that, he decided to book a date there and then.

He threw an email together:

"Dear Carla,

I have decided that after today - I require a holiday, just to get some R&R time. With required notice, I'd like to select the 7th until the 18th November, inclusive.

Would you please mind confirming that this would be okay?

In the meantime, I intend to rectify any lost efforts due to my error today.

Regards,

Tom."

EJT

October 28th, 1860

Edward's game was going well!
"Oy! Teamwork, young Edward!" Lewis, his football coach screamed from the sidelines.
It didn't deter his actions, as he felt invincible, looping through his opposition, and booting a strong kick straight into their goal. A field of cheers and matching level of booing filled the air. Edward ran with an arm high up, celebrating his own efforts and encouraging the small crowd.
William was at the field edge, shouting his praises, looking a little worn from a long night of romance!
Edward kicked a long stretch, allowing another one of his team mates to pull the ball in, and kick it directly into the net, once again. They all cheered in great gloating satisfaction.
"Alright, alright! Time is pretty much up lads!" Lewis seemed protective of too much insult to the other team.
The team players were all buzzing with joyous energy and bundled themselves into a victorious hug.
William paced up and down, keeping within range of Edward's kit bag.
As Edward approached, William studied his mud-ridden appearance, longing to have a conversation about the night before.
"Thanks for coming!" Edward was always incredibly grateful for his support.
"Hey, local team and all that..."
"Yeah, we beat that lot easier than I anticipated."
"I'm surprised you were able to play so well this morning." The probes began.
Edward smiled. "Well, an over-protective father saved an over-done night."
"You mean..."

"I do. We didn't see one another beyond the dance."
"Oh, I thought that was why you left fairly early on."
"It's a sorry affair to admit... Hold on one moment," Edward studied his friend's face, "I am sensing you went a little above and beyond with your new acquaintance last night?" Edward suddenly recognised the need for this conversation.
William looked extremely guilty.
"Well, you know that I would always respect the lady. We did however have a night of chatting and generous kissing."
Edward laughed with joy for his friend, with some remaining breath of exertion from the game.
"Changing times Will, changing times!"

They both walked along the street, moving closer to their regular view of buildings that brought them to Edward's shop.
A little side-door opened to a flight of steep stairs, allowing the two men to climb up to Edward's home upstairs.
As they climbed, William took deep breaths, realising the tiring result of staying up all night.
Edward moved up effortless, aiming to scrub the dirt from his skin and change into his regular clothes.
William walked straight into the living room and took a comfortable rest on one of the seats, as Edward focussed on rearranging himself in the bathroom.
"So when will you be seeing your pretty dame again? Only I was thinking we should perhaps go to the park together - all four of us, I mean."
Edward listened from the distance.
"To be honest, Will, I haven't had more than a couple of sentences-worth of conversation with Ann yet."
"Aha! Well, perhaps a group gathering will make her feel comfortable about getting to know you."
Will could hear the trickling of water and rustling of items in the bathroom as he relaxed deeper into the seat. Edward cleaned

himself up relatively quickly and walked out into the living room space. William noted Edward's fresh, crisp-looking shirt.
"Are you heading off somewhere Ed?"
"Not particularly. I would like to think we may head out at some point however, especially as the weather is so fine."
William knew of his friend's outdoor lifestyle preference.
"Well, what if…"
"Here we go," Edward interrupted, "What if we tried to encourage the ladies to meet up in the park?"
"How do you read my mind so well?"
"You know I can read you like a book. The only trouble is – I don't have any knowledge of Ann's residence."
"Why is it that you two haven't communicated anything at all?"
"Will, we've had one dance and a chance meeting in the shop. Her Dad smothers her, and I'm really shy when I'm around her. I can't jump into the subject of homes, marriage, children."
"Well, that *would* be jumping the gun now wouldn't, it my friend. One subject at a time."
Edward could sense the sarcasm from his friend but recognised his dramatic response certainly called for it.
"Shall we head out for a walk, or go to yours?"
William heard the same suggestion almost every weekend.
"You know, we need to make the most of our time if it is just ourselves. These ladies may end up *becoming* our time, as children will come, and family will grow. Perhaps we should do something different, something wild."
"What can we do that's wild, Will?" Edward was pulling his shirt cuff buttons together.
"I don't know. Perhaps we could head to the Inn and drink some ale with the big guys."
"Argh, I need to be at work tomorrow with a clear head."
"Ah man, Ed, you need to relax a little more. You often drink my amazing concoctions and work fine the next day."

Edward questioned his life within a few seconds. Was he becoming too habitual, or was William simply pushing something he just simply wasn't in the mood for? Was William suddenly worried about settling down?
Edward's analysing thoughts filled him, bringing a hopeful diplomatic response.
"Will, I love how we have been the entire time we have known one another. I do not wish to change things just for the pressure of new chapters in our lives. Can we stay focussed and go with the flow instead of forcing something just because we expect to get tied down?"
"Ed, it is just because I appreciate our friendship and want to make the most of it."
"I hope we shall always make the most of it. New relationships do not need to come between us. One makes it sound like an imprisonment. Surely our intention is to retain a strong friendship," Edward breathed a sigh of submission however, "Perhaps it *is* worth a thought. Let us go to the Inn and hope we get out alive."
"Yes!" William was instantly filled with excitement!
Edward was expressing his fearful words to attempt to dissuade William, but his joy demonstrated a completely different focus.

They both rambled their young, nimble legs down the staircase and exited the little door, heading out into the cobbled street. They walked swiftly and confidently to the local Inn.

The main door opened with a slight creek, entering into a heavy rush of voices, some celebratory and some slightly argumentative. The lights were relatively dim, with some corners of the large space so dark, that the figures were barely shadows.
People gave a slight, rugged stare at the two young entrants, plainly obvious that they weren't regular visitors to the venue.

Thankfully, the stares didn't last too long, and they made their way relatively comfortably to the serving space.
The large man behind the bar held such a heavy, long beard, that some of the end tufts contained the frothy foam of a beer head or two.
"What can I get for you two gentlemen?"
He appeared pretty welcoming. They both felt an improved sense of calm, although William held such excitement from the time he left Edward's home space.
"Two of your finest ales please Sir?" William asked swiftly.
The man weighed William's face up for a moment before preparing their drinks. William couldn't help but feel a bit guilty for something he hadn't done!
When they paid up, the seating arrangement looked a bit limited. William kept an elbow on the bar, his body language suggesting they remain in position for a while.
"Where-to then Will?" Edward almost whispered under his breath, feeling out of his depth.
"I suppose we wait a moment Ed. Perhaps a study of our new environment first."

Just as they were observing while attempting to navigate a space for themselves and their drinks, a man with a thick set of arms gripped William by his shoulders, making him feel as small as his eleven-year-old-self!
"Hello you boys! You look a little fresh faced to be in 'ere! What's say I help you settle over by my fellas?"
The accent didn't appear local, but he was friendly enough to take guidance from. They both went with the action and sat among a reasonable group of strong, large looking men.

The men were extremely welcoming and began asking questions of their origin and lifestyles.

As they spoke with much interest amongst themselves, Edward sensed some *drilling* eyes into the side of him from a different table in the near distance, forcing him to look in their direction. He recognised some of the football members of the opposite team from his earlier game.

Edward leant into Will slightly, trying not to make his nervousness obvious.

"Psst, Will... My football rivals are to the right of me, staring a hole into my shoulder."

Will briefly looked in the same direction with a friendly expression, noting their strong stare.

"I suppose we have made it obvious that we are aware of their stare now. I would think it is best simply to ignore them. We are with a good crowd. I am certain they will fear these large gentlemen."

Edward and William slipped back into the present company's conversation and before they knew it, they were soaked into the crowd's fun and jolly behaviour.

Drinks were roughly smashed on the old wooden tables on occasion, creating slight splashes, just adding to the atmosphere. It grew late, and the darkness of the drinking house hadn't permitted the perception of time.

Edward started to feel a bit heavy in the eyelids, so suggested to William that they depart.

There was always a mutual respect between one another on any social departure times, as they usually matched on feelings, as if they were synchronised in some shape or form.

"Away we go!" A slightly merry William shouted joyously to his new group of acquaintances, standing with obvious plans to leave. Edward felt grateful for his instant response and stood with equal intention.

They all hugged with heavy slaps on one another's backs, wishing wellness and prosperity. Another one or two of the immediate group decided to leave mutually, which made things feel well-timed.

Both Edward and William walked slightly 'out of sorts' as they departed the building. The other men watched on and made friendly jokes in their direction.
"Don't trip over your legs!" Came from one of the blurry faces seen by their intoxicated eyes as they tried to focus forward. Laughter and encouragement followed right to the exit door.

William and Edward held onto one another's shoulders now, walking down the uneven ground of the cobbled street, hoping to get to one of their homes in one piece, at least.

A familiar figure walked slightly behind, shouting over to them.
"Edward, is that you?"
The voice was that of his football coach, Lewis.
"Ah no. Don't stop Will. He'll hold it against me. He always says no girls or alcohol when seriously training."
Edward managed to throw this loud whisper into William's ear, amazed at his ability to throw important words together, as if sobering up swiftly.
Will attempted to speed them both up, moving his arm down to Edward's mid-back to push him a little.
"It's okay, I'm fine. Let's just hurry back. I shall deny all."
"Edward!" Lewis persisted, still sounding distant.
"Don't respond Will, just keep moving. I shall deny that it was me."
Edward wasn't sure if he was living in some kind of dream world with the hope that he wouldn't be recognised.

They both picked their speed up and took a corner, swiftly attempting to hide in an arched doorway.
They stood silently for a moment, trying to sober themselves up.

"I've got my reputation Will." Ed held a layer of sweat over his forehead.

"Ow! No! No! Get away from me! No!" Lewis was now screaming in the distance as if *he* was the one in trouble.
William and Edward looked at one another with surprised expressions, trying to remain unseen.
"Ignore him Will. He is most likely trying to gain my attention."
William grew concern, however, and reached his neck out into view to see what the shouting was in aid of. He noted some younger people pulling Lewis back and forth, some landing some heavy punches into his body.
"Oh boy Edward, it looks as if some young men have gotten a hold of your coach. They're beating him to a pulp!"
Edward grew a new sense of responsibility and moved out to attempt to rescue him.
Rain started to fall, growing heavier by the minute. The darkness of the sky combined with a cluster of gas lamps on a tall stand, made the scene shiny and sharp to his eyes. The effects of the drink made him feel invincible. His stability and strength felt amazing, suddenly, perhaps with the combination of adrenaline rushing through him.
William tried to stop Edward from his running launch, before losing reach space, but it was too late. He couldn't stop his fast movement! William didn't want his friend to get involved in something that could land him in hospital or prison.
"Ed! No! There are too many of them!" William was trying to shout without too much volume.

William witnessed a brutal fight.
Lewis was being pushed and punched by four young men, each taking their turn on this poor human punch bag.

Edward sprinted wildly into the zone, shouting, and intervening, causing two of them to spin their focus. The rain was heavy, but Edward felt light and untouchable.
He focussed in on the attackers, recognising them to be the opposition football team seen in the public house.
His mind was disappointed with their primitive behaviour before redirecting his thoughts on his pending fight intervention.
"Leave him alone!" Ed shouted without raising his fists, hoping his words may be enough, but prepared to use his pent-up energy on those who decided to take him on.

William stood in a dry doorway, feeling a coward, but not knowing much in the ways of fighting other than in observations. He wondered if he could replicate what he viewed when watching and supporting Edward's boxing lessons. Some of the things were retained in his mind, but infrequently practiced in action. He initially hesitated, but then with his lack of confidence, decided not to intervene. If things grew dangerous for Edward he would most certainly run in and try something, however.
Edward was unsurprisingly attacked! A very obvious, pre-empted roundhouse punch came in from the most immediate man, allowing Edward time to duck and shift back up into using his bodyweight to use an uppercut under the man's chin. As his opponent's head swung back, Edward stepped forward to throw an open palm under the base of the jaw, forcing them to fall back onto the extremely hard, cobbled ground. Edward felt no worry for the man who landed unconsciously, as he refocussed on the second attacker who came in with a couple of straight punches. Edward dodged them easily with his trained eye, moving side to side, avoiding their sloppy fists, allowing him to slip in from another angle to throw a hook, hard into the man's ribs. This caused an instant buckling, allowing Edward to use the same arm to throw another downward hook into the receiver's jaw, making him spin slightly into a sideways fall onto the ground.

Will was impressed with what he was viewing. It all seemed so surreal, yet highly impactive. He cheered quietly in the background, hoping for complete success, still praying that he wouldn't have to get involved.

Edward noticed that Lewis was still being held by the other two men. He wasn't sure if it was to keep him in some strange hostage position or because they were dumbfounded by the unexpected change of events. Despite the questioning in his mind, he began to approach them threateningly. They looked at Edward with fearful eyes, letting go of Lewis and running away, occasionally turning their heads to ensure they weren't being chased.

Edward wasn't going to chase either of them, particularly when Lewis was needing some medical assistance.

William came out of the shadows to aid with the potential carrying of Lewis.

"That was phenomenal my amazing fighter friend." William looked very white-eyed in the moonlight.

Edward smiled and turned his full attention to Lewis.

"We need to get you back to mine, to clean you up and check you over. You may need the doctor." Edward appeared completely sober now! Lewis didn't respond as he appeared to be in and out of consciousness.

William felt a bit late in assistance, but still offered his thoughts, "Ed, it isn't too far to *mine* from here. We don't want to be carting him up your steep stairs."

Edward noted the logic and agreed with a simultaneous nod and grunt when they both began to lift the weight of Lewis' body. Lewis wasn't coherent at all, although obviously still breathing with the rise and fall of his chest.

They both had an arm each over their shoulders, either side of Lewis, encouraging him to walk with them as his head hung forward.

An occasional mumble came from Lewis as they walked.

Edward thought he could just-about hear the words…

"Drinking... after... drinking and football... They don't go... well." Edward chuckled slightly under his breath, although still holding onto a surge of adrenaline.
"What did he say?" William recognised a connection between them.
"Well, he still disapproves of me drinking when I'm playing football seriously." Edward informed William, then turned to Lewis," and if it means *that* much to you, even after all of this... then I promise to take things a little more seriously. The drink won't happen again."
Lewis raised and dropped his head in an attempt of approval.
"No more drinking?" Will contemplated the end of his fun evenings with his home brews.
"Sorry Will, but I guess Lewis wants to see me do well." Edward winked at William, who was confused as to whether that confirmed this new promise, or if it was simply to please Lewis at this moment in time. William wasn't holding hope, and childishly wondered if *he* was becoming the victim in all of this.

They finally managed to get Lewis into William's home, and on his sofa with propped up cushions.
With some light on their wounded subject, they observed the blood pouring liberally from Lewis. His nose and mouth ran quite worryingly, leaving William and Edward uncertain of what to do.
"Not on my Maple Gilt Bronze!" William grew possessive of his expensive piece of furniture.
Edward couldn't believe his ears with the selfish tone.
"Well perhaps we could sit him up in the front garden?"
William sensed his tone and felt slightly dizzy and half-drunk, with added stress. He walked out to gain some form of cloth to wipe the blood from Lewis's face. At first, Edward thought he was fleeing from the scene, noting his pale features.
When he returned with a cloth, he was relieved to see a useful, kind action, even if it *was* to prevent blood splashes on his

furniture! William knelt down to apply the cloth to the nose area, when a clunking noise hit his floor to the side of him, instantly revealing the *crystal* they had both forgotten about.

Edward's mouth opened with confusion as to why the crystal was sat in William's pocket the entire time they were in one another's company. Before they had time to speak openly, a blinding white light illuminated the entire room, forcing their hands and arms to cover their eyes swiftly.

"Oh my..." William was the first to express his shock.

"Touch the crystal, Will... I think that's what you did last time to dim the light!"

"I can't see it to touch it!"

"Just fumble around Will! How can anyone help Lewis when we can't see?"

The light suddenly, and instantly went out, with Will's hand firmly finding and clasping the crystal.

When all of their eyes adjusted, Lewis sat up, looking fresh-faced and back to full health!

"It's a miracle!" Ed was flabbergasted. They both stared at Lewis as he fumbled around himself, trying to find the same pain and wounds he held only a few seconds ago. Old dribbles of blood were simply dried on his clothing.

Edward and William both looked at one another, wondering about the crystal's effects once again.

"What were you doing carrying that crystal, Will?" Edward wanted to know about his secret loyalty to this unknown stone.

He looked guilty.

"I... Well, I just felt a comfort with it. I don't actually know *why*... and besides, look at the new discovery we've made!"

"Well, we don't know for sure what this stone holds. I thought we'd moved it aside and forgotten about a potential situation."

"What situation can it bring Ed? I mean, it only seems to be doing good, right?"

They both looked at each other as if one wanted to understand the other's thoughts instantly. In the meantime, Lewis stood, still checking his body. "I feel unbelievably outstanding! I am certain my body has reversed to only twenty years of age or so!"
Ed wanted to give reasoning. "Well, you couldn't have been much older anyway, surely!"
"I certainly felt older than I do now Edward!" His eyes were revitalised and bright, staring at the crystal with some kind of *knowing*!
William and Edward stared at one another once again, both with the same fresh fears. Edward was the first to begin some form of protection to their findings.
"Listen, Lewis," He grabbed both of his shoulders head on, looking at him directly. "Not a word of this can be told. You know what happens to witches. We don't know what this is!"
"He is absolutely right Lewis. I was going to bury this item out of sight, but I am now risking a lot, foolishly. It needs to go in the garden right away!"
"What are you talking about? The garden? I have healed instantly. It is a miracle!" His mind was transfixed on his miraculous recovery.
Edward tested the theory of Lewis to see if he'd noticed the connection to the crystal and his healing since he'd stared at the crystal.
"Do you think it is a miracle Lewis?"
"Absolutely! I have been cured, instantly. What else could it be?"
William held the stone behind his back now.
"People will think you are mad and attempt to lock you up if there is any word of this Lewis."
Lewis held such radiance in his skin, and a strong energy in his body. "You are right! This must be our secret boys! No matter what! This must be *our* secret!"
William and Edward looked at one another with more of a comfort in their expressions.

"Well young men, I must head back to my wife right now!"
They all grinned at the possibilities.
Lewis ran from William's home, leaving the two friends full of adrenaline, yet relief for a resolving situation at the very least.
They both sat with a thud of huge sighs. Edward leant back on the head of the wooden frame of the sofa and attempted to calm his body.
"We've got to control that stone or bury it as you said." Edward held an obvious fear.
William knew something needed to be done to protect the two of them, but he felt there was such an amazing potential financially. Edward sensed the desire William had to retain it.
"Look, William, I know how you've suddenly become attached to this item, and I know I have a huge story to tell of it if I wish to, but I am certain that it will risk our livelihoods."
"Ed, last time you went somewhere amazing and then returned. I know that we have dismissed it in conversation since, but after yet another extraordinary event, we cannot ignore that this is some kind of beneficial item to have in our possession. Our friendship is strong enough to work together on this and find out what it holds. Surely we owe the opportunity to something or someone. I feel it belongs to someone important. Do you not remember your words on sensing a purpose for it somehow?"
"But *how* do we know who it belongs to and *what* purpose it holds? Since the first experience, I decided we would go into mysterious territory that could perhaps risk our lives. I hoped that we had conveniently forgotten of it, and that you had physically disregarded it."
"We should have had a reasonable conversation about this the first time, but I assumed we had moved to ignorance. I know as much as you however, Ed. Perhaps if we hold onto it and discover the reasons for our possession and the gifts that it holds, learning patiently, one day at a time."

"But what about our normal lives that I thought we had relaxed into, Will? The ladies we have just met. We can't put any of this burden on these wonderful people."

They both sat in silence for a moment, feeling uncertain – thoughts racing around their heads.

"How did things get complicated over a bag of gems?" William questioned.

They both looked at one another.

"The other gems. What if there are others?" Ed grew concerned.

"I think we need to sleep on our thoughts. Tell me what you think in the morning. Feel free to sleep here, and we can chat with fresh minds."

They both grinned, knowing sleep was going to be interestingly difficult.

Present Time

Tom wanted some answers this weekend day so decided to head to the local museum and library. He wanted to know about the area Ethan had moved to and if there was anything unusual about it. He knew of the famous Avebury and Cherhill areas that were nearby, but he couldn't find anything related to the monument inscription or of any events that could describe his experiences. He felt he couldn't speak to anyone about them either, for risk of being ridiculed.

His day felt a little wasted, so he decided to pop into his own local pub for a relaxing drink. He lived a ten minute walk away from his local pub so decided to leave the car at home just in case one drink turned to a few more, although he didn't have any intention of wasting his evening either.

He sat with a pint, wondering if he should at least speak to his brother, and just say that he's been having strange dreams rather than full-blown visions and unexpected deep sleeps. His life was a bog-standard one before helping Ethan move home, which made him question the timing. Tom knew he was of sane mind and didn't need it proving, but he didn't want his sane mind proving otherwise!

Being deep in thought caused him to phase out of his surroundings.
He heard his name called in question.
"Tom?" The familiar face of Megan stood above him, with another lady.
This sprung his mind into urgent focus on "normality."
"Oh, hello Megan! I didn't know you were familiar with this pub."

"Ah, I am in unfamiliar territory. Perhaps you could tell us all about it." She began pulling a chair out for herself and the company she had. "Unless you're here to zone out, which would be weird in this sociable place."

"Oh, please do feel free. I was just thinking about Ethan and his new home actually."

"Oh, not much of a thought then," Megan assumed, "This is my sister, Abby." Megan introduced a beautiful, curvy, dark haired similarity of herself.

They both made themselves comfortable on the chairs surrounding the small table.

"Did you want drinks? Have you just come in?" Tom was observing their fresh action.

Megan grinned. "Actually, the man behind the bar said he'll bring our drinks to us. I hope you had that service too."

Tom looked at the beautiful ladies before him, not feeling surprised about the special service they were receiving.

"I bet that was Ben. He's known for going out of his way for the ladies. *That* would be my first bit of info on this place."

"Oh, so there's nothing unique about us two then." Megan looked a bit disappointed."

Tom gulped, knowing his nerves were complicating his thoughts.

"I'm only kidding." Megan comforted his obvious thoughts, "Whoever it was, was nice anyway. It seems a nice place. So, I think you live this way don't you, as I'm certain Rachel was saying?"

Tom felt a little more at ease with her friendly, relaxed tone.

"Yes, just around the corner more or less. Let's just say I don't need any other transport than these." He slapped his thighs with his palms.

He heard Abby chuckle a little bit, which made him feel even *more* relaxed.

"We decided to have a look around this area – heard this was one of them nice country pubs that serves great food. I hope we can give them a healthy review." Megan smiled with very shiny, lipstick filled lips.

"Can't escape the judgment from the technology world these days." Abby allowed her first confident sentence.

Tom smiled, thankful that everyone was making an effort with the conversation as he didn't know where to begin.

Megan opened further opportunity. "What are you doing drinking here on your own then? I'm sure Ethan is just floating around today. Rachel said they're pretty bored this weekend, but grateful for the rest."

"Ah, well, I was trying to do some research on his new dwelling, but without much success. I didn't want to drag them into that kind of boredom. It took me all day just to browse through a little bit of info in the library, and then the museum."

Tom worried when he spotted their faces looking a little more on the serious side.

"Oh, so I guess that's the kind of thing a bored, shy person gets up to." There was another pause with both ladies still staring directly at his eyes. "Erm, well, I guess that's why I'm still single too!" He grinned nervously, hoping for a small smile or chuckle.

Abby saved him swiftly, noting his emotional reach. "I'm an avid reader, so a library is actually second home to me."

"My sister is the academic one, who excelled in English Literacy." Megan was expressing pride in her sister, with a twist of humility.

"Well, Megan is the academic one with mathematical genius." Abby showed a similar amount of pride and humility!

Tom grinned at their behaviour. Their childhood was predicted in his mind.

"Well, if you put both of your genius minds together..."

Megan and Abby looked at one another with an element of perhaps a previous trial of working together somehow.

"So, have you worked together in the past? You're looking as if I've hit a nail on a metaphorical head." Tom wasn't sure if he was asking the question correctly, knowing he was with two very intellectual people.

"Almost, Tom. We wanted to open a small school of tutoring, but we couldn't agree on some minor things. Thankfully the idea didn't last long as we both slipped into our own careers that we're still in now. I guess we missed that metaphorical *boat*."

They all chuckled.

Abby reverted to the museum and library actions. "So, what were you trying to uncover about the area you mentioned?"

Tom felt comfortable with the company, so spoke quite liberally, trying to hold back a little bit.

"So, since Ethan, my brother," he ensured Abby knew of the finer detail, "moved to the area he's in now – I have noted some coincidences and wondered if there was any history that could unravel some of the questions I have in my mind. Just by convenience, there was a chap in the museum who claimed to be an infamous historian, who couldn't even answer what I wanted answering." He chuckled with slight embarrassment.

Abby was frowning with interest. "What kind of coincidences have you been having?"

Tom was beginning to wonder how long this drinking session was going to be, but told his mind to relax, since this was what his overall plan was meant to hold anyway.

Ben, a broad, strong-looking man came over suddenly, working a couple of drinks through the opening of people's space to get the two drinks on the table.

"Ah thank you!" Megan sounded and looked grateful for the brief break.

Noting Megan's expression, he wondered if the conversation was too intense or if everyone was more nervous than they were letting on. Abby still appeared to be interested, so he spoke slower and sat back in his chair to attempt a calmer outlook.

"Coincidences... You see, Ethan's name is pretty much inscribed on the monument really close to his home, which dates back to 1861.

Our first run up on his local hills, and we come across it. That was the initial thing."

"Wow, that's pretty cool. What were the other things then?" Abby was definitely interested. Her tone of voice was bright.

Megan looked slightly bored and paid more attention to the taste of her drink.

Tom didn't intend to mention any further coincidences. His continuation tease was in error since they were extremely *unusual* experiences.

"Well, we have had a few strange things occur, but perhaps the others weren't so coincidental, more *unusual*."

"What kind of *unusual*?"

Tom gulped, knowing he was making things worse. He tried to keep things sounding normally-explanatory.

"I guess I can summarise it by saying *he's* had unusual visitors, and *I've* been having unusual dreams... May I add that I haven't told him about my unusual dreams. Not yet anyway." He hoped that this didn't sound too crazy to them.

"Oh." Megan added. "Something that's only happened since Ethan moved there then?"

Tom felt he needed to somehow change this particular subject.

"Yes. It's all been a bit, well... different, that's all." Tom paused, "But how long have you known my brother and his wife? How come I didn't know of you before their move?"

Megan looked a bit startled by the sudden turn of conversation.

"Well, in actual fact, I'm surprised we didn't bump into one another before. You know they haven't moved too many million miles away from their previous home, so I knew them in their previous place. Rachel used to look after Sky for me on occasion, and we grew quite close I guess. One of them natural bonding friendships."

"Oh right, and do you live with Sky's father?" Tom asked the question before he had chance to recognise that his words sounded like a probing on whether or not Megan was single.

She looked at her sister with knowing eyes. Abby seemed to speak up for comfort of her sister.

"Things didn't quite work out as they should have with Sky's Dad."

"Oh, sorry if I…"

Megan smiled and touched his forearm briefly. "Trust me, I've had this conversation *so* many times, it's absolutely fine."

Although this felt slightly awkward, Tom was also relieved on the change of subject.

He looked down to notice Megan had almost finished her drink. Both Abby and himself had only been taking light sips.

"Did you say you've ordered food too?" Tom swiftly added.

"We have indeed!" Abby had a broad, beautiful smile.

Tom drank a little quicker. "Well, I'm only staying for a little while, so I'll be gone when your food arrives."

"Why don't you share some of our grub?" Megan offered. "I can order another set of cutlery."

Tom took extra gulps of his drink. "Ah no. I need to get back to…"

"Your history books?" Megan only meant for a bit of banter.

He smiled. "Actually, I'm meeting up with a friend of mine. I'm secretly keeping an eye on the time."

Tom gulped some more, noting he was nearing the end of his filling pint, hoping his impending walk will help him burn the calories.

He stood with only a centimetre left in the glass.

"Well, it was a really nice surprise Megan. Nice to meet you too, Abby." He slowly edged his way around the table with side steps, trying to remain polite and unrushed.

As he approached their side, they both stood to give him light hugs of departure.

"Bye." Abby called, as Megan waved with a keen eye.

Tom kept moving forward, feeling slightly uncomfortable about two very attractive ladies paying him such valuable attention.

As he walked, he looked back, noting a glimmer in Megan's eyes. It was such a notable glimmer, that he took a second glance.

Upon the second glance, he noted a familiar colour shining. He couldn't quite figure out the familiarity, but continued to walk briskly away from them, the pub, and the entire experience, bringing him to the road of sudden ease.
The walk along the windy road permitted calmer breathing and a relaxed mind.
It wasn't until he reached to open his front door with his key, that the familiarity of Megan's eyes hit him!
They had a similar glimmer of colour to the tall, unusual person that so threateningly entered Ethan's home recently!
"Them eyes!" His body felt shock with the connection as he spoke the words loudly in his own company.
Another coincidence perhaps. He hoped!

29th October 1860

Edward sat at work, preparing to open the front door for the day, wondering why the football players decided to beat his football coach up. It was *meant* to be a friendly match. All football games are meant to be friendly matches, perhaps with a little tension for the pressure of winning.
His thoughts were moving away from the events of the violence and turning now to the strangeness of the stone or crystal. This item held such mystery, yet uncertainty. He often checked his thoughts to see if he was still sane of mind, but just as regularly correcting himself, knowing that the *two* of them were experiencing the same situations. The healing of Lewis took them to new levels of mystery. William and Ethan discussed how they were slightly concerned that Lewis's excitement may not help the overall secrecy. They hoped that he may retain his assumption that it was an unmistakable miracle!
With all of this on his mind, Ethan attempted to focus on the possibility of Ann entering his shop this fine morning. His memory of how beautiful she looked at the dance started to fill his mind and leave his worries behind.

Edward realised how deep he was in so many thoughts and tried to look outwardly at his present space. As he did so, he noticed the familiar face of his best friend staring in through one of the large glass-paned windows. At first Will gave him a fright, as if a ghost, just standing there, all tall and still!
After the initial shock, Edward chuckled under his breath and invited William inside.
"Oh, Will, you know first thing is my busiest time for preparation."
He realised his initial words weren't the best!

"Thank you so much for the kind welcoming, my dear friend! Besides, I have come to inform you of news travelling fast just the same as always!"
"What are you talking about?"
"Pleasant as always when you've been drinking the night before, young Edward."
"Sorry my friend, I must be a little vexed."
"I thought it was important to inform you of an article in the local Gazette."
William placed the large article of paper on Edward's desk.
"I am not sure how they acquire information so swiftly these days." He pointed to the piece he needed Edward's attention to be on.

"...The young men, both of 24 years, were beaten and left for dead on the streets. For any witnesses, please contact Constable William Cole at the local Police Station as soon as possible."

William noticed Edward's change of complexion.
"This is all we need Will. We don't need attention drawn to ourselves."
"Who said it will draw attention to *us*?"
"There are too many secrets Will, and the footballers know me. They know Lewis. Maybe I should go and speak with the Police Constable and let them know that they were beating on Lewis and that my intention was to save his life. I did not believe that I left them for dead, and I'm assuming that they did not in-fact die."
William placed a hand on Edward's shoulder.
"Come on, let us think clearly and see what we think a little later on in the day."
"They will ask why we didn't go to the Police the following day."
"Please keep yourself on the level. If you still think this way later on, then we may visit the station after you finish work."
"Okay, I think you are right, as always, my level-headed friend."

William collected the newspaper back up into a messy grasp, not realising his informative plan would have stressed his friend as much as it had.

"I hope that your day brings some greater joy my good friend. I must depart and ensure our focus lands on a successful income."

"Please forgive my concerns Will. Consequences sometimes hit hard. Let the day certainly bring us sunshine and hope."

"Very well! Until the later hour!" William tried to extend good vibes.

They gave one another a hardy hug of goodbyes, as they parted for both work ventures of the day.

As soon as William departed, he bumped into a mutual friend and stood to talk for some time in the cobbled street.

Edward smiled at William's usual sociable habits and settled back into his little work of creations, putting gems on top of lanterns. He watched every person dwindle in and out of his shop, either pondering or purchasing their greatest treat. His day was working out tremendously, much to his gratitude for improvement.

As he sat, sipping his fortunate cup of tea amongst the hardships of these days generally, he recognised the feet-pottering noises that were those of Ann's! He felt a strong heart fluttering and looked up slowly to take in the beautiful dress, leading to her blushed cheeks and healthy, vibrant eyes.

As always, she left her protective father on the other side of the closed door.

Ann clocked Edward's excited expression, followed by the observation of her dad's presence.

"I know he always appears to be with me, but he just loves me and wants to protect me. He tells me it will end when he knows I hold a strong husband in my arms. That way he can relax knowing that I am in another set of fresh hands."

That's one way to start a conversation!

"Well, that makes complete sense. If I had a daughter as beautiful as yourself, I believe that I would do exactly the same." His instant response surprised his own mind!

Of course, Edward would prefer to have Ann arrive completely solo during her visits - but accepting her the way things currently were would only enhance her trust for him.

"That is wonderful Edward. I really enjoyed our time at the dance. I hope that my early departure didn't upset you."

"To the contrary dear Ann. I prefer a good hearty recovery on a Saturday evening in order to play football with great spirit on the Sunday."

Ann's eyes seemed to light up at his responses. Edward appeared to be a very respectful and understanding gentleman.

"You are a very orderly person." Ann offered.

"Perhaps we could exchange a form of contact so that I don't need to wait for your visit to my work premises."

Ann pulled out a piece of paper from her purse and handed it to him as if she predicted the conversation. Edward received it with a gentle grip to prove his respectful handling.

The paper contained a very well handwritten note of her address.

"So, you trust me enough to visit your home?"

Ann smiled. "Well, it is a very well protected home."

Edward smiled broadly, also wondering if she lived in a huge manor house of some sort, with guards and maids.

"I hope to see you one weekend day perhaps. Choose a lovely one so that we may walk through the pleasant gardens. Be prepared for an introduction to my father initially, however."

Edward felt excited and nervous all at the same time. He realised the potential expectations of a wealthy father. He wanted to be the traditional breadwinner should things progress between the two of them. He instantly envisioned a plan to sell more items in order to obtain a large dwelling for great impressions.

"Money is not everything." Ann surprised him, "In fact, it can make one feel rather lonely at times."

Edward realised his judgemental mind. He saw things from a different perspective and felt an instant relief of pressure.
They both smiled at one another with great approval.

The entry-bell of the door heavily rang this time, with the father watching on at someone brushing by.
In walked a very tall, broad, and sharply uniformed police constable, instantly paying attention to Edward's face!
Edward's blood felt as if it had all dropped within an instant. He knew what this was going to entail.
"Sir, we have word that you may have been involved in a serious brawl. If you wish to see as little commotion as possible, I insist you close up immediately and walk with me to the station."
Edward must have looked as white as a sheet, as the policeman grabbed his arm not only to detain him, but also to ensure he remained upright.
Ann's face dropped with an equal shock, and at the same time, her father approached to encourage her departure for safety.
Edward shouted with defence as the two of them departed swiftly. "I did not do anything wrong! Do not assume I have committed any crime! I am innocent!"
The father swiftly turned his head to give a glance of disgust, leaving Edward feeling as if his entire world was crumbling within an instant.

William, *still* talking to his acquaintance on the street, looked over, shocked at the drama before his eyes. He reached out, shouting his friend's name, but knew he needed to stand back from the sudden crowd that was forming. He felt useless but attempted to formulate a plan in his mind.

The Globe

The woman sat, staring at the *being* right before her eyes. She waited for her registration of details in order to allow access to her new accommodation. Swift disruption to her home left her feeling numb yet shocked at the same time.

She stared at the perfect and pure white suit, that seemed to be part of the skin of this tall-bodied existence.

She looked up in fear of the long-face, whose nose and chin almost touched one another, blending into the neck that she assumed was a separate section of the body. Every part of this *being* seemed to blend into an expression of length without much separation of parts.

Although she held much fear, she also noticed the kindness of this character. Their words were *attempting* to bring comfort.

The lady looked up to note a queue of others looking equally lost. Some were being carried on huge, strange bubbles of solidity, transporting them off to another section of this huge place she was not yet familiar with.

This being's voice was gentle and masculine, with some touch of radio-noise likeness. She wasn't sure if this being or person was purely organic, or partly, if not wholly artificial intelligence. The voice came to her again, with eyes that looked directly into hers. The eyes looking at her were thin slits, that had dark moving parts behind, just enough to notice. The lady now listened to words of calm.

"You are extremely safe here. You will be taken care of wonderfully."

This wasn't enough for the fear to calm at this point, particularly as information was about to be gathered for this unusual registration.

"Please provide your given name." The being suddenly requested officially.

She shivered, uncertain of the specific need.
"Please provide your name at birth."
This made more sense.
"Sue," she shook inside, "Sue Alexandra."
"Please provide your *time* and *date* of birth."
"The nineteenth of October nineteen sixty five."
"Please provide your *time* of birth." The being repeated the specific request.
"Er, er, I don't know my *time* of birth, just th-the date."
"Please provide your medical detail."
This *being* must have been taking the detail and storing it simply from the verbal information, since there were no notes taken traditionally or earthly-modernly.
"I just have an injury to my foot, but all else is well."
"Duration of injury."
"I'm not sure. About five months. I was playing…"
"Cause of injury."
"I was about to say that I was playing tennis with a friend, and I went over it. Perhaps ankle more than foot. I didn't get it checked properly."
"Please move to sector four."
"Where is sector…?" Sue was lifted instantly by what appeared to be one of the solid bubbles that transported others about this highly technical place.
The bubble moved to an area of others who were now seated on similar platforms.
Everyone looked terrified and uncertain.
Another shaking lady looked over at Sue, offering words.
"Where are we? Is this heaven do you think?"
"I still feel alive. If we're shaking, I swear we're alive."
"What's your name? I'm Jess."
"How did we get to come here do you think?"
"I'm still trying to figure it out myself. Are we in a dream?"
Sue touched the bubble, which now felt more slate-like.

"It feels solid to me."
"We are confused."

Another vehicle moved to the collection of people in this given section.
A gentle white, long-faced being, just the same appearance as before, revealed a small item and placed it on Sue's hand.
"This is a calming effect. Please digest it. You are safe here."
Sue felt an unusual sense of trust and reassurance, so took the small item, similar to a pill, yet much shinier, and with a perfect roundness. As soon as this pill-like item touched her tongue, she felt full relief and understanding.
"Oh!" She exclaimed with instant confidence.
Jess looked on with confusion, still shaking but about to take the same type of pill.
Other identical beings were moving around, offering the same substance, creating instant calm for the people here.
"Sector four is free for mobilisation." One of the beings stated clearly to all of his assumed colleagues.
As soon as this statement was made, all of the people stepped from their transportation platforms and down onto a huge arrangement of pure, white pavements. They instantly had knowledge of their location and surroundings.
Sue turned to Jess again. "You know where your room is? I think it is right next to mine. We should make a friendship."
Jess noted Sue's calm and healthy glow, just the same as Sue noticed Jess's equal refreshment.
They all walked along perfect, shiny white pavements, looking around the assortment of available places of social and restful areas.
They approached their individual homes, which were compared to extra-large igloos, made up of pure whiteness. Each of these igloos were so clinical and of perfect temperature.

Sue inspected her place of accommodation and noted her bed space; seating arrangements; and screen of entertainment that didn't appear to have any controls.
Jess entered Sue's living space. "I see each one looks exactly the same."
Sue looked over. "We have a new home. All seems to be well."
"Are we unusually calm? I hope it stays this way. Those pills are so amazing – and instant!"
"Shall we take a look around?" Sue jumped to another subject, not intending to be ignorant to the futuristic medication effects.
Their friendship seemed instant with a swift bonding.

Sue and Jess walked throughout the local places, taking note of their surroundings. The light was always bright, white, and clinical. The entire place felt calm, yet buzzing with activity, which was a strange and controversial combination. They felt completely sane and stable, with a need to investigate their surroundings, despite some kind of background knowledge in the back of their minds, somehow!

Observing multiple areas, they noted a space of reading and calm; a place of drinking and nattering; an area of official workspace for these other beings; a communal space of bathrooms; an entertainment area with gentle music, and a huge space with mixed images, like a futuristic cinema with a combination of holograms and different dimensional occurrences.
They both looked up and around to note vehicles passing from one side to another, with some not remaining within the walls of this notable, vast space. Sue watched as one cigar-shaped flying vehicle passed vertically, well above their heads. She took note of the shape of the huge domain that they were dwelling in and watched as the vehicle aimed for an opening that allowed it to exit the globe. She was gaining an automatic knowledge of this place,

but she still had an underlying feeling of missing her true home, wondering what the necessity of being here was.

Jess and Sue walked comfortably together, deciding to stop for a warm offer of drink in the sociable area. This drink was so tantalising on their tongues, giving every part of their bodies a wonderful buzzing feeling.

"Although I know this place and the functions, I don't quite understand why we are here." Jess offered.

"Whatever we took, gave us calm and some kind of information, but there are parts missing. I love what we have here already, but I don't have that love of home feeling."

"That's exactly how I feel. It's a bit blank. Why are we here? That's my question."

An almost-transparent screen instantly fell before the drink table they shared, taking the two ladies aback slightly!

On this screen sat a friendly human face with an open smile.

"Welcome to your temporary home. We do hope that you are comfortable with pleasurable food and drink. If there is anything you need, then please call out the word QUESTION and ask what you wish. Someone will pick the word up telepathically and come to your zone."

Jess and Sue managed to retain their strong sense of calm.

"I *do* have some questions!" Sue shouted at the screen.

The face looked on with patience.

"How did we get here, and what are we here for?"

The person on the screen smiled broadly.

"You are here for temporary safety and to aid one another's species. I would like to elaborate on that question, but more of this will be revealed when you are more settled. Simply relax and enjoy, knowing that you will be returned in good time."

"We are going back to our normal home?" Jess sounded happier.

"Most certainly. Conditions are monitored for your return."

"Thank you." Sue offered without the need for relief since they were both so calm.

Present Time

It was an evening of pizza for Ethan, Rachel, and Tom with an extra twist for a change.

"I can't believe you're making it really obvious!" Tom was responding to Ethan's invitation for Megan to join them, "I simply wanted to relax in these rugged jeans with my brother."

"Yeah but it's obvious you like each other." Ethan encouraged, then turned to Rachel, "She likes him hey babe?" He wanted Rachel to give further encouragement.

"She's been speaking very fondly of you. Maybe relax and see what happens. What's the worst that could happen?"

"Rejection! I'm too emotionally vulnerable for rejection! I also hate the secretive planning behind my back. We're not kids anymore." Tom added to his complaint.

Rachel reached over to hold his forearm. "You know what? You're absolutely right. This was a childish move. It's just that neither of you seem to be making a move, but you both want to."

"Do I?" Tom couldn't believe he was responding with a stressed tone to the girl he truly admired, "Gosh, I'm sorry Rach, I know you just want to see me happy, but if this doesn't work, and with such pressure, then there's a lot at stake! An awkwardness with your friendship... then there's Sky, and then there's... well, it's not easy."

"All relationships bring a bit of risk, and baggage these days. Come on bro, just give it a go. She's hot as hell and you've been eyeballing her."

Tom grew silent with recognition of the truth, but he still felt betrayed in some way for the set-up.

Ethan got up to collect a set of beer cans.

"Here you go. Now come on. She'll be here in a minute for the movie, and you need to be in a better frame of mind, otherwise you'll give her a bad impression of yourself. Act normal as if it's all simply innocent."

"Ah gee, thanks. Get the drink inside me. That'll do it."

Rachel gave him a disappointed glance. "Tom, please. She finds you really attractive. Surely we're giving you a head-start to a bit of joy."

Tom softened as always, with the secret crush-of-a-lady with such reasoning. He just wished he had met Rachel *first*. In his head, *that* was the cure to all things, but as far as he knew, she could only remain in his wishes and dreams.

Rachel noted his change of expression.

"There you go. My Tom's coming back."

If only you knew. He wished once again.

Ethan was really gulping some beer down as he carried some more into the lounge area.

Rachel looked over with a frown, "don't get too drunk. You know how quickly it affects you when you've tired yourself out."

Tom thought they were going to start moaning at each other too, feeling guilty that he may have started a negative atmosphere.

Rachel looked back at Tom, touching his arm once again, explaining their day, "he's been digging a lot, creating a huge pond at the back of the garden. You should have seen all of the stones and heavy rocks. He was getting aggressive with it, and I think I kept annoying him by suggesting things."

Tom was only interested in the tingly sensation he was feeling by her touch.

"Well, is this pond just about done yet?"

Ethan was about to answer, but Rachel threw her words in swiftly, "He's been digging on and off for ages – whenever the weather is dry enough. It looks as if it's taking shape."

Ethan thought he may as well continue drinking since Rachel was speaking for him.

Tom was about to give some tips that could have potentially continued to wind his brother up, but as if perfect timing, the doorbell rang, giving them all a fright.
"That strange event with the tall lady has given us all some kind of doorbell-trigger-fear!" Ethan offered with observation.
"He-yeah," Tom replied, exhaling his negative concerns.

Megan entered the room looking incredibly attractive, offering a smart/causal appearance, yet with the perfect fall of hair and figure-hugging clothing.
Tom reconsidered his initial negativity. He studied her eyes and noted that they didn't have that strange glow about them this time, much to his relief. His previous observations may have been imaginative given the recent stresses. They all needed some relaxing times. Perhaps the movie would bring some fun to relieve any tensions.

They all sat comfortably on a c-shaped sofa, big enough to fit an entire family of about six.
The two couples were tightly together at either end, ready for the entertainment to fill their senses.
Megan's closeness in position gave off some deliberate perfume aromas. He now had confirmation of expectancy.
He thought he would offer a respectful arm around her shoulders to see what response he'd receive.
What *success* he discovered when she leant into him, encouraging a tighter hug. He felt the move was a little bit too early in the evening however, criticising himself internally!
Dating seemed to be so long ago!
He realised the head start came from the previous introduction and the recent public chat. Perhaps she already felt quite comfortable with the familiarity of mild interventions.

The movie began, and they all sat, gazing at the large television, the light filling the colours of their eyes. The volume was quite high, deliberately in order to make it as true a movie-night as possible.
Ethan and Rachel were obviously a long-term couple with their natural looking cuddle, while Tom felt slightly hot and uneasy with the slight pressure. Tom sensed that Megan felt relatively comfortable as if she had dated fairly frequently.
He sipped his drink more often than he would usually have liked, but it seemed to help. Megan had a glass of wine that was so lightly sipped that it lasted the entire movie.

When the movie *did* eventually end, Tom asked to move in order to get to the toilet for much needed relief. He got through more drink than he realised.
His first few steps felt slightly wobbly, making him recognise his inability to be driving home. His thoughtless actions annoyed him slightly, but the mild intoxication gave a little less concern.
When he returned to the living space, he noted Ethan was half asleep and that Rachel was trying to sneakily remove herself from the tangled arms of movie-cuddling.
Megan was sat upright, looking awkward. Tom was attempting to decipher whether she'd hoped for another cuddle or if she was planning to leave for the night.
Tom stumbled in, wondering what the next act was going to be. Not being at home, he wasn't a hundred percent happy about helping himself to a spare bedroom.
Rachel appeared to read his mind.
"Tom, we have a little bed in the spare room you can stay in now, unless you fancy the sofa."
Megan stretched, "Ah Tom, it's a good job I controlled my drinking! I need to get back to the baby-sitter."
Tom flumped himself on the sofa, not certain if Megan was annoyed at his state. She reached over however and kissed him

fondly on the lips. As soon as the feeling tingled his sensations all over, she stood to leave. He appreciated the control, but also felt the tease of it all.

"I'll walk you to the door." It was the only way he may receive yet another *controlled* kiss.

He noted the cunning grin of his brother and Rachel, feeling a little fooled by the plan for not wanting too much complication in his life, but excited about the attention.

At this point he was grateful for her well-timed departure.

They kissed briefly at the door, but Megan was obviously keen to get back to Sky at home.

Perhaps she was nervous of complications too! Particularly with a child of her own.

Circumstances felt odd, but he was happy to know he would be sleeping alone in his slightly messy state. If "it" was going to happen, then he would normally prefer a coherent state.

Megan kindly slipped her business card into his nearest hand, stating that her mobile number was for both work *and* private use. They both exchanged pecking-kisses as Megan was demonstrating her urgency to leave. Tom picked up the vibe and understood her needs, wishing her well, exchanging a hand grip and release to confirm their goodbyes. Megan walked off in a rush, without looking back, and climbed into the car.

When Tom slipped back into the living area, Rachel and Ethan were looking very sleepy. The conversation was non-existent, so Tom grew accidentally comfortable on the sofa and quickly fell into a deep sleep. A fly on a wall would have said that they were all open-mouthed and in an unconscious state until sunrise.

30 October 1860

Edward couldn't believe how badly he was being treated. He wasn't the criminal the police made him out to be.
He spent the night in a harsh, miserable cell, enough to think thoroughly about his work reputation as well as his chances with Ann.
Just as Edward was writing everything off in his life, a Police Officer came along and clunked a huge key in the lock, opening the door.
"Okay, you can leave." His tone dropped at the end of his sentence as if he was disappointed in allowing his release.
Edward couldn't believe his ears initially, so looked up, wondering if it was some prank he'd get smacked back down for with the truncheon.
The serious gaze received gave him permission to leave, along with a head nod to the side as if to say, "get out!"
Edward stood, ensuring it was genuine. He walked cautiously past the Policeman, half expecting a wallop, but all was comfortable and clear.
He walked down a large, old corridor, hoping for a loved one to greet him at the end.
Reaching the main entrance and reception, he noted his football coach smiling on! He walked up to Edward, offering open arms. It created quite a strong welling up of emotions that he needed to control. To cry at his age was frowned upon in these times. He just needed to get out of the building.
After a signature upon a huge-looking form, he left with his head hanging low, telling a tale of intense emotional suffering.
"I've never been through anything like that coach. How did you manage to get me out?"
Lewis grinned. "How could I leave you suffering in there when you've given me such a great new life? Besides, my best friend, Herbert, is a Police Constable. When I went to visit *your* friend,

William, he said you were in the slammer for beating them young ones up. It was self-defence - you saved my bacon. They brought it upon themselves!" Lewis took a breath and then continued with further comfort, "Herbert agreed once he heard the full story. Even the papers will read differently once the news travels."

"I *hope* they write it truthfully! I need my work sales! I am also in love with the most amazing lady. She witnessed my arrest. I don't know if she will ever attempt to visit me again!"

Lewis felt Edward's concerns. "It will all be fine. Time heals anyway. Those idiots need kicking off their football team! I'll ensure that happens. You may even look like the hero once things are straightened up. Hold hope!"

Edward felt so much better having had such an encouraging conversation.

"I am so grateful Lewis! Perhaps we could re-live a drinking session and end it all well this time." He bantered.

"I owe you, and William. You came in for my rescue and took me indoors to heal. The speed of my recovery was nothing short of a miracle! This is the least I could do to help. You certainly are not the prison cell type!"

Edward looked at the healthy complexion of Lewis and wondered how the light of the stone or crystal could have performed such a powerful action. He was relieved at the remaining mystery in Lewis's head.

As they walked, Edward realised he needed to get back to the shop. Thankfully, his key was submitted and recollected upon release, but he couldn't recall whether or not the door had been locked with the dramatic scene.

"If you don't mind, Lewis, I must make my way back to work!"

Lewis wasn't concerned at his need to rush, as his feelings were so immensely good, that he almost assumed everyone else around him must have felt just the same.

"You go for it, young man. I hope all will be in order."

Edward ran along, managing to get to the front door of his shop. The front door was closed securely, much to his relief. He wondered cautiously through the front door, moving in with the intention of ensuring all was exactly as he left it.

After a few moments, the recognition of all being well brought a great feeling of calm.

He caught sight of himself in an old, framed mirror. His hair looked straw-like and sitting in all directions.

The front door jingled, and Mrs. Phelps walked in as if nothing had changed in her external world.

Edward smiled at the familiar scene, not caring about his appearance all of a sudden.

"Oh, dear young Edward, you look so seriously ruffled. I do not believe I have ever seen such a sight with you."

He smiled. "I do apologise Mrs. Phelps. I had some over-night dramas occur, but all is well now. I just need to tidy myself up."

He tucked his trousers in, buttoned his shirt back up to the top, and located his tie that conveniently remained in his trouser pocket. He may have felt slightly dusty and less crisp about himself, but re-capturing his view in the same mirror, he thought his swift tying-up and hair manoeuvring looked reasonably close to his usual appearance.

He caught sight of Mrs. Phelps studying him in his peripherals, but the joy of his swift escape made him feel almost whole again. In some ways it was as if he hadn't even been away!

His thoughts of Ann returned to him, wondering if all was lost romantically. He couldn't envision being with anyone else.

As his fresh guest was busy looking about his self-praised creations, he walked over to his usual desk, retrieving his long-term journal. He pulled his pen to make elaborate notes of his recent events. Always wanting to retain a secret, life-long dairy of his life, this would remain in his possession until the daunting *clearance* someone would need to do at the end of his time. Someone would hold his history as if a "time capsule-equivalent" one day.

As he poised his pen to write, he was surprised at the few items that his regular customer had decided to purchase on this occasion. Mrs. Phelps placed them gently on the desk before him, looking extremely pleased with her choices.
A jewel-framed painting; a stone-designed lantern; and a pair of cufflinks managed to fit on his large desk.
He took the charge of money she willingly submitted, creating a sense of abundance for Edward.
His mood was already beginning to improve tenfold.
Mrs. Phelps left with a large, satisfactory grin on her face, knowingly uplifting Edward's mood for the day.
Did she purchase the items out of sympathy?
Either way, he felt satisfied about the kindness, knowing that she was an already-wealthy person who didn't need to watch her expenditure too closely.
Edward hoped that he would one day feel financially abundant enough to feel *that* free.

William now raced through the front door – a charging bull as always.
"Ed! I'm so happy to see you back here!" He reached over to kiss his forehead with a combination of slight aggression and appreciation. "Lewis said that he would rescue you just as soon as he heard the news."
Edward gave a weary smile. "I'm so grateful. I know that violence is not a pleasant resolve. It was seemingly forced upon us though, do you not think, Will?"
"Oh, without a doubt young Ed. Justice always serves so well, but I do hope that we taught a lesson with our actions. Hopefully they

will not attempt to harm another if they have felt the wrath of your fists."

Edward didn't feel the peaceful words had landed with him too well, but in this present moment, his gratitude of friendship filled his heart beyond care.

"I feel we need more caution next time Ed."

"With our entertainment?"

"Yes. The drinking in harsh places may need to be reconsidered. I feel your caution is wise on your young head, so we should go with *your* preferences in future."

"The crystal is the greatest concern of mine. Should we not bury it deep within the ground?"

"Oh now, your caution with the crystal specifically needs *two* heads! We need to understand its full capabilities. It now appears to *heal*! To know that it can transport you from one place to another, and now that it can repair a greatly wounded man, we need to investigate further!"

"But what of my wisdom you speak of Will? Since your gem collection arrived, we have been experiencing some unusual events. Would it not be better to return to normality?"

"I think we could test the stone *cautiously* Ed. I've been playing with it and want to show you a few things when you next have some free time."

Edward grew concerned. "How have you been testing it?"

"It is better to demonstrate before your eyes Ed!"

"Are you just looking for another disastrous drinking event?"

"Not at all! Please trust me! It is all extremely cautious times, with no drink involved. In actual fact, think the *drinking* sessions have created the odd situations. The stone, or crystal – whatever it is – is sitting innocently, awaiting our actions. So far we have only approached it with dramatic situations!"

Edward frowned with new trepidation, but realised William was talking sense. Perhaps gentle investigation and testing under controlled, calm circumstances would enlighten them more so.

William noticed Edward's agreement in his softening expression. "I can see that you are seeing the same sense as me now, Ed."
Edward nodded, looking down at his open journal, placing a gentle new entry.
"What are you writing there Ed?"
"I want to keep a log of all of our events Will."
"Good idea. Good idea!" William saw a different perspective. "Once we have enough work and evidence, we could take your written works and our joint experiments to someone who could make further sense of it."
Edward looked up. "At this point, I believe it is safe to keep this information to ourselves. We don't want any further trouble. Last night was extremely stressful for us."
William gave a sympathetic smile. "Moreso for you with the fighting, and the prison." He leant on the table, "So what *is* a prison cell like?"
"Please! You truly do not wish to know. Thank goodness it was one night. Although saying that, it was one *very* long night!" Edward looked William directly in the eyes.
"You were thinking about Ann weren't you? I'm certain all will be resolved."
Just as William's kind words began to comfort him, he reached into his pocket, finding the scrunched up piece of paper. With the drama, he'd forgotten about his swift movement to secure Ann's address. He unfolded this crumpled piece of paper on top of his journal.
"Her address!" William was pleased to confirm the wise move they had made for future contact. "All is not lost!"
Edward held doubts about her father's permission, but he needed to do something brave if he was to have any chance of seeing her again.
"Let time slide for a little while Edward. The dust needs to settle to allow further truth to escape. In the meantime, we must have a great adventure with this secret stone."

They both smiled at the thought of some adventure they didn't understand at all!

Edward still thought of his need to improve his reputation, however.

"I hope the truth of our innocent saving of Lewis is shared with the local people. I do not wish for my reputation to be tarnished!"

"Oh, Ed, your works are desired by many, so those of twisted morals would only miss out."

William was sounding so wise, comforting Edward instantly.

"Thank you my good friend." Edward placed his palm on the side of William's arm in appreciation.

"I must return to work now young Ed. If you have time after work, then please pay my home a visit. I wish to keep you up-to-date of my experiments."

Edward felt uncomfortable about the word "experiment" again. It sounded ultimately crazy!

William gave Edward a friendly handshake and rushed away, through the front door, looking energetic in his movements.

Edward felt strange at the end of his working day. His initial return was more in order to check on the security of the premises, but with Mrs. Phelps' sudden appearance, it created an instant work-time without any plan of it!

The consolation of this random continuation of "normality" was that it wasn't a long day.

He now felt like resting in order to catch up with his thoughts and emotions but didn't fancy going upstairs to his own company. Instead, he thought the distraction of William's crystal discoveries may be good for him at this time, provided that it wasn't too dramatic!

Edward took a casual walk to the front door of William's home. Knocking with his usual "coded" pattern, William answered swiftly with the recognition, welcoming him so well, as he always did.

"Now then, I am sure that you may prefer to relax after your trauma yet knowing that you don't want to get into a drinking mess, I shall offer you a mild drink with your choice of quantity."
"There's no need to be polite with me, Will. If you pour your latest experiment into the glass, then I plan to control it."
"I hope you have control over *this* one!"
William felt proud of his latest concoction as he allowed a swift flow into two glasses.

They both sat and sipped for a moment or two. Edward cringed at the sour taste but tried not to be impolite. He also felt guilty for going against his word of total sobriety.

William stood with a keen interest to get his information literally on the table.
"Let me show you my latest findings Ed." He placed the familiar crystal in the centre of his table.
Edward stared at the beauty of it. The main clear structure of the crystal held a beautiful section of blue that wrapped so naturally around it. The glimmer was captivating.
"Don't stare too hard Ed!"
"It is so beautiful though Will. What *have* we found here?"
"I agree completely. I still do not hold the answers for you but let me show you what I know so far."
William touched the crystal, instantly creating the immensely blinding light! Edward covered his eyes to protect them, already knowing of this particular action.
Within another second, the light was eliminated just as soon as William touched it again. Edward then dropped his protective arms.

"So, Edward, as you can see, I can turn the brightness on and off with a simple touch."
Edward was relieved at the control of the item so far.
"Okay, now watch this…"
William retrieved a sharp, jagged blade and pressed it against the end of his finger, letting out a painful whinge.
"What?!" Edward was shocked at his actions.
William wanted to point out the trickling blood on his finger, before activating the crystal with a simple touch yet again. Edward tried to monitor his friend's actions through the intense light. William didn't appear to do anything other than sit comfortably, allowing quite a bit of blood to flow!
After only a short few seconds the blood flow stopped, and his cut sealed itself tremendously! He then tapped the crystal for the light to instantly diminish, whilst demonstrating the instant healing of his finger.
"Wow Will! We knew it had healed Lewis, but you seem to have worked out some finer details. What have you been doing to yourself to find out?"
Edward had pushed his chair back with all of the visual adventure. A combination of fear and excitement filled his body.
"We could literally look at performing miracles if you want to Ed, but perhaps in an extremely private manner."
"How though, Will? How can we do it without getting locked up or creating chaos? We seem to be coping well, but how will others, when we are only used-to knowing one way of life? This is so life-changing!"
William's eyes had moved to the side as he began to think about the possible approach.
"That's so true."
They both sat, sipping their drinks with deep thought.
"Will, we have also dismissed the fading memory of me having disappeared somewhere. We do not fully understand what this is all about."

William changed colour slightly, realising he had perhaps only touched the surface of it all. Literally!
"You are right Ed."
They both sat silently, obviously continuing some future plan.
"Ed... What if you *were* to go back through? What if you could risk going back to wherever you went, to see if you could gain more answers? Can you remember how it transpired?"
Edward's body tensed instantly with the concept.
"Oh, Will, could we perhaps have some time to think first? I feel a little worn from our recent adventures."
William realised his insensitive suggestion.
"You are so right. A little rest for a while. When you feel ready."
Edward thought for a moment. "William, have you tried to see if this could actually happen to *you*? You seem to be quite able at the moment."
"Oh, but Ed, it was extremely stressful to watch you separate into mini pieces and disappear. It could potentially be something more stressful than the experience itself."
Edward laughed at the prospect. "You could be right. Perhaps some time for both of us to contemplate for a while."
"Wise. Wise." William gulped his drink more abundantly.
Edward found himself indulging accidentally too.
They both sat back in their chairs, staring at the beautiful crystal.
How could one beautiful stone change their lives all together?

Present Time

Tom had plucked up the courage up to ask Megan for a date of his *own* choice. He managed a long weekend break away from work, ahead of his *expected* holiday plans.
A cautious text message with a little humour, hoped to entice Megan for a bit of time in nature. A sunny day would encourage a gentle stroll near a pretty lake, followed by a rucksack full of prepared food. Tom thought that a cute picnic may demonstrate his self-arranged efforts.
The date was agreed thankfully, so they met in the gravel car park, commonly used for the pleasant area.

Tom arrived first, feeling slightly apprehensive about their private arrangement, but within a couple of literal minutes of his arrival, he spotted Megan's car approaching. He hoped that his pacing wasn't showing his nervousness too obviously.
He could see her large smile through the windscreen as she swerved to park near him.
He walked around to meet her, hoping to open the door for her, if security locks allowed.
A gentle pull of the handle unclicked the door, uncertain if this was a gentlemanly move in today's equality preferences.
The continuation of Megan's smile proved a positive reaction.
"Hi, alright?" Tom wanted to demonstrate a sense of confidence, thinking she may be feeling similar in nerves.
"Hi!" She almost bounced to stand, encircling her arms around his middle, and tucking her head into his chest.
Tom was a bit surprised by the action but felt more comfortable about her interest.
Megan let go to retrieve her handbag from the passenger side.
"So, what is this place?" Megan started.

"I'm glad you asked. If it's new to you, then that's good for fresh entertainment!"
They both smiled and began a placid walk towards the lake, making gentle conversation.

They walked and talked for quite some time, until Megan's feet began to hurt.
Tom encouraged the picnic-time once they reached a nice green patch with a welcoming wooden bench, conveniently placed for great views!

Eating and talking brought some amazing discoveries about one another. The things they had in common were uncanny. They both admitted to great hurt from previous marriages. It amazed Tom to hear that Megan enjoyed the same sports and past times too!
Their conversations were easy and agreeable. Tom admitted that he never thought he could find anyone worthy of dating, which was also agreeable by Megan. Tom couldn't help but think that all of this was too good to be true.
They spoke for hours, noting the sun moving its way down.
Tom wanted to encourage their walk back to the cars before the temperatures plummeted too much. Megan was due to collect her daughter from her sister, who could only babysit until the evening, adding to the time limit.

They walked towards the car park, noting a small cemetery on the side-lines. As they gazed at the rolling green hills slightly beyond, a tremendously large white and blue feather dropped between some gravestones in the distance.
Megan noticed the beautiful colours and structure of the feather.
"Ooh, I must grab that feather! I have a thing about feathers!"
Tom paid attention to her interest and thought about collecting any different looking feathers for the next time they met in order to score some future dating points!

They both walked into the cemetery, noting the exact location of this huge feather. It encouraged Tom to look up through the sky space, wondering what type of bird this would fall from.
"I'm thinking the same." Megan offered as she grew close to pick this large feather up from the ground.
As Megan collected the feather, she felt the hardness of the ground. Leaning over, she felt cement under some roughage, encouraging her to scrape the plant life apart, leaving Tom to question her actions.
Megan revealed a headstone that was lying flat.
"Help me uncover this Tom." She seemed frantic to unveil her discovery.
He knelt down without words, aiding her delicate fingers and nails by ripping some dead, intertwined plants apart. He stood to scrape the stone clear with the grip of his shoe.
"I hope this isn't disrespectful." He added, "But it's becoming clear now."
Megan tried to help again, finding the words more defining.
"E. Taylor… 18… Is that 18 years of age? Or is it 186… Ooh, it could be a year, but I can't quite unravel the final digit."
Tom listened with surprise, hearing the name matching his brother's, once again!
Megan noticed his expression. "What is it Tom?"
He gasped to answer. "Well, I'm starting to wonder what's going on. This is the second time I've seen my brother's initial and surname on some kind of plaque, in a short space of time."
Megan brushed it off. "Ah, the surname is a very commonplace one, and the initial could be of a *lady* for all you know."
Tom contemplated things for a moment and thought Megan sounded very logical. He felt his jaw and shoulders loosen instantly, thinking about his assumptions.
"You know, you're right. Some odd things have been happening lately, but I think you may be my source of logic."
Megan stood, feather in one hand, and arm around his shoulder.

Tom appreciated the kindness at first and then realised the hug had worked in his favour, breaking some physical boundaries, gently.
He turned to face her, looking for approval of a gradual movement in for a kiss.
Feeling like a teenager, he was so grateful for the mutual kissing action that Megan had reciprocated.
Her lips were so gentle and perfect, encouraging him to move in tightly for a wonderful, passionate kiss.
They were there for quite a considerable time.
Megan felt the coolness of the air bringing goosebumps to her arm, making her realise the later hour!
"Oh my gosh! I've got to get back to my sister. She'll be going mad!"
Megan gripped Tom's hand tightly, trying to bring his mind to the present situation. He complied, slightly docile from the wonderful feelings he was experiencing.

They managed to get back to the cars in good time, joking about being rushed and out of breath. Megan clipped herself into her car seat and promised a more relaxed time for the next event. Tom kissed her one more time through the open window as she began reversing, making him turn his head before losing the connection.

Megan drove off, throwing a wave as she grew into the distance.
"Bye!" Tom shouted into a receipt of no listening ears.

Tom sat back in his own car, wondering who he could share his date news with. This was a big deal to him, considering his fear of new potential relationships.
He pulled his phone out of his pocket, deciding to send a text to his brother.

Hi Bro, just plucked up the courage to kiss Megan.

He then sat in his car, hoping his kiss was good enough to encourage another date. Recalling a song by Cher, with the words, "It's in his kiss," made him smile.
His brother didn't hesitate to reply.

Are you still with her?

Tom replied with a "no."
A call came straight through to Tom's phone. Ethan was obviously after the juicy details.
"Come on over. We've got too much pizza. It needs eating up. Tell me your date details. We could do with a chuckle."
Tom laughed at the words and started his car engine with full intention.

Tom pulled up to his brother's house within a short time, making an entrance to the front door, where Rachel had noticed his approach.
He walked in with a well-received welcoming hug from Rachel.
"Hello Sweet!" She sounded desperate for the extra company.
"What's going on?" Tom sensed some upset or tension.
"Come in and crack open a can if you want." She diverted.
"Ah no, I'm okay for that. I've been running a bit more lately, so keeping up some healthy habits."
"You might want one when you catch-up with misery-guts."
"Oh, what's up with him?"
"Come in and grab a seat."

They both walked in on a dark-eyed Ethan, who sat with his knees up on the sofa. He looked as if he hadn't slept for weeks. Tom's observations weren't far off.

"Hey Bro!" Ethan stood to offer a handshake and sat back down with his knees close to his chest.

"What's going on?"

Rachel sat at a distance, which wasn't a normal scene for the two usual lovebirds.

"Oh, I've been having these nightmares. They're so real! I don't want to keep having them."

"Yeah, but he won't see anyone." Rachel added with frustration in her voice.

"Aren't you a little old for nightmares?" Tom didn't quite understand.

"Age has nothing to do with nightmares, man. Show a little compassion here."

Tom grew a huge sense of guilt, looking at the dark shadows under his eyes.

"If it's that bad, maybe you *should* see someone."

"Na, I reckon they'll eventually stop anyway."

"What are they about?"

"They seem so real. I'm fighting someone and I'm stabbed. The blood pumps out of me so fast!"

"Woe!" Tom was surprised at the idea of the gore.

"It literally seems so real, that when I wake, I'm not sure if I'm here or still in the dream. It takes ages to come back around."

"That's seriously gross! Is it the same every night?"

"Not far off! Sometimes I'm boxing this big guy so hard and almost getting there, but then I just can't stop the bit where I'm bleeding so badly. I don't understand it."

"You know, in some of my dreams I can take control and choose how it ends, like my mind decides to get involved the way I *want* it to be."

"You can do that? Maybe I should try that. It's weird because it's only been since moving to this house." There was silence for a while, and then he continued, "So tell us about your date. We want to know every detail."
Tom lost the exciting feeling with hearing such a horror story and seeing his brother looking so worn. It was sad that he was experiencing this but keeping it to himself, until now.
Tom wanted to snap into a positive role, so forced himself to step up a gear.
"Megan is great! I get that she has a kid and responsibilities, but I hope I get to see her more as time goes on."
"Did you have a kiss 'n' stuff?" Rachel asked with a cheeky smile.
"We had a proper kiss. There was definitely a connection, perhaps too much of a connection. We literally have too much in common. I just hope she felt the same chemistry."
"Aw, that's so nice." Rachel sounded happy for Tom. "Have you arranged your next date?"
"No, Megan suddenly realised how late it was and needed to rush off, so we didn't make any other official arrangements."
"Hmm, well that's got to be a great start if she lost track of time." Ethan added.
"True." Rachel was encouraging.
They were quiet again.
Rachel piped up to get the remaining pizza and brought it in on a large plate for Tom to devour.
Tom spoke about the dreams again, as not to ignore the circumstances.
"Maybe you should see if there's someone who can interpret your dreams." Tom asked with a fun tone.
Ethan responded with a declining expression.
"Thing is, I can imagine they'll ask me about my life and what I do and crap, but my life is generally great! I've had a great upbringing, and I have a great time here with Rachel. I have *you*

and our folks, our friends and stuff... Rachel thinks she hears stuff in this place. She's thinking it's the house too, maybe."
Tom looked around as if he may catch sight of something. "Really? It doesn't feel horrible or anything."
Rachel gave Ethan an unusual look and then looked at Tom to clarify. "Well, I swear I have seen odd things and felt strange feelings. I can't actually put my finger on it though."
Tom started feeling uncomfortable.
"I guess you might need to move – again!"
Ethan looked frightful at the idea. "I really don't want to do it all over again."
"Yeah, but if it's definitely the house... I mean, why don't you try some time away to see if it makes any difference?"
Rachel smiled, "That's a brilliant idea! I can't believe I didn't think about that."
Ethan grinned, "Well it's like our brains are a bit dumbed down at the moment."
"That does it then. Let's check out some holiday time for you."
Tom pulled his phone out, wiping pizza grease from his fingers onto his trousers, much to Rachel's disgust, who quickly pointed to the napkins she'd deliberately placed next to him.
"Oh yeah, sorry."
"Gross on your trousers."
Rachel seemed touchy, but Tom didn't care about a small bit of grease on his jeans.
He chewed away, looking at some ideas.
Within the time he ate the remaining pizza, his two holiday subjects had agreed to a great deal that he'd suggested. They looked quite excited about the prospect now!
Tom felt content about being able to help his brother out.
"Just one thing though Tom." Ethan was hunting for further favours.
"What have I missed?"

"Oh, I was just wondering if you would consider staying here when we're away. Maybe see if you pick any weird stuff up."
"Err, wow! Now you're making me nervous... I guess it's just a house." Tom couldn't believe he was hesitating, making it obvious that he was a little concerned. "I suppose I could. It's about the same distance to work from another direction."
He convinced himself as Ethan and Rachel noted the fear in his expression.
"You don't have-to, but we'd be grateful for the added security."
"It could be fun and investigatory. You guys have a bigger house. Would you mind if I invited..."
"Megan?" Rachel completed his sentence, "Of course you can!"
"It's done then." Ethan completed.
Tom smiled with his agreement.

31st October 1860

Edward felt immensely refreshed and grateful to be sat at his work desk, allowing guests to enter as they pleased.
Thankfully, the gossip surrounding his arrest was that of a positive nature. People were asking him directly of the details, allowing him to clear up any misunderstandings. With living and working locally, everyone knew one another's business, which was sometimes useful, but of course, people will always form their own opinions no matter what the truth is. With the news travelling fast, it did in-fact appear to be beneficial to his business. Playing the ultimate hero brought him some wanted (and unwanted) attention.
Edward wasn't proud of the fact that he needed to intervene with violence, but at the time it felt as if he had no option.

In his deep thoughts, a figure interrupted his imaginary dreams of Ann walking through his shop. He looked up to see a police officer, bringing back some horrible feelings!
"Don't worry fine Sir," He obviously noticed his change of complexion. "I just wanted to say that although we don't approve of taking crime into your own hands, we are grateful that you weren't held any longer than necessary, now that we have the finer details of the incident."
Edward was taken back by the words, not certain if this was a means of apology.
"That is so impressively kind. Thank you, Officer. I appreciate you coming in to clear things up."
"If there is anything we can do to help build your reputation back up with any business losses, then please let me know."
Edward was surprised yet again.
He considered a few things within a few second's-worth of time.
"Well, there is one thing I wouldn't mind help with."

"You're probing me to ask what that would *be*."
"Yes, I suppose I am. You see, there is a girl…"
"There is always a girl, son."
"Yes, but there is a young lady who was frightened off on the day you arrested me. We were only just beginning to find some common ground and my arrest ruined everything. Her father is very protective, so…"
"I understand where you are going with this, but please understand that I was only following orders. We don't arrange dates, young man. I do wish you luck, however. If it is meant to be, then you will both find a way."
Edward thought he may have had better luck with the idea but was grateful for the kind comment all the same.
"I shall bid you good day, young man." The Policeman tipped his hat and casually walked out of the shop.
"Good day to you too, Sir."

As the day moved forward, Edward's nerves calmed, allowing him to enjoy a few conversations and purchases by customers. His business was suddenly booming! He needed to speed up his creations at the desk.
William popped in briefly, offering a 'good morning' message, but noticed how busy the shop was looking, so didn't stay for his usual length of time.
Edward felt guilty about it, so decided he would pay a visit to him at closing time.

With it all being so busy, the time of the day moved so swiftly!

Before he knew it, he focussed on the present moment of walking up to the front door of William's.
William opened the front door willingly just as he always did. He was always grateful for his visits. *This* time was slightly different however, as he was moved into the sitting room area. In the room

sat his new lady friend, cross-legged with an obvious offering of William's homemade alcoholic drinks.
Her eyes looked slightly glazed, making Edward wonder if he'd interrupted a private plan. William could almost see his thoughts.
"You do remember Eleanor don't you Ed? We are just having a chat over a drink. Would you like to have one?"
"I remember you dear lady. It is wonderful to see you again. Please forgive me, but I have overdone the drinking times with Will as of late. I think I should leave you two to your affairs. This was just a casual visit without knowing of your plans."
"You do not need to leave." Eleanor had a very strong voice, with confidence.
"It is absolutely fine. I can visit another time." Edward was already turning his feet to leave.

William walked with Edward to the front door.
"I am so sorry Ed. I can drop into the shop and catch-up tomorrow. We just so happened to bump into one another in the street, so I invited her back to mine."
"That's perfectly fine Will. Please enjoy her company. We can catch up any time."
They shook hands at the door and Edward walked hurriedly away from the awkward scene. As he walked on, he realised the reality of the changes that were so obviously due. In his mind, he could see a slow division of friendship and a gradual increase in courtship with ladies. In many ways this was an exciting change, but he knew he would miss his regular time with his best friend.

Edward climbed the stairs to his humble abode and sat comfortably on one of his seats. He pulled an old book from one of his shelves and began to read, realising he hadn't had an opportunity to rest completely like this for quite a long time.
After reading for a lengthy stretch, he noticed the darkness creeping in heavily, making his eyes feel slightly heavy. He walked over to the window and looked up at the blackness, noticing the odd star beginning to twinkle.
A blast of light seemed to come from the distance, but he dismissed it and continued to stare.

He found comfort in his bed early this night, and snuggled cosily, wondering if having more time to himself may actually do him some good. Feeling better about potential change, he drifted into a deep sleep.

As the dawn chorus began to find its way back into the air, he woke with a start with some heavy banging at the front door. At first he was reluctant to investigate the rude interruption, but after a second lot of banging he decided he needed to rise from the comfort of his warm bed.
In his pyjamas, he reached out for his robe and threw it around him.
After a third round of banging, he started to truly wake up and wonder who would be so rude at the crack of dawn.
He opened the door to a terrified-looking William.
Edward was disappointed, "Oh no Will, what has happened now? Can we not have a peaceful moment?"
"May I come in Ed?"
In some ways Edward was happy to know that he was still needed by his friend, but in others, he wasn't open to hearing any negative stories first thing in the morning.

Without word, Edward stepped to the side to allow entry. William walked up the stairs with more speed than seemed normal for this weary time of the morning.
Edward followed behind without the same spring in his step.

As they both reached some seats, William sat perched on the edge of one.
"Ed, she stole the stone!"
Edward felt slight dismay, but then thought the pressure had been released from the two of them if there was no further sight of the item that seemed to have changed their lives in a strange way. He then had more clarity of mind and wondered how she would have even known about it.
"Why would she steal it? How did she find it?"
"It's a long story."
"I thought we were meant to keep it between the two of us. Perhaps the three, if we count Lewis."
"Well, you see, she got so drunk that she grew ill. I panicked and used the crystal to heal her. She felt so amazing and clear. Her excitement was kind of overwhelming."
"So, she took the crystal and ran?"
"Not straight away. I think I fell asleep a bit later on, and when I woke she was gone, and I could not find the crystal for looking. I certainly looked everywhere!"
"Did you actually point the stone out to her?"
"She witnessed my use. You can not exactly miss it when it shines so brightly. I told her it would help her. At first she was so drunk that she cared-not, but when she felt so amazing it was as if she became addicted to it. I switched it off with my touch."
"Did she try touching it when you were both together?"
"Do you mean to see if it had the same effects?"
"I am just wondering if you are the only one who can activate it. I know it doesn't seem to light up when I've tried touching it."

"You simply disappear into it somehow, Ed! What will happen to *her*? It may do something entirely different to different people."
"It is certainly a possibility."
"We need to get it back Ed."
"Do we? We could simply get on with our lives instead perhaps."
William was disappointed that Edward wasn't feeling the same sense of distress.
"Can you not see Ed? This stone may bring eternal life – no suffering. I suppose because I've felt the results of the healing with my experiments, I can truly feel something magical about it."
"Will, there is no doubt that it brings something truly amazing, but without it in our lives we have no responsibility for what *could* happen. We've only seen the *good of it*, assuming that it only *brings* good. It is a power that has concerned me since the time I disappeared somewhere."
William sat with distress, feeling alone with his concerns.
"Let me get us both a cup of tea. It may bring some clarity to us."
William grew impatient. "I need to get the stone back Ed. I need your help. It needs to be back in our possession swiftly. I feel we are the safe-guarders."
"Will, please calm your mind for a few moments. Sit comfortably here and bring some logic to all of this. We can go and look for this stone later if you like. Just drink some of this tea and try to relax." He handed a hot drink over to a shaking hand. "Please Will. If you're *that* worried, we can have a look for Eleanor later. The light of the stone shines so brightly that I'm sure we shall be able to locate it quickly, *assuming* she is able to light it up. She may not even have that ability. If it is meant for us, then perhaps it will only light for us."
William fidgeted but began to calm with the more helpful approach Edward was now offering.
"You know Ed, there is no certainty to this, however I thank you for your flexible offerings. I also appreciate your tea." He sipped his drink with gratitude, beginning to calm now.

They both sat drinking tea for a while. Edward could see continual improvement in William's nerves.

"So, Ed, I have decided not to go to work today. I will see if I can locate Eleanor and pop in and out of your shop if you do not mind?"

Edward gave a gentle sigh. "If you truly want to do that, then of course, you're very welcome."

William looked sad. "You know it's just hit me that Eleanor isn't my future wife. I thought we were getting on so well."

Edward realised the same. "I am so sorry Will. That crystal has a lot to answer for though. If the stone didn't exist then things may have been different."

"It proves that she would steel from me though."

"True." Edward stood to begin organising himself for work whilst keeping within hearing range.

"So, what about Ann? Are you going to look for her?"

Edward was pulling his tie together and beginning to straighten his hair in an old, heavily framed mirror.

"I'm not sure how to approach her. Do I go to her address? Or do I wait for her to visit the shop on her own accord?"

Despite the conversation about their potential relationships, Edward was secretly happy to hear words that deflected from William's concerns.

"If it was me, you know what I would do."

"Sure, I do." Edward imagined a trip to her address and a clash with Ann's father.

"I can read your mind, Ed. I know she has a protective father, but if you win *his* respect you might get somewhere."

"You know, you're right Will. I should aim for *him* first."

They both grinned with the idea.

"Strategic plans always feel so wrong though don't they?" Edward felt strange about it.

William smiled at the imagined plan.

"Right!" Edward displayed courage, "I must head downstairs for work. Feel free to hang around for a while."
William stood in acknowledgment, at the same time noting the useful viewing window ahead.
"Ah, I remember you have a great view over the streets from here. Perhaps I should keep an eye from this height."
"Feel free Will. I must go. You know where everything is."
"Have good business Ed. Thank you for helping me out. I don't deserve it, having been so careless with the stone."
"You were only being helpful when you were worried about the lady being unwell. I am certain I would have done the same."
Edward smiled, walking casually down the stairs, leaving William to stare intriguingly, looking like an illegal spy!

The Globe

Sue and Jess relaxed in a sociable area with provided coffee. They looked out at this sparkling white and silver globe that they had suddenly come to dwell in.
Their nerves remained amazingly calm in this new environment, remembering the unusual medication that brought such a lovely sense to their body and mind.

In another section of this vast space, stood a conference of some kind.
Three *"beings,"* all with the same longer features, and white complexions stood in a very wide triangle.
Above these fellow beings, moved a silent, hovering vehicle that slowly descended in the centre of their triangle. This vehicle was a slightly miss-shaped pyramid, the size of a small garden shed. As it gently surfaced, another being stepped through one edge of this pyramid shape, as if walking through dry water. This life form appeared to be just as tall, and with great confidence. Their features were of a light purple, with larger eyes and an almost-flat face, with a very small, attached piece of breathing apparatus running into a small hole into the centre of their facial area. It was like a replacement for a nose or mouth. The top of their head didn't seem completely solid. In-fact, from a human perspective, the *entirety* of their presence didn't appear to be *completely* solid. The three white figures had a voice that projected from their whole being and not from their mouths.
"Welcome again Trion."
"Thank you friends. I come to your centre-point to request a removal of power, for our home purpose." This lifeform didn't *move* a physical form of voice either.

The conversation from all seemed to be a telepathic form, which projected enough to feel like an open announcement of conversation.
One of the three white beings responded with a protective sentence.
"We cannot release power from our centre without *imbalance* occurring at this time."
The being in the centre appeared to change colour slightly to a darker purple, like a mood-changing body.
"It is essential for the survival of our transportation between planets. Our sources are close to depletion."
"We have offered our services within our home for your temporary dwelling until we can build our sources enough to distribute liberally. The plan is to liberate our sources successfully once we are in abundance." Another white being responded.
"We cannot *wait* for this abundance to manifest further. We are almost depleted. We require an amount for survival in order to trade. This must be available to us in immediate time."
The white life forces remained strong but appeared cautious, with expected retaliation but hope of continued peace. Trion historically held aggressive behaviours in desperate times, but there were frequent attempts at mediation and collaboration to retain as much calm as possible.
 "With desperation comes force. Please do not allow this force to manifest over a small sacrifice for the sake of others."
"Our source is required for our survival at this point too. All we request is further patience. We have said that you are welcome to dwell here until such time."
"All life force is free to all life forms within our Universes. We are simply requesting a portion of your gatherings in order to survive." The purple being was looking more rigid in body.

The three white life forms stood still, offering private telepathy, attempting to agree on a resolving action. Communication was

changed simply with intention. Privacy or public volume could be amended through the power of decision.
One of them spoke with outer volume again.
"You are welcome to take one seventh of our portion, but it is with our delivery to you after the next cycle."
The purple being was now beginning to pace with impatience.
"You go against the law of compliance. Stashing without sharing is illegal in our system, as you are well aware."
"Taking with force is also against the law of compliance. There is currently a project in place to build the power source which we shall ensure you also benefit from."
"My actions are of kind request out of desperation."
"Your *intention* with this source is in question. This is our reason for resistance against sharing much at this time."
"The truth now escapes you. You do not trust my reason of need."
"We have many reasons to distrust you Trion."
"Previous actions are creating your uncertainty. At this moment in time, we are in desperate need of source-energy. This is for survival purposes only. In time of desperation, you are required to comply. Request the evidence you require, and it shall be provided."
"What can you demonstrate for verification?"
The purple-coloured life form lifted a finger to his right side and scrolled through the air, allowing an image to appear. The image was almost transparent, with outlines of forms. A couple of shapes formed to show similar beings without much life force in them. Poverty and illness was before their eyes.
Some digits of time were at the base of this image, showing a live feed of what was going on in his home world.
"You can see my fellow community – we are at the point of collapse. Our power has faded. We need some original source."
The three white-faced beings stood in telepathic communication yet again, trying to resolve this awkward situation. While they were communicating, the purple being, remaining in the centre,

began to grow more impatient, interrupting their internal conversation.

"Please, this is not up for discussion. It is of pure *need*, and I must not transport back empty handed."

One of the white life forces communicated to someone in the near distance, allowing this extra body to arrive at this gathering. This body was shorter, but the face longer. It appeared to be a younger version of the three communicators in the triangle formation.

The shorter body reached out to deliver an item to one of their hands. A taller one received the item willingly and handed it to the centre purple *being*.

"Thank you! Can you not offer any further amount at this time? We plan to recompensate once we have grown sufficient amount again."

The white formation of figures all offered a gentle, yet relatively firm confirmation of no further offerings.

"You can manifest an abundance simply using that *one* piece in gradual time just the same as we have been doing."

"Your energies are greater than ours. Our manifesting powers are currently weakened. It would be worthwhile to start with something more energising."

"You are beginning to push our already-generous nature. We can advise that you have the same potential to build on that *one* piece. You are knowledgeable enough to understand this."

The purple being looked as if a haze of steam rose from the top of his head, perhaps in frustration or anger.

"Trion, you will now depart and rebuild with your already-provided strong source."

"So be it!" The being walked back into the pyramid transportation device and disappeared behind its solid form.

The craft lifted silently again, directly upwards.

The three white beings watched on with distrusting eyes, ensuring the safe departure without disruption.

An opening at the top of the globe formed to allow the exit, but just as the hole was fully formed for the transportation to make its way through, the pyramid vehicle moved so fast to create an almost-invisibility, diverting diagonally down to another area of the globe. The pyramid scooped through a doorway which held the globe's power sources, and retracted, knowingly successful to have removed valuable items.

The white beings stood in shock and dismay at the robbing actions of Trion. An instant feeling of regret for not forcefully escorting him off site filled the three white life forms. They should have predicted his cunning motivation from previous eventful situations. A new dread filled them now as their own flight-ships moved in with new security measures to ensure his complete departure.

The leader of the three white forms was known as "Spreckley." He spoke with his two trusted advisors and team members of this highest order, attempting to run through an emergency procedure. They moved swiftly on the foundations of large, floating flat stones – hovering items of transportation - taking them intentionally (as if a life form of their own) to the storage room that usually held their power sources.

As they entered, they noticed the items that were missing. They were left with approximately one third of the original amount. "This was a swift theft! I don't think it would be wise to chase after Trion despite our temptation to retrieve things." Was the wise advice of Spreckley, "I believe we need to retain what we have remaining and build upon *this* whilst keeping Trion and his counterparties disqualified for entry into *our* space."

Spreckley was confident upon inspection, that the remaining items were enough to survive on for a useful power source. He knew that they could build the same level of power in a short space of time with their positive intention. He then considered his greed and wondered if he should have offered a little more to Trion. Either way, the theft was unnecessary where energy sources had

the ability to increase in power using the force of *intention*. His reasons for the small offering - were based on Trion's laziness for building upon what he often had, coupled with his occasional behaviours of unnecessary crime.
"I need the energetic ones to spend some time here building on what we *now* have. We need to build to be much stronger this time, with control of access at full capacity from now on."
One of his advisors held a small thought. "I am concerned of Trion's intentions. Do you feel he may have a plan of action *against* us?"
Spreckley pondered at the thought. "I think he has what he wanted, even be it by force. I hope that we shan't see him for some time."
The others around him hoped that he was right.
"Just to be on the safe side, let us see if we can connect to his intentions once things are more balanced."
The others agreed that things needed monitoring and protecting.
"Bring the humans to this area. We need them to begin sooner than we thought."

Sue, Jess and approximately ten others were requested to join Spreckley in this power-house room.
They all travelled on the bubbles of transportation that carried them around the vast space, in swift time. These bubbles collected them like automatic taxis, drawing them to their destination.

Sue watched with keen observation, still holding her calm, wondering what this new literal move was all about.
They stood on the huge, flat bubble-appearing items that felt extremely solid under their feet. They travelled through new areas, passing extreme white structures of such bespoke design. One structure looked similar to that of a temple, while another looked like a large, enclosed wall with pure white seats encircling a centre stage.

Sue wondered what kind of events occurred within this huge, futuristic dwelling place. Everything was so grid-like, but comforting and homely. It seemed an odd contradiction.

The flat transportation items carried everyone towards a large doorway, opening up to a high set of walls and bright coloured lights. It blurred everyone's vision at the initial instance, until clarity formed the view of large rock formations as if in a future-styled cave. Sue remembered caves that held stalactites and stalagmites that formed in caves that she had visited as a child on the Earth. The formations were that of a futuristic version. The view was extremely captivating. Everyone's eyes and mouths were wide with the amazing beauty in front of them.

Spreckley spoke with power, this time moving his mouth to project his voice in the way he knew humans understood.

"Welcome fellow friends. I can see that you are amazed by the view. Please take a while to take in the sights. It would be wonderful to bring you all a tour of what we have here. This is our area of power source. We began with a few formations that developed and grew with the power of manifestation. We witnessed that humans had the *greatest* power of manifestation through the power of intention and visualisation. Humans don't understand their great power and allow themselves to be ruled by weaker beings that only seek to control them."

Sue grew interested by Spreckley's words and listened intensely. She looked about to note that everyone else was so captivated by the view with their eyes and the words hitting their ears.

"We weren't going to display this view to you for a while in order for you to settle in and enjoy some pampering, but we now have a necessary need to inform you of your great purpose here, in this planetary system."

Most of the human expressions frowned with curiosity.

"This great room is full of natural growth, with rock formations that – as you noticed – hold immense beauty. They are our power source that provides our energy to transport from planet-to-planet in order to trade with our balanced system. We usually trade peacefully with immense success, but we have lost some of this formation due to an untimely theft. Our source of power, like many other power sources, is in great demand and is often depleted and then sometimes abundant, dependant on how much we use and how much we trade. Are you following this so far?" Everyone nodded with mumbles of an occasional "yes."

"So, we here, are going to teach you of your own power. You are the most powerful being in our system. The power of your minds are beyond our capability. You are able to visualise, and grow your visualisation, like planting a seed and watching it grow into something magnificent. It has been held from most humans, as I said previously, in order to control and stop your development or progression... Some may even say that you are being controlled in order to prevent your progressive *Evolution*. There is always a battle for power, but there is always a hope for peace."

Sue felt excited and wondered if others were sharing the same feeling.

Jess was stood nearby and needed to share a thought. "So, what about being controlled by *your* species? We have taken some kind of medicine that is keeping us calm, and I can't even remember how I came to be here when I was resting in my own armchair not too long ago!"

Sue acknowledged that this was actually quite a reasonable question to ask.

Spreckley smiled.

"Let me explain wonderful people... We have probably given away the fact that we do *need* your amazing abilities and have – in your language – abducted you from your homes."

There was a shuffle amongst the crowd of people.

"You abducted us? I knew there was something I had forgotten. I couldn't remember how I got here. You've medicated us somehow, haven't you!" A strong male voice spoke from the far side of the group.

"Please note that you have the most amazing purpose here. Not only that, but this experience will be forgotten once we return you. You will also be so vastly compensated for helping us out... One further amazing factor to understand is that when we return you, you will have only been missing for approximately five minutes of earthly time. You will be in this place of living for several weeks, but with our ability to manipulate space and time, it will be as if nothing ever occurred. If you could please enjoy this moment while you remember your present experience, knowing that an abundant life will be awaiting you upon your return."
Jess spoke up with much bravery yet again. "What is your measurement of abundance then? What sort of abundance are we talking about?"
"You will return with a greater ability to manifest a life of great riches. Riches in the way that you determine riches in your own unique way. You will have installed within your mind - a greater knowledge and understanding of your power. You have the potential to bring a great power to your own planet. You can use it any which way you decide, but trust me, you will know about it."
"But we will forget about it too?" Another man's voice in the distance questioned.
"You will forget these events, but you will hold your own ability that has been ignited, tenfold."
Spreckley had slight doubt about his group of people but knew that they wouldn't be able to read his concerns.
"Do you all wish to proceed? This will be such fun creativity for you, bringing a heightened ability to your subconscious. It will benefit all concerned. Moreso, yourselves. Otherwise, my colleagues here are happy to return you without any adjustment or enhancement. You will not be *any-the-wiser* as you say on your planet. We have studied humans greatly. Please speak now or raise your hands if you wish to be no part of this, and we shall instantly return you. I promise you will be extremely well cared for."

They all stood, uncertain, knowingly placed into this circumstance that wasn't *apparently* by choice.

A kind sounding gentlemen spoke from within the group. "I was living quite a dull life, so this is quite an amazing thing to be part of. I'm in."

Sue looked at Jess and then turned to Spreckley. "I guess it sounds as if this may improve our lives. Can I just ask why *we* were selected over millions of others though?"

"Most certainly!" Spreckley seemed pleased of *this* question. "You were selected as you seemed to have the biggest vibrational energies. Notable to *us*. You just don't know how to use your well adapted energies. Once you know what we teach you, you can never go back from your new abilities. It will be in your subconscious – your automatic mind."

Jess was still confused. "Do you steal humans often to create your power for you? When did all of this start?"

Spreckley looked a bit guilty. "That is an extremely valid question. In the past we would work in hidden caves upon the Earth, and disguise ourselves by shape-shifting. In other words, we would make ourselves appear human-like. When visiting, we would encourage some people of the Earth to sit with us and visualise this energy growth. This was a long, long time ago. Once we had more than many lifetime's-worth of power, we transported it back here, where it continued to develop at a very slow rate. The source gradually depleted over many years, so we grew desperate. The small amount that we can manifest is very slow compared to the output.

Our problem with returning to the Earth, is that the population and general surveillance on your planet is now vast. It would be difficult to hide in caves and work in private in the same way. Apart from your own monitoring methods, you may not realise how widely your planet is monitored. Many of us so-called Aliens have means of viewing you and your planet so productively, it's almost like the creative movie that you call "The Trueman Show."

"I've seen that one!" A familiar male voice said from the back area.

"I am sure that many of you have. In fact, there are many *very telling* movies that people watch for entertainment, without being any the wiser. That aside, I am simply saying that we are able to monitor particular strengths of energy from a distance, which brings us to our selection process. You should all be very grateful for your heightened abilities that you are not fully aware of."

"I know you said it'll only be like being a short time away when you are able to put us back, but how long will this take in *your* time? How long are we going to be working for you?" Jess wanted accurate answers.

Spreckley grinned knowingly. "Jess, we know you are of strong character, so we expect these wonderful questions from you. Once we have shown you *how* to use your power, it should only take a few short weeks, as mentioned, to manifest another few life-times of power source for us."

There were mutterings between people and then a strange, uncomfortable silence.

Spreckley spoke again. "Another important thing to mention is that in the *silence*, we can hear your *thoughts*. Our *kind* speak telepathically to one another. You were once able to do this and can find this ability once again within a short time. Be aware that when we return you home, you may prefer not to hear the thoughts of your fellow beings. Their words can be harsh. This may sound very judgemental of me, but the human life forms are still very much like children trying to express their words for the emotions they feel. Forgive them either way. This is the biggest lesson you will learn. We plan to install this *knowing* within you too."

They were all silent again, looking at one another's eyes, wondering how this new knowledge will begin.

"We lost a lot of our power source through theft, so we do need to begin our training session today. Please help yourself to fluid and food for approximately one hour before we begin this exciting process."

Sue and Jess looked to see an abundant spread of food on long tables only a few yards away. They both looked at one another, obviously wondering the same.

"They must have thrown that together when we were distracted." Jess always wanted her questions answering.

The crowd of humans walked over to the food and drink like hypnotised people following a strong smell.

"They know what they're doing." Jess spoke quietly to Sue as they walked over.

"I guess they're more advanced than us."

"I mean that they know how to keep us satisfied. I'm surprised they aren't offering us sex on a plate." Jess was obviously making it clear that she speaks her mind.

"Are you annoyed with them?" Sue focussed on her expression.

"I don't know *how* to feel. They steel us; use us and bribe us into helping them out. They've also given us something to keep us calm, perhaps so that we don't get out of control. They say we are kind people, maybe convincing us to act kindly *here*. I'm just not sure."

"Well, I remember how I felt when we first met. I was terrified, so I kind of like this wonderful feeling. I'm not sure on the morals of it all though."

"I guess we just have-to go with the flow. So long as it truly *does* benefit us, even if we don't remember any of it."

"We *do* have the choice to go back though. It's best to speak now before they get started. It would be a shame, as I kind of like how we've gone through this together so far."

"I guess you're right." Jess started to see the bonus of their companionship, "I think I'll stick around. Sorry, I think I needed to go through the whole thought process. I probably sounded really difficult." She reached out to encourage a hug.

"It's not like our everyday existence on *Earth* is it?" Sue acknowledged and reciprocated the offered hug. "I think you're just saying what we all want to say. At least you're brave enough to express yourself."

They all ate the amazing, abundant spread of food, lapping up the goodies whole-heartedly.

Present Day

It was a weekend, and Tom grew bored of the house-sitting for his brother. There were no strange events, and everything appeared to stand still in time. Megan had plans with Sky, leaving him feeling *very* single.

He decided to head out for a trip to one of the small, local towns to see if any events were occurring.

He took himself to the town of Devizes, which wasn't too far away from the house.

Parking up on a side street, he walked around randomly to investigate various views. A pretty water feature and some bespoke shops carried his eyes, until he followed a road up to some more prominent shopping zones.

As he walked about, he felt a strange pull toward one particular direction, not knowing if it was his imagination or not. A gentle, magnetised feel encouraged him to walk through to an area he was certain he wouldn't have consciously picked. The walk brought him to the local museum, making him predict the need to purchase a ticket for entry. He knew there was little else to do, encouraging him to go with the flow.

Once he settled into the atmosphere of the museum, he felt particularly drawn to the history of the local castle. The interest made him wonder if they allowed public visitation. After some reading, he discovered the details of private ownership, confirming an assumption that the option wouldn't exist.

After about an hour of searching through the museum, he decided to attempt to *find* the castle, since it was his biggest interest prompted by this visit.

A brief study of an available map within a pamphlet, gave Tom local familiarity. He left the museum and took a new direction.

Tom walked in the direction he remembered well from the map, and found the main gates to the castle, with the disappointing "no entry" signs.

The external grounds were quite interesting, allowing some view of the structure.

As he walked through a pretty pathway, he wasn't certain of an alternative public route to gain nearer distance to the building but decided to continue through anyway and risk a mini telling-off at *most*. The walk was a very quiet, tree-filled pathway around the circumference of the castle grounds. He wasn't sure how far the path would take him, but he continued with hope.

Some trees gave quite a bit of shade to the pathway, almost a bit too much shade, creating a sudden darkness. His eyes needed to adjust quickly. When he came to another opening, there was a tall figure in the near distance, seemingly walking along the same pathway.

Tom continued on, hoping to keep the same pace so that they didn't need to clash in the narrow area.

At a random corner of the path, he noticed a change in the volume of everything all around him! There was a sudden and uncomfortable silence! The bird tones he was hearing throughout had suddenly stopped, and traffic in the distance had even silenced. Everything felt eerie all of a sudden.

A light whirlwind formed in the near distance, turning direction, and gaining size. This whirlwind twisted and turned from an upward-moving action, to tilting into a sideways moving whirlwind, forming a strange, transparent tunnel. This stopped Tom in his tracks, making him wonder what to do to escape it. He shifted off to the side, into some light shrubbery.

Thinking it may move through the air and bypass him, it seemed to remain in the same position, swirling and hovering. Tom was baffled, looking for an immediate exit route. A wall needed climbing if he was to escape in a sideways direction. He was about to find his risky climb over the ivory-filled, cracked-rocked version of a wall, when he decided to stop and look back first, checking to see if he was overreacting to a bit of wind. The whirlwind now seemed smooth and inviting rather than frightening and threatening.

Tom calmed his mind and studied his surroundings. Everything appeared to be the same in terms of the tall person in the distance and the odd patch of the castle in view. The whirlwind turned fast, but gently, like a hovering mystery. He retracted from the dodgy wall and took his mobile phone from his pocket in an attempt to take a video. The filming was clear, without any expected resistance or experience. The tunnel of wind continued in the same spot, defying any logic that *he* was aware of. He began to realise that this wasn't a threat to him of any kind, thankfully. The tall person along the pathway was now much further away, completely oblivious to any of this.

Tom wondered how much investigation he should do. The thought of leaving it for someone else to find now crossed his mind. The captured footage was enough for him to show anyone who could potentially explain it, hoping for it to be a natural phenomenon. Tom slowly walked back along the path he originally came from, checking back to ensure he was safe of any unexplainable, illogical chasing!

He grew considerably distant, when he gave a final turn of observation, but this final view gave an unusual image that left him curious yet again! The whirlwind looked definitively and distinctly like a tunnel. He stopped in his tracks to face it with a squinting stare. It still remained in the same position.

Thoughts raced through his mind, as an image inside the tunnel reminded him of the blue haze he saw in his car! The external parts of the tunnel grew a brighter white, with a blue item shining more obviously in the centre.

For a few moments during a stare and trying to make sense of it all – he decided to face his fears and move back towards it. He pulled his mobile phone out yet again, thinking the capturing of it would at least prove to others that he wasn't imagining things.

The phone was recording the scene before him really well!

He grew in excitement, replacing his initial fear.

There was a disruption to his privacy, when he noticed the shape of the tall person in the distance turning to face *his* direction. Tom wondered if this person could see a similar scene from the opposite angle.

Strangely, the figure picked up speed and ran towards Tom, nearing the whirlwind! His hairs stood on end, noting a familiarity to this person. He squinted to note the same unusual lady that aggressively entered his brother's home without permission not all that long ago.

He held his phone momentarily, to attempt to capture some features of this approaching person before swiftly dropping his hand in preparation to run in the opposite direction.

Just as he was about to take off on foot, his eyes noted the shrinking whirlwind that reduced swiftly to the size of a coin – from his literal point of view.

The tall figure attempted to reach out to capture this miniature version of the whirlwind, but it dispersed just in time as if attempting to save itself.

Tom spun and ran now without further observation, running back in the direction of the semi-busy streets.

The tall figure noted Tom's movement and threw full attention to *him* now, prompting them both to increase their speed.

Tom's adrenaline pumped hard, wondering what he had gotten himself into, and how coincidental it was that this figure had reappeared to be a threat, yet again! Was this person a yet-to-be-labelled-criminal? He couldn't understand the personal vengeance.

Tom ran along a pathway that emerged to a road full of passing vehicles. People were glancing through their windows, but not stopping to be involved. He felt the gain in distance from his threat, so attempted to sprint harder, tilting his head back to add some serious intent.

A noticing of calmer traffic allowed him a swift crossing of the road to attempt to blend with some of the public members of the town. His assumed-enemy gained distance swiftly, like a terrible chasing nightmare that he was certain he had experienced as a child.

Some people made little noises of shock as Tom ran between groups and couples, barging his way through, hoping to find a way to blend in!

His intimidating predator felt really close, but Tom didn't attempt to look back. He found a heavy crowd of people paying attention to a marketplace and jumped into the centre of the group. Unfortunately, people dispersed with the uncertainty of his behaviour, making him feel open and even more vulnerable. The tall figure slowed their pace and walked, feeling confident of a successful approach.

Tom panicked and shouted, "Help! Help!"

People looked on, wondering what he needed help for. Onlookers were confused at the scene of an extremely tall, elegant woman walking towards a frightened man.

Tom could see their frowns of uncertainty but felt his voice would be the only saviour. "Help! This person is aggressive and wants to hurt me!" He turned to inspect expressions again, "Please help! Call the police!"

The unusual-looking figure grew close with the same frightening eyes. Their voice boomed with a cold aggression.

"Just give me what is mine and you know I will leave you in peace."

Tom was gasping for air from his panic and long sprint. He felt his head begin to spin, but he told his body to hold on. His usual fitness would surely cope with his run, but the sudden stop and mix of fear took control. To his surprise, a blackness, like the closing of curtains at an old cinema - took the view before his eyes. All of a sudden there was nothingness!

Tom didn't know how much time had passed, but when he opened his eyes once again, a beautiful red-haired lady with beautiful green eyes hovered above his face. He thought she was blowing puffs of air onto his eyes!
He attempted to sit from what he realised was a lying position.
"Don't try to move. You had a nasty fall."
"Wha'?" Tom looked around, noting a few others fussing around him.
"You just fell to the ground. You were shouting for help and just fell like a sack of potatoes. Luckily, your head fell on a cardboard box that only had bananas inside. The owner wants new bananas though." She grinned, looking up at an obvious market-stall man.
"Oh shi'." He started to swear but noticed kind faces looking down on him with concern. "I've never fainted before. I take it that's what I did?"
"Confusing innit!" One of the concerned faces said, obviously having had a comparable situation themselves.
Tom started to sit himself up.
"This weird person keeps finding me and asking for something. I need to report them to the police. I don't know what they're talking about, but they are so threatening. It's the second time I've seen them. I don't know them, but they are stalking me or something." He babbled quickly!
"Alright, calm yourself, you need to regain your circulation nicely." The beautiful red-head offered kindly.
Tom looked at her again. "Are you a nurse? Thank you for helping me either way." He slowly gained height to stand without any issue.

"I'm not a nurse, but if you'd have been out any longer we would have had paramedics out to you."

"I can usually run for miles and have no issue, but I guess suddenly stopping... and the panic..."

"That'll do it!" Another member of the crowd offered.

Tom realised his sudden luck. "Did my stalker leave?" He looked around in all directions with hope and relief.

The lady stood with him and offered comforting words.

"I guess whoever it was couldn't do anything when you fainted. How could anyone rob a collapsed man when everyone ran to your rescue?"

"Wow!" Tom rubbed his head.

"Is there anyone we can call to get you home?" The lady was so thoughtful of every single detail.

"Ah man, I parked the darn car, but I'll call someone to get me just in case." He reached for his phone, recalling the video capture at the same time.

"If you sit with us, we'll make sure you're collected safely. I'd report that weirdo to the police too while you're waiting."

"Good thinking." Tom muffled whilst multifunctioning.

Looking at his phone, he wanted to view the video before calling someone. He noted the captivation was perfect! This would need great analysis!

The Evening of 31st October 1860

William waited patiently for Edward to return to his home space upstairs. It had grown relatively dark, and a couple of fairly large bonfires were in view. The sudden realisation of the date made him realise that it was Halloween! Local fires always marked the occasion, hoping to ward off evil spirits.
William always longed for All Saints Day and wished for a swift arrival of Christmas.

Finally, with much relief from William, his friend came up the stairs looking slightly dishevelled. The obvious question came.
"Busy day? I thought you mostly created gems at your desk and caught up with conversation with the local people."
"So, you say that I am not entitled to have tiredness from a long day?" Edward asked light-heartedly with a peaceful grin, changing the subject immediately, "I take it you haven't had any joy in locating your thieving friend?"
"I don't know what label to give that lady at this moment in time, but I cannot give her friendship status." William seemed to have formed more permanent frown lines from the stress.
"Oh, dear my friend, perhaps if I change into a casual form, we can scour the streets. You look as if you need some time outdoors."
"I am concerned for the crystal and for missing a day of work!"
"If it is affecting you *this* badly, then we do need to retrieve the stone." Edward was now changing into another set of clothes in the background.
"Thank you Ed. I know you think I am a fool, but I do feel a connection to our responsibility with this power."
"I have been thinking similarly whilst at work, Will. I hope we are not too late." Edward picked up some bread and offered some to William. They both chomped into their food whilst working their way down the staircase as if there was no time to spare.

The streets were dark, but their eyes were accordingly adjusted in a very short time.

"Do you know where she lives Will?" They walked swiftly in a direction that seemed full of intent.

"Ed, you know that strangely I do not know the lady's surname or her home address." He looked embarrassed at the admission.

"Well, it has been a new relationship." Edward noticed William's expression, feeling the need to change his words swiftly, "I mean it was a fresh acquaintance."

"You don't need to worry about using the right terms with me Ed. I am only disappointed in myself."

Edward felt some relief from the need to tread on eggshells.

"I do know that she said she lived not too far from our community hall, so that could be a start."

"We are dependent on a sign though Will. Don't get your hopes up too high."

They walked without word for quite some time, as they focussed on their breathing at the swift pace they were walking at.

Both of them gained distance with their close arrival to the Community Hall.

"Can you think of any other connections or clues Will? Anything else that she may have said to give her location away?"

"She did say that her father is a supplier of the sweeping materials for chimney sweeps. She suggested I go into business with him, but it was such a brief mention that I thought she couldn't promise anything. I took note of that though, thinking I might benefit from it one day."

"So, you're thinking there may be a hint of sweeping materials, or a business sign somewhere perhaps?"

"It's worth a thought, isn't it?"

"Absolutely."

They both walked through the street in line with the community hall, keeping a keen eye on the details of every home.

William spotted a plaque on one of the walls by the side of a front door.
"Bingo!"
"Shush!" Edward reminded his friend of their need to be stealth-like.
William cringed with his own lack of discretion.
The plaque said, **"Robert's Chimney Sweep Materials."**
"It seems strongly coincidental. Let us take a good look around first. We can't *confirm* that this would be the house." Edward suggested.
"It all makes sense. The house is close to the hall and the work is exactly as she described."
There was a gate between two homes, encouraging them to both walk with the intention of gaining access to other angles of the house.
"Who goes there!" A very deep and dominant voice came from a sudden opening of the front door in question.
William stepped back, attempting to look innocent.
"Oh, I am sorry Sir, I was wondering if Eleanor was free for a moment. I am her friend."
"She is in bed after a hard day of sewing. Perhaps you would like to return at a more convenient time!"
Edward noticed a light shining from an upstairs room.
"Oh, I am sorry Sir. You are right. It is an hour of unsociable times."
The man was of tall, broad, solid structure. He had a heavy moustache and beard.
"We shall be going." Edward answered.
The onlooker watched with suspicion, noting their detailed appearances.
William whispered as they walked.
"That is indeed her home."
"Darn good luck."

To William and Edward, it felt like the man was staring so hard that he could bore a hole into the back of their heads. They walked away swiftly, hiding behind the house at the end of the row.
"What do we do?" William had a brisk intention for resolve.
"Well, we can't just barge in there. It is one thing to do our own detective work, but we are not equipped to break into homes."
"I wonder if we could sneak in through the back when they're all sleeping."
"Don't think hastily. I think we need a time to plot something."
"She will know that we know where she lives. She may have time to plan something hastily herself. Her father took a good look at us. She'll know it is us! I feel we need to act relatively swiftly."
"Oh Will, I don't know what we can do without getting caught."
William had a recognisable smile that made Edward feel extremely uncomfortable.
"Ed, you go home and relax, and I'll sort my own mess out."
"No! Don't get yourself all messed up. That man looks very heavily set."
"I don't plan on getting caught by him. Go home and all will be resolved by the time you wake up." William hand signalled with a shooing action, "Go on. I promise it will all be perfectly fine."
Edward looked deep into William's eyes, noting his confidence, so began to shuffle away. Just as he did, a recognisable light shone extremely brightly from the upstairs room!
"She can activate the stone?" William's words were loud, but the screaming from the house was even louder.
He looked at Edward, hoping he hadn't walked too far along. As he spun his head, his eyes caught the sight of Edward dispersing into small particles yet again and vacuumed up towards the light!
"No! Come back!" William panicked again and wondered what to do with these *added* factors. His adrenaline was pumping so hard that he couldn't think straight. His only guiding action was to race back to the house and slam on the front door.

Eleanor's screams were loud enough to fill the street, causing lights to go on in the entire row of houses. William's eyes were catching the action of the lights, whilst his ears were struck by the thunder of his own fist banging on the door. Nobody answered the door, so he ran back toward the side gate and forced it open, leading him to the path he suspected would run through to the rear of the house. He ran through, still hearing the confused screams.

The house looked solid, with all doors and windows completely sealed. He realised the lack of ability to gain entry, so decided to knock equally hard on the back door. As he did, a lady's frightened face glanced through a window.

"Please! Let me help! I understand *that* light and know what to do!" He shouted at the top of his voice.

The lady looked extremely uncertain and began to move back, and out of sight.

"Let me help! I know Eleanor!" His final plea saw the face of the lady look through the window again. She reached over to open the window by an inch.

A weakened, shaking voice understandably questioned him. "How do you know my daughter?"

"We were dating and then she stole something of mine that she has no understanding of. That item she's screaming about isn't safe in Eleanor's hands." He lowered his voice to bring a sense of compassion.

She looked into his eyes, studying for a fleck of honesty.

Her face disappeared with the window gently closing.

He heard the clunking of locks to their backdoor. He felt a huge sense of relief and resolve when the lady opened the wide gap for his entrance.

Just as he walked through, he felt an immense pain work through his skull. His first thoughts were that of some power from the crystal upon entry, but there wasn't a time for thoughts after that, as he went into a deep darkness.

William could *see* again, through small slits of his eyes, but they were stinging so much with some fluid.

"You've been out cold for some time." The recognisable voice came from the beautiful face hovering over his head.

He realised he was regaining consciousness, not quite understanding the cause at this point. His hands patted downward to feel a mattress, bringing recognition of a bed he was lying on.

"What happened?" He didn't move through fear of the unknown situation. His stinging eyes brought a vulnerability.

Eleanor sat next to the bed in a gold-framed chair, achieving comfort in order to speak with calm.

"My father bumped you on the head with a heavy frying pan with true intention. He thought you were robbing the place."

William wiped his eyelid on one side and noted his own blood on his hand.

"How bad am I?" He worried, trying to sit up.

"You're okay. I told Father who you were, so he asked the family doctor to come over and check you over. You might have a bit of concussion and a headache for a while."

Recalling events, William looked about for sight of any white light.

"Everything is fine now. I wanted to apologise for stealing that stone from you, but I didn't know how to. I placed it somewhere and couldn't even remember where it was."

"You don't know where the stone is? You know that it has the power to heal, after what happened don't you?"

"Yes! It was the reason I took it, of *course*."

"Yet you lost it somewhere? I know it is in the house from what has just occurred."

"How do you know that Will? I placed it somewhere in my room I am certain, but I have had other priorities."

"Wow! I have been trying to find you to tell you how important it is to retrieve the stone for the safety of all. You didn't know that it was the cause of the extreme light?"

Eleanor seemed concerned and confused at the same time.

"You mean to say that *that* was the cause of that frightening light? We thought it was a frightening miracle. I was terrified!"

"Eleanor, that same light occurred when I healed you from your drunken state!"

"Will, I was drunk! I don't recall a *light*. I only recall the after events of you telling me that you healed me with the stone you held in your hand."

William remembered how she returned to consciousness *after* the sickness, and the terrible drunken state.

"So, you don't remember the light?"

"If it is the same light that we had this fine night, then I do not recall it from previous times. I screamed so loud with fear that my father came to investigate, causing a slight blindness to him. He ran downstairs, fumbling with his hands and said that this was when his eyes began to see, allowing view of the figure of *you* entering our home. It was a chaotic run of events."

"Well that certainly makes sense." William lifted his legs to dangle over the side of the bed.

"Wait one moment – so you came to attempt to steal the stone *back* from me?" Eleanor's face looked vexed.

"Well, you stole it from *me* Eleanor. I knocked on the door, hoping that we could ask for your attention and retrieve our item in a sociable way."

"Wait a moment. How did you find my home?"

"You ask me that *now*? Did you not wish for me to know? We were meant to be together. You stole the item from me, yet you ask a question upon morals? Where has the light gone now, Eleanor?"

As he asked, she looked even more confused.

"I thought *you* knew the actions of this stone?" She paused, "The light came into my room somehow, for no apparent reason. After a short time, I noticed a lot of small particles of dust fly in through the smallest gap of my window."

William stood with urgency. "Ed!"

"What?" Eleanor wouldn't have understood the next possible explanation, leaving William to request more detail. "Where did the dust land Eleanor, can you remember?"
"Well, the dust didn't settle William. I expected to find some once the light had settled. I tried to sweep it up, but there was nothing to sweep. It was part of the mystery."
William was beginning to realise that Eleanor would find a full explanation extremely difficult.
"Could you please show me where the dust was expected to have settled?"
"Well, directly under the bed you were lying on."
"This is *your* bed?"
"I wanted you to heal in comfort after my father and the doctor lifted you from the floor."
William decided not to confuse her anymore and knelt down to look under the bed. He brushed his hands over the carpet, causing the light of the stone to spring into action once again! As Eleanor decided to scream yet again, a rush of strong particles erupted from under the bed, forming the gradual figure of Edward on the opposite side of the bedroom.
"Oh my Gosh!" Eleanor's face grew almost grey, leaving her slumped in the chair, obviously having fainted.
William studied her to ensure she was breathing, confirming that she was okay. He then moved swiftly over to Edward to ensure he was focussed enough to return to his surroundings.
William reached under the bed again, to feel the stone with the tip of his longest finger. The light extinguished immediately, allowing a better focus on the entire situation.
He managed to grab the crystal and place it in his jacket pocket. He held no fear of leaving the house, even with the extra-dazed person in toe. The returned crystal and his friend filled his entirety with relief.

He took another look at Eleanor, who continued to breathe. She began to move slightly, encouraging William to grab Edward's arm to guide his direction for them both to swiftly depart.
William directed Edward through an upstairs corridor and gently down the staircase, hearing the distant moans of Eleanor demonstrating her return to consciousness.
"Quick Ed!" William shouted in the highest whispering volume. Edward was obviously moving subconsciously, not fully aware of who or where he was.
They gained distance to the ground floor, seeking out a corridor with hope for an exit door.
William caught glance of a candle-lit lantern hanging from a distant wall to the far right, with the mother of Eleanor knitting in a comfortable chair, half dozing into a sleep state. The back of another large chair held the view of the rear of her father's head. William knew he would need to be swift and silent. The dry blood on his hand and the slight sting in his eye reminded him of his personal safety.
He crept past, pulling a zombie version of Edward along, keeping slight view of the mother in his peripherals.
Reaching the old wooden door, he hoped for a smooth catch and opening. A big key sat in a main lock. He knew the metal would clang the lock open. Standing still for a moment, he had a sudden realisation of not actually needing to creep out of the house. He looked down, took a deep breath, and shouted in a surprisingly confident manner.
"Thank you for your hospitality!" William shouted with fake confidence, surprising even his own ears. Pain struck through his head, reminding him of his injuries. He heard the creak of the chairs after announcing his presence.
Knowing he was out of sight, nearest the front door, he needed to swiftly turn the key, which he did with an almighty clunk. One-handedly once again, he tugged at the latch to pull the door open.
"I'll be leaving now!"

He could sense the father was on his feet and beginning to walk in their direction, so just as soon as the two of them were the other side of the door, he swiftly pulled it closed, pulling Edward with all of his might.

"Come on Ed! I need you to come round! I need you to run with me!" He tried to run and encourage Edward to pick up speed in unison.

The adrenaline pumped through William as he ran, dragging his friend as hard as he could, managing to get to the end of the row of houses. He turned into a corner that was easier to get out of sight with. Pausing to catch his breath, he hoped that they weren't being followed.

William tried to look at Edward's face in the dark.

"Edward, I need you to realise where you are. You did your little travelling thing again, but you are back in your normal body."

William wasn't sure if anything was working. Edward was still looking vague, so he grabbed his arm and told him to run with him yet again until they eventually arrived at the shop.

William fumbled through Edward's pocket's attempting to retrieve the key to the front door. He kept an eye out for any followers, hoping the father hadn't caught up with them somehow.

Thankfully, he managed to retrieve the key and gain access to the property.

William sat Edward in his work chair just inside the dark shop. He looked through the front windows to ensure yet again that they were both safe of followers.

Edward's head started to move, followed by a more life-filled set of eyes beginning to view the scene before him.

"Oh, what has happened?" Edward spoke with a croaky voice. "I feel as if I had left my body again."

William breathed a huge sigh of relief. "Oh my, I didn't think you were going to return this time. I believe you did that strange transportation into the stone again. Do you remember being at Eleanor's house at all?"

Edward looked a bit dazed and confused, taking sudden note of William's blood.

"What in the world happened to you?"

William touched the tender spot of his wound.

"Oh boy, this is going to take a while to explain." William removed the stone from his pocket. "I am starting to realise I have a connection with the stone that activates it simply with the intention of my thoughts. I realise now that when we were stood at the front of Eleanor's home, I activated the stone by visualising my connection with it once again. I knew we were close to one another."

"That sounds like madness." Edward didn't realise the contradiction of his words.

"Well, *you* did your usual thing by slipping into the stone somehow. You seem to lose your body and become particles. Eleanor noticed dust flying toward her room through a small gap. I think *that* is madness."

"Do you think we are mad Will? Do you think we need help? Is this all our imagination?" Edward had a concerning look on his face.

"Maybe this is all you Will! You could be knocking me unconscious somehow and making me believe all of this."

William was shocked at the accusation and frowned intensely. His voice grew serious and extra deep.

"I cannot believe you would say such a thing. Did you not witness enough with the light? Did you not experience a journey once again?"

Edward looked down with thought.

"Oh, I am truly sorry. I am beginning to recall things now. I think it has taken me time to fully bring myself back to the here and now." William's stressed shoulders dropped with a little more relief. He couldn't handle the loss of his friendship during such a time. Edward looked up at an old clock that he had decorated.

"Three o'clock in the morning? How did that happen? I need to get some sleep!"

William walked close to touch Edward on the shoulder.
"I am so sorry Ed. This wouldn't be so ridiculous if I hadn't had been so careless. From this day forth, I plan to keep this in my own hands. Perhaps you could make a wallet for its safe keeping."
"You know, *that* is quite a good idea." Edward's eyes looked extremely heavy as he looked at William. "My body seems to be forcing me to sleep."
"Okay Ed, it could be valuable to get some rest. If I help you upstairs, would you mind if I kept you company by sleeping in the living area? In the morning, we could rationalise things together."
"Good idea Will."
William felt wounded by the injury to his head but needed to aid his friend from what seemed like a severe trauma to his entirety. Edward went to sleep almost immediately upon landing his head on the pillow, leaving William to grab blankets of familiarity from previous stays, and finding relative comfort on a fortunate sofa.

Present Time

Archives within gold-edged paper were so deep and thorough, with much detail.
Records were held with such intelligence, with extremely accurate calligraphy. An occasional blob of ink looked unfortunate but obviously largely avoided.
The book was heavy with a leather cover and browning crisp paper. Tom turned the pages with caution for preservation, making the conscious effort to retain the words he read.
Words of interest struck him in the mind just the same as a strong feeling in his body. Words of healing made him feel good, but words of injury literally gave him nerve pain. He seemed to *feel* the words!
He knew he was retaining a lot of information so easily but couldn't understand how. The words appeared to come away from the pages now, flying towards his face in gold lettering. It became a little bit overwhelming. This wasn't something that normally occurred! He felt beads of sweat form on his face as the gold entered his eyes, making him take a big gulp of air!
He flung his body forward, sitting upright, taking time to focus his eyes into the present moment. Two worlds seemed to be merging, confusing him slightly, but realising he was waking from an extremely vivid dream.
He lifted himself up to the edge of his bed and stood to shake himself back into his physical mind. Standing, he rubbed his head and neck, bringing back normal feelings and realisations. His clothes were flung on the floor, so he lazily reached down to grab them, placing them wearily onto his body. He walked over to a full-length mirror and ruffled his fingers through his hair, pleased with his swift improvement of appearance. Tom wasn't expecting

to go anywhere today. He felt as if he was still recovering from his frightful experience of being chased by the mysterious person.
He wanted to make the house-sitting for his brother a little bit of a recovery event – somewhere with different walls and views generally.
As he splashed his face with water in the bathroom, he wondered about the vivid dream, thinking that the recent fear-provoking events had impacted his mind somewhat.
Walking down to the kitchen area, he prepared himself a glass of water, rehydrating his mouth to feel even more "normal."
He looked into the garden, noting the digging Ethan had been so busy with. The pond was taking shape, but there was still some serious work to do. Soil and rubble sat either side of the large hole. Tom wanted to help finish the job, but he wasn't sure about the shape or depth Ethan was aiming for.

Tom sat to eat breakfast, shuffling through some paperwork, feeling a bit guilty for being nosy, but still wanting to snoop through, as if something mischievous was driving him.
Nothing of excitement or importance sat in any of the papers, and he'd finished eating his breakfast at the same time as his paper shuffling.
His mind was now focussed on a desire to go for a walk and possibly build it up to a run. The idea was that it would help to clear his mind and reduce the recent stressors.

He stood, stretched, and placed his breakfast tools in the sink. His training shoes were by the door, so he placed them on swiftly with the exit plan for fresh air.
The air was fresh, clear, and wonderful for October, in England. Tom walked with ease, feeling a lot calmer, aiming for some beautiful green hills within view and reach.
He looked up to admire a large Buzzard flying through the sky with the beautiful set of large wings and the wind directional tail. The

bird appeared to be enjoying the clear blue skies too, and Tom felt some interesting connection to them, noting their little head scouring over the land, looking so free but with obvious intent for prey.
He could feel his body working calmly on the food he'd eaten, making him feel alive and wonderful. If the weather was slightly warmer he would have been tempted to remove his shoes on the impending green grass up ahead.
This break was doing him good. He wanted to keep the same good feeling for a full rest, recovery and recouperation for the next few days.

The grassy land grew close, and he considered a faster pace.
As he grew near, he followed a well-used path, rambling over styles and climbing the gradient that helped him to work slightly harder.
He remembered the monument at the top of the hills and noticed it in the far distance, knowing he could reach it relatively quickly if he wanted to pick up his speed with a jog.
His eyes felt rather strange at this point, and there was a slight haze that covered the hills now, uncertain if this was a visual impairment of his own, or something that was building in the atmosphere. He frowned with wanting to confirm this, but as his attempt to refocus was in play, a golden haze covered everything in the distance. Tom started to wonder if this was real or if it was his imagination playing tricks on him.
A warmth filled him, increasing with an immense sense of calm. He couldn't help but feel a sense of being drawn in, deeper into the golden warmth of air. It felt so protecting and encouraging. His walking pace grew faster without effort, and his aim appeared to be towards the same monument at the top of the steep hills. He felt a slight vibration on the ground that his logic questioned, leaving him uncertain of what to do. Continuing his fast pace of walking however, he noticed gold swirls growing stronger in his

peripheral vision - spreading and spreading - eventually enveloping most of his view. This caused him to stop in his literal tracks and shake his head.

The golden swirls caused everything to appear blurry other than the image of a strange-looking person walking through the most golden part of the haze. His head seemed taller, and his chin blended into his neck. Tom squinted his eyes to make sense of his view just as *another* person interrupted the unusual scene! Normality hit him as a dog barked alongside his human companion, causing the golden haze to disintegrate completely all of a sudden, creating a slight imbalance to Tom's feet. His grounding to the Earth felt unsettled for a few seconds. He looked at the person with the dog who spoke confidently with a "Good Day to you!"

Tom took a while to find his normal words, sensing that his expression may have appeared stunned. "Hi there."

The dog owner looked at Tom strangely and encouraged his dog to hurry along beside him, gaining swift distance.

Tom looked ahead to see that the golden haze was completely gone and that there wasn't a sign of any other being around him at all.

"Weird." He whispered to himself.

He spun his head in all directions, trying to recapture the wonderful moment, but nothing returned. He was almost at the monument, so continued on to reach the foot of it, just to have achieved *something*. The memory of the inscription caught his mind, so he decided to view this again, remembering the similar golden haze running alongside his finger when he rubbed over it. He tried this action again to see if the same strangeness would reoccur. Another walker moved past nearby, distracting him from his intense thoughts. He decided to look on instead and take in the wonderful view at the top of these rolling green hills, wondering what the magic of this place was all about.

His life had taken a strange angle, but he decided to keep this to himself and investigate further in his own time. The feeling of the gold and whatever presence there was, left him in a wonderful state, so there wasn't a necessity to speak with anyone in particular. Life felt strangely exciting!

The Globe

Spreckley monitored the humans eating their food and enjoying the liquids provided for them. He listened to their thoughts. They were all questioning the motives of this event, with some primitive, critical thoughts of one another's appearances. Spreckley was used-to the way humans thought and accepted their views as *normal*. He wanted them to evolve to be more loving towards one another, however.

Memories of communication with other humans came to his own mind. He used-to teach some people in the past whilst analysing them, in order to attempt to understand *why* they were the way they *were (*or *are* the way they *are)*... Allowing their freedom to choose what they wanted to believe without any intention to control them.

Spreckley noticed that people struggled with the idea of their uniqueness, bringing a lot of division, although division was also encouraged by the odd few.

His own species had evolved to higher levels of understanding, along with the (unrelated) advanced technologies but were ahead enough to bring wisdom to other life forms if they *chose* to take note or listen. The universal laws of *choice* and *allowing* are irreversible, which knowingly only allows advice and inspiration from Spreckley and his team.

One of his colleagues, Shayze, moved smoothly over to him and pointed upwards to catch the fresh sight of a hovering vehicle taking entry into the globe area.

Spreckley gently questioned the observation, "Is this authorised entry? We need to be tighter on things now. I hope the team have increased awareness at this time." Both Shayze and Spreckley were uncertain on the hovering vehicle as they watched on.

This vehicle was the shape of half a circle, with the flat part as the base. It could be described as a dome. It moved without noise and passed through the opposite side of the globe, with a natural opening and closing action of the nearest portal.

"That was just a cut-through." Shayze - his almost identically-featured-colleague commented.

"Please speak to the others to ensure awareness of identification is vital since our recent theft." Spreckley gave a comforting smile with his request.

Shayze moved backwards with peaceful acknowledgement and aimed towards another group of beings in the near distance. They had already discussed the heightening of security, but their previous need for such things was usually so minimal that they didn't take swift action with their lack of desire for feelings of hostility. It felt very unfortunate, but the hope was that this situation was temporary.

Just as Shayze moved to communicate the necessary need for heightened awareness, the dome returned from a different angle. This time the dome swooped down into the area of the relaxed humans, suddenly disturbing their peace with small noises of very slight distress, given their calm-induced states.

The dome flew effortlessly with ease, moving into the power-based cave-styled area. Spreckley stood with surprise, moving like the wind to attempt to stop yet another-assumed-theft from their energy storage!

A swift movement was enough for Spreckley to recognise the image of Trion, collecting very large pieces of their items of power and shifting them speedily into the dome-shaped ship. Spreckley knew that this was now *severely* risking their own global energy. Trion was a crafty character full of such deceit, stealing for the greed and laziness of his own species, unwilling to build upon his already-stolen items. It was easier for him to steal what

Spreckley's team had been building. His thieving actions were getting less predictable, particularly when a theft had occurred only shortly before!

The dome held four huge chunks of this energy-rock-source (that Spreckley could witness as he ran toward the event).

Shayze gathered a team and attempted to block the entry and exit points, using their own movement vehicles of various oval, pyramid, and cone shapes, but Trion was so swift in escape that the action was completely wasted.

Shayze was a character of passion and strength, so moved swiftly with his own vehicle and attempted to chase Trion. Spreckley held the sides of his head in despair, hoping a battle wouldn't erupt from the fresh clash. He didn't think an act of harm or war was worth some further energy losses when they had the advantage of the new manifestation plans. They would certainly need to move swifter with a re-accumulation of energy sourcing with what remained, but it was still possible, even with the smallest item to work with.

Shayze moved in a swift, flatter disc-shaped flying technology, able to gain distance and find the dome-shaped vehicle of Trion's, making its way back to the neighbouring planet.

The disc moved so adaptively, reaching the dome easily. Shayze intentionally reached to a clear screen within his own ship, making a motion that threw a yellow coloured beam of light out of his vehicle, capturing Trion's dome, cutting his power, and causing the dome to remain completely stationary.

Trion's ship suddenly held a *brighter* yellow colour and managed to regain power. Shayze remembered the stolen items within Trion's ship, and how the power of *that* would outweigh the power being carried by the minimal source of the disc vehicle. With this new realisation, Shayze grew frustrated, considering alternative options.

Trion's transport managed to escape the controlling beam of light and swiftly moved through the black atmosphere, creating an urgency of action for Shayze. He called for a flock of back-up vehicles, using an emergency button, and within a few seconds, a few other similar shaped vehicles were surrounding him, ready to take action.

Shayze led the group of supporters, sighting the target on a large navigation screen. They all connected in on the same form of technological communication and shot forward to attempt to stop Trion. The assumption was that Trion's plan was to stash and hide the stolen power source.

As they neared his vehicle with ease, they attempted to surround him and block him from entering the atmosphere of his planet. From a distance, Trion's planet was a very bright, colourful planet, with shades of white, yellow, orange, and tinges of green.

Trion tried hard to shift through any gap but noted their clever tactics to continue to trap him. Trion decided to attempt a diversion by aiming for a non-predictable destination. His dome shot off into another zone extremely quickly. He slipped into a different Galaxy, with another planetary system in view, swiftly selecting a random planet, and allowing his vehicle to crash into a vast space of water. As Trion monitored the health of his transportation in his new depth of water, he noted the reasonable level of safety. He also noticed that the deeper he went, the less visible he was to his pursuers. He couldn't locate them on *his* screen, so knew that he would be invisible to them too.

The vehicle was moving, but slightly sluggishly through the water, so he realised he needed to make quick decisions.

Trion glided until the water grew shallow and his dome began to shift along rough grit. He intentionally moved forward into a large space of green roughage, including many tall trees, enough to hide his location from direct vision.

The crowd of pursuers were now on his radar once again yet remaining at the outskirts of this particular planet. He still felt vulnerable to attack however with their knowledge of his location. He looked through some analytics of this planet on his highly technical screen, newly understanding that this particular galaxy had strict universal laws in order to protect the lifeforms here. To his pleasant surprise he realised he'd discovered an area of importance within the universe - a planet of which had high focus for evolution! Furthermore, he pulled up information confirming this planet was protected from the unknown life beyond its' own. In other words, he discovered that the lifeforms on this planet were not meant to be interfered with, without a higher form of consent. He realised he'd broken some universal laws by entering the boundaries of this planet but equally decided that this is *also* what would keep him safe! The others would know their inability to chase him! Trion didn't care about breaking any universal laws! He was simply keen to escape at this point.

Having more time to ponder, Trion began to plot some more unlawful ideas. He realised how primitive things were on this planet (yet full of extreme evolutionary potential), therefore began unfolding a new plan. The plan would be to gain gradual control of any intelligent *being* in order to create total power of this planet.
For the immediate moment, he needed to stash his power source! After some gaining of immediate local knowledge, he managed to find a location in order to bury a large item of the crystal power-source. This item was extremely large and heavy, but his vehicle held the power of light-beams to lift and shift items into the ground. One large crystal, three times the size of himself was strategically placed deep within the ground. He noted a circle of trees, which he decided to remember as his location identification when it was time to retrieve the power source.

He regained his position inside the vehicle and shifted swiftly and stealth-fully to another location at an opposite end of this planet.

This time the land was pure, green, and extremely hilly, perfect for another delve into the ground with another huge chunk of crystal power. This particular chunk of crystal was successfully buried too. He could tell that his pursuers were hovering a little further away, in near distance to the external atmosphere of this planet.
They were obviously uncertain of their permissions to enter, leaving Trion feeling benefitted by his pursuers foolishly sticking to the Universal Laws.

Trion moved to a vast area of sand and dust, finding this another secret location to bury yet another source of extreme power deep within the ground. He wasn't sure how to remember this location, but noted some structures in the distance, so decided to remember the view and hope that his memory would serve him well.
At this point, a small chunk of the crystal fell away from the latest large chunk and sat comfortably in his hand. He looked down to admire the beauty of this piece, wondering what to do with this part that held potential power. This piece shone brighter and pulsated in his hand. As he felt this pulsation, he could sense that his own energy combined with the crystal. With this momentary pause of awareness of present-moment, he noticed that this crystal connected to the power of *all* of the crystals that he had *just* buried. It pulsated and magnetised strangely.
This was an unusual surprise, yet suddenly realised as a useful locator and energiser!
This hand-sized crystal felt like a *deliberate* source of connection to all of the crystal power sources. This was a new sensation to him. He looked at this planetary atmosphere and wondered if it held something more energising. He felt a buzzing light around him, so enjoyed this energy-enhancing moment for a while, not wanting to leave the item, or this new planet.
He noted an area of flat land in the near distance and buried this smaller, broken part of the crystal well, noting the landmarks. As

he buried this *particular* crystal, the land seemed to vibrate with it as if the land was activated by it! He started to wonder if this planet had an unusual life to it.
Upon re-entering his vehicle, he took an extra note of the location on his screen. He attempted to imprint the location in his mind. This couldn't be forgotten!

He now looked at the remaining power source within his vehicle and pondered over the final location for this.
Looking at his navigational screen, he noted six of Spreckley's crew still encircling the planet from a distance, obviously hopeful of an eventual capture. Trion smiled at his luck so far in his criminal adventure. He moved his vehicle to another vast space of water and dove it into the sea life.
Just beyond the view of sea he pleasingly spotted a large cave space. He lifted slightly to shallow waters, placing the final, large piece of crystal inside this very deep cave, allowing it to sink into the depth of the waters.
His vehicle now held just enough energy source for him to move elsewhere to escape.
Trion quickly moved away from the cave and turned almost vertically, allowing water to slip violently over the dome, giving him the power to move directly upwards. He took a sharp move to the right of him, scouring over land, hoping that the speed he moved would make him invisible to the primitive life below. Trion knew the limitations of some of the eyes on this planet. If the vehicle moved swiftly enough, he would be too fast for their vision.
Suddenly his speed reduced, and his vehicle felt slightly sluggish. He looked back inside this huge compartment of a ship to note small shards of crystals, foolishly realising that this wouldn't be sufficient power to travel a huge distance.
What a fool! He cursed himself.

He now wanted to attempt to gain access to his original planet with yet another plan in mind.

Trion managed to exit the atmosphere of the planet, and hover in the darkness of open space. He pressed a button that was meant to convert his vehicle into stealth mode, but his power was insufficiently low, so the dome flickered in and out of visibility. He held onto a piece of crystal and attempted to manifest more of the same, but he wasn't relaxed enough for his thoughts to focus. Before he knew it, a crew of vehicles surrounded him, and several streams of light captured his dome as if in a sudden spotlight of attention.

An item of flat material forced its way into his vehicle and lifted him from his feet, surrounding him in some form of life-sized tube. He was bound by this tube that lifted him into the depths of darkness and down into one of the fleet of vehicles.

Inside this different vehicle, a *being* looked at Trion, informing him of his capture. Trion didn't speak, as much as he wanted to respond - with sarcasm.

Trion was transported back to the *Globe* within a short few minutes and placed within a specific department.

Spreckley was seen approaching, making Trion angry and frustrated.

"Remove me at once Spreckley!"

Spreckley approached swiftly, knowing his thoughts.

"You will now receive the therapy required to heal you of such negative actions. Once we are satisfied, you will be released and returned freely to your home planet."

"I do not need such therapies Spreckley. You know my actions define my purpose in order to bring experiences others can learn from."

"Trion, we are desperate to regenerate our power following your actions, so the therapy is required for two purposes. One of

stalling you in order to regain our sources, and the other is to hold hope of some change to your behaviours."
"Oh, all high and mighty Spreckley who borrows other beings in order to stash such powers, yet you are so morally right. Perhaps *you* are in need of therapy."
"I enhance their lives Trion, as you well know. These beings benefit without interruption to their lifelines. They have increased abilities once I return them. Unless of course they prefer to stay."
"The beings have the power of choice, yet you break the laws of the universe by making the choice for them."
"Some breaking of laws can be beneficial. Your breaking of laws do not benefit others."
"They do in terms of helping my *own* planet Spreckley. If you use and abuse, then I should benefit also."
"We are all in the mind of sharing, but you are not aiding the sharing by stealing an abundance of what we are creating. By accepting what we share should be sufficient to you and your planet. Your stealing is simply greed."
Trion stood tight-lipped, not having a good response plan.
"And what of my ship?" Was all he managed.
"You shall retain possession when the time is right."
Spreckley knew the conversation had ended and asked his colleagues to help Trion feel comfortable in his new therapy space.

1st November 1860

William needed to focus on his work, as he noted his earnings were dropping with all of his recent distractions.
He woke to the sofa that he found relatively comfortable, feeling the soreness on his head from the previous attack.

"Good morning." Edward's voice was clear, with his approach comforting. He carried some bread and eggs to William's lap.
"Eat this. I believe it will do us both some good."

William rubbed his head and focussed his eyes.
"You are a great friend Edward. Thank you so much."

They both sat and ate comfortably, enjoying one another's company, knowing of their individual need to recover from only a short few hours ago.
Edward looked at William, noting his pained face.
"I guess you will struggle with work today if you plan to return."
"I think so. How about yourself?" William asked without looking at his friend.
"I had quite a refreshing sleep in all honesty. I just feel a little tired. I know you took quite a blow to the head."
William enjoyed the food on his taste buds.
"I shall be fine young Ed." He spoke with courage.

They both sat in silence for some time, just eating and relaxing. It felt therapeutic and bonding.
The food was warming and energising, encouraging them to start their day well.

They both stood without word after some calming moments and placed their plates and utensils in the sink not too far away.

Edward led the way down the stairs, wishing William a good day as he made his way through the front door with a gentle wave. Edward worked his feet toward his usual position behind the creative desk.

William only felt a slight pain in his head, leaving his good friend, and casually walking down the road. He felt a sense of relief for his beneficial youth for a swift recovery of things generally. He wasn't sure why he couldn't take a simple walk home after the night's events in order to be in his own bed though. Perhaps the comfort of his best friend dictated a lot of his actions.
As William walked, he looked ahead to notice a familiar figure standing at the entrance of his own home. Eleanor was stood with her tall, slender figure, peering through any available gaps or windows, hoping to gain attention.
He quickly slipped behind an available tree trunk, planning to spy with hope that she might give up and walk away.
Watching her actions, she wasn't going to give up easily. He chuckled at the thought that she may be expecting him to suddenly appear like some kind of ghost popping up.
"Come on lady. I need you to head off now." He whispered, looking at his watch, truly desiring preparation for work.
She didn't seem to want to give up. William wondered why she was so insistent when it was clear that he wasn't at home. As he continued to hide whilst spying, he looked at his watch again, noting she'd been waiting and looking for over five minutes since spotting her. At the second he decided he may have to face her presence, she started to dwindle away from his property. He breathed a sigh of relief and slowly unfolded himself from his chosen hiding place.
Eleanor walked away, occasionally turning her head to face the house as if his head would suddenly pop up!
William walked cautiously, waiting for her to fully take stride in her departure. She finally moved out of sight enabling him to gain

access to his own home! He kept a keen eye on the surrounding walkways to ensure he was most certainly free.

Entering his front door, he moved into the dining room to place the crystal on the table from his trouser pocket. He attempted to keep his thoughts unintentional on igniting the crystal as not to draw attention to himself. Any bright light from the crystal would give his whereabouts away.

Looking at the crystal, he wondered what this item was bringing to his life. Should he bury it? He stared in deep thought, noticing the reflection of his face on the nearest side. As he looked with a serious face, another smiling face of his own looked back! It frightened him initially, causing him to pull back and try again. This time he looked at his reflection with a smile, but the reflection looked back with a serious face. He pulled back in shock yet again!

"What?"

He stood back, uncertain as what to do. This was such a puzzle to him. His life was so simple before the crystal came into their possession.

"That's it! It's too much for me!" He picked the crystal up and began walking over to the back door with intention to bury it deep within the ground.

As he grabbed the crystal it grew so cold in his hand that it felt unbearable, forcing him to drop it.

Particles began to unfold from the crystal! It was the same formation of particles that would create the structure of a person, just the same as the view of Edward returning from the item, although this time, obviously, it was someone or something else! The small particles moved out of the crystal with such strength and force, forming a figure right in front of his wide eyes! He stood back, leaning on the wall behind him, his palms flat against it. The figure formed as a mirror image of himself. If he had a full length mirror, he would be seeing himself in full form very similarly but in full depth.

"William." The voice was identical to his own, but very gentle. He gasped to listen with a tension he'd never felt before.
"William. I am you. You are me. I need you to understand some things."
William stood in horror, trying to remain stable in mind.
The hand reached out and touched him gently on his left shoulder.
"Please be calm with my body. I need us to be strong."
William still couldn't speak or move. He could only feel the cold wall on his palms, that were pressed with such tension.
"William, please listen. I am *you* from another dimension. I need to explain things that will help you understand the reason you need to keep persevering with the crystal."
William slowly began to lower his shoulders and calm his breathing slightly.
"That's better. Please listen to me and know that you are completely safe. I wouldn't harm you. I wouldn't wish to harm myself."
"Y-Y-You are me?" He managed to muster.
"I am indeed. We all exist in many dimensions. You need to be grounded here so that you are consistent in the choices you make in this solid, three-dimensional space. The concept will sound crazy to you."
William shook a bit, really trying to calm himself. The words wouldn't have been understood even if he held clarity.
"Please calm yourself. Pick the crystal up and place it over the centre of your chest."
William was too afraid *not* to follow orders, so performed the action within the shortest few seconds possible.
Placing the crystal on his chest created a huge force of energy. Beams of light surged through him and all around him, creating so much courage within him that there was no place for fear anymore.

William's entire posture changed. He stood like a hero of some kind. His chest looked larger, protruding like an extremely proud lion-version of a human.

"That is *so* much better." Was the voice from ahead that now seemed timid and weak to him.

William looked down at himself to check the reality of his new feeling.

"The crystal has more power than you could ever imagine William. I need to give you quite a lot of information, so there is a way I can do this without needing to give intense lectures.

William didn't reply. He felt too strong to express himself, so stood in silence looking down at his hands, still inspecting himself.

"Place the crystal between your eyebrows now."

William concurred with the action and gently allowed the crystal to sit between his eyebrows, wondering what power he may receive from *this*!

Instead of receiving power, he had a vision of a future event. Words in a gentle, but crispy, feminine clarity came to his ears in the background, saying that he needed to be the protector of the crystal and of his great friend, Edward. There was a fight scene of an attempted capture of the crystal. He tried to gain a clear view of the vision. A man with a very strange pair of deep, dark eyes attacks his friend, Edward, in the scene. There's a lot of gripping and wrestling with the three of them. During the scene, William is reminded again and again to protect Edward and the crystal. The message comes through in a kind, but repetitive manner, stating the importance of protecting Edward and the crystal. The voice tells him that his guarding of the two, is, in-fact a vital purpose of his. The voice tells William that it is his entire life purpose, as it is all meant to happen exactly as it does for a very large, overall reason in life.

William's view came back to the stable room that his eyes were used to. His "other-self" had disappeared, and he caught sight of some final particles that were vacuumed into the crystal that still sat between his eyebrows.

In a sudden panic he dropped the crystal and caught his breath, looking around himself to attempt to understand what had just happened.

"How the heck am I going to explain *this* to Edward?"

He spoke to himself, wondering if anyone else could hear his words as he felt *watched* after the event.

"Are we always observed?" William questioned the world he *thought* he understood.

He bravely retrieved the crystal from the ground and looked at it again, thinking it may be a good idea not to stare into any reflections until he had time to digest what had just occurred.

He placed the crystal on the dining room table, deciding to place it in the centre, and then step backwards, to slip away from the room.

He needed to straighten his head out and get ready for a working day somehow. The immense bravery that he experienced seemed to be reduced, but he still felt courageous enough to deal with what had happened and psychologically place a line under the event for now.

William decided that he would ask the questions in his mind later, when he had time at the end of the day. For now, he needed to ensure he literally placed his work boots on and departed the house. He frowned with slight confusion but needed some reality for now.

Present Time

Tom was waiting for his brother to return home whilst cleaning up any final mess in the kitchen. He was expecting Ethan and Rachel to return any minute.

Spinning to a car noise, he recognised the vehicle of his brother pulling up. From a distance, they both looked happy and well. He hoped the break had given them the time and space they needed. Tom answered the door to two very happy people offering him a loving hug.

"Hey, you guys look as if everything went to plan!"

Ethan had a big grin on his face.

"Well bro, I do have-to say it was a great idea of yours. We had a fab time."

"Thanks Tom." Rachel offered with the mutual hug.

"So, what did you get up to?"

"Ah no, you first! The whole trip home we've wondered if you had any weird experiences in the house."

Tom shrugged with a slightly cynical expression.

"Nothing happened the entire time?" Rachel wanted confirmation of the observed body language.

"Nope."

This made Ethan feel slightly odd about being the only person with any unusual experiences.

"I'm hoping, if anything, that I've changed the energy of the house to be better." Tom was offering something comforting.

"Ah, thanks Tom." Rachel could feel the sentiment.

"So shall I leave you guys to it, or did you want to tell me about the trip?"

They both placed their bags down untidily in the kitchen.

"Let's have a drink and catch-up." Rachel offered.

Ethan still looked comfortable about things and grabbed three glasses in agreement. "I'll grab us the usual ones unless you let me know any different."
"Well, actually, I fancy a coffee." Rachel gently suggested whilst walking over to their machine.
Ethan looked at Tom, his expression asking if he wanted the same.
"Go on then, a coffee sounds good. If you don't mind?"
"You guys settle down and I'll bring them out." Rachel wanted to make the coffee to her own literal taste.

Ethan looked incredibly happy and refreshed, much to ongoing observations from Tom.
"You know, I hope I can keep this feeling. We had such a wonderful time." Ethan walked with conversation to the living room.
"What made it so amazing then? I'm happy for you, but this is a huge transformation from your previous appearance. I was worried."
They both sat comfortably, overhearing Rachel's spoon clanging in the mugs.
"We spent a lot of time in this peaceful, nature-filled space. There was a lot of talking, relaxing and…"
"Don't give him all of the details honey!" Rachel walked in with a tray of hot mugs and a smile. "Thanks for heating the water up Tom."
"I wouldn't give too much of our stuff away Rache." Ethan smiled.
"We have some good news." Rachel offered along with the angle of the mug handles available for grabbing.
Tom knew what was coming but asked anyway.
"You're setting a date?"
Ethan laughed. "Is it *that* obvious? We wanted to trial living together, and we do support each other really well."
"Whatever makes you happy brother." Tom offered his mug first in an offer of a celebratory clang.

Rachel placed the tray down to join in.
They all gently raised their mugs with gentle clings of celebration.
"That's got to be the best news I've heard for ages." Tom smiled broadly, giving into the fact that he would never be able to take Rachel away from his own brother even if he wanted to, no matter how great the secret love and desires were.
Ethan studied his brother's expression, noting a genuine smile that lit his eyes up well.
"I didn't ask *when*!" Tom didn't want to seem un-attentive.
"What are we like? We meant to say!" So, next September. We thought the ninth would be perfect for some reason.
"Cool! Will it be a big affair, or are you thinking small?"
"Big man! We want cousins, uncles, aunts, friends - the whole shabam!" Ethan was definitely excited in his tone!
Tom felt the good vibes and sat comfortably, knowing better things were coming. He also hoped that the previous bad dreams and events were all over.

They all sat with their coffee, chatting excitedly about their relaxed break and future plans. Ethan mentioned Megan and Sky, hoping things were heading in a good direction for Tom too. Tom wasn't in any kind of hurry, but realised he needed to demonstrate a level of interest in order to retain the good things they had so far. He looked over at Rachel, noting her happy glow, continuing to wonder if she ever had the same feelings for *him*. He couldn't help feeling a strong, natural chemistry that he never felt with anyone else. It was always the same, straight from the initial meeting. He was never able to explain it. He secretly wondered if Ethan would mess up one day, but never wished for their unhappiness. His thoughts seemed so wrong!
Tom looked over at Rachel again, studying her pretty eyes and hanging onto her every word as she spoke about the type of flower arrangements she was envisioning. It felt wrong listening about her wedding preferences with his admiring thoughts but

knew that if it was himself taking care of things, he'd bend over backwards to ensure her complete happiness. He turned to Ethan, wondering if he noticed the gaze he suddenly snapped himself out of.
He then turned back to Rachel, and for a very swift split second, her face seemed to have an unusual light of someone else's features! Tom had to blink multiple times to ensure he could see normally again.
"Are you okay Hun?" Rachel looked directly in his eyes.
"Yes! Yeah, I'm fine. The light from the window behind caught me in a strange way just for a moment."
Rachel smiled a comforting smile directly at him. It sent tingles down his spine, really enhancing his desire to ask if she felt the same. Retaining his frustratingly logical mind, he decided it was a good time to leave.
"Right guys! I must depart! I have plenty to do and my break here must end before I get too comfortable!" He stood to match his words.
Rachel's eyes instantly grew big with hearing the decisive, louder voice. Ethan was secretly keen to have his space returned, so felt an instant relief, trying his best not to reveal his true feelings.
They all walked to the front door and said their hugging goodbyes. Tom collected his belongings and walked over to his car, throwing his large bag into a back seat.
He drove off, waving happily, trying to shake his mind into forward thinking.

As Tom drove he noticed the benefits he was feeling from the break he managed to have at their home. The observations of their happiness also filled him with good feeling. He felt a slight uncertainty about how he observed Rachel's odd face change, very briefly. He wondered if he was becoming someone of gifts that many people see as peculiar. So many odd things had been happening. He thought about these recent events and needed to shake them from his mind, keen to keep a happy mindset for the foreseeable.

His car drove smoothly, with some encouragement of a good few tracks of music to sing to. He pondered his new relationship with Megan and wondered if it was a lie if the only person he ever truly wanted was Rachel. He also wondered if Rachel was always the reason for his failed relationships. An old memory of his ex-partner, Lisa, came back to his mind. *She* could see his feelings for Rachel despite his honest loyalties. Tom would always deny any infatuations.

A scene hit his mind: Lisa and Tom stood in their kitchen. Lisa was in a raging mood on their final night together. The memory alone caused a sweaty forehead for Tom. Lisa was a very strong character anyway, but with a triggered temper she became quite frightening.

"So, you know where the frig *I* am, and I know where you're fucking hiding, so why are we wasting our time?" She threw a kitchen towel hard on the kitchen worktop. Her long, curly red hair spun over one of her rosy cheeks.

Tom stood back, trying to avoid another argument, but the more they both avoided the truth, the worse things bubbled up.

"Okay, okay. I think we just need to accept that things aren't working. We can't hide like this anymore."

"No shit! I'm going to divorce you on account of having an affair." Both of her hands were now planted on the surface of the counter. Tom noted the pressure on her hands gave some of her finger-knuckles a pink tinge.

"I told you before, I am not having an affair! We are drifting, and I don't know what to do to save us!"

"We don't spend any time together to even attempt to salvage anything Tom."

"How can I reason with you when you're always shouting at me? You hate the sight of me now. We can't spend two minutes together."

"How the frig can you expect me to treat you right when I know you're obsessed with that woman? It's the only reason you go to your brothers."

"I am not obsessed with *anyone*. *You're* obviously the one getting attention elsewhere. I'm just keeping out of the way. I go to my brothers for *his* company. You could come with me. I always ask if you're free to join me."

"Yes but why? Just to watch you gawk? We just need to face the truth Tom! We'll sell up, go halves, and get on our merry way."

Tom looked down in sadness. "Well, I'm sorry it's come to this. I wouldn't have deliberately tried to ruin something we built upon so much."

"Are you accusing *me* of deliberately trying to ruin us?"

"Ah, Lisa, there's nothing I can say to make any of this better. You've set your mind on things already."

"You never fight for us. We'll never win with that attitude."

"I think you're always going to do the gaslighting. I'm not doing anything wrong other than keeping out of the way, knowing you don't wanna be with me anymore."

"Us ladies are very sensitive to things. I know you don't love me. I know who you *are* in love with, and it truly is sick."

"Lis, please. I've done nothing wrong. I know you're assuming I am, so you're doing something with that tough guy to get your own back."

Lisa stood with a more aggressive lean on the counter.

"I *am* seeing Matt, but you no longer love me. You left me in your head much sooner. That's what ruined us. I'm just saving myself."

Tom's head began to spin with the new admission.

"Saving yourself?"

Tom realised he was slipping deep into a reality that no longer existed. The horrible memory of such an emotional battle he no longer wanted to revisit. He shook his head, throwing the images and words out of his mind, knowing he couldn't change the past. He knew that his ex-wife instinctively sensed the feelings he had for Rachel, but she always had some underlying respect not to say anything about it to anyone other than him. She didn't appear to worry about the criticism of being seen with someone else however!

Tom always denied his feelings, naturally. How could he tell the truth? He didn't ever wish for his marriage to fail, and he loved his brother, so would never wish to ruin that blood-relationship. He knew he was only ever able to *admire* Rachel, but always assumed his admiration was hidden in his own thoughts.

As he drove on, he realised the thoughts flying around his head were due to the difficulty accepting that final commitment for Rachel and his brother. He thought he was okay, but he had such a strong pull towards Rachel. Megan was lovely, but he wondered if the same issues would arise again in time. He gave himself a small telling off in his mind, knowing that he couldn't live life that way, and that if *they* were meant to be, then it would present itself at some point in his life.

It was at that moment that he set himself a strict rule to make the most of his time and just to accept that things are the way they are. He remembered reading an article about many people being in love with people that they can't be with for various reasons. He knew he wasn't alone by any means.

Tom turned the music back up in his car and decided to snap back into the feeling of the present moment. He was gradually improving in making better choices of emotions.

After an assortment of thoughts during his car journey, he realised he needed to allow the future of his brother and fiancé to occur... with his blessings!

2nd November 1860

William decided to visit Edward after their working days, uncertain on whether to mention his latest crystal experience.
The nights were drawing in relatively quickly now as winter was edging its' way in. He walked towards Edward's shop, hoping to find his front door still open.
Thankfully, he spotted the view of his friend, all smartly dressed, sat behind his usual sales desk with the lighting still strong.
William was always tempted to play a mischievous prank of surprise upon arrival. He held back this time when he caught sight of the regular Mrs Phelps having a glance at the beautiful creations.
Edward was relatively swift at creating new ideas to sell. He still had plenty of gems to decorate various items with.
Mrs. Phelps was in the middle of purchasing a pretty broach when William gently pushed through the entrance. He wondered if her husband was aware of all of her abundant purchases. William instantly threw his judgemental thoughts back and walked quietly into the shop, noticing Edward's awareness of his presence.
There was a kind wrapping of the item and the money exchange, followed by a satisfactory "goodbye" set of words from Mrs. Phelps. As soon as she was the other side of the door, Edward greeted his friend with much gratitude.
"How was your day Will?" Edward looked fresh-faced and radiant in health.
"Wonderfully successful my good friend. You appear to be joyous too."
"Without question. All is magical and calm at the moment."
Edward gave a questioning look on the selected words for a moment, then looked down to tidy his desk from the remaining items of the day.

"I'll pick this up again tomorrow. I think I can close for the day if you wish to enjoy some social time."

Just as Edward brushed his final miniature items into a large, brown bag, he noted a familiar figure approaching the front window, under the darkening shadows of the evening.

"Ann!" He spun to look at her through the window in great surprise.

William's heart sank slightly in opposition, instantly predicting a potential heartbreak for his friend yet again.

Ann's figure grew close to the front door of the shop, allowing her eyes to spy through, to catch sight of the internal scene.

Edward glanced over to notice William's slightly disappointed expression, knowing his thoughts.

When he returned his view to the door, her figure was already moving away as if she lost her confidence to approach things. Her change of mind brought on a swift-escaping walk.

William felt bad for his friend now, noting the disappointment after such excitement!

"Go get her!" William offered in part resentment, but care for his friend.

Edward looked at the keys in his hands, and parted them over to William, opening the front door in the hope he wasn't too slow in finding her.

He ran into darkness, observing some shiny wetness on the pavement from some rain, not thinking about his inappropriate attire for these conditions.

Looking about, he found the swift-walking, slim figure. She appeared to be moving very fast as if she had no intention of speaking.

"Ann!" He walked with a puffing breath, "Ann!"

Ann turned her head slightly, not fully attentive, or intentional on responding.

"Ann, please talk to me." He picked up to a running pace.

It was strange to see her retreating behaviour, uncertain of her thoughts.

He gained distance and touched her gently on the shoulder, hoping she would turn to acknowledge him at the very least.

"No, Edward! I cannot be seen to speak with you!"

He was surprised, allowing himself to slip back in pace.

"Ann, you know that I am innocent. I was falsely arrested! I was only attempting to save a friend's life from some violent bullies!"

He shouted clearly to ensure she captured his snapshot of explanation.

Thankfully, she stood still, but retaining the direction of her stance.

"Ed, I have walked past many times, discreetly, just to see your face and figure to admire what we had."

Edward's hair had flattened against his head in the wet weather. He listened on with a wonderful relief but wanted to comfort her mind into knowing that he missed her.

"Had? Ann, we can still have our magical world. My feelings haven't changed."

Ann stood still, encouraging Edward to remain still, respectfully, not too far behind. He wanted to reach out and touch her hair, which glimmered in the combination of moonlight and rain.

There was a pause before Ann spoke again.

"My father threatens me if I am to come anywhere near you again."

It was predictable, but still a blow to Edward's hopes.

"I need to see you somehow Ann, you are my one and only, I just know it."

Ann spun with tears obviously flowing, unable to hide her feelings.

"I am embarrassed to be so upset."

Edward grinned, grateful that Ann was finally expressing her feelings openly!

He walked forward. "May I hug you Ann? I truly missed you. I wish for you to be in my life."

Ann was the first to grasp Edward around his waist, tucking her head into his chest.

"I am so sorry that you were judged so wrongfully. I knew that it could not have been right. At least I had hoped. I was so upset that I could not face it all."

Edward felt so warm and free now that all thoughts were out in the open.

"I am guessing your father is protecting you a little bit too much. I wish he knew me a little better. I hope that he does not suspect any of your walks, however."

"I usually return home with a little milk or bread. This time I have been carrying a bag of nuts. The only time I get a little more freedom of shopping is just before Christmas when I collect the bread, cheese, wine, nuts, and oranges."

Edward laughed at her future prospects.

"Is it truly that bad? Your level of freedom?"

"My father thinks I am his little girl. I am the only one who needs to stand up for myself."

Edward began to view her circumstances in better light. He was the controlling father in view of her protection; and she was allowing it to occur with fear of hurting his feelings. He obviously found it difficult to accept that his daughter had become a beautiful woman.

They continued to hug tightly, with Edward's arms around her back, tightly expressing his affection and desire to keep her close.

"I know where you live, remember? I have your address. I could come and speak with him, at least to prove my worthiness."

Ann gasped at the thought.

"I need to resolve my own issues Edward. Perhaps give me a little more time and we shall be together with freedom."

"What do you plan on doing? I need you to be safe."

During their conversation, Edward noted another familiar figure approaching their zone. Eleanor was walking with intent in their direction from a distance.

"Ann! Quickly! I need you to walk with me swiftly." He hoped the dark was leaving them slightly out of recognisable-sight.
He gripped her waist and encouraged her to walk swiftly back towards the shop.
"What is going on?" She walked compliantly yet whispered in fear.
"Trust me. I shall explain in just a moment."
He walked them swiftly back into the shop and secured the front door, eliminating all lighting.
William came closer, about to speak in a congratulatory way for seeing them holding one another. The sudden elimination of light stopped any words from leaving his mouth.
"Will, get down for a moment." He signalled for the three of them to crouch down.
"Why? Wha'?"
"Shshsh!" Edward discouraged noise.
They all crouched out of sight, behind a counter, all hearing the same attempt at the door handle.
William peered cautiously around the side of the counter, wondering who could have been so threatening to the three of them. As he caught sight of the figure, he gulped and encouraged the continual hiding!
"What is *she* doing here?" He whispered.
Ann wanted to know more. "Who are you speaking of?"
"Eleanor is becoming a bit of a stalker. Will is keeping away from her." Edward explained.
William looked at Edward in agreement.
"She sure is becoming a bit of a pest. I've avoided her at home and work, and now she's obviously trying to get to me through you!" William spoke in a low volume.
"What are we going to do? I wonder how far she plans on going!" Edward was growing in concern.
"She's no threat to us really. She is simply a pest!"
William took another clear view around the counter, noting her disappearance.

"I think we're clear now." He carefully stood to monitor all of the windows.

"What am I going to do if she comes in during the work times and causes a scene?" Edward grew slightly annoyed at the potential inconvenience.

"What can she do at worst Ed? Just ask where I am I suppose?"

"True."

They all stood gradually, with Edward and Ann looking a bit dishevelled from the weather conditions. William chuckled inside at the circumstances until a smile developed enough to create an outward giggle. They all began to laugh at the situation, realising how light-hearted it all was *really*.

"I mean, what the heck is the threat of Eleanor?" William offered between the laughs.

"I think things have been a little bit too serious lately." Edward offered an explanation of recent moods.

William looked at Edward and Ann, admiring the two.

"I suppose this means you two have rightfully rekindled."

Edward smiled at Ann in agreement, causing them both to look into one another's eyes.

"Okay! I'm out of here!" William made an alternative plan in his mind, with his feet beginning to walk toward the exit door.

"Actually," Ann offered swiftly, "I cannot stay. I was explaining to Ed that I have a tight leash upon myself at the moment. There is a situation that needs cleaning up in my life." She unclasped her hands from Edward's and walked towards the door. "Please stay with your friend as intended. I would not wish to come between you this evening."

Edward tried to re-attach their hands, but Ann was adamant on her departure for now.

"I understand." Offered the tone of a slightly disheartened Edward.

Ann walked up to him again quickly and offered a slow, engaging kiss, then took herself away with a sympathetic smile.

"We know where we are. Be patient for a moment longer."
Edward and William watched on as Ann walked out of the shop in an extremely elegant fashion.
"I shall be waiting patiently." Edward wanted her to know how he felt within a short, few words.
The two men were left standing with slight grins on their faces.
"Well, at least you know there aren't any hard feelings between the two of you." William smiled broadly now.
Edward brushed his hand through his wet hair. "Yeah."
"I am sure she will find a way to sort things out." William offered some comforting words.
Edward ensured the property was now fully secured, without flaw. Both of their eyes had adapted to the dark room, so they didn't attempt to lighten the place up.
"I came by to see if you wanted to enjoy some relaxing drinks and company." William's whites of the eyes were quite bright in the darkness, watching on as Edward was finishing off his securing tasks.
"That would be good for us."
"Do you like the idea of returning to mine?"
"I suppose. These clothes need washing, so I could leave them on for the evening." Edward looked down at a perfect set of attire. His standards were becoming impeccable.
William chuckled in his mind at the thought of washing perfect-looking clothes but knew him well enough to know his reputation needed retaining.
They both walked back to William's without any further situations and enjoyed some relaxed drinks for the evening.

Present Day

It was a sunny weekend with the approach to winter, and Tom was helping his brother complete the digging up of the garden in order to finish the planned shape of the pond. They knew it needed finishing before potential snow and regular downpours of cold rain. Ethan had purchased a huge plastic mould in the shape of the planned pond. They needed to dig an almost-identical shape to the mould and lower it in. On a couple of occasions, they attempted to lower the mould into the space, but continued on, knowing it needed more effort and accuracy than originally expecting.

Tom was trying to focus on the job at hand and ignore the regular interruptions from Rachel, offering them a sympathetic drink or an energy-building snack.

The two men were beginning to admit to aching backs yet were so close to achieving completion.

"Come on! It'll be dark in a bit." Tom was encouraging Ethan in order to escape another torturing hour.

They now attempted the mould-lowering again only to find that it was pretty-much perfect!

They both smiled, holding their palms downward against their lower backs.

Rachel looked on from the kitchen window, recognising the similar traits of brotherhood.

The men went down on their haunches now, brushing the external soil to fit into the surrounding edges, tidying things up well.

"Who's gonna pick that pile up then?" Tom pointed to all of the rubble and garden waste that they had created over time.

"Ah, I'll worry about that later." Ethan was too tired to care about any extra work at this moment in time, "Look at this amazing pond! It'll be great when it's filled with life and creative features!"

Tom admired the tidy mould that filled a messy digging session, feeling happy to see the final result.

They both stood, checking the boarders visually for complete stability.

"We're done!" Ethan spoke with expressed joy. "That's a load off my mind. I thought the unfinished hole would just sit there for another couple of seasons."

"Ah, I'm glad it's done, although are we meant to support it with concrete or something?"

"Ah man! I'll ask a builder friend later, but thanks so much for your help!" Ethan tapped Tom gratefully on his shoulder.

"No problem. Anything to see you happy."

Ethan looked at Tom's expression as if he'd picked up a tone of sadness.

"How about our usual celebratory pizza to say thanks?" He offered.

Tom smiled, "You know me too well bro."

They both walked into the house, closing the door to an appreciated, warmer space.

"Done then I see!" Rachel was happy and relieved for them.

They both sat at the table, leaning back into comfortable, back-supported chairs.

"Fancy Pizza?" Ethan hoped Rachel would be just as easily influenced.

"I want a load of pineapple this time." Rachel confirmed.

The men smiled, with Ethan pulling his phone from the opposite side of the table to make the online order.

He was obviously over-familiar with the task, and their favourite choices, as he completed the order within an extremely short time, sliding the phone back to the opposite end of the table.

Rachel carried an equally-confident drink option to the two of them. Two hot and steamy mugs of coffee sat right under their noses, making them feel wonderfully smug at the treats ahead.

Rachel joined them in a seat at the head of the table with her own hot mug.

"I bet you'll both sleep tonight."

Ethan and Tom grinned politely in her direction, uncertain of how to respond.

Tom admired her glimmering eyes, trying to keep his admiration to a minimal split second.

For the first time in their entire time of friendship, Rachel caught a glimpse of his approval. She took a quick gasp of air and stood in order to pretend an ignorance.

"The coasters!" She reached out to grab some protective coasters for their drinks.

"I didn't know you cared so much about this old table." Ethan made her feel revealed.

"I just thought we should start to preserve in order to save for the wedding. We can't buy new furniture for a while huh." She felt sufficient in her cover-up, but she noted Tom's eyes questioning her behaviour.

Tom looked at her nervous finger movements and wondered if she was growing anxious about the wedding, or perhaps having second thoughts. He obviously hoped for the latter, but despite such hopes, it would always be impossible to betray his brother. She stood, taking her mug with her, pretending to prepare the table with further placemats in preparation for their food order.

"Are you okay my darling?" Ethan was detecting the same nervous energy.

"Ah yes, I'm just a bit twitchy. I think I've sat down a little bit too much today. I need a good walk to rid of my excess energy."

"I can think of ways to..." Ethan was interrupted by Rachel, who had predicted his obvious response.

"Indeed, you can! But let us save that talk for later."

Ethan was used to messing about in front of his brother and thought that Rachel was behaving unusual where she usually held placid humour. He frowned, knowing that they would need some private conversations later. Ethan looked head-on at his brother now, looking to change the subject.

Tom felt the atmosphere change but went along with the swift adjustment.

"So, with impending rain, do you think I should allow the water to fill the pond naturally? Or would you go with tap water?" Ethan seemed a little rigid in his tone.

"Erm, I suppose it might need a mix. Unless you wish to hurry things along." Tom looked over to study Rachel, whereas Ethan was trying his hardest to keep attention on *him*.

The wait for the pizza seemed horrendous. Rachel occupied herself with little jobs in the kitchen, leaving a forced conversation about pond creation plans between the two men.

Finally, after an uncomfortable thirty minutes, the pizza person finally arrived.

Tom rushed to the door, giving the young delivery lady a generous tip out of huge relief. He was very hungry to eat, but also desperate to leave the uneasy atmosphere. In his mind he wanted to eat relatively swiftly and then play on tiredness to allow early departure.

He carried the boxes of food easily into the kitchen/diner and placed everything in the middle of the table as they often did. The three of them made pleasurable noises as they munched away, satisfying their taste buds and hunger pangs.

Tom took a side glance at Rachel, watching her lips become greasy, leaving a tinge of gold over her lipstick. She lifted her eyelids to catch his admiration again, forcing her to look down swiftly in a pretence not to notice. This second eye-connection confirmed her thoughts, making her wonder how long Tom had been thinking of her in *that* way. She always felt a buzzing feeling around him, with him being extremely cute and seemingly caring, but didn't consider anything with the focus on her relationship. She also assumed that with his marriage break-up that he was in a completely different zone in life. Rachel and Ethan always had a natural intention to comfort Tom with his single life, with hope to see his happiness build. They played a little game of cupid with Megan, with much secret plotting that came into fruition.

They all finished their pizzas in extremely good time. Tom sat back, feeling comfortably full. Rachel and Ethan looked at one another, as if knowing one another's thoughts. Tom felt the tug to leave now.
"Well, I should leave you two love birds to it. I wanna get back before the intestinal exercise starts causing the overwhelming tiredness."
Rachel gave an unusually high-pitched laugh at his words, then wiped her greasy lips with a napkin.
The two men both looked at her with a frown. They both knew her well enough to know she was behaving differently.
Tom stood to escape the awkwardness, pretending not to notice any unusual behaviour.
"Okay guys. Thanks for the pizza. Fun digging… Great exercise. I might be aching in the morning though." He started a polite, slow walk, aiming for the front door.
"Thanks brother. If you need any help with *your* place, you know what to do."
The two men walked ahead, with Rachel tagging behind, giving an awkward wave from the back.
"See ya then!" She played it cool.
Tom offered a manly hug to Ethan and waved casually in response to Rachel's gesturing hands.
He walked over to the car, keen to get in and hold an honest expression.
The car started nicely, allowing him onto the escaping streets with ease.
He hit the dashboard with anger. "Damn it!"

His feelings were of frustration and disappointment. He wasn't sure what Rachel was displaying, but she seemed to be extra appealing and awkward, all at the same time.
The battle he had driving away seemed to get worse every time. An energetic pull toward Rachel seemed to be getting stronger. He decided he needed to spend less time around the two of them and to work on his own life. With himself potentially in the middle, he risks confusion of two, or three people's lives.

As he drove, his dashboard connected to an incoming phone call. Rachel's name came up on his screen. His heart felt as if it had shot up into his mouth.
"Oh my…" He spoke to the air!
Answer it. Answer it… Act normal!
He hit the receiver button. Rachel was the first to speak.
"Hi Tom. I think we need to talk."
"Erm." Tom gasped, "we do?"
"Of course, we do. Let's be open here. I am good at reading people, especially *you*."
Tom didn't reply, feeling awkward.
"Tom, I know when someone looks at me in *that* way."
"Erm…"
"Honestly, it's okay. It's okay to have an attraction, even when they're unavailable."
What's she saying?
"Erm… I guess." He decided to play it cool.
"Oh, come on Tom. Look, let's meet for a coffee tomorrow if you can spare some time. We can talk this through."
Tom felt uncomfortably hot.
"Do you think that's wise?" Was all he could offer.
"I think things are better spoken about, don't you? We can be honest and open. We're only human. These things happen, right?"
Tom was surprised at the way Rachel was dealing with this.
"So, this is why you were behaving a bit off?"

"Ha! I guess this was the first time I noticed the eye thing."
"The eye thing?" Tom still felt the fool.
"Relax Tom. Honestly, nothing will be said to Ethan. I think we just need to talk it over."
"Uh, okay. I guess."
"Okay, tomorrow, at eleven? Our local coffee shop?"
"Okay." He knew the place she spoke of.
"Okay, bye."
"Bye."
Tom didn't want to press the button to end the call, but she didn't hesitate to. His music suddenly hit the car at a high volume, forcing him a rush to turn it down.
"Jeepers!" He was stunned.
Nothing will be the same again.

The Globe

Trion knew there was no way of escaping the contained room. He didn't feel any desperation to escape anyway, as he knew he'd be psych-evaluated for a while, just until they were satisfied that he demonstrated large elements of peaceful, satisfactory behaviours. He had plenty of time to reconnect with his own energy.
Trion had a very strong, powerful body, with quick reflexes and youthful nimbleness. As a known thief, he was always slightly feared for his abilities. He wasn't known to hurt anyone, but certainly knew how to steel large, useful items and didn't usually allow others to stand in his way.

The globe was a peaceful space, full of tranquil actions, allowing time now to replenish the crystal power within the futuristically, large cave-space.
Spreckley continued to teach the kind and willing humans to manifest the crystal shapes and sizes, creating wonderful shapes, colours and powers that would replenish and enhance, to the benefit of the population that lived within the immediate area and surrounding planetary systems.
Having Trion contained, gave the staff of the globe an opportunity to enhance the security and monitoring systems.
The globe was now energising extremely powerfully, and for the greater good.
Spreckley ensured the humans were well compensated with great comforts. It wouldn't be long now before they would be returned to the Earth with evolved abilities, but a rightfully-forgotten experience, so that they could live abundant lives as a graceful reward.

As Trion sat in his space, he meditated, allowing a great energy to fill his essence, noting his *own* development of power. He had too much time to contemplate his future actions.

During this time, he decided that once his freedom was regained, he would return to the planet of primitive life and consume the power there, for his own benefit. The hidden crystals, coupled with the knowledge of forbidden access, would bring him a lifetime of freedom and power. His secret planning would allow him the ability to grow and develop, consuming a planet that could potentially evolve enough to rule an entire galaxy, with technology that would only be available to those he would personally select.

His plan would take him to a new home, with disregard to his previously-exposed planet. He had no reason to return to an almost-barren land, especially when his newly discovered planet was so freshly untouched and inviting. He wished to collect a companion to join him (should they wish to).

Trion needed to be careful of his thoughts, as he knew the telepathic communication was strong. He could only think freely when he knew Spreckley was distracted. Thankfully, he had studied the Globe for quite some time, knowing their structured habits and peak times of events. If everyone was consumed in their own events and thoughts, then *his* thoughts would be muffled amongst many others – not enough to be unravelled specifically.

He expected his psychiatric assessment at the same time each day. Everything was structured so predictably here, which always helped him work against the grain.

He would soon be free.

3rd November 1860

Edward and William decided to head out for an interesting stroll on this fine Saturday. They put a basket of food and drink together, wishing for a time of male bonding, with plans of becoming slightly inebriated.
They took themselves to some green space near a railway line, hoping to hitch a cunning ride to a random destination. At times their mischievous plans got them into trouble, but at their age it was an urge for random excitement. They knew it wasn't respectable behaviour, but they wanted to create some daring fun. The risk of getting caught was the exciting feature, knowing they were fast sprinters if they needed a swift escape.

They sat, eating initially, enjoying the taste of fresh bread and boiled eggs. William had carried a bottle of his latest homemade brew, impatient for them to give it a whirl.
"Do you think Eleanor is wishing to apologise to you?"
William was surprised at this particular question.
"I thought we were going to forget the stressful conversations on this very fine day."
"Oh, I am sorry Will. It crossed my mind, I admit. The stone may have confused her for a short while. I wondered if she could be genuine during *normal* times."
"It's okay Edward. She is still the apple of my eye when I think of her. I just don't know if I can trust her now."
"Do you think it will work with Ann and myself with her controlling father?"
"It depends how much you wish to have her in your life I suppose."
"Let us try your latest drink concoction then my good friend. I am in the mood to risk something."

William willingly poured some of his bottled contents into two flask cups.

They both took initial wincing sips, followed by braver gulps.

"Sharp, Will!" Edward found it the strongest of his blends so far.

William laughed under his breath, wanting them both to benefit from the alcohol strength.

"Perhaps you need to eat a little more first." William pretended to care about the level of intoxication.

Before they both knew it, they felt invincible with the alcohol levels.

"I think my blood is more alcohol now." William offered in jest.

"I think I might be matching you there, my good friend." Edward's words were slightly slurred.

"What about this picnic basket?" William questioned, with a desire to leave it behind for the potential train journey.

"Nobody will want this heap of wicker." Edward lacked care in his inebriated state.

They both stood, aiming for the trainline.

When they arrived at the train tracks, they both walked on an outer edge, finding their way into some underground space.

"Where are we going? Is this the tunnel?" Edward didn't like the feel of the route.

"There's some huge building space down here. Something exciting to investigate."

They walked for a while until William took a stumble and fell on his knees, chuckling heavily at his clumsy drunken state.

"Get up Will!"

William was giggling uncontrollably, unable to regain the energy to stand.

Edward reached down to attempt to encourage him up, but William wasn't aiding with his deadweight. He remained on all fours, giggling like a teenager.

Edward joined in a little, giggling along at nothing in particular.

A noise from the distance sobered them up slightly with the sudden adrenaline. It was a heavy thud such as a heavy rock having fallen from a great height.

"Get up Will!" Edward warned with a serious tone and feeling of urgency.

William found the strength to push himself back up.

"Can you see what that was?" Edward continued.

"It's too dark Ed." William reached into his pocket, intentionally pulling the crystal from his trousers, and lighting it up to shock both of their eyes!

"What?" Edward was surprised. "Why did you bring that thing with you?"

"I don't know Ed. I felt I needed to for some unknown reason. It is coming in useful right now though, isn't it?"

Edward admitted the light of the crystal was extremely useful at this moment in time despite the extreme brightness of it. They could both make out the fine detail of brickwork that formed the huge tunnel that they were in.

"I feel extremely sober and strong all of a sudden, Ed. I thought we were a drunken mess only one second ago."

William looked different, almost alternate-human in some respects. Edward studied his stern features which changed tremendously within a second.

They were both then immediately distracted by a figure, deep within the tunnel. The figure looked unusual in shape with a colour they couldn't figure out from that particular distance. The clothing looked tight against the figure's body, giving a different impression of the fashion they were used-to on a daily basis.

They both tried to zoom their eyes in for more detail but felt at threat. They decided to turn with intention to escape, back in the direction they came from.

William felt powerful in his legs and began to retreat with a fast sprint! He noticed Edward was running equally as fast - only one leg-length behind him.

They reached a space of public gathering, suddenly feeling vulnerable to observations or scrutiny. They both needed to retain their reputations for their work statuses in such a tight community.

William was suddenly aware of the bright crystal in his hand, which thankfully blended in relatively well with the sunny day that it *actually* was. He swiftly and intentionally deactivated it with his mind, replacing it within his trouser pocket, much to Edward's relief. They both looked back, wondering if they had imagined the creepy-looking character inside the tunnel.

They both looked at one another, attempting to blend in with the gathering of a few, who were obviously celebrating something outdoors.

People were holding expensive-looking glasses and selling items on tables. Thankfully there were enough people to blend into, disguising their location and gaining space at the other end in order to find William's home in very near sight. They both gained speed with a strong run, right up to the front door.

"What was that?" Edward spoke, slightly out of breath.

"I don't know my friend, but I need to say that I feel fabulously strong."

Edward realised they must have healed themselves with the crystal after being inebriated. He could see that William was thinking the same.

"I do think you should be leaving the crystal at home though Will. We still don't fully understand it! It could be bringing trouble to us."

William looked guilty. "I agree. It does seem to attract the wrong kind of circumstances."

Edward knew this had been said somewhat before, so was quite annoyed at the risk William had taken.

"Can we please make a plan to bury it once and for all?"

"I feel quite an addiction to it, Edward. I'm not sure that I can."

"Do you wish to bring stress and danger to our daily lives?"

William felt a disagreement coming on, so became the subservient one.
"Perhaps I should bury it once and for all."
This discussion seemed repetitive for the two of them!
Edward studied William's face to be a mixture of disappointment and submission.
They both walked into William's home and relaxed at the large, dining room table without further event.
They lifted the mood with the thought of potential hallucinations inside the tunnel, due to William's strange drinks. Large, warm drinks were relaxing their bodies and minds as the dark night began to creep in.

Edward noticed time moving along swiftly, so decided to leave to go home for the night, leaving William to check an old diary of his, running his finger down to confirm a significant date. As suspected, he remembered that the coming Monday was the day he was expected to make a trade with his supplier of gems.
Meanwhile, Edward, having arrived at his shop, pulled his heavy book out from under his work desk and began to record the latest crystal event, hoping this would be the final entry in *this* regard. This was a journal of positive preference. He keenly filled in detail of how Ann returned to his life and how his thoughts veered toward a hopeful commitment in the future. He noted his feelings as he wrote. Her father's control was a huge stumbling block in his mind.
Continuing to write with his heavy pen, he wondered if Christmas would be the only safe time Ann may have a few spare moments, even if he could help with her "food shopping!"

Present Time

Rachel looked as nervous as Tom felt as he approached her from the other side of the coffee shop. He faked a brave face as her eyes spotted him.
He pulled the chair out, opposite her.
"Hi Rach, how are ya?" He hoped his overly-casual manner wasn't too easy to analyse.
"Hey. I'm glad you came. I know this is super weird, right?"
"Well, yeah." He noticed the two hot mugs in front of them.
Rachel knew what to order.
"So, you got me the usual huh?"
"No point trying to guess otherwise. A good starting point, right?"
The small talk was grinding on the both of them.
"Okay, Rachel, you got me. I hoped you'd never see through me. I kept my feelings to myself from day one. I can't interfere with you or my brother. I don't intend to. I just find you mega attractive, but that's it." He immediately felt cold-hearted with the words but couldn't admit to loving her inside and out.
Rachel looked hurt and fidgeted as if she was contemplating a departure already. Her face dropped and she stared into her mug. Tom felt guilty and reached out to hold her wrist in a supportive sense. He tried to tidy his words up now.
"I'm sorry. Obviously I like you very much. You caught me out somehow, but there's nothing we can do, right?"
Rachel looked up with hurt in her eyes, leaving Tom feeling helpless already.
"I guess we're getting straight to the point here. I'll tell you my truth too."
Tom waited for the continuation of her words, admiring the lipstick she didn't normally wear, making him wonder about the added effort she made for their meet-up.

"Ethan and I have been struggling. Since we moved in, he's been so stressed and unusual. He covers it up. He seems to have changed. That isn't what makes me think about *you*. I don't want you to think that you're an alternative, or a safety net. I want you to know that Ethan and I got together innocently..."
Tom was confused, but listened with extreme intrigue, not expecting her to make any of her *own* confessions, "Although I love your brother, I've always felt some kind of unusual connection to you. I thought it was just that you're so handsome and sporty – easy to admire. Your brother is good looking too! I didn't think I had any feelings for you until you gave me that *look*! I've felt all butterfly-like since – you know the kind – like a real chemical connection that people talk about? I've never felt like that... Like this! A look from you that's opened something up!"
"I didn't mean to give away the look in my eye." Tom smiled, hoping to lift the mood a tad.
Rachel smiled too, connecting eyes, feeling the strong chemistry again.
She looked down with slight guilt to speak again.
"You see, your brother is great. I just don't get the same feeling. I think it's been a gradual progression with him. Perhaps I didn't know until now though. This is all so strange for me."
"Gradual progression?" Tom wanted to clarify.
"Well, Ethan makes an effort on words and actions. Perhaps we can fall in love with anyone we choose to get to know."
"But you do love him?" Tom laughed awkwardly.
"I'm starting to understand the phrase of loving someone and being *in-love* with someone."
Tom grinned. "Do you think we have a natural, lovable chemistry? Something like that?"
Rachel smiled with compliance.
"I genuinely didn't think in this way until you looked at me *that* way. Ethan and I were always trying to focus on your happiness. It's like you opened a surprising door!"

Tom put his head in his hands. "So, what do we do?"
"Do you think we need to live with it as things are?" Rachel surprised him with her draw-back suggestion.
Tom looked up with a frown. "Ignore our natural pull towards one another?"
"I don't know what to do." Rachel's eyes seemed to well up, "Ethan would be crushed, and I know it would destroy your relationship."
"Yeah I totally agree. I just don't know how to address this. I've been struggling, trying to hide my feelings, but they seem to be building out of control by the second. It's all happened so suddenly... So it seems!"
Rachel's expression changed to a slightly scrutinising one.
"Perhaps we *are* just confusing sexual chemistry."
Tom was horrified by the suggestion.
"No! It is a deep sense of closeness, like a magnetic pull of feelings. It's a feeling of very strong respect and value."
Tom released his honest feelings, making Rachel's eyes open wide.
"That's beautiful. I truly appreciate this opening-up. I'm just worried about our feelings. Is it truly real? Or is it a connection that we don't understand?"
"For me it feels like a connection of two people destined to share a life together."
"Oh gawd!" Rachel reached over to hold Tom's elbow crease.
"At least we are both being open and honest now." Tom offered, "I think the only thing to do is take a break from Ethan to be certain about what you want."
Rachel was surprised at his swift suggestion.
"Have you already practiced this scenario?"
Tom paused, realising his words were simple compared to the actual action that would need to be taken.
"Oh, sorry. I know it wouldn't be easy just to walk away like that." Tom put his head in his cupped hands, rubbing his face and then looked directly at Rachel with a confused expression.

Rachel took some large sips from her cup, noticing the temperature of the liquid had dropped significantly. She pointed to Tom's mug. He knew what she meant and gulped a few mouthfuls of his coffee.

There was a silence for a short moment, with glaring into one another's eyes. Both of them seemed to know what the other thought.

Tom spoke first, after some final gulps of his drink.

"I wish you hadn't noticed my glance."

"I'm so glad I *did*! I now know how we *both* feel."

"Wow."

"So, I know we are both confused about what to do, but what the heck *do* we do?"

They both looked down at their pretty-much-empty mugs as they thought.

"I think it's all in *your* court sweetie. I know it's a cruel thing to pass over, but you're the one who needs to know if you wish to pursue this or take the path you have already made headway for." Tom tried the approach of harsh reality.

"I can't get married, Tom. I was kidding myself anyway. I got washed up in our holiday excitement. Once we were back in the normal routines, I knew I'd given into something I was simply swept into without much thought."

"But you both seemed so excited and said so many convincing things."

"The holiday excitement spilled over slightly until normality kicked in. Oh boy." Rachel looked a funny shade of pink.

"I can only help on the quiet. If we do aim for something in the future it's got to look innocently gradual, as if we never expected it. The first step needs to be departure though. I guess I'm jumping in with thoughts of action again." He started biting into one of his fingernails.

"Well, I suppose it's a mess I got myself into, so…"

"You seem braver already."

"Between our words I am realising how young we are, and how I mustn't make a dangerous marital mistake."

"It's gonna break his heart, ya know? I'll need to help his emotions, like some kind of traitor." Tom felt the bad side of their plotting.

"Why does someone always have to get hurt when we can't help who we fall in love with? This one is tough. Ethan is my brother!"

"Hmm. This is a good and bad situation. I think we should take time to think before rushing into anything."

Rachel chuckled slightly. "We were brave one second ago and now we're back-tracking."

They both chuckled.

Rachel looked at Tom, deep in the eye.

"I am so glad we had this conversation though. I'm not gonna make calls or send messages. I want to do this without further risk, okay?"

"Gotcha." Tom grinned with confidence and elevation of new potentials, noting her action to leave the coffee shop.

Rachel stood and kissed Tom on the forehead, leaning on his shoulder before walking casually away. He felt the pull of her departure but held thoughts of patience. Her amazing figure carried a beautiful walk into the distance and out of sight.

He sighed, realising he could purchase another drink and stare into space, since *that* was the mood he was in. His alternative was to leave and make a fresh plan to distract him for the day.

Not so surprisingly, he felt a pull to purchase another hot drink. He treated himself to a hot chocolate and relaxed back into the comfortable chair, staring out of the window right next to him. He noticed a glance from another solo-drinker across the café but didn't care to socialise at this time.

He sipped, savouring the flavour and comforting warmth of his drink. The familiar figure of Rachel walked past the window, giving him a surprise, making him sit upright, but he noted her expression was that of intent as if she had forgotten to perform a task whilst in the area. Tom admired her tall walk and striking features. At the time of his staring, he sensed his eyes were playing tricks! The scene of Rachel flickered like a faulty nineteen-eighties image on the television! She flicked into an image of a lady in a Victorian dress! He blinked his eyes and regained view of her, noting that Rachel was simply *Rachel*, walking speedily over to a shop in the distance. He questioned his mind and eyes over the view, but everything appeared to be normal again. He took more comforting sips of his drink, noting the stranger ahead, take an interesting, deeper stare at him, making him realise his exposure of odd behaviour. His sips became gulps, forcing him to leave in order to avoid unwanted small talk with the stranger who was obviously trying extremely hard to connect with eye contact. As Tom stood to leave, he started thinking about his poor brother. He couldn't help how he felt about Rachel, but he started to wonder if this was all a huge mistake. Questions came to his mind such as whether or not Rachel was simply finding the next-best-thing if she was unhappy in her relationship. In all of the time he knew Rachel, he hoped he had judged her character to be a stable and honest one.

He felt that they hadn't come to any agreement at this time, leaving them both even more confused.
Could he really do this to his brother?

As Tom left the café, he noticed another familiar figure in the distance. At first it made his heart feel as if it had dropped into his shoes! The very tall, slim figure that had behaved aggressively – twice now – was spotted in the distance!

Tom swiftly hid behind a corner of the nearest wall, taking his phone out, preparing for some filming. He realised he was yet to show someone his already-captured footage of the unusual experiences with this tall person. Perhaps this was an opportunity to capture their features for better recognition. He carefully viewed the street around the corner and noted the speed in which the person was walking. Tom decided he would take a chance and follow this person but retain a great distance behind.

As he followed, he was able to view them easier. Their features were feminine, with a strong, elegant walk and longish stride. He noted the same short hair, but took a longer look at the colour, which seemed to be a very light shade of grey – almost white. When she looked to cross to the opposite side of the road, he noted her nose to be quite small and delicate. If she wasn't such a strange, aggressive character (for some unknown reason), he would have been intrigued by her appearance. Tom felt a strange mixture of attraction but unexplainable danger.

They were almost out of range, so he shuffled faster into a mild jog, paying attention to a turn taken through an alley. Tom felt uncomfortable about them getting into a quieter zone. He caught up however, to note her walking stealthily now, looking over people's fences, simply with the lengthening of her neck whilst walking forward.

What were they looking for?

Tom watched on, still keeping far enough back to feel safe, knowing the public eye was still in relative range.

Tom suddenly realised they were nearing *Ethan's* residential area! He felt his adrenaline pump a little harder and decided to stop the discreet filming in order to enter into the phone's functions. He scrolled through his contacts to make a call to his brother. Almost at the second his phone had called out, Ethan's response came, much to Tom's relief.

"Tom!" Ethan's voice was of positive tone.

"Ethan, thanks for answering so quickly! Are you at home?"

"Ah, no. I'm running some errands. Rache said she was going to do a bit of coffee-ing and shopping, so I thought I'd head out to get some pond features."

Tom was relieved that he was away from danger and gave an obvious sigh. There was a pause as Tom continued to watch the direction of the tall person.
"Are you okay?" Ethan could obviously sense the distraction.
"Oh, yeah. Sorry bro. I don't want to worry you, but you remember that really weird person who came to your door that one time asking for something we didn't understand?"
"Yeah?" Ethan started to breathe in unison with his worried brother.
"Well, I'm following that person, and they seem to be aiming for your road."
"What? Did you want to call the cops?"
"Well, the person hasn't done anything yet. They look a bit kinda, well, full of intent, but it's hard to say what they're up to at the moment. I guess we don't know what state of mind they have. We didn't even get the *initial* reason for the odd behaviour huh."
Ethan was obviously thinking.
"Where are you then? Are you following them?"
"I'm following *her*, and she seems to be approaching your area. I don't know what to do. I'll keep spying from a distance. She hasn't spotted me... I'm hiding behind the corner of a fence at the moment."
Tom monitored the person and observed the strong movement towards Ethan's home itself, confirming his worst fear.
"Ethan! She seems to be going to yours, for sure! I'll film her actions and let you know if anything happens. If she tries anything weird, I promise I'll call the police, okay?"
"Tom..."
Tom didn't give his brother chance for debate and adjusted the phone to record the actions before his eyes. Zooming in with both his naked eye and the phone, he could see that she was trying the doorbell. He watched as she waited in a very tall, rigid manner. Tom frowned at her strange stance.

She moved to look into the front window, placing a cupped hand to the side of her eyeline to get a better view.

Tom knew his brother had intricately placed many active cameras in and about his property and that he'd probably be attempting to check in on these, using his phone.

There was a pause followed by another doorbell ring.

She's obsessed!

He thought he would call the police if she continued to be so invasive.

He took a breath, realising how he needed to calm himself slightly. Excitement strangely took hold of him now. His actions were that of a private detective. He recalled some of his childhood heroic-action figures. His mind drifted for a moment, until he noted the tall person viewing her surroundings. Tom quickly moved back, panicking slightly about being caught. He held his place behind the corner of a fence for a few seconds, before managing to find a gap enough to look through. This person had reverted back to the view of Ethan's front door.

She obviously wasn't giving up in any kind of hurry. He chuckled at the thought of her sitting on the front door mat until someone had emerged. It wasn't funny after a few dodgy realisations, however.

As he monitored, she moved backwards and then used some super-human movement to jump extremely high! Tom gasped with disbelief! He compared the action to that of a *cat*, as her thighs did a squatting action, followed by her landing on all fours on top of Ethan's porch roof! It seemed absolutely effortless!

He almost lost grip of his phone with the shock, attempting to film the new view!

This person now jumped up to the main roof of the house and moved swiftly on all fours to swiftly climb over to the other side! Tom managed to capture the crawling action and then wondered what to do in all of the unusual behaviour. If he told anyone about this, he would be seen of as delusional. As she obviously crawled over to the other side of the house towards the back garden, Tom decided to call Ethan again to clarify a call to the police.

Ethan answered his call instantly, with panic.

"Tom! What's happening?"

"Erm, this so-called *person* has climbed over your roof! I have no idea what they are doing, but they're aiming for the rear of your house!"

"Oh yes! I can see them on the camera now! The garden camera is showing this weirdo shuffling through that pile of soil we dug up!"

"What? Is this a weird human that digs into people's gardens? What do I do? I think it's time to call the police, don't you?"

"Trespassing is enough, surely."

"Yeah! I'm on it. I just needed to hear it from *you*."

Tom switched the call off and immediately called "999."

He gave the details of events and expected progression. His voice was in a swift, panicked tone. Thankfully, the police were willing to attempt to catch the intruder red-handed, stating that they just-so happened to have a car at the nearby High Street that Tom had just walked from. Relief filled him, although he couldn't help but worry for their welfare with not fully understanding her abilities after what he had just literally witnessed. He kept a watchful eye after the registered call, not able to see much with her being at the other side of the house.

Tom noted the police car arrival and hoped they would remain stealth-full and vigilant. He wanted to follow the police up to the door to get a closer view. With a vulnerability for leaving his hiding-place, he walked nervously up towards the house. He watched from afar as the police officers cautiously looked through the edge of the windows.

He noted their idea to go to the neighbour's house and request access to their garden. Tom knew he needed to keep out of view, so remained at the edge of the street, looking casual and ready to duck into someone's garden, even if he was performing the same trespassing act!

Ethan called his phone, frightening him with the vibration in his hand.

"Hi. The police are here. They're monitoring her from the neighbour's garden I think. That's how it seems."

"Yeah, I'm still watching on the cameras. She seems very interested in finding something in the damn garden!"

"Maybe your previous owners kept some kind of secret."

"Ooh! Something is happening. I'd hide if I were you!"

Tom took his brother's advice and ran to hide behind a low wall nearby. He sat down without intention of spying this time. Ethan was still on the phone, so Tom whispered.

"What's happening?"

"The police jumped in, but that lady jumped like some bloody Tigger character over the other fence. It left them looking confused, but they're out of sight now, so I'm guessing they're in pursuit. Be careful you don't get seen bro! I'm coming back now, okay?"

"Yeah, I witnessed her jumping. She looks like some kind of cat woman!"

"I wonder what she's looking for in my bloody garden."

"Maybe some rodents for dinner. Ha!"

Ethan didn't find his words funny.

Tom lifted his head to allow his eyes to capture the view. The police car was now driving off at great speed, obviously to chase her. Tom now stood confidently, knowing it would have been enough to fear the unusual character.

"She's gone... Along with the police chasing her."

"Okay. Can you stay for a bit? I'm on my way back."

"Sure." Feelings of guilt over Rachel filled him now, even with all of the current excitement. His brother always needed him.

Tom regained calm of the current situation, knowing all was in hand. After a few breaths he called Rachel. She answered with a disappointed tone.

"Tom remember we need to keep the privacy thing. If Ethan notices many calls..."
"This is *unusual* Rachel. If I didn't call I would be heartless."
"Unusual? In what way?" Her tone changed to that of slight concern.
"That aggressive woman that frightened the shit out of all of us not too long ago, went back not your house. I followed her and called the police when I noticed she was heading into your property."
"What? I'm just coming back now!" Rachel disconnected her phone immediately, not allowing further conversation.
Tom placed his phone in his pocket and sighed with the drama.

Later that day found Tom, Ethan and Rachel sat in a police station discussing the dramatic events.

"So, you let her get away?" Rachel was speaking with disgust and distress.
"You need to understand that she was highly skilled in some athletic and acrobatic behaviour that allowed her to escape with such ease. We did our best, with a heavy pursuit. We plan to do our best now, with surveillance."
"Do you think I feel safe going back to my home, knowing this crazed lunatic could do something stupid and invasive yet again?" Tom looked at Rachel with genuine concern.
"You guys could stay with me for a while if it helps?"
Ethan looked on with disappointment, trying to express gratitude.
"That's really kind of you bro, but we shouldn't stop living a normal life. Fear of a tall, athletic person seems ridiculous. If she was gonna hurt us, I'm sure she would've done that by now."
"We agree." One of the police persons responded.
Two police officers sat on the opposite side of a large, granite-styled table. One of them was an extremely pretty lady with a comforting voice, and the other quite the opposite. He was heavily set with deep, dark eyes, a tidy beard, and an extremely definitive jawline.
Tom observed the officers, wondering how they could even hope to catch the unusual criminal after his observations.
"I have some video footage that you guys might want to see. I was going to hold onto it, for it being extremely weird, but then this seems the most obvious time for sharing."
"How far back does this footage go in terms of time?"
"I have actually seen the lady before."
"We *all* experienced her aggression and weird appearance." Rachel added.
"Actually, I have seen her in between things. She spotted me walking around the local castle and found it necessary to chase

after me. I have no idea why! I don't know if it was out of recognition, or if I was somewhere I shouldn't have been."
The lady police officer was already observing one of the videos, with a change of blood flow to her face becoming quite apparent.
"Why didn't you say anything before?" The lady police officer was demonstrating that she was capable of switching to a firmer approach.
"Yes, Tom. Why haven't you even shared this with us?" Ethan looked angry.
"I've had a lot going on. I also fear for my life with this person. It's like facing a fear. An unknown fear. She gives off such a force that makes me…"
"It's okay Tom." Rachel interrupted him and placed a hand on top of his.
Ethan witnessed the strong support from Rachel, making him frown further. He spoke over the *footage* discussions now.
"I want to know who this strange person is, and why the hell she is playing with my garden! We are the victims here. I expect something done, and now!"
Ethan surprised the entire group and walked solidly to the door that gave the impression of freedom to leave as and when decided.
"I'm sorry officers. We are all a bit stressed. We aren't accustomed to crime." Rachel felt the need to explain.
The police officers nodded in agreement.
"We need to retain this video footage for analysis and possible evidence." The lady Police Officer continued.
Tom's hand gestures gave a calm agreement.
"That's fine."
Rachel stood, gesturing for Tom to join her.
"I think that's all we have. I hope you can build on it." Rachel offered as she spun to leave.

As they walked together through the premises, they both noticed Ethan in the distance, leaving through the large revolving doors toward the car park.

"Let's leave him to stew for a bit." Rachel wanted a private word on the side.

"We can't say much here. Maybe later." Tom pulled gently on her wrist.

Rachel felt disappointed but knew he was right. The intertwined relationships may become Police observations despite it being knowingly irrelevant themselves. Her underlying frustration was knowing that she'd need to support the less approachable brother at home.

4th November 1860

William stood at the docks from an early hour to allow plenty of preparation and transportation of the abundance of wood he had collected for his latest trade.
He felt an urge to give more than he ever had on this occasion.
The boat came in as promised and always predicted.
The ropes tied the boat to a steady, halted position. The men walked slowly and tiredly from their places, onto solid land, obviously accustoming to adjusted leg use.
One of the men, Charles, walked directly to William and offered his usual handshake, which was enthusiastically reciprocated.
They greeted one another with their usual hellos and then broke the small talk once William began with his curious questions.
Walking and talking seemed relaxing for the two of them.
"Charles, I'm always grateful for our exchange as you know, but do you mind if I ask about a particular crystal?"
Charles looked slightly confused.
"You can ask anything my good friend. I cannot say I am over-familiar with these crystals, but I can only do my best."
The men from the boat were already beginning to load the offered wood onboard as they conversed. One of them carried a heavy brown bag of gems from the boat for a swift exchange. They ran over to the space of William and Charles as they were walking further away from the harbour.
William took the bag of lumps and bumps of various sizes and threw it over his shoulder, retaining eye contact with Charles, with the hope of a kind answer.
"Let us continue to walk and talk William. It feels good to land on solid ground momentarily."
Charles and William continued their chat whilst walking slowly away to enjoy a business-like conversation.
The air was fresh, with a bright blue sky and mild few clouds.

"May I ask about a particular crystal then, Charles?"
"You can ask anything, freely, but I'm not sure I can give you a fantastic answer. Everything is acquired in bulk my Sir William." He reiterated slightly differently.
"Okay. In such case, where do you acquire the crystals?"
Charles had a very dirty, heavily-wrinkled face from too much weathering at sea. His beard was only slightly darker than his skin.
"Are you in some sort of trouble, William?" He sensed.
"Oh no, not at all. Do you care to come to mine for a welcoming cup of tea perhaps? That way I could show you an unusual crystal from one of our trades. You may know more about these things than I do. This is all I wish to discuss."
Charles smiled. "A welcoming cup of tea sounds wonderous. If I come to yours, could I trouble you for a freshen up?"
William smiled at the small request.
"You are very welcome to freshen up." William looked at the shape of Charles and offered, "You look relatively similar in shape and size to me. Would you care for some fresh clothing for your next trip out to sea?"
Charles smiled broadly, exposing his frequent smile-action by filling the same wrinkles. He reached out to hold and tap William's opposite shoulder in gratitude.
"You are always very kind to me young Sir."
"And you me, Charles."

They both walked heartily, eventually reaching the front door of William's home.
William realised he hadn't moved the heavy bag once it had settled on one shoulder, so the sharpness of too many individual stone-like penetrations to the skin were suddenly felt.
He didn't demonstrate any weakness as he unlocked his door and ushered Charles kindly into his home.
William encouraged the two of them into his sociable dining area and lit his fireplace, encouraging warmth to build up swiftly.

He warmed some water enough for the two of them to enjoy a hot drink of tea each.

The fire strengthened, warming the room up as hoped!

"I shall warm a big bowl of water up for you shortly Charles."

"That is wonderful William. May I offer you a cigar, carried across the seas for many miles?" He reached into an internal pocket, lifting out two chunky cigars and some loose matches, placing them clumsily onto the table.

"Oh wow! That would be a heavenly treat."

They both sat with drinks and lit cigars, relaxing with shared tales, until the opportunity came to answer the biggest question on William's mind.

He retrieved the life-changing crystal from a hidden space and placed it on the table between the two of them.

Without any knowledge of previous circumstances, Charles lifted the beautiful stone and studied it closely.

"Is this the one in question?"

"It is. It appears to hold some unusual properties. This is why I have so many questions. I can-not part with this one. My friend and *ongoing* trader consumes the majority of my gems, but this one seems to have been created for a very special reason!"

"What do you mean?" Charles looked at the crystal and then returned his eyes to William.

"Well, I was truly hoping you could tell *me* something about it first."

Charles looked slightly vexed but held his politeness.

"I have been getting familiar with *some* of the names of these crystals, or stones, or gems. This one looks like a combination of Lapis Lazulu... No, Lapis Lazu-li... and Clear Quartz."

William wasn't any the wiser, so knew his blank face may have given his thoughts away.

When Charles looked up, he smiled at his friend's confusion and continued.

"There is a theory that the Egyptians used the blue crystals, like this part here," he pointed to the most beautiful, blue part of the crystal, "to connect to the heavens. I suppose because of the connection of colours. They loved this colour with the thought that it gave an extra *intuition* – I suppose the word is."
"Oh, okay." William answered briefly.
"Quartz, I think are mostly for protection and energy building."
"To build up energy levels?"
"I am not entirely sure young man. Why are you asking about this particular crystal?" Charles looked at the crystal from many angles, noticing how the two parts wrapped around one another in a beautiful state. He felt a heaviness, in the hand that held it, and a buzzing, pulsating sensation. He dropped it with slight fear.
"What is wrong Charles?"
"I, I thought I felt a slight buzzing in my hand, but I am not certain."
"Yes, you see, there is a power about this crystal, hence my unusual questions. Do you know where it originates from?"
"Young William, we collect these from poor classes, who have travelled far from places of the east. I couldn't tell you where they unravel them from directly."
William sighed with slight disappointment, knowing of the ongoing puzzle that may never be answered.
"I would like to let you know that many people believe in a great power enhancement from these crystals. Some say that it is useful to allow healing, enlightenment, or clarity of thought somehow."
"So, how would one tap into the power of such things?"
"I am not entirely sure. I have only seen images of people sitting in silence with them. I know they have blended with make-up, or jewellery, perhaps with the Egyptian tombs or coffins.
I think with silence and connection somehow, that something may come to one's mind. I am not sure if one should delve into such things, however. If you do not know what things are involved, then one should not play."

Charles was speaking freely, noting William's facial expressions of intrigue. "What have you been experiencing William?"
William found it difficult to hide his truth as he fidgeted and looked in different directions for a distraction.
"Do you care for another cup of tea Charles?"
Charles grew intrigued.
"William, you have experienced something very unusual haven't you?" He pressed.
William was standing, reaching to stoke the fire, then returning to the kitchen utensils to attempt to re-fill both mugs.
"Charles, I would say that the crystal seems special, so I have been holding onto it, but a friend insists that I should bury it. Perhaps I *should* bury it deep with the confusion that it brings. I just can't seem to bring myself to do it."
"Why does it bring confusion? Why do you keep it despite the others?" Charles was frowning, trying to relax with the cigar and currently-remaining tea.
"I feel attached to the crystal, like it is meant for me personally."
"William you can-not tell another about this. People do not understand such unusual talk."
"I know, please do not worry. I am aware of how ridiculous this all sounds."
"Okay William. I hope that I have helped with some information. I am sorry if it is not as useful as you may have hoped."
William carried a large pot of water to the fire in order to warm it up for Charles to wash with.
The scene was tranquil, but the feeling within William was of a slight tenseness.
"William, come and relax with me some more. Now that you have *some* answers, we can put that to the side. I can tell you of some interesting sea stories. I only have a short time before I need to leave, so make the most of this company."
William felt comforted by the words alone, acknowledging the need to relax and have some fun.

They both smoked some more, and with such relaxing luxuries (for them), this encouraged William to collect some of his infamous homemade drinks from one of his deep cupboards.

They both grew merrier than they intended to within a short space of time. Charles looked rather glazed over, glimmering in the light that shone from the comforting fireplace. William enjoyed the joy that came from their fun interaction.

Charles became aware of the time and stood with a wobble that made the two of them giggle.

"I somehow need to make it back to the men. We are heading out again. I hope you find another interesting crystal among the bag of goodies."

"I look forward to any unusually powerful ones. I hope the wood serves you well."

"The trade is always good!"

William linked arms with Charles, attempting to help him with stability to the front door. They both knew it would be an interesting test of agility and control as they continued to giggle at the state they were both in.

Charles somehow sobered up swiftly in the fresh air. William felt behind in the recovery process but wanted to hold onto the liberations. It made him feel warm and comfortable inside with the colder nights slipping in.

They both walked for a short while, nearing the harbour.

"Goodbye my good friend," Charlie offered with a very slight slur, nearing his workforce. "Until we trade again…"

William realised their forgetfulness on Charles's intention to freshen up. He looked at his departing friend, noting the worsened state of his features, hoping he'd appreciate the fun more so. William watched his friend walk down the cobbled road with great effort to remain straight and upright. He smiled at the scene.

William was about to head back indoors to retain the heat of the fireplace and enjoy a sobering sleep, when he caught sight of Edward walking towards the house, waving.
Edward passed Charles, not having met his acquaintance at all, giving a friendly nod as they crossed paths.
William hoped he could hide some of his drunkenness.
"Hello my friend." Edward bellowed, approaching swiftly.
"Hello young Ed. To what do I owe…?"
"I finished early to speak with you." He interrupted.
"Oh, well I hope you are able to attain some sense from my interesting state."
Edward grew closer to note the inebriation behaviours and strong odours emanating from his friend.
"Oh no, Will. Was that one of your friends from the trading I passed? He looks as if he tried one of your interesting concoctions."
"Ah, well, you have not been wrong young Ed. We have been having a few chuckles. Please do come back to mine and enjoy the warm fire I created."
Edward followed William back to his very warm home, occasionally feeling the need to help his friend walk steadily. It would be a short visit before William would fall into a deep sleep, especially in warm comforts.
"You live like such a man of leisure!"
"Is that good?"
"Ha-Ha! I suppose."
"So, what doth thee here young Ed?"
 Edward noticed how drunk William truly was, so wasn't sure if he'd gain much detailed sense from his friend.
"I remembered one was going to be trading today and that you were planning to ask for some detail on the crystal. Did they have any information to benefit us?"
"Oh yes. We grew a little distracted as… you know. I did ask, and he said that the blue one was called… Lapis Lazuli. How did *I*

remember that so easily? It is a strange name to remember. Wow! I impress myself. The blue one was known to be a connection to heavens or something. I hope I remember that correctly. A bit like the blue sky I suppose. The clear part was meant to be a Clear Quartz. Wow! Perhaps I am not as drunk as I thought."

"I'm impressed Will. So did they know that the crystal may be a little bit unusual?"

"I suppose I chose to remember, and it wasn't all that long ago really. He didn't appear to know much otherwise. I think he stared at the beauty of it for a while. The two crystals and colours are so amazing though, are they not?"

"They truly are well intertwined. You didn't tell him…"

"Do not worry yourself young Ed. He is none the wiser, although I did notice he felt something when he held it."

"I hope you can trust him then." Edward looked around to see where the crystal was.

"Do not worry yet again. The crystal lies deep within my pocket." He reached down to feel the safe, solid features of the stone and took it out to comfort his friend's mind.

"Thank goodness. You did well, but you still plan on burying it right?"

"I don't think I can give it up just yet without answering some questions."

"Considering you are influenced with the special liquid – you do need a clear mind to plan such events." Edward laughed outwardly and continued with his thoughts, "I wonder how else we can find out more about this piece."

"It is difficult when we also need to protect it from sight."

There was a heavy knock at the door!

"Are you expecting someone?" Edward's face looked surprised.

"I don't think so." He walked to the door confidently, opening it to a face of hope!

"Eleanor!" William's heart fluttered and sank all at the same time, not knowing how to feel after his long attempts to avoid her.

Edward realised it was an error of William's to have opened the door.
"Can we talk?" Was the gentle, extremely feminine voice.
"He may not be in the right state of mind at the moment Eleanor!" Edward spoke with volume and freedom from the near distance.
"He's right you know." His eyes were growing heavy with an attempt to stay awake.
"It won't take long, I promise."
"I suppose. So long as my friend, Edward is here to witness your actions." His voice was distrusting.
William stood sideways on, inviting Eleanor to enter if she wished. He took a scanning eye over the immediate outdoor space to ensure there were no followers of any kind.
The three of them sat in the lounge area, awkwardly waiting for Eleanor to speak. She looked at Edward, feeling uncomfortable at the lack of privacy.
"William, I do really like you and I am here to beg you for forgiveness of my actions. My family acted out of protection, and I acted out of unusual desire for the item of which I don't fully understand. I wish for us to start again out of fondness for you."
Edward now felt awkward and wanted to leave them in peace but needed to keep an eye on her for obvious suspecting reasons. He could see that William wanted to admit his feelings too but held an element of caution.
"I feel that we did make an instant connection at the ball. If we could return to that time and start again it would be wonderful." He grinned with very heavy eyelids.
"We could draw a line under our recent events and try again if you wish."
"What would your parents think?" William wanted to feel supported.
"They are the ones who asked if I would feel better to clear things up. My mother can see that I am desperately in love."
"In love?" He was shocked at the words.

"I have a strong fondness for you." She smiled and clasped her hands together on top of her knees.
Edward raised one eyebrow and looked to study William's thoughts.
"That is wonderful to hear Eleanor. I suppose we need to build upon the trust initially and see where things are headed."
Edward smiled at the lovely reunion hoping that it was truly genuine.
"We have had unusual circumstances." Edward attempted to justify everyone's recent behaviours.
William and Eleanor both looked at Edward in a way that told him to leave them in peace. He felt uncomfortable but remaining protective of William's vulnerability.
William reached over to hold the top of her clamped hands.
"I am so grateful that you took such bravery to speak this over with me."
Edward cringed at the awkwardness now.
Eleanor felt so comforted by the warm touch of his strong hands but could see that his eyelids were reaching a point of closure. She smiled at his uncontrollable tiredness and forgave him since she visited so randomly.
"I shall let you have a fine sleep and visit at a more convenient time."
Edward nodded in agreement and immense relief as she met his eyes to confirm her need to depart.
Edward stood to encourage movement, which she complied with immediately.
They both walked calmly to the front door and gave polite words of goodbye, leaving Edward to close the door, knowing that it wouldn't be long before he'd also be at the other side of it. He just wanted to say goodbye to William if it was still consciously possible!
He walked into the lounge to see that his friend was sound asleep in a slump on his sofa. Edward crept out and walked into the

dining room to ensure all things were safe and secure before leaving quietly. The fire had weakened, confirming a burn-out shortly. He casually left, ensuring all doors were securely closed.

When Edward returned home, he quickly made a note in his retained journal. He wanted to ensure the names of the intertwined crystals were remembered so that he might be able to investigate further. The spelling of such names were guessed, but he thought it was best to write them in a way that they were said. His calligraphy pen moved smoothly without any blotting:
>Lapis Lazuli and Quartz intertwined.

He felt satisfied at knowing a little more, even if it was a simple labelling for identification.

The Globe

Trion was tried and tested to his limits within physical confinements. Spreckley knew he could only do his best to aid Trion to do things for the good of his planet and all neighbouring planets. He frequently observed Trion's thoughts and words to ensure he was safe to depart his captivity. Despite the containment, it was a good one, with an abundance of food, water, and entertainment.

He was screened and questioned with their inter-planetary mind therapist visiting him frequently to ensure his intentions were improved in preparation for fresh freedom.

The almost-invisible, transparent doors of containment were now opened with peace-keeping members of staff monitoring his expected departure.

"You are free to leave now, Trion, but it is imperative that you remain peaceful and retain distance from our atmosphere from this day forward." Shayze was in charge of this process, giving out his rights of passage.

"It was wrong to retain me for as long as you have." Trion added as he walked calmly away from his temporary dwelling.

"It was necessary in order to allow us time to create a better security system from your theft threats and to ensure that you are thinking in a more peaceful manner." Shayze wanted to ensure the words were clearly heard by Trion in their defence.

Trion walked proudly away from the staff of The Globe, ignoring the comments, and walking into his dome-shaped transportation vehicle.

"We have kindly provided some crystal power of our own creation in order to get you safely returned to your own planet. The system of your vehicle has been programmed to return you home, with a retention of restriction, keeping you in permitted zones.

Trion turned to face Shayze with anger in his eyes.
"You messed with my *own* vehicle? That is an invasion that is illegal in itself!"
"It was passed by the Legal Guardians. Here is the evidence." Shayze unveiled a pocket-sized screen that unfolded from a metal rod the size of a long matchstick. It could have resembled a futuristic version of an old scroll. On there, listed a long digital form of literal jargon that Trion didn't have the patience to waste time on.
"Keep that home-created rubbish to yourself. You have no right to mess with my property."
"I don't think you have the right to talk about other people's property."
Trion knew any form of debate was simply a waste of time, so he entered his vehicle and allowed all doors to secure themselves behind him. The transportation lifted with the usual swift ease.

Trion watched with much relief as he entered the atmosphere of his own planet, despite the harshness of life on there. It was still freedom to him.
The dome landed, allowing him to exit the vehicle. He hoped his own planetary aid may have a way of reprogramming his transportation for individual control yet again.
Three friends came to greet him with much joy having missed his company for the time he was away. They all huddled around him, thanking him for his previous efforts to gain great power sources for their planet.
"I have a plan to gain access and control of another planet. One more habitable and pleasant. I stashed the huge crystals there." Trion started without any introductory conversation, "I have been extremely keen to tell you about this."
One feminine being looked on with keen interest, staring into his deep eyes. She was good at transfiguring into different forms and

decided to use her slender appearance, with bright blue eyes, enhancing her encouragement of attraction towards herself. Trion noted her attempt to grab his attention.

"You do look wonderful in that state, Bo." He offered, reaching out to her hand.

The other two friends were of masculine form and discouraging of their behaviour. One of them had extremely large hands – completely disproportionate to the rest of his shape. He spoke in curiosity of Trion's plans.

"So, tell us more of this plan of yours."

"It will bring us freedom and abundance. I also sense it is a relatively primitive land. One that we could potentially take full control and ownership of."

The second male was an extremely tall, strong figure, with bulging arms, who stood broader when hearing of the potentials of this planet.

Trion continued, "We could live such a life of freedom and ownership. I sense the crystals would work and retain themselves well there."

The feminine *being* held Trion's hand extremely tightly now.

"This sounds wonderful for us. After all of this hardship, you have done well."

Trion felt invigorated by the encouragement.

"We need to leave things temporarily, in order to behave unpredictably, but if we remember what we are heading for, we at least have a great new life to look forward to."

Four of them stood in unison, smiling at the prospects of the new venture.

Trion took Bo, his feminine friend, gently out of sight, promising to hold an official meeting when the plan could proceed.

"You and I could do this alone, in partnership if you want full control you know?" Bo offered in cunning thought.

"Oh Bo, we can still have *our* private life there. It would be good to have as much strong protection and friendship just in case we need the extra aid. I don't know much about this planet as yet." Trion attempted to encourage the preference of a strong team. Bo had a long, elegant stride. She transfigured her features to a softer, shorter bodied person with long, lightly shaded pink hair and purple eyes.

"I love it when you pick an appearance that fits our feelings."

"I want you all for myself Trion. You are my hero, my confidant. I want to live my life as your partner if you will allow."

"You sense my feelings Bo. I know that you're aware of how I wish things to be. We make a great partnership, so I fully intend to remain in partnership with you."

"That is wonderful. Nothing can tear us apart any longer."

"The containment on the Globe was completely unlawful. Spreckley had no right to keep me like that without prior warning."

"It made my heart grow fonder, Trion. It taught me everything I needed confirming."

There was a strong, green glow shining abundantly from Bo's chest confirming the love she felt. The green energy twisted and turned, filling the space in front of her very clearly. Trion admired the beauty of the light movement. She could shape-shift at will, but Trion could always identify her. They were closely bonded in love.

Bo huddled against his body, making him feel deeply loved. They both stood face-to-face, with their chests pressing comfortably into one another.

"Bo, I need you to help me keep these energy sources safe with me. You're the one I trust the most, but we also need the strength of others, so the four of us must move together and without any of the others knowing our full plan."

Bo stroked a finger down the side of his arm, teasing his senses. "I will always keep close. We can keep the crystals safe. The others here are so conditioned to daily repetition. I doubt they'd notice anything unusually exciting if we ran away together. I prefer it to be just the two of us."

Trion noticed the majority of the beings on their planet were distracted simply by the monotony of day-to-day occurrences. "You are so right. They wouldn't notice our ventures." He looked over immediate scape of the dry planet, noting figures continuing on with their usual behaviours, almost zombie-like. "It's almost as if we are the only ones that are awake." Bo added.

"I guess we might appear the same to them if they stared in our direction, but I suppose if we zoomed in on their lives, they may have some things going on."

Trion pulled her close into his chest again. "Perhaps you and I *alone* are good, but I say we give it a little time and then take ourselves to the heavenly land I've mapped out for us. As simple as that."

Bo grinned. "I think we need to use those small ships over there though."

In the distance sat very swift and manoeuvrable vehicles that could be identified by the shape of a sharp beak. They were big enough to carry two beings at a time, along with average baggage pieces. The planet called these vehicles "Sharps," just as they appeared. They were popular for chasing or shooting down any enemy vehicles but used a lot of energy. The faster they move – the faster they burn! This was a reason they couldn't use them unless it was absolutely necessary.

"I think we may have just enough power to get one of them to the new place."

"Did anyone hear your thoughts during isolation?" Bo worried for a moment.

"I managed to contain my thoughts to be those of very general ones." Trion grinned.

He spun Bo around in excitement, "We are going to be free!"

"Where is this place?" Bo grinned as she spun with Trion's strong grip.

"I found it purely by accident. I need to keep it under wraps until we get there."

Bo stood higher, changing shape to that of a tall, strong woman who didn't look safe to upset in the slightest. "You must not tell a soul!"

"Oh, trust me, if I did tell anyone our entire plan would be ruined. It is a forbidden planet for those who follow the laws of the Universe."

"Then it is important that we are naughty-naughty!" Bo grinned at their cunning thoughts.

"I like naughty."

Trion picked Bo up with a lot of effort from the sudden height of her but managed to carry her over to a tent they often hid in!

The two male figures watched from a distance, knowing they'd need to keep a close eye on the two of them. They wanted part of the promised plan.

Present Time

Tom and Ethan were hurriedly raking through the garden waste, re-arranging the piles, attempting to work through every single section in order to figure something out.
Tom had a very long rake in use, but occasionally got his fingers in, breaking up heavy clumps of mud.
Ethan seemed to have his eyes really close to the ground, taking an exceptionally long time to work through each section with an older rake that wasn't as strong.
Rachel watched through the kitchen window with a hot mug cupped by both of her hands. She couldn't help but feel as if she was watching some crazed movie.
They all needed to find what the "unusual lady" was seeking out in their garden, so hunted for something out of the ordinary.
Previous conversations brought them to consider extreme value of an item, perhaps that of antique nature.
Rachel questioned her distracted mind as she watched on. She felt so drawn to Tom but cared very much for Ethan. Knowing them both so well made it all so extremely difficult. As she watched on, the doorbell rang out of the blue, making her feel nervous. The two men obviously hadn't heard it, so she went over to look through the front window of the lounge initially, noting the familiar figure of a friend, much to her relief! Seeing her friend stood there brought such comfort, making her run to the front door with a big smile.
"Hello!" She opened the door to her good friend, Tanya.
"Hi Rachel, I'm so sorry to bother you, but I was walking by and thought I would see if you had time for a cuppa. It's been a while."
Rachel felt so warmed by the thought and invited her in with an encouraging hand on the shoulder.
"You have no idea how much I need a friend right now." Rachel declared as she prepared another fresh brew.

"Why? What's going on?" Tanya had a concerned expression. Rachel noted her heavy lipstick as she prepared her reply. Tanya always wore bright red lipstick that stuck out incredibly boldly. Her eyes were a very unique pale green colour, which added to her striking appearance.
"You look great!" Rachel encouraged as she handed her predictable cup of black tea into her hands.
"We could do this blindly now couldn't we." Tanya smiled at the prediction of drink choice.
Rachel smiled and wondered if she made the right decision to assume.
"So, come on, let me lend you an ear." Tanya helped herself confidently to a dining room chair. She looked up then to meet Rachel's eyes.
Rachel looked out to ensure they had full privacy.
"What's that all about?" Tanya wanted to know what the secret behaviour was for.
Rachel switched the power to the camera system off, wishing to keep all things private for obvious reasons.
"There's some shit going down." Rachel looked serious, but Tanya chuckled inside at her choice of words.
"You sound like a crazed actress!"
"Sorry, that did sound a bit ridiculous."
"Well come on then, spit it out!"
"Shush. I want to tell you some secret crap."
Tanya held either side of her mug not knowing how to behave.
"I think Tom and I are in love."
"What the hell!" Tanya shouted.
"Keep it down!" Rachel insisted, "I need to keep this away from their ears. There's other stuff going on. I'm meant to be marrying Ethan, and there's a crazy lady who keeps trying to get something from us."
"What are you talking about girl?"

Rachel changed seats so that she could face the garden and still talk openly to her friend.
"So, there is this threatening woman trying to find something we have no idea about. She has been trespassing in our garden, hunting for something. We are assuming a stolen good or goods. The police are keeping an eye out for us, but the guys are out there trying to find what she's hunting for."
Tanya's expression was that of concern.
"What have I just walked in on then?"
"I guess a heap load of weird stuff."
"Do you think the stress is making you think insecurely? What's this about you loving Tom? You love Ethan."
"I have always had a secret pull towards Tom, but I thought I loved Ethan, that's for sure."
"They are both hot though! You are lucky to have the choice!"
"It's not as easy as that. Obviously I'm messing with feelings here, including mine."
"Wow, that's a lot of stuff to work through. I guess you have the police looking out for that crazed lady, so leave *that* crap to them. You just need to sort your heart and head out with the brothers." Tanya paused, "I guess that's stating the obvious. When did all of this new situation begin?"
Rachel felt alone in her thoughts, but it was nice to have a friend over for comfort. Tanya's timing was really helpful.
"Have they been doing that all day?" Tanya asked, looking out at the two hard-working brothers.
"Mostly all day. They've been looking through that muck for hours... With the guys - I guess the new stuff with my feelings has suddenly popped up, but it's all coming to a head." Rachel didn't realise she was going into a moment of thought.
"Hey, if you need me to do anything, then please just ask."
Rachel was grateful for the set of words, but knew it was just useful to have somebody to talk to. She looked down at Tanya's

extremely long and pointy red nails, thinking they could be useful digging tools, chuckling to herself at the thought.

"Will you keep me company while the guys do the digging? It's strange when they work together. I feel like the odd one out sometimes. I know this is an important task for them, but I don't fancy digging with them! They often do things I can't involve myself in, like playing with car fixings and things. It would be good to have someone with me. Maybe we could find something of our own to indulge in."

"Wow! Of course, I can hang out for a bit. What did you fancy doing? We could stick a soppy movie on or something?" Tanya paused for thought, "I bet Tom usually feels like the odd one out when you and Ethan are together though."

"Yeah, I guess that *is* hard. I never thought about that, but we tend to involve him in so many things we do. Sometimes I wonder if Ethan knows something but keeps silent. He never says anything. I guess that's trust. Oh gawd, what am I going to do? I'm not to be trusted, am I!"

Tanya reached over to touch the top of her hand in a gesture of emotional support.

"Only *you* know what you feel. You can't help who you fall in love with. It's just bloody awkward when it's close family connections. Shit, have you had a thought about watcha gonna do about the-getting-married-bit then?"

"I haven't a clue Hun. I thought about putting him off me, little by little, but that seems cruel and plotting."

"Tough call sweetie."

Rachel realised she'd been so focussed on her own issues and was about to open conversation about Tanya's life, when Ethan walked through the door, looking cold and mucky.

"Oh, hey Tanya. What brings you here? It's been a while."

Tanya put a fresh face on in response.

"Hi Ethe! I note your digging efforts. I hope you can find what the heck it is you need to find."

Ethan laughed slightly in the madness of it all.

"You know, this is all a little crazy. I'm thinking to just leave the cameras on and let the police take full control. We can't find jack in all of that rubble and dirt. I've even smashed old rock up. I feel like we're hunting for a microscopic piece of gold!"

Ethan walked up to the sink to wash his hands in an obvious conceding action.

"You turn the cameras off hunny?" He sounded slightly off with the disappointment.

"Oh gawd, I'm so sorry, I thought it was a waste of footage when I was watching you intently, but I forgot to put them back on."

Rachel stood to switch the power back on, appearing a bit sheepish.

Tom walked through the door now, making Rachel take a surprise gulp. Tanya looked up, feeling self-conscious with the two handsome men in the room.

"Maybe I should head off Rachel. We can always do the movie when things are a little more settled. I can see it's a trying time right now."

"Oh no." She sounded disappointed in her decision but could equally see Tanya's reasons, noticing the brothers were about to settle down with the onset of sunset arriving.

"Don't you want to stay for pizza? We were just deciding it needs to be one of our post-labour-pizza-treats to make all of the effort worthwhile!" Ethan offered in a very welcoming manner.

Tanya looked at Rachel for approval.

"It would be nice to have an even number in the house for a change." Rachel smiled.

"Great! Okay, so long as I can submit an order of pineapple in the topping arrangement somewhere."

"Cool!" Ethan offered.

Tom looked at Rachel in a way that said it would take the pressure off the awkwardness for a while.

As they all sat in calm and comfort in later moments, watching some background television, Tanya was noted to have long, joyous conversations with Ethan. Rachel couldn't help her plotting thoughts with the observations! Tom looked on with awareness of her potential thoughts, grinning slyly, but with guilt. They all got on famously well. Tom wanted to hold onto the peaceful moments, knowing there may be an emotional storm ahead.

Somehow, alcoholic beverages were involved in the evening, and everyone grew comfortable with the satisfied digestive systems and mild merriness. For Tom, the déjà vu of the movie night with Megan and himself made him feel peculiar. He loved this kind of social activity however, as it was very comforting with the abundance of conversation, food, and drink, but he wondered how the evening would form.

Tanya was obviously beginning to flirt with Ethan as the late hours crept in, but Rachel didn't know if it was to help out or if it was a genuine alcohol-induced set of behaviours. Tom didn't mind what he was viewing, taking an occasional glance at Rachel for her equal thoughts. Ethan was enjoying the attention but kept it all in good behaviour. Rachel filled his glass on several occasions, knowing his tolerance levels. Tom bit his lip every single time! Tanya appeared to ease off when she noticed Ethan's slurring, with her conscience kicking in. The evening was weird and childish but strangely tactful.

Tom stood with intention to leave once he sensed the tittering-over-the-edge signs!

"I think I should go now." He wobbled when he stood, however.

"What? You're well over the limit." Rachel looked in surprise. Tanya looked at him with criticism too. "You can't leave this party!"

"How did it become a *party*?" Tom added in a naïve sense.

"Oh, come on bro. Relax. Sit down. You know you have the spare bed marked up already. No responsibility! Relax, have fun!" Tanya sounded forceful.
Tom moved in a plot to concur but advance to a better seated position. Sitting hip-to-hip with Rachel now, he felt complaint yet rebellious.
Tanya noticed with glazed eyes, but managed to retain her attained, secret knowledge to herself. She didn't have any intention to make serious sexual advances upon Ethan. The tease was fun, and her night was light-hearted in her head.
Rachel still secretly hoped for an advance since it would take some pressure away.

As they grew messy in their head states, the tall, elegant, unforgivingly-determined thief had crept into their back garden! She camouflaged herself well in the darkness with black attire that even covered her facial features!
She hunted for some time, uncovering soil and large clumps of ground.

Hours had passed and sunrise brought beams of light into the kitchen, bringing rays that touched every one of their faces.
Tom woke first, on the sofa, recognising their obvious dropping-off. He stood in an uncomfortable, startled state, wishing he hadn't wasted such a lot of time on pointless behaviour. His arms and legs ached from the lack of rest following hours of digging. He rubbed his hand through his hair, feeling a tenderness. Rachel started to stir in movement, but he took focus on the taps in the kitchen, wetting his lips and throwing water into his hair and liberally splashing his face.
He looked up through the window ahead, admiring the nice sunrise, noting how peaceful it was outside and wondering how it must be for nature in these quiet times. His thoughts went into how the homes of humans built comfort, but how nature was able

to take care of itself so well. He wondered how birds were able to build their own nests and collect daily food; how spiders could build webs and catch their own pray; how foxes and rabbits could dig their homes and still find natural food for themselves. As he pondered these thoughts, he caught sight of a squirrel walking along a distant fence, enjoying the golden warmth of the sun's waking day.
Why can't we live without these elaborate brick-built homes? We must be aliens disturbing a natural planetary cycle...
A hand touching his shoulder, made him jump with a noise that made everyone in the house stir into motion! Rachel laughed silently at the fright she had given him.
"Sorry," she whispered, "I couldn't help myself when you were so deep in thought. She continued to snigger.
He bowed down to grab her, playingly, around her waist, lifting her up to a playing, swinging action.
Ethan followed the movement into the kitchen, watching the frivolity, wondering how their heads could even consider it with the way he personally felt.
"Oh, morning messy brother." Tom quickly diverted the attention to him.
"How can you mess about after the stupid session?"
"I don't think we had as much as you did." Rachel offered in defence, clocking a rough count of deliberate refills.
Tom and Rachel held smirks that made Ethan frown. He didn't suspect any foul play, but thought they were unusually happy.
Tanya was heard by the three of them, rattling around her handbag, obviously realising she would need to check her make-up. Rachel grinned at the thought of her friend needing to swiftly arrange her appearance.
"I'll get some coffee and eggs going." Rachel offered.
"I think they need something more hydrating." Tom tried to help, collecting a set of glasses, and pouring fresh water into them.

Tom handed the first glass to a fumbling Tanya in the lounge, offering words of comfort. Her response was to attend the toilet before any food or drink.

Ethan reluctantly drank the water, but Rachel refused Tom's kind drink offer, stating her remedy was always coffee, somehow!

Ethan looked out at the garden, noting the welcoming blue sky. His eyes caught sight of a disorder however! He bashed his glass hard on the nearby worktop.

Rachel and Tom looked at him with swift movement, assuming his morning feelings were causing some discomfort. Instead, he pointed to the garden without word.

Tom and Rachel walked over to view the same sight. The garden was completely torn apart as if a huge digging machine had been permitted to silently work overnight.

"What... the... hell!" Rachel's mouth dropped open to join the others with the shock of it all.

Tom wondered how he didn't notice the destruction when he stared outwardly in deep thought.

"Has your camera got night vision?" Tom was the only one trying to think straight.

"I'll have a deep look on the laptop." Ethan kept his eyes on the garden for a moment, "They even lifted the fucking *pond* back out. How come we didn't hear any of this?"

"I guess we were stupidly occupied, or busy with heavy alcohol-induced dribbly sleep!" Rachel was able to retain some sort of humour in her tone.

Ethan was too angry to see *any* humour at this point. He began sifting through the camera footage of the night.

Tanya emerged again, looking adjusted to the day, with perfectly brushed hair and heavy eye makeup and lipstick. Tom was surprised to see that she was so desperate to hide her hangover appearance. It was obvious that everyone was a little below par this morning.

"What are we all admiring?" Tanya asked obliviously.

"Someone has hunted through our garden a little more than we could ever be capable of." Ethan offered, attempting a kinder tone.
Tanya had a look and gasped. "Wow! Did this happen while we slept?"
"Uh hu." Rachel's tone was still pleasant.
"Well, if it were my garden, I'd be calling the police."
"Yes Tan. I'm gonna get to it. I just wanted to look back on the camera footage. We can offer a bit more to them then." Ethan still sounded half-asleep.
"Get to it! If you waste time the police will question why it took so long to report it." Tanya was typically pushy.
Ethan's mind was shocked by her louder voice, encouraging him to rub one side of his head.
"Alright! Alright! Is that what everyone wants?" He couldn't hold his tolerance too well.
"I guess we shouldn't stall or demonstrate any weird behaviour online. It would be best to report it first." Rachel did her best to bring calm.
Ethan grew in anger.
"First this effing woman interferes with our lives, and then she effing digs our effing garden up!" He walked to his phone and hit the relevant number.
"You can swear in front of me you know. I am used to it." Tanya thought he was trying his best to restrain his anger in front of her - being a guest.
Ethan grumbled under his breath, feeling like a growling bear.
Tom and Rachel looked at one another in awkwardness, wishing that they could hug one another for comfort.
Ethan's call was swiftly responded to, so Rachel gave a gesture for Tom to follow her out of sight.
Tanya felt she needed to leave, feeling awkward with her knowledge. She knew Rachel and Tom were creeping off to talk in secrecy, making her feel that she was left to support and distract

Ethan. She wasn't having it, so walked into the lounge to collect her large handbag in preparation to leave. Ethan spotted her actions as he was fumbling for a pen to note down a given crime number for insurance purposes. Tanya noticed his difficulties, so reverted to help him in the instance, thinking it might be better to wait for the call to end. She had a pen working on a scrap piece of paper, preparing it swiftly for him. His mood was swiftly changing, offering a kind wink in gratitude. Her rush to leave was halted momentarily, suddenly realising it would be good to hear the latest news first.

Ethan wasn't on the phone for long, switching it off in a slightly better mood.

"Sorry Tanya. It's hard to be pleasant when someone is trying their best to ruin your home."

"Oh, please Ethan. I get it. I can't do anything here though and I'm also feeling the effects of last night, so I just want to head off and leave you to sort this stuff out, whatever it is. It seems a bit of a weird situation."

Ethan had a flash back of the evening, remembering the fun they actually had despite the background events.

"I had a good time with you over, Tanya. Thanks for coming over." He reached in to offer a good hug.

Tanya gave him a hearty kiss on his cheek, leaving a heavy lipstick mark.

Ethan held on longer than he felt he should have. She moved back, feeling his hand, slowly slipping from her back. It was a gesture of fondness, but she tried to ignore it and moved her actions to leave for sure this time.

"I'll see you and Rachel later. Send me a message to let me know how things go on."

"Sure thing." Ethan looked comforted.

Rachel and Tom must have heard the changes in the room, so re-entered with a sheepish appearance.

"Are you leaving now then?" Tom asked with a faked casual behaviour.

"I'm leaving you guys to it, yeah." Tanya was keen to escape now, feeling a strange energy between them all.

"Come back again soon won't you honey?" Rachel gave a swift hug around her shoulders and opened the front door.

Tom asked Ethan about the call in the meantime, noting the lipstick mark.

Ethan explained the obtaining of a crime reference number for now as he opened his laptop to continue to view the nightly occurrence.

Rachel didn't say anything about the obvious lipstick mark, despite her temptations to use it as a cheating catapult for her potential future plan.

The three of them started to huddle around the laptop, noting strange motions from around one o'clock in the morning. At first it was a shadow of movement, followed by the obvious figure of the tall lady. She walked around, looking as if she was scanning the ground with her eyes. It was so dark, that the detail was useless at this point.

Things got even stranger when some large item was suddenly on the ground, as if it had arrived from out of nowhere! It looked like a metallic cabin. Again, it was too dark to obtain details, but it appeared to move around the garden swiftly.

In another shot, the metallic item wasn't there. It seemed to be there in one second, then moved around with the lady like some magnetic pull, and then suddenly they had both disappeared. It was like an elaborate magic trick that left their garden a complete mess!

The three of them looked at one another with frowning confusion. "I don't know what the police are going to think of this!" Tom felt nervous.

5th November 1860

William and Edward were sat in the shop frontage together, holding warm drinks. They were talking about the usual 'Guy Fawkes' evening, and possibly joining in on a "penny-for-the-guy" event that was always planned. There was a gathering in the picnic area they had visited not too long ago.
Edward was expressing how frustrated he was that he couldn't have a liberal arrangement with Ann, since she was so controlled and allegedly contained. William wanted to invite Eleanor to begin a process of getting to know one another *properly*, but he didn't want Edward to feel uncomfortable. He was happy to sit with Edward for the day, for one another's company.
They shared every single detail on their experiences with the crystal. Edward did his best to recall what he could see whenever he went "through the crystal" to an unknown, futuristically-advanced place. William explained his confusing experience of his other-dimensional self, letting Edward know that he was informed of his purpose to protect the crystal. William didn't feel it would be fair to let Edward know every single detail, however. Giving information on having-to protect the crystal and Edward alike, may create a nervousness about what he would need protection *from*!
They shared every detail other than that however, to update one another thoroughly. William couldn't continue with the concept of needing to bury the crystal out of sight forever, so it was vital to talk everything out.
They both had no idea of exact details, but they were getting some information bit-by-bit.
Edward decided to write it all down in his journal. He felt it was important to keep detail, as then they had a full "story" if they were ever questioned or captured for any reason. They knew they held a huge secret that could potentially land them in trouble.

They didn't know if it was something extremely valuable, but they were brave enough not to report it to any form of authority.
His writing was held in a very heavy, thick book. He loved to write anyway, as he'd often write his thoughts down. The used pages would become slightly stiffer with an enjoyed crinkly noise with every turn. This book was about a quarter-filled, but he was always keen to use its' entirety. After the day's conversation, he felt that William's purpose was to protect the crystal and that he, himself, was meant to write about the experience. Even if it was an invented purpose, it helped his focus on the unusual circumstances for now.

The day was extremely quiet, which gave the two young men ample time to catch-up with their thoughts and words. Edward decided to close up early since everyone appeared focussed on the annual celebratory day.
It grew dark swiftly on this short day-lighted part of the year. People were beginning to walk past with lanterns and fired-up sticks to celebrate the evening. Some wore home-made masks that were actually quite frightening to see.
William glanced over at Edward's observations and grinned in knowing.
"Come on Ed, let's head on out. We've been sat in all day."
Edward smiled in agreement, loosening up his tie to begin the evening plans.
They both eliminated all of the shop lights, taking a couple of already-provided lanterns and lit them up ready for the streets. People filled the cobbled roads, dancing and singing with fun in their movements and voices. Edward and William were beginning to get into the mood of it all, feeling youthful and energetic again. They rolled into a good crowd of people who were encouraging the good spirits. Some of them were drinking traditional mulled wine that they scooped from a huge barrel.

William spotted Eleanor and another lady in the distance, walking together in very pretty dresses. He looked over at Edward, noting his comradeship with some other young men, singing with heart, and dancing with conviction. He smiled at his fun. This all moved forward with great speed! They felt as if they had swiftly shifted from one dull environment to a highly energetic scene within one second of walking out of the shop door!

Edward started to fill himself with the mulled wine when he was offered an old mug to refill at his will. He realised he hadn't kept his sober promise to Lewis at all!

William wanted to control his intake, knowing the chances of bumping into Eleanor was increasing by the minute.

Edward didn't notice any of his friend's reservations, given his own spiking inebriation. It was good to lose himself for a while.

William continually monitored Edward to see if he had the ability to sneak off for a moment to say hello to his lady, but there seemed a keen eye between the two of them. William suddenly had a ringing of words falling back into his mind. He needed to keep his friend very safe. The crystal was also sat inside his pocket, as always, as of late. He held on with the memory of importance, watching Edward like a well-paid bodyguard.

William's keen eye spotted another familiar set of figures walking up toward the crowd, making him feel excited about the potentials!

Ann and her father were obviously taking a look at the local features of the night.

When they grew closer, William walked a short distance in their direction, deliberately, in order to walk into their path.

"Ah, good evening young Ann." He offered a respectful bow.

Ann looked slightly unnerved, trying to hide her face.

Her father gripped her arm and encouraged her to walk in another direction.

William grew angry at his control and walked swiftly to follow.

"Sir!" William gathered his distance in their direction again.

Ann looked back with a panicked look, but her father looked straight ahead and encouraged them to walk with ignorance.
"Sir!" He wasn't going to give up.
Ann gave a "go away" glance, but he knew it was a fearful act.
"Sir! I demand that you stop at once!" William was shocked at what had left his own mouth.
The man actually stopped and slowly turned his head, removing his top hat. William caught his breath.
"What is it that you want?" The man was extremely stern and angry in his tone.
"Ann is a friend of mine and I find it incredibly rude that you deny her the opportunity to at least speak with her friends."
The man actioned for Ann to stand behind him as he walked up to fill William's personal space.
"I find it incredibly rude that you forcibly intrude on father and daughter time, and if you continue to behave so threateningly I shall not hesitate to contact the local authorities!"
William took note of his dark eyes, puffed-out chest, and sharply-styled hair. He looked like a young, strong father-figure indeed!
"Look, sir, you are denying your daughter's happiness. If you clip a bird's wings…"
The man's shoulder moved backwards to prepare for a full fisted swing, giving William the chance to duck just in time!
The wind of his arm was felt over the top of his hair. William stood back up and pushed him forward, right into the back of his exposed ribs from the turn of his punch. The push made Ann gasp in shock. William was seeing everything in slow motion with his adrenaline.
A couple of people noted the fight and pulled the two men apart. Attention fell on them, making the whole thing feel one hundred times worse than it needed to be.
"You need to give your daughter a life!" William shouted as loudly as he could. "You can't keep her tied up for ever! She is living *no* life!"

More people gathered around, causing Edward to take note and regain a straight mind. He walked over, trying to calculate the occurrence.

Ann's father picked his fallen hat from the ground and tapped it against his legs to shuffle any dust away.

He pointed directly at William's face. "You stay away from me you complete moron!"

Edward quickly caught on now and ran over to a shaking William. "What the hell are you doing?" Edward was confused more than anything.

"I tried for you Edward. I had words about allowing his daughter freedom. He threw a punch at me, so I defended myself without seriously hurting him."

Edward looked at his stressed friend and grabbed his shoulder to try to support his emotions. The crowd dispersed gradually once the theme of the event had crumbled.

Ann was seen looking back in distress as they walked away.

"I don't know if this has made things better or worse." Edward was dumbfounded.

"I thought we might have been able to have a man-to-man conversation, but he just took to violence." William was straightening his clothing out, regaining his usual breathing despite the ongoing adrenaline.

"I think I can see what you attempted to say my good friend."

"Thank you Ed." He appreciated the comforting words.

"At least it didn't get *too* out of hand. There are plenty of people around thankfully."

"I thought you would have been blinded of the event. I thought you were too inebriated to notice."

"I am rather drunken." Edward laughed and tilted slightly forward and backwards.

"You are holding it well."

They both chuckled slightly and wrapped their arms around one another's shoulders, walking back to the abundance of fun. The singing picked up again, with dancing recreating the energy to be that of heightened joy.

A ladies' figure came from the edges of the group, looking awkward and vulnerable. Edward recognised Ann!

"What are you doing here?" Edward's surprising words captured William's attention too.

The two men stood in front of her, just staring.

"I thought you'd be proud!" She had some shiny eye features from crying.

Edward walked in and gripped her in a tight cuddle.

"What happened?"

Ann cried in his arms for a moment. William looked on with wonder and amazement.

"Yes, please tell us what just happened."

Ann leant to the side, still having an equal cling to Edward's supportive cuddles.

"*You* happened, William!" Neither of the men had heard Ann's voice at such a volume before. They both didn't quite understand her meaning either.

With the confusion, Edward made a suggestion to head back to the shop for all three of them to have a relaxed conversation over a hot drink.

The three of them walked in a wobbly huddle of support, not needing to reach a distant destination with the events occurring only a short distance away. Some acquired lanterns that they carried were guiding the way.

Edward unlocked the front door, allowing the other two first entry. William wilfully arranged some seating from what was available. He then went to an out-of-sight room to heat up some water to make some drinks.

Edward and Ann had some time to hug and speak, but Ann was insistent that an explanation was due when they were all settled.

William carried some hot mugs into the room, one by one. They sat in a triangular form, and looked at one another, trying out some hot sips for comfort.

Ann spoke first, knowing that the two men were keen to know details of events.

"William's actions triggered a serious conversation that my father and I desperately needed. I was terrified."

Edward reached in and held the top of Ann's thigh to support her.

"Did he hurt you in any way?" Edward frowned as he asked.

"Not at all. He was so upset. I now feel sorry for *him*."

"Wow!" William offered.

"After we walked away he was so angry, accusing you of being so judgemental and aggressive."

"Aggressive? Me?" He thought it was a twisted view.

"I suppose from his opinion, you came out of nowhere, accusing him of something he wasn't particularly aware of. When he finally asked me if he *was* controlling, a few feelings were spoken of."

"You told him how you felt?" Edward encouraged.

"I told him how I feel I have been treated. He wasn't aware of his extremely protective ways. He didn't know that he was making me unhappy with confinement. He thought he was keeping me safe. *That* was his only intention, ever, apparently. I told him that I need a little bit of protection, but that I also need space. I need the opportunity to learn for myself; to mix with others; to live in varied ways; to find friendships; to find love in others."

Edward felt nervous for her!

"Wow!" William wanted to bring the encouragement.

"Wow indeed!" Edward added the encouragement.

"Following our discussion, he said that the first test of trust would be to see how I survive at the street party without him. He explained that it would rip his heart out to allow such a thing, but that if I returned home before midnight, he would truly try his best to loosen the reigns a little more. He cried in pain at knowing that his daughter was wishing to fly the nest."

"Well, this is better than I could ever have guessed!" Edward felt delighted.

William was more concerned of the time, so checked his watch accordingly.

Ann smiled at the innocence of the two men in front of her.

"I do *also* need some adjustment time. I haven't had time in free-time as such. Please understand that this will be a gradual process. If you want our friendship, or relationship to grow then you will need to be incredibly patient with me."

Edward smiled. "I guess we are all growing up here. I think it is only natural to allow a steady pace for these things."

"Indeed. My father does not approve of some youthful actions *either*. It is partly why he has been so protective. He thinks I'll be influenced in many ways. I guess he wants me to remain his pure little girl, but we all need to learn in our own way, right?"

William and Edward looked at one another this time.

"We totally agree with your father." William wished to comfort, recognising his need to calm his drinking-side down.

"So, you wouldn't like the idea of trying some of William's strange alcoholic concoctions?" It was almost as if Edward could read William's mind.

"Oh, come on, that isn't fair at all!" William laughed at the thought of their drinking experiences.

Ann sat in silence, enjoyingly observing the banter between the two close friends.

The three of them spoke for quite a while, keeping an eye on the time in respect of a father's needs.

Edward felt amazingly grateful for the spectacular turn of events.

As the time grew near to Ann's required departure time, Edward suggested a brave offering.

He walked Ann back to her home address and ensured her father's view of his approach. His intention was to demonstrate his *own* protective support.

The arrival at the property was very enlightening, even in the darkness! Huge gates gave access to a very long driveway that walked them to the sight of an extremely large home.
Edward had never been in or around the grounds of such a big property, so his eyes were circling the entire premises to attempt to take in how such a place would feel!
Ann noticed Edward's expression during the walk and felt a strange mix of pride and guilt.
They both walked up to the large, castle-sized front door. Ann placed her large key into the keyhole, giving a loud unbolting noise, that would certainly give notice of entry to anyone inside. When the door opened wide, a comforting light of candles and lanterns glowed very invitingly. As Edward gazed from the entrance, Ann's father almost-instantly appeared with a sense of high authority. Edward wondered if he had been stood behind the door with the speed in which he had appeared. It was enough to bring surprise to both of them. Edward was prepared, however, having imagined this moment many times.
"Sir, I just wanted to assure you that I promise to take good care of your daughter whenever she decides to…"
"Thank you for returning her in good time." His voice interrupted Edward's, with a depth of intimidation.
"That is okay indeed, Sir."
The door was closed with a delay enough to demonstrate domination.
Edward was left stood, facing a large, wooden door that he couldn't quite make detail of in the darkness. It took a few seconds for him to turn and begin the return walk.
As he walked, he occasionally looked back. He hoped to make an ongoing impression for a gradual build-up of trust for both parties

but felt that it may bring quite a personal challenge. He grinned at the prospect of himself, and Ann's progression should his father approve over time.

His legs took him from a strong, lengthened walk to an impatient run all of the way back to his shop and accompanying home.

This was the beginning of something very exciting in his head.

Present Time

"Did you wanna go then? It could take our minds off things." Rachel was suggesting some time out of the house. They had all lazed about in the house, recovering from the night before. Tom and Edward felt the pressure to keep an eye out for the strange lady, but Rachel was growing frustrated with the imprisonment.
"It sounds good! Even if it's just for a walk." She continued, trying to show the small advertisement in the local magazine that she had gone through in boredom.
"It sounds okay I suppose." Tom wanted to comfort her.
"Na, you guys go ahead. I think I wanna stick near the phone and make sure the doors remain secure." Ethan was zoned out, eating his third slice of toast whilst staring into the garden.
Rachel and Tom gave each other a cunning eye-glance, both recognising the potential of a private trip.
"You don't mind?" Rachel wanted a strong confirmation to avoid any accusations at a later hour.
"Sure. I don't have enough interest at the moment, besides there's also a chance the police might get in touch. You guys head out. I'll be fine."
"Alright then. Off we trot!" Tom stood to gather his car keys, working hard to hide his excitement.
They both climbed into Tom's car, looking back at the house in unison as if hiding mischievousness from parents.
"Hee-Hee! Let's go!" Rachel couldn't contain herself.
Tom started the car, taking one last look at the house.
"He'll be fine. We won't be long." Rachel was grinning so broadly when Tom looked at her to confirm her conviction.
"I don't think he's paying attention. When we get back, I guarantee he'll be miffed that he wasn't listening properly." Tom knew his brother well.
"Well, he needs to do exactly that! Pay a little more attention!"

Tom smiled mildly in agreement as he drove away from their little road, eventually gaining speed on a slightly larger road.
"I thought this would be a cool thing to do actually. A big place to hide in too!" Rachel was still holding the magazine with her first finger pointing to the advertisement.
"I can see you're keen ma 'lady."
The local castle had an 'Open Day.' The private owners of the huge estate very rarely offered access to the public.
"It's an opportunity to get lost with you. You seem keen to discover the local history, and I can hold your arm in secrecy."
"You can hold more than my arm my good lady."
"Ooh, now, now. A little respect and less haste. I am needing a little emotional foreplay before any of that mindless groping. You need to work on my mind first."
"I thought I *already* captured your dear heart!"
They both chuckled at their teasing.
"Just you wait young man!"
Tom drove swiftly around the local corners, with little patience to get to the destination.
He spotted the signs to the car park in a short time and pulled into a designated bay marked by cones.
"It looks quite quiet now." Rachel noticed.
"I guess most got in there this morning when we were still nursing our heads and witnessing the scary garden thing."
Rachel reached to undo his seatbelt after swiftly undoing her own. She placed her palm on his nearest thigh and rubbed firmly, surprising him with her almost-instant tease. He felt himself jump initially, checking externally for wondering eyes.
"I've already done that. As I say... It's quiet." She teased again.
Tom twisted to face her the best way he could, turning his posture in her direction, encouraging her hand to continue with the rubbing. He held the back of her neck and reached in for a gentle touch of lips initially, growing harder into a heavy, deep kiss with such passion.

They were both driven by something they didn't quite understand. Their energy felt intense and somehow *knowing*. Tom was so comfortable with their actions, moving his other hand to the top of her chest, slowly moving it down to caress her left breast. Rachel moaned with such enjoyment that her hand moved up to his crutch, which made Tom move his pelvis forward and backward.

They both groaned into one another's mouths.

A car's tyres hit their ears on the gravel, deciding to park next to theirs.

"What?" Tom moaned. "Of all the places!"

Rachel sat back and chuckled quietly.

"I think that's a sign for a pause. Shall we have a look inside the castle so that we can tell a story once we return?"

Tom smiled agreeingly, trying to calm himself for a moment.

"I hope they don't mind the public using their toilets!" Tom was innocently thinking about a deceiving wash of hands with strong smelling soap to disguise their body smells.

"Oh, my my." Rachel offered with alternative thoughts.

"Come on my beauty. Let's take an internal look."

"You're such a tease you know!"

They both unlocked their doors and slowly stood to the side of the car, meeting at Tom's side to walk to the main doors, hand in hand.

A familiar face stood behind the main entrance, taking the entrance fee and providing a small ticket.

"Shit." Tom let go of Rachel's hand, noting a work colleague.

"Tom!" The lady didn't waste any time acknowledging his familiar face and frame.

"Hi Carla! What? Have you changed jobs now? I thought you were doing well."

Carla sniggered at his attempted humour.

"Tom, what brings you here?"

Rachel stood back, wondering who the lady was.

"Erm, this is Rachel." He placed his arm around Rachel to bring her equally forward, "Rachel, this is Carla, my boss at work."
"Oh, hello Rachel, Tom speaks about you on occasion. I think you are his sister-in-law to be?"
"Aha! You do pay attention!" Tom let go of Rachel's shoulders. "Her husband-to-be is taking some time out at home, so I'm jumping in to get us both out for a bit."
Tom wondered why he was making a fool of himself with explanations.
"Erm, boring day… and hangovers throughout." Rachel tried to help.
"Alright then. It's a fiver each to head on in. Hopefully a walk around this place will shake the cobwebs."
"Wait a minute," Tom paused, realising he could turn the attention to Carla, "Do you know these castle folks? The owners?"
"Ah, well, you see, I try to get involved in local stuff and one of the household members asked if I fancied helping at the door. Bit of a loose end this weekend…"
"Oh right." Tom felt better at transferring the awkwardness.
The exchange of money for tickets was made, and the two of them looked at the huge entrance hall, trying to appear patient in their desperate desire to escape!
"See you later Tom!"
Carla's voice became distant with the two of them walking swiftly out of ear shot.

"What are the chances of that?" Tom gripped Rachel's hand and pulled her into a faster walk.
"Well, she seems friendly. Is she a good boss?"
"She treats me a bit like a teacher's pet at times. It can be a little embarrassing with the others in the office, but heck, I haven't been given any special promotions or anything." He laughed out loud at the thought of such awkwardness.

"Are you looking at these walls?" Rachel realised they weren't paying attention to the scene they had paid for.
Tom smiled and pulled her shoulders in close to his with joy.

They both walked, looking at huge paintings and golden furniture. The carpet was a deep red with a gold stitching around the edges which was extremely soft under foot, making them both feel like taking their shoes off.
Tom began to bounce like a child in acknowledgement. Rachel joined in mildly until someone in the distance looked as if they were going to turn to walk in their direction. They both chuckled at their childish behaviour and walked sensibly now, looking at the impressive surroundings.

After looking around the internal parts of the castle, they had the opportunity to scan around the external walls and gardens. The memory of being chased by the threateningly tall lady came flooding back to Tom's mind, making the trigger cause a slight internal discomfort. He didn't want to ruin the mood, so literally shook his head to throw the thoughts away. Rachel was distracted by an interesting carving of wood, thankfully.
"This is great!" Rachel smiled, "I know Ethan and I had the holiday not too long ago, but to be doing something different with *you* feels good."
"That's so sweet of you to say!" Tom squeezed her hand with joy, "I really can't believe we've had secret talks and admitted how we feel. It's like a dream to me. I've always felt we were meant to be together, but never been able to explain why."
"You mean it's not because of my beautiful face or body?" She said in jest with an encouraging smile.
"Oh, it's so much deeper than that."
"I know, I'm just playing with you." Rachel lifted their adjoining arms in expression.

"Ah sorry. I didn't mean to seem serious then." Tom grinned with embarrassment. "Do you honestly feel it too though? I've never had such a pull or chemistry. Sorry if it's annoying to say. I think we are so cool together."

"I am extremely excited to share what we have. I just feel the yukky pull of tidying up I've got to do with your brother."

"Ah yeah. How about Tanya though, hey?" Tom said 'tongue-in-cheek.'

Rachel gave him a nudge into his shoulder, smiling at the impossibility, with knowing Ethan well.

The reality of hurting Ethan hit them both during a few moments of silence. Their jesting seemed so immoral now.

The two of them walked in the beautiful green shades of garden space, relaxing into one another's comforts.

A familiar golden haze came into view from the distance, extremely notable to Tom's eyes. The strange, familiar figure with the previous golden haze on his solo walk, came into view. He gasped, looking over at Rachel who seemed oblivious, still smiling, and almost skipping with her walk.

Tom felt his palms begin to sweat, and his pulse race, wondering how he was going to deal with this situation, preparing to run with Rachel's hand attached to his.

"Can... you... see..." Tom stared ahead, hoping Rachel would catch on quickly to the scene.

"I can see a golden haze ahead. Is that what you're trying to say? It's so beautiful."

Tom remembered how he felt the first time he noticed the golden light, so tried to go with the good sensations he felt before. He just prayed in his mind that it wasn't a build-up to another chasing. It would be difficult to protect the both of them.

Rachel noted his sweaty palm now and looked at him to see what was going on in his mind. "Tom, what's going on?"

He didn't feel he could speak, with not knowing how to prepare. His adrenaline built the muscle tension as he just stared.

The familiar figure with the slightly taller head, and a chin that appeared to blend into the neck area - suddenly appeared in front of them. The golden haze surrounded all three of them, creating an intense calm yet encouraging sensation. Tom and Rachel looked at the unusual-looking person with intrigue, and then looked around themselves to notice intense golden light swirling around them.

The person ahead didn't move a single facial muscle but expelled the volume of an unusual, crisp voice!

"Finally, I have you in my safe hands. I need to reveal something of importance to you, Tom."

Rachel and Tom retained their extreme calm as well as a crisp logic. They both looked at one another with a frown, wishing to know more.

"I need to show this to you."

The *being* that appeared extremely pale in a grey/white shade of thick skin, held out an item in the centre joining part of both of his hands. This item grew into a large book as if by magic! The size increased, with golden edges of the pages coming into view.

Rachel and Tom looked on at this *magical* book, wondering why they were being shown such a thing. They assumed this scenario was some kind of planned act.

"This book is of importance. It is within the grounds, where the railway line and the largest brick in the wall..." The unusual being instantly stopped speaking, sensing a nearby threat just the same as a vulnerable mouse, noting a bird of prey!

The golden swirls of light were sucked into this person, along with the book, forcing their disappearance, leaving Tom and Rachel standing rigidly.

"What the..." Tom held his breath and looked about for safety.

"Tom, what just happened?" Rachel held Tom in a tight grip, leaning her head into his chest in an attempt to feel safe again.

"It's okay. I'm sure it's okay. Is it some kind of themed act for the Castle Opening Day?"

Tom looked about and suggested they run back to the car just in case it wasn't part of the event.

Both of them sprinted harder than they ever imagined they posslbly could and sat in the locked car, attempting to catch their breath and calculate the purpose of the shared experience.

"I don't think I can handle a relationship change until all of this weird shit…" Rachel started to babble in a fearful state.

"Rachel… Rachel… Please, let's keep our heads. Nothing needs to change yet. I agree, there's too much weird shit going on. We just need to calm our thoughts first. Let me think… Let me think." Tom was trying to be helpful but needed to level his own thoughts out too.

"That seemed really… I mean… *really* freaky. If we both experienced it together then we can't leave each other. I can't leave your side after that!"

"Rachel, Rachel… We just need to calm… Just calm." Tom was trying to repeat the importance of allowing their minds to settle before acting completely irrationally.

"Tom, what is going on lately?" She looked tearful now.

"Rachel can you remember how calm and wonderful that felt, in the golden colour?"

"Yes… Yes. I can remember how good it felt."

"That's got to be the good guys, right?"

"You mean there's the good guy and that maybe there's a bad guy around?"

"Rachel, I have sensed this guy before. He's tried to be in touch before when I was on a walk on my own. When you guys were on holiday. I wasn't sure if it was my imagination… Oh, and the book! The book! I have seen the same book in a dream! Only in the dream - the pages had golden letters coming out of the pages. I'm sure it's the same book. The same cover."

"You've had this guy come to you before and able to cope with it on your own?"

"I wasn't sure if I was imagining it, or if it was an act arranged by the Castle this time, but now that I'm thinking about it, there are connections to these other experiences. I'm just as confused as you though!"

"What do we do Tom?"

"I genuinely don't know right now. The thing to remember is how good the experience felt. We need to know that it is something amazingly magical. I mean who can tell such a bloody weird story?"

"Who and how? You'd be accused of being completely unstable." Tom was starting to feel okay. His thoughts were rationalising and growing quite excitable.

"We can do this Rachel. Have you noticed the strange, tall lady hasn't *actually* hurt us? She's only been after some-*thing* we don't understand. And this odd being we've just encountered certainly has the kindest energy about them, don't you think? Maybe they can't hurt us. Maybe they're connected."

"What makes you think they're connected?"

"Well, maybe the tall lady is looking for the book. It's the only thing that makes sense to me. The signs are all coming together. I think… Why would that person come to us, to show us *that*?"

"Good point." Rachel said in a rush of breath.

"But what are we supposed to be *doing* with a book?" Tom added.

"Maybe the book holds some kind of ancient secrets." Rachel was starting to calm slightly with some unravelling offerings.

"We need to help find the book!" Tom grew slightly excited through the remaining nerves.

Rachel looked over at him, wondering how they could find a book that they had the most limited clue over.

"I know what you're thinking. How can we find a book with a bloody riddled message? He gave a message about this book."

"He said it was within the grounds." Rachel tried to join in.

"Wait!" Tom held a thought, "How did this person *actually* know my name?"

Rachel gasped at the thought too.

They both looked at one another for a while, still feeling perplexed, but calming gradually by the minute.

"This seems to be quite an important thing, just as he said. What if I am some kind of chosen one?"

"What? You?" Rachel started with a slight chuckle, "This isn't some kind of movie with…"

Tom interrupted with a loud laugh. "Ha-Ha-Ha! Okay, I went too far then, but it helps to think a little crazy, huh? I mean this is the craziest thing…"

"Within the grounds." Rachel remembered, "We still have our tickets. We don't need to get past your boss again. We could legally take a look around. Maybe this was all planned to the date and time!"

Tom's eyes grew slightly. "This is the moment I guess. When will we have another open day opportunity. It must be vital to try, right?"

"Within the grounds… The railway line…" Rachel was recalling the words again.

"What was the bit about the biggest brick in the wall?"

"Oh, it's fresh in our minds. We need to write this down."

"We can remember those points, can't we?" Tom was confident, "I mean, there are two of us and not a lot was said other than what we've just repeated, right?"

"Railway line?" Rachel repeated.

"Within the grounds?" Tom started chuckling at their repeating behaviour.

Rachel scoured with her head, wondering if it was safe to depart the car. She felt relatively protected within the metal tin on wheels.

"I know. It's going to take some more bravery. How do you feel now? Brave enough to face more weirdness?" Tom was trying to offer support, knowing they must be feeling the same in heightened nervousness.

"I think we should just do it. Get it found. Get it done... so that we can move on with our lives. Watch this weird crap disappear, and the two opposing forces come to some conclusion!"

"You're right. We just need to make sure this book gets into the right hands!" Tom knew the challenge wouldn't be too easy.

"Hold on. What if we haven't judged correctly on who the nice person is and who the dodgy person is? What if the tall lady is the good person? What if this strange pale person is good at behaving or acting?"

"If you remember that nutty tall lady well, she tried to force her way into your home, and I would say she had a huge bit of aggression about her. I had a horrible feeling with her. With this little white guy, I felt a nice kinda energy from him. I trust my feelings on this one."

"Oh man, I'm not sure Tom." Rachel started biting into her nails. Tom reached over best he could to try to hug her with comfort.

"Either way, I feel we need to get this book. If we have it safe in our hands for now, then at least we know it's literally safe with us."

"What if we can't find this book and realise we've been hallucinating or something?"

"Ha-Ha! Come on Rachel. Let's go on an adventure. Replace your fear with excitement. Change your way of thinking like that. It's helping me to do *that*."

Rachel breathed in fast and breathed out really hard, trying to expel strong nervousness.

"Okay, Tom. I guess we haven't been given an option. These two characters might give us a battle for ever if we don't act upon this now. Maybe it'll stop the stupid bitch digging up our garden."

"That's the spirit! We've talked it out! I think we should do it now. I know we hoped not to face Carla again, but I think we need to. Follow my lead." Tom also breathed out heavily in preparation.

The two of them exited the car cautiously and walked back up the long stretch, into the main entrance. Once again they had-to speak with Carla. Tom had a plan of words.

"HI again, Carla."

Carla looked up. "Are you starting from the beginning again?"

"Ha! Actually, I was wondering about the history of this place. We were walking around the grounds and wondered if there was a railway line here, somewhere. Would you know much about that kind of thing?"

"Of course, I *do*, you young fools." Carla was almost insulting with her condescending tone making Tom frown in surprise.

"A railway line used-to run under a tunnel. It was constructed around 1857, some say 1862, but closed off in 1966. This is what I have read anyway."

"Can anyone look at that? I love old track lines. It's a bit of a hobby of mine."

"If it's a hobby of yours, then you should know a little bit about railway lines that are here and gone, surely."

"Well, I mean in a little bit of a different way. I love how clever they are in the construction, but I don't know about where they run." Tom was wondering why Carla was being difficult.

"Ah, sorry, I believe it was all ripped up."

Tom and Rachel looked at one another, confused about their next move.

Carla continued, "There *was* a tunnel for it, but one side has been bricked up."

Tom perked up again with an idea. "Are we allowed to look in the tunnel?"

"Ah, I'm sorry, it's now used as a shooting range and part of the commercial property that it now is. The old station has been replaced by the public car park over there, and some of them properties on that side." Carla offered with a waving finger and a kinder tone this time, "...the tunnel is a shooting range. In other words, it's a separate business."

"Is it a shooting range *nearby*?"
"Just up the road. Have a look on your phone. I'm sure your Sat Nav will guide you there."
Carla was quiet firm, behaving to be more of a boss than she was at work!
"Okay. We'll head that way I guess." Tom looked at Rachel to confirm that it was a good time to leave anyway.
They both left the entrance area, looking back at Carla, wondering why she was behaving quite closed.
"Maybe we're asking too many weird questions." Rachel whispered as they walked out of hearing range.
"Could be." Tom comforted, "I was thinking that the bricked-up part of the tunnel would be of the most recent decades, so maybe we need to get into the deep parts of the tunnel."
"The shooting range then?" Rachel started looking on her phone for some opening time information.
Tom walked, holding onto Rachel's back, scanning the area like a stalked animal of prey.
"Ooh! It's open! It's open quite late." She paused, "but how do we get to look at the brickwork without acting weird?"
"Come on, I have another plan. Can you navigate us?"
"Yup!"
They both picked up their pace to a gentle run, reaching the car and climbing in, feeling out of breath, partly due to the exercise and partly out of concern. Tom hit the "lock" button, causing a clamber of door locks to seal in unison.
They both held their heads back for a few seconds, then looked at each other, giving a good chuckle, helping them both to feel better about the situation.
"Ready?" Tom checked for their next set of moves.
"Let's do this."
Tom reversed without effort and moved forward speedily. Unfortunately, it brought unwanted attention. A police car must

have been around the corner, as the sirens came up behind them almost instantly.

"Oh crap! We don't need this!" Tom pulled over in compliance, feeling beads of sweat form on his forehead.

"Just be cool. Pretend we've had an argument. We need a reason to be acting crazed."

"Good idea."

Tom remembered reading a piece of information about how to behave when being pulled over by police officers. His memory of this encouraged his action to turn the engine off and get out of the car.

His exit caught a very tall, authoritative figure indeed!

"Do you realise how dangerously you were driving?"

"I am so sorry officer. My partner and I were stressed from a stupid argument, and I stupidly took it out on the pedal."

"Well, that's not uncommon. I appreciate your honesty. Let's take a look at your licence though."

Tom swiftly complied, hoping for a quick escape from the uncomfortable scene.

The officer took a look at his licence and a strong glance at Rachel in the passenger seat.

"Would you assist in a Breathalyzer test?" The strong officer pulled the test kit from his pocket as if prepared a while ago.

"Most certainly."

Instructions were given and followed. Rachel was sat worrying, thinking about the amount they had drunk the night before, hoping it was out of their systems at this time.

The officer went back to the car to answer a radio call, holding onto the test, stalling the entire stressful situation.

He returned to confirm that the test was okay. Tom felt extremely relieved.

"You seem rather relieved to hear about the test." Suspicion seemed to rise.

"Oh, I had a few last night and suddenly realised I've never checked to see how long it stays in the system, but we were recovering this morning before heading out."

"Never drive after drinking, that's for sure! It usually takes a few hours, depending on how many you've had. It doesn't matter though. You're clear. Just be careful in future."

"Oh, I will Sir."

"It's still an issue that you were speeding and driving slightly stressed though."

Tom screwed his eyes up in realisation he was still in trouble.

"I'm really sorry officer. I can't believe I drove like a pratt."

"Have you both resolved your argument?"

"We have indeed officer."

"Where are you headed?"

"We were sightseeing today. We heard that the shooting range is part of the old railway line tunnel which was part of the castle grounds. We don't plan on shooting but asking the owners if they'd mind us having a snoop around *after* shooting hours."

The police person seemed to hold an interest in his words.

"That's quite interesting." He paused, "You seem a reasonable person. I'm going to give you the minimal fine for this event, but I'm going to follow you to this shooting range to ensure you have a good head about you, simply for your safety."

Tom felt relief. "That makes sense."

The police person handed the licence and fine over, with a grateful, receiving hand.

The stall frustrated both Tom and Rachel as they re-clipped their seatbelts, but it was a reality check enough to slow them down a little bit.

They both wondered privately if they were wrong about the strange 'treasure trail' they decided to take part in.

"Pfff!" Tom offered Rachel as he tried to regain his calm for a slow pulling-out of the car, with indication to demonstrate competence.
"Bloody timing!" Rachel gave, in return to his noise!
"I swear we are being stopped somehow. Sometimes I feel as if we live in a goldfish bowl and there are hands that reach in and play with our daily events to see how we respond."
"A bit like 'The Trueman Show' movie?"
Tom grinned broadly. "Yeah, I guess that's the closest comparison."
Tom looked for parking as they grew near the shooting range.
"I guess we need to park a little bit further away and walk over, but how is the police officer going to think?" Rachel tried to get view of the patrolling car behind them.
"Well, I'm sure he knows from fathoming out things from our perspective." Tom parked in the nearest parking zone and pulled the handbrake up.
"The car has carried on past us. Does that mean we're free now?" Tom asked Rachel but knew they'd guess the same.
"He hasn't parked up beside us..."
"Are you ready for the next venture?" Tom grew interested again. Rachel tried to remember to turn her nervousness into excitement. She nodded in readiness.
Tom opened his door as an action to encourage the two of them to make the motions. "Once we get going we can get into the role of it all."
They both walked with scanning eyes of their surroundings, hoping for a few moments of peace.
Finding the correct structural parts for the entrance, they both walked to find their way in, noting complete silence.
"Well, it seems quiet today!" Rachel's volume echoed in the large space.
"We're only just reopening really after a fire to the place." A strong, male voice approached them, "But there are some people

having a go at archery in some grounds if you fancy giving that a go? They're beginners, so if you've never had a go..." The gentleman was kind and inviting.

"Oh, actually we were extremely interested in the castle's history and the structure." Tom was quite straight from the start.

"I get a lot of that. I could show you the tunnel while it's clear of people, but I don't have much time to give you a thorough tour." The man was fixing some pieces of string together whilst talking.

"That would be amazingly generous of you. I am *so* willing to pay an entry fee if you want something for your time."

"Ah na, heck, I've not asked for anything yet for a little look, so why would I treat ya any different. Just gimme a minute."

Tom and Rachel watched on, standing innocently still as he was obviously trying to fix something very fiddly.

"Ah stuff it." He dropped the items on a small desk to his side, "I can do that later. I think it'll take longer than five minutes. Follow me."

Tom and Rachel felt a bit awkward about taking up his apparently-productive time, but followed with gratitude and haste, knowing the urgency and need for the opportunity.

"Did you notice the top of the tunnel before coming in?"

"Oh, I noticed it looked like part of the castle with the battlements." Tom was swift in pretending to know *something*.

"Well done! Great observations. The structure clearly proves that it's part of the castle. Did you check the other structures out in the nearby area? Have you looked at the hotel?"

Tom looked at Rachel, then back at the kind man.

"Well, actually this is all new to us. We've recently moved here. We didn't think we could look at anything with the castle being privately owned, but with the Open Day it brought us here, and one thing seems to be rolling into another! We're excited about getting the chance!"

The man raised his eyebrows. "Impressive! I'm Keith. I meant to say, sorry." He offered a hand of introduction.

"Oh, Tom." He reciprocated with a linking hand, "This is my partner, Rachel.
"Nice to meet you both. Right, come through here. Look at this amazing space."
They both looked up and through a huge tunnel, both obviously thinking the same thing – that they surely wouldn't have the time to scour through such a structure simply to find the largest sized brick!
"You guys look shocked. It's not as impressive as the castle itself. It must be important to you."
"It's amazing!" Rachel gave a fake smile to play along.
Tom started walking along, gently rubbing the ends of his fingers along the structure on one side.
"It's nice to feel the energy of the *old*..." Keith offered.
"Yeah, I love to see if there are any markings or inscriptions. Have you ever come across anything like that? It's like linking with someone from the past."
Rachel smiled at Tom's idea.
Keith looked at Tom with intrigue. "Are you into history generally then?"
"Not particularly. I just find it so amazing, like remembering someone, when we all become part of history so quickly."
Keith's eyebrows raised in a happy agreement.
"It's nice to meet people who care so much. I tell you what. If you don't mind, I must get back to the archery crowd, but if you want to take all the time and then maybe when you've done, just make sure you get mine or my wife's attention at the main entrance to show you're actually leaving. That way I don't need to worry about my head-counting numbers. After the fire, I'm extra aware of head counts."
"Oh, of course!" Tom grew excited at the freedom of their search.
"I'm happy to please some genuine people. Just make sure you give one of us the wave, okay?"
"We promise." Rachel gave a reassuring expression.

Keith walked away with a brief look back at them to throw a smile their way.

Tom and Rachel acted innocently, and convincingly looked along the tunnel walls.

"I think it's okay to hunt well now." Rachel whispered.

"There may be discreet cameras in here, so just look as if we are hunting for markings. Look for a bigger sized brick."

The two of them looked hard at as much of the tunnel as possible, worried about how it must look to be so fanatical and for a long period of time.

"We need to leave before they think we're too weird!" Rachel whispered after about an hour of simply scanning the old tunnel structure.

"I don't think we're gonna be able to do this. What do you think we should do?"

"Shit." Was all Rachel could offer, "I guess we've got to think about leaving."

"Well, nobody has come to shuffle us out yet. Maybe just a few more minutes."

"Ah Tom, it's just impossible honey. Too crazy. I mean, just look at the length of this tunnel."

"Keep it to whispers darlin', we still don't know about surveillance."

"Soz, I just think we should go before we look suspicious. Two police dealings in one day isn't gonna bode well."

Tom felt helpless, "Ah man. I guess today is our first scary adventure. Maybe figure a new thing out in the morning."

Rachel went up to Tom and hugged him for reassurance, then encouraged the two of them to start walking outward.

Just as they did, a sudden haze of the familiar gold swirling energy hit their eyes. They both lifted their arms to cover their eyes, in a natural motion to protect their vision.

"I am sorry." The gentle, familiar voice gave in comfort.

They both lowered their arms gradually to unveil their view. The pale figure stood within the golden light yet again, forcing Tom and Rachel to look around them for reassurance of privacy.
"Don't reply to what I say. The owners can't hear or see me, so if they see you responding, it will appear an unusual action."
They moved their eyes side-to-side, almost frozen by the scene anyway!
"Just watch." The pale, unusually shaped figure moved in an almost-gliding manner around the side of them and down the tunnel, to an area that seemed quite far away. The figure pointed to a particular location.
Tom spoke despite what he was told. "Why can't *you* retrieve what you're hunting for?"
The being moved their fingers over the area, obviously not "physical" enough to make any difference to the three dimensional, solid state.
Rachel placed her finger over her lips with indication to silence Tom. He acknowledged her but was pleased he asked, with the being's limitations confirming the reason.
"It's like he's a hologram." Tom offered as a whisper.
They both walked up to the same area to meet this being and looked at the brick directly in front of the pointed finger.
Much to their surprise, there was an engraved name that was extremely faded in time. Tom retrieved his mobile phone from his pocket and swiftly took a photo.
"Tom!" Rachel whispered with volume.
"Sorry, but I need to know I'm not going mad!"
"Well, you're not if we can both see the same stuff!"
The golden haze and the being disappeared swiftly, leaving the two unsure of their next action.
Tom rubbed a finger over the edges of the large rock that formed the shape of an old fashioned brick! He noticed the seal around it wasn't completely full of the dividing consistency. The height of

this brick was just below eye level, making it easier to have an attempt to do something.

"What are we meant to do?" Rachel asked in confusion.

"I'm not entirely sure, but one thing I *do* know is that this isn't completely covered in the pointing cement, or whatever they used-to use. With some effort, I may be able to pull it forward."

"It's a huge rock!" Rachel feared a failing action.

"I know, but I need to try something."

Tom wiped all surrounding edges and did his best to figure out if he could make any movement of the brick, or rock.

He pushed his fingers in any gap and attempted to pull, making him almost fall backwards in the surprise that the brick was very thin in depth! He now held this brick in his hand!

"Is that a fake brick?" Rachel was staring in surprise.

"No, it's just not very thick. It's had the appearance of length and width, but it's a very thin piece of rock. Weird!"

He stared at it for a moment. He wished he could take it home with him, but it was quite heavy despite the thinness of it.

"Wow!" Rachel exclaimed, looking at an opening in the space it came from.

Both of them stood in amazement at the gaping hole it left!

They looked at one another, both knowing that one of them needed to look inward.

Rachel retrieved her phone from her pocket this time and engaged the torch option to look in with detail.

"Imagine the original person of the eighteen hundreds looking on at us now, with today's technology." Tom was looking in the gap, but aware of all situations in the present moment and in historical amazement. The timeline of things was bringing such curiosity.

"I can see something!" Rachel spoke louder than they both wished, making her cringe and tuck her neck into her shoulders. Tom placed the held stone down on the ground, leaning it against the wall with caution.

They both looked into the hole, nervous about what was sticking out. Tom noticed a familiarity! With this, he stepped back in shock! Rachel noted his behaviour and wondered what was wrong. His face went a funny shade of pale, and his legs literally looked trembly.
"Tom, what's going on?"
"You won't believe that I've seen this before!"
"What do you mean? That's crazy."
"Exactly!" He reached his hand in to pull a very thick, leather-bound book out of the hole.
As Tom was pulling the book from the large gap, they heard footsteps on the hard floor, gaining space.
"Oh shit! What do we do?" Rachel whispered.
Tom quickly checked the hole for anything further, noting the space was completely empty once the book was removed. He handed the book to Rachel, who swiftly placed her phone in her pocket, allowing Tom to lift the rock and cautiously place it back into the correct position.
A figure came from around the corner of the tunnel structure, giving Tom just enough time to tuck the book under his armpit, attempting to look calm and natural.
"Are you guys okay?" Keith was obviously starting to wonder why they were spending so much time pottering around.
"We are just leaving! We were getting a little bit too comfortable down here I guess. This would make an amazing open-plan house." Rachel spoke up with a high pitched voice.
"Okay, well I hope you've seen it enough to kill all curiosities about the place!" Keith shouted from the distance.
"Oh, heck yeah! Thank you so, so much!" Rachel was hoping Tom was acting steadier on his feet.
Keith looked at the book under Tom's arm.
"I didn't see you carrying that book. It looks old."

"Ah, I did bring it in. It's a historical manual I thought I'd bring in to compare images, like a now-and-then comparison." Tom felt he didn't make sense but tried his best to be convincing.
"Oh right, well, if you are heading off now, that'd be good 'cause the archery is all done and dusted. I wouldn't mind closing up."
"Thanks so much Keith. It's been an amazing day of adventures, and this place was the most intriguing part of it!" Tom added.
Keith smiled, looking slightly weary now. He started his slow walk away to encourage their following.
Tom and Rachel looked at one another with tension in their faces, agreeing to speedily walk, to catch up with Keith's desire to lockup. He wasn't quite as friendly now, making it obvious that they'd outstayed their welcome.
Tom was trying to regain his logical mind despite everything being extremely strange for him right now.

Keith waved a courteous goodbye as he closed the main doors following their rushed departure. Rachel attempted to apologise, but he wasn't really interested now.
They both walked back to the car with tension, but as soon as they climbed into the car, they both breathed extremely heavy sighs of relief!
"What a crazy time!" Tom shouted, attempting to lock the car doors with his fumbling fingers. He heard the click work and allowed the weight of his body to fall into the car seat.
"So, what the hell have we just been through? I think you have quite a bit of explaining to do about this guy in the gold stuff, and the book you said you've seen before! What the frig, Tom! Have you set all of this up or something?"
Tom looked over with honest eyes.
"I can understand you thinking that."
"You said you've seen the book before too, and you gave the police footage of that tall woman that we never knew about

before. You dragged me into all of this crap without even knowing the consequences!"

"Oh, come on Rachel, you know I love you and that I would never intentionally drag you into anything that would compromise your safety. I expected the same as you... A nice bloody day out in a castle!"

"You love me?"

Tom was surprised at his slipped words, realising he sounded a little bit like a character in a cheesy soap drama series of some sort. He reached to touch Rachel's hand.

"I think we both know deep down that we love one another."

Rachel was quiet and savoured the moment of comfort with the holding of hands.

"Can you give me five minutes of explanation of recent events?"

Rachel gave a "yes" with the body language of a tight grin and very short nod.

He looked forward.

"Okay, so I've had a dream about this book..." He tapped the book, not expecting the obvious dust to come up close to his nose, "So that's where I've seen the exact same image. I know it's important, but I have no idea *why*! Then the tall lady chased me once on the same day that I had my very first glimpse of a golden haze and some figure. There weren't any words between us, so I'm still confused by that. Then there was another time I was taking a nice bit of exercise up in the local hills, when there was that nice golden haze which made me feel so wonderful. It's like a drug, as you probably know with that immense sense of calm we had. These are all bits of things that I can't quite put together. I kept it all to myself because I wasn't sure if *some* of it was just my imagination, but I was also afraid. I was going through it on my own."

Rachel looked at him and calmed herself.

"Well, you've got *me* now. That's the first thing. We need to figure all of this out together. We need Ethan in all of this too. Everything

else will fall into place in good time. We need to figure out the importance of this book and work out what the frig to do with it."
"Ethan! We left him on his own. What if that crazy lady has been back?" Tom started the car's engine.
"Wait! Wait! Look in the book!" Rachel wanted to know some of the contents before heading off.

Tom left the engine on, allowing some warmth to comfort them. He handed the book to Rachel to allow her the first viewing. She willingly rested it on her lap and turned the hard leather cover over with a paper-creaking noise, exposing some golden-edged pages, and extremely well-written calligraphy script. The paper was a pale brown, with thick, heavily-inked words.

She skimmed through the pages, with the thickness of it all, not knowing where to begin.

"Maybe read the first few lines." Tom offered.

My Private Journal

Edward Taylor

Rachel read the introductory parts, noting some loose pieces of paper tucked behind some pages that were obviously letters to the author. Tom watched her unfolding pages and noted the deep colour of the golden edges. Some pages looked dented in the centre, encouraging Tom to reach over and flick past a lot to get to a section that held a small hand-made envelope. There was a note on top: -

William's Requested Rings.

Tom reached in to pick the envelope up and felt the weight in his palm, then felt over the top to feel the shape of two rings!
"What? This is incredible!"
"What is it? Rachel wanted the same excitement Tom was experiencing.
"There are rings in here!"
"Wow!" What have we found? It might not be the book. It may be the rings that are important!"
"Shall we look inside?"
"Or shall we take it to the police? Or maybe a museum? Leave it to someone else to worry about."
"Oh Rachel, we have done something so brave and could uncover such an exciting story! I want to see more before rushing to do anything else with this!"
"Okay then, I guess we deserve this excitement after the risks we've bloody taken!"
"The doors are locked, nobody else is about. We're okay." Tom scanned all of the mirrors and looked thoroughly, in all directions. Tom carefully unravelled the very-brown, folded paper that held the items, and confirmed that they were indeed two extremely old rings!
"Wow! Oh wow!" Rachel shouted with amazement.

"I want those rings so badly!" She carefully reached to pick them up with her fingertips.

"Are you sure you should…" Tom tried to discourage her.

"These rings are mine! I feel they are mine!" Rachel seemed to be acting obsessively.

Tom looked at her with a deep frown.

"They are too valuable with the age of them. We need to get them checked over somehow. I don't know how yet. I don't think we can make rash decisions just yet."

Rachel had already placed the rings on her wedding finger!

"What are you doing? That's not the finger to put them on!"

"They *are* Tom. These are *mine*!"

"What are you talking about? We can't take them. Maybe they will give us a portion of the money for finding them."

"No, Tom. I don't understand it, but these are definitely made for *me*!"

Tom looked at her again, and then down at her fingers, noticing her very slim fingers were a perfect fit for the two rings!

"That is extremely weird!" Tom grew confused, "Just when we thought we were over the strange parts!"

"These are mine, Tom. I can't explain it."

"You look strange, like in a haze of something I can't explain. Maybe we are both getting a bit delusional."

"No. I feel saner than I have ever felt, as if my life is suddenly making sense."

"What?" Tom was growing concerned.

"These were meant to be found – for me! For me, Tom!"

"Look, I know they are very attractive and extremely valuable indeed from what I'm guessing, but you can't claim them as yours!"

"I can *feel* they are mine Tom. I just don't know *how* I know, but I know!"

They both sat there in silence, forgetting about the large, heavy book, but staring at the beautiful rings that sat perfectly on Rachel's fingers.

Tom noted the design and colours of the rings. Both of them were made of a very-old looking silver, with imperfect shaped circles, which indicated the obvious hand-made efforts of someone. They both had crystals encircling a main stone in the middle. One was an extremely clear stone, and the other was an interesting shade of blue with some lighter shade of pale blue running through it. The stones were large, and the main part of the ring was a thick strength.

"They don't make them like that anymore." Tom offered, breaking the silence for a moment.

Rachel seemed drawn into the rings.

"Rachel, what is going on in that head?"

"Erm, I can't explain it. I'm so in love." Her eyes were fixated.

"I think we need to get into the words of the book. Can you pass it to me, carefully?"

Rachel closed the book and handed it over to his lap, feeling the heaviness of it, trying not to catch the edges of the rings on it.

Tom opened the front cover again, repeating the entry words.

"Edward Taylor. Hmm." Tom felt a feeling of familiarity hit him suddenly. A mild trance came over him, and visions came to his mind.

The engravement on the local monument!

The name on the gravestone when with Megan!

His mind now looked at the inscription on the rock inside the tunnel!

It wasn't clear until now. Something was bringing close attention of this to his mind. He zoomed his mind into the same name, "E.Taylor!"

"Tom! Tom!" Rachel's voice came clearly to his ears, bringing him back to note their seated positions in the car, "This isn't a time to fall asleep! I think we've got to re-focus and get back to Ethan - tell him all about this weirdness."

Tom was surprised that Rachel was returning to her normal, logical behaviour, leaving *him* feel slightly disillusioned now. He tried to return to his own reality. His mind was now racing however, with realisation of an obvious connection or crazy coincidence!

"E.Taylor! Edward Taylor! I've seen this name numerous times. It was on the brick or rock we just pulled out of the tunnel! It's inscribed on the local monument, and I was meant to note the same name on a gravestone. Now the book, written by Edward Taylor! Why are we meant to find this?"

Rachel was looking at him with concern. "Is this a puzzle you've been unravelling? Maybe your curiosity has drawn you into this situation!"

"It could be! Or it could be some kind of destiny." It felt cheesy just saying it.

Rachel and Tom looked at one another with confusion, but excitement at the same time.

"I am so attached to these rings, I don't understand it, but at the same time it makes sense! You are so drawn to the name and the person who helped us find his book, but neither of us know what's going on. Are we in some kind of dream?"

"I don't know, but I feel a pull to get back to your place for safety, and to check on Ethan, as we keep suggesting."

"Can you drive safely do you think?"

Tom grinned. "This is so exciting! I just hope we're not being watched by a hidden police car again!"

Rachel looked around. "I can't see any monitoring going on. Do you think by finding this stuff we may get left alone by these weird people now?"

"Quite the opposite. I think we'll have a battle on our hands. We need to figure out what to do. Maybe we should get to safety to read this book. It may hold the clues!"

EJT

Rachel knew he made sense.

The Globe

Trion and Bo popped their heads from the tent, noting the haze of light for the day hitting the horizon of the planet. They knew they needed to be extremely quick to avoid the stir of others waking.
"Are you ready? Are you sure this is right? Just the two of us?"
Trion was holding his palm over Bo's upper back to prepare the motion for action.
"I am indeed, and yes, it's just for the two of us!"
Trion's eyes scoured the area, ensuring the coast was most certainly clear.
"Go!" Trion pushed Bo's back.
They both rushed their legs in aim for the 'Sharp' vehicle on standby, after secretly preparing it over the recent days.
They both felt the rush of urgency and excitement of their escape plan. If this was a successful escape, they would have a new world all to themselves in an expected paradise.
Surprisingly, they were able to gain access, without interference, to the vehicle, and secure all access for their departure.
The two of them sat in comfortable seats at the front view, with screens of faint lights, recording all directional and measuring shapes and figures.
Trion was familiar with most vehicles, so took to this machine with ease, and placed his finger into a slot that lit the vehicle into function. The internal passenger area gave a light humming noise. They both looked at one another with the positive possibility of their formed dreams of the future. Trion slid another finger in an upward direction over a flat screen and began using controls that lifted the ship up, and into deep space within seconds.
They both grinned at one another once they dropped into the galaxy they needed to access, knowing of no following, or sighting of them.

"Have we done it? Is it *this* easy?" Bo let out a cry of excitement and a colour of yellow that omitted from her lower chest area.
"You can't hide your feelings can you, Bo!" Trion observed with a smile and then continued to focus on the control panel ahead, knowing he would find the destination of their aimed planet in a short time.
"There it is!" Trion grew excited once he noted the ease of access to the atmosphere.
The ship almost fell through the haze of the entrance to the planet's atmosphere, dropping down to note the shape of beautiful green land.
"That is incredible." Bo gasped at the natural beauty.
Trion smiled at her agreement and moved down to the greenest space with hills, and privacy.
"Is there life here?"
"Primitive life. We will have freedom here. In the state that these beings are, that I sense, we can have them believe we are some magical Gods. We can have them serve us. They will be putty in our hands."
Bo sensed how it would feel to be treated like a Queen or Princess.
"We will truly love it here. I see no other form of life like ours, so we might have the entire place to ourselves! That would be much preferred."
"There could be life forms in the water, or inside the ground, but we can investigate. It's the first planet I've seen that hasn't had *obvious* life on it, or within it."
"I hope we don't come across some nasty surprises then! I want this to be our perfect move."
"If we stick together it'll be perfect. I can see we have technology that is lightyears ahead."
Bo grinned with the mutual observations.
"Water... land... clear atmosphere... I see nothing interruptive." Bo looked about, sensing they'd picked an untouched planet.

The ship landed comfortably on soft ground, opening the automatic doors to allow the freshest air they'd ever felt enter their bodies.

"We know we can breathe here too!" Trion offered.

"This is too perfect, Tri. We need to inspect it thoroughly before relaxing."

Trion pressed some parts of his useful screen, allowing access to the details of this planet. An image popped up in front of their eyes. It demonstrated a heated core of the planet, with layers of cooler parts. These layers could be compared to the layers of an onion, however the centre being warm, and the outer layers getting cooler and cooler.

"Can you feel a bit of life with this planet?" Bo asked, feeling a bit of a rhythm within her chest. "I can feel a faint beat, like a heartbeat. Do you think this planet is a natural one, with a lifeforce to it?"

"Well, if it is, you're the only one sensitive to it. It hasn't spat us out yet!"

"That's a point. Let me see if I can connect to it."

Bo stepped out and sat on the beautiful green grass that her eyes felt captivated by. She allowed various colours to leave her body's energy, controlling them with her mind, closing her eyes and allowing them to swirl in all different heights within, and without of her body.

"Oh gawd." Trion knew Bo's habits from old.

The two of them were quite the opposite, like chalk and cheese, as the old saying goes!

Trion was purely active and physical with quite a rough, forceful way about things, whereas Bo was sensitive to feelings and intuition. They complimented one another well, as Trion was the one who ensured their physical survival with food, water, and comforts; Bo was like an inbuilt security system, always letting Trion know about her intuition and foresight. Neither of them were perfect in action, but they always managed to find a wonderful connection.

"What do you think?" Trion asked, expecting an unusual answer.

"I think you're right. It's very primitive here. There is land, air, water, perhaps a hidden power that we aren't quite aware of yet."

"So, where are we going to settle do you think? We could make comfort of the ship until we figure out the structures we need to live in."

"We didn't even think about food."

"Don't worry Bo. I already have the maker in the ship prepared for several meal arrangements."

"Good job you were aware of that! I thought we might be able to make something edible out of the plant life I've spotted, but it may take some adapting."

The "maker" was a machine that reversed food to the size of seeds, but when ready to eat, the machine can reverse the seed-sized item back to the full-sized food source that it originated from. It was extremely useful for preserving the food and re-producing it with ease.

Trion and Bo sat together on the hillside they'd initially taken the landing to. It was a wonderful scene for the two of them, admiring the sun movement.

Trion tried to make sense of the planetary system, noting a white planet making an appearance in the distance, and a golden planet making a disappearance in order to exchange the lightness for darkness.

Trion and Bo leant into one another and inadvertently fell asleep in one another's arms.

A few hours later, and they both woke with such a wonderful feeling of comfort. Trion noted the golden ball of light rising at the edge of the horizon, bringing warmth to their bodies.

They both stirred into movement and admired the view of green shades on the land.

Trion looked at Bo, noticing the light around her heart, swirling in green and pink colours.

"You seem extra bright in your energy this morning."

Bo stretched, "Oh, it feels so wonderful. I'm not surprised."

Trion joined in on the stretching.

"My body feels different here."

"In what way?"

"A bit limited I think."

"I feel like I can use my energy more here." Bo stood and looked over the lovely view, "Wait! I can feel something."

Bo walked over to a tree and moved her hand toward a branch, closing her eyes and just *feeling*. The branch moved closer to her hand.

Trion was watching with interest.

Now Bo leant down and hovered her hands over the tips of the blades of grass. The blades of grass directly underneath her hands grew slightly taller, moving up into her palms, with the surrounding blades all pointing towards her like a pulling magnet. She then looked up and lifted her hands to the skies, encouraging cloud formations to move together.

"What are you doing?"

"Everything is part of us here. Everything is one energy. We can connect to all life. It's beautiful."

"Wow!" Trion stood to see if he could do the same.

"You may need a little more assistance, as you're not so grounded. You're also not so connected. You know I am sensitive to things."

"I do know. So how can I be helped?" Trion asked with slight jest.

"You need something to enhance your energy. Go and collect a piece of our source – a piece you can hold in your hand."

Trion walked back to their vehicle and rustled through some small items to find a small shard of crystal. He returned with a smile and hint of curiosity.

"To what benefit is it to play with all of this?"
"Oh, Trion, we can hold great power here! If everything is an energetic connection, that we all are, then we can create whatever we wish!"
"But we can do that at our home planet."
"Not as flourishingly as we potentially have here!" Bo was excited.
"So, we could build more of the power source on this planet?"
"We can build so much here. We just need to connect with what we want and have excitement and intention, just as we know. This was an amazing choice of planet, Trion!"
"Wow! Can we have a little play?"
"Let me try a few things. Just hold onto the power in your hand and follow me."
Trion held the crystal, wondering what feelings he should *feel*.
An unusual noise came from a distance, making them look at one another in surprise.
Trion swiftly opened a keypad of lighting on his forearm - an advanced piece of technology that was futuristically placed within them as a useful piece of artificial intelligence. The lighting on his forearm formed the image of an advanced keyboard that he pressed to connect with their 'Sharp' vehicle. Once he pressed a few digits, the ship disappeared to the naked eye, camouflaging it.
"I suppose we haven't discovered this planet fully." Trion explained his caution.
"Well, I suppose it's a good idea just in-case."
They both looked around for a few moments not recognising any threats to them.
"This is going to be fun!" Trion felt experimental again.
Bo led the way down, through a few green field spaces and found a source of water. The water was so pure and clear, allowing a perfect reflection of their faces looking down. The body of water was only a small lake, but big enough to drink from if needed.
"Watch this. If it works then I have proven my theory."

Bo placed a hand over a portion of the water, causing a mild ripple of movement that impressed Trion.

"Look closely now. Can you see a pattern?"

Trion looked down to notice a pattern that looked similar to the design of a large snowflake.

"I think I can see a pretty pattern in there. Is that what you mean?"

"Indeed. Now allow me to try again." Bo appeared to do the same thing, and asked Trion to look again.

Trion looked at the water, and noted a different pattern that didn't look pretty at all.

"Do you notice a difference?"

"I did. This one is a less pretty pattern."

"I'm connecting to the energy of the water and giving it a feeling from my own energy. If I give the water happiness, then the patterns look nice. If I give the water sadness, it shows a less pretty pattern. Everything is super enhanced here, making it really obvious that everything connects with our energy. Everything responds to what we are putting out. We could encourage plants to grown swiftly and healthy, allowing our food to grow so well and healthily too. We can choose happy water to drink. We can even encourage the air around us to feel good. The trees can grow with joy around us. This is all we need. A planet with everything so easily formed."

"So, we just need to stay happy, and everything grows well so that we can eat and drink well. Have I understood this correctly?"

"Yes." Bo smiled broadly.

"Wow, then we can change with such abundance. I think the more abundance, the happier we will be. The happier we will be, then the more abundance of good things will be!"

"That is perfect thinking!"

"Hold on." Trion pulled a small gadget out of a piece of his clothing.

"How did you get hold of *that*?" Bo noticed a small testing probe in his hand.

"When I stole some of the source of power, I helped myself to some of their testing kits too."

The testing item was a small gadget that looked like a mini probe with a digital screen.

Trion knelt down and offered the probe-end to the base of a blade of grass. The properties of the grass came up on the mini-digital screen.

"This particular item is seventy-five to eighty percent water content."

Trion walked over to a tree and allowed the probe to test a main piece of the root at the base.

"This one also holds a relatively high level of water, but also carbon, oxygen, hydrogen…"

"What are you doing, really?"

"Well, most of this life source is made up of water."

"You can manipulate the element of *air* and *water* relatively easily here, on this planet, from what I can sense." Bo offered.

"We are going to have fun investigating!"

"I just hope we are the only advanced beings here. We want to avoid competition when things are so delicate."

"I *truly* hope we are the only ones here. Even if we can stay here, in *this* section. I don't see any other *being* with eyes, arms, or legs. This plant-life, water, and air is all we need. We have the warming planet in the distance."

Bo closed her eyes and felt the warmth on her face.

"We also have our Sharp to travel or escape with just in case. I feel we won't need it much though."

"I think we will be super happy here!" Trion laughed with excitement.

The crystal he'd picked up from the ship started to tingle in his other hand! Bo noticed his observations.

"Can you feel the power that the crystal holds?"

"I can actually. What *is* that?"
"Crystals hold energy. We can decide what kind of program we choose to give them. It is super enhanced on this very-much alive planet!"
"Can this help us to create things?"
"We have a lot of fun ahead of us Trion!"

They both looked around in silence for a moment, hoping their new lives will continue to be as good as it appeared to be. Bo felt that the planet was almost untouched. The natural life and cycles that occurred didn't seem disturbed at all. They both felt excited at the new prospects.

6th November 1860

Edward woke with a sense of joy. He always knew he was extremely fortunate in life and felt strong gratitude. He knew others had such hardships and tried to offer generosity where he could.

The weather was beginning to get quite cold in the evenings and some people were beginning to get winter illnesses with their poor conditions. He would periodically make jewellery that sat in a basket with extremely low price tags so that those who didn't have much could enjoy such treasures, and potentially pawn them for much more. His customers knew the timing of his sales and valued his kindness. It aided attention to his store, with some travelling from distances when they grew desperate. He did his best to keep both the rich and the poor satisfied whilst filling his own pockets for success. Edward was always comfortable with what he already had and gave a big portion of his profits to William to encourage their ongoing trade. They both knew the value of one another, but mostly in friendship. They supported one another in all of life's ups and downs.

Edward walked into his shop front, ready for business, noting a small crowd waiting to enter, making his heart flutter with more gratitude. He opened the door relatively swiftly and retrieved items section-by-section as not to keep his customers waiting as he prepared his display.

Some of the people were familiar-faced, with three other new faces on this delightful morning. He smiled with a welcoming appearance, encouraging their custom.

He retrieved his lower-priced basket of goods, and many of them moved in to peruse the items in a slight bustle of excitement. It brought a smile to Edward.

Most of them retrieved an item of satisfaction to their eyes and handed over the exchange of coins.
Edward noticed one lady in the final two customers of the initial rush. She wore some tatty-looking, stained clothes. He instantly felt sorrow for her and hoped she would be the final decider on an item in order to offer it to her for free. Thankfully it worked out perfectly as the other person selected something relatively swiftly, allowing private time with the poorer-looking lady. He knew there were always clever tactics of some *posing* as less fortunate people, but he sensed that *this* person was genuine. At this moment in time, he was able to speak openly with her.
"Which is your favourite, Madam?"
A tired-looking set of eyes looked up at him, followed by a pointing action to a shiny diamond set on a thin, silver ring. Edward picked it out and handed it to her willingly.
"You can have this one for free."
An extremely broad smile offered a broken set of teeth and deep wrinkles around her mouth. She didn't speak, but she danced lightly on her feet for a few seconds before leaving the shop, looking back a few times, demonstrating happiness.
Edward felt good about his decision and sat back with hope of more custom after his early rush.
Mrs. Phelps arrived with a casual door-opening, noting Edward's satisfied expression.
"Good morning, young man."
Edward grinned at his regular customer.
"I am happy to see you Mrs. Phelps. Is there anything that you would love to see today? Perhaps something that you would love for me to adjust to your preference?"
"Oh, you are such a good businessman. I would love to simply admire your work for a few moments. If something pops to my eyes, I may surprise you."
"That is absolutely fine Mrs. Phelps." He grinned broadly, knowing her usual habits, and not wishing to interfere too much.

William caught Edward's peripheral vision, walking in line with the shop front, intending to walk through the door for a morning chat. The door opened, allowing a mutual greeting. William spotted Mrs. Phelps and noted her usual judgemental eyes. She offered her regular frown over his regularly-rough appearance.
William moved to Edward's side of the sale's desk, almost as if it was safer there, behind some form of barrier! Edward always laughed inwardly at his behaviour.
As they sat there, expecting normal daily events to occur, a person who looked extremely worn and tired almost-fell into the door. They gasped with their words as they attempted to catch their breath. The man was tall but hunched over as if he always needed to bend down to match everyone else's height for hearing.
"Can someone please help me? My mother has fallen and hurt herself badly!"
William instantly touched his pocket, and Edward knew his thoughts. The crystal immediately activated within William's pocket, causing the usual, extremely bright light! Edward urged him to deactivate it swiftly for them to at least see clearly! Thankfully, the stranger didn't react fearfully to this blinding light, but simply blinked several times to regain his normal vision. Mrs Phelps continued on in the background area of the shop, completely oblivious to anything unusual.
Both Edward and William stood and ran from the desk to see to the said emergency.
When the three of them ran in the same direction, the taller man drew them to a street around the corner.
"She was *here*!" He looked with genuine concern with his palms out in question.
By this time William had activated the light of the crystal in his pocket yet again, forcing Edward and this man to cover their eyes.
"William! Put it out!" Edward shouted without thinking.
A frightening figure came around the corner, lifting a lady, with one arm!

William willingly deactivated the crystal with immediate compliance.

"That's my mother!" The weary man shouted with a primitive pointing of the finger.

William and Edward were confused about the scene, trying to make sense of it all. They semi-recognised the unusual figure. Edward looked hard to note a relatively flat face, not appearing to have a nose in the centre. He gasped, also trying to take in the view of coloured clothing that fitted the body tightly.

This tall, different-looking being spoke clearly from a distance.

"I wish to retrieve something in your possession that you know you have no control over."

William held the crystal tightly in his pocket, assuming the original owner of it had finally come to claim ownership. The three men stood in silence, trying hard to understand what their eyes were telling them.

"This can be over within a few seconds. This lady can be helped, and I can go away with the item that belongs with me. This is a power source that belongs to me."

William took in detail of the being, making note of the small apparatus that ran into the centre of their face, not understanding the function. He was surprised to see large eyes and a strange haze above the head.

They all stood in shock without word, not even retaining any words spoken to them.

This being threw a small ball along the ground, that found a section of stillness just in front of the three shocked gentlemen. This ball omitted a haze of blue, that the three of them innocently took into their respiratory systems, causing an overpowering calmness.

"Can you see clearer now, my friends?"

Edward's eyes looked side-to-side with uncertainty of what had just happened, but knew he was suddenly calm, with clarity of thought. He looked back at the two figures ahead.

"That lady needs help!" Were his first words.

"My mother needs a doctor!" The stranger shouted in their direction.

"What do you want?" William offered with confidence.

The unusual figure before them looked contented at their fresh interaction attempts.

"My name is Trion from another planet, but at this point in time, you wouldn't understand. I wouldn't want to bombard your brains with too much information, but I believe you have something of mine that you *also* do not understand. It belongs with me. I need it to complete a process that needs *that* part for the planet to function."

"Please help my mother." The stranger shouted in desperation.

"Your mother will be fine. She's breathing and is just in a little bit of shock."

They all focussed on the lady's condition and knew she was drifting in and out of consciousness, as this being held her in an upright stance with one arm. It was worrying to note how strong this person appeared!

"Right! I need you to pass me that stone from your pocket. I don't know how you managed to gain access to it, but you are playing with danger, and it isn't worth your life!" A rigid finger was pointed at William along with the words.

Everyone looked at William, hoping that he'd make the decision to hand it over, however, in William's mind, he was remembering his recent experience of his other-dimensional-*self* making communication.

"*Protect the crystal and Edward. My life purpose...*" William whispered for everyone to hear.

"What was that?" Edward asked with concern.

William didn't reply, as he knew the others wouldn't understand, and he felt unable to summarise the events in his head within a short time enough! Instead, he looked ahead and asked an unusual question.

"What do you want it for? I have paid for this item, so I have not stolen it." His lie was strong.

"It is of great value. I am willing to give you the monetary value that you are familiar with." The being responded, still holding the lady up without effort.

"I believe this is invaluable. I cannot sell it." William stood strong.

"You say you purchased it however I can purchase it for whatever fund you request. It is valuable to all life on this planet. I am willing to give all funds that I have."

"What would a measly stone do for the benefit of a planet?"

"You believe that this rock we stand on is a simple rock that you build further rocks upon for homes, churches, and statues. There is a lot more at stake. There were lives before your civilisation, and there are lives that still come and go without your recognition. My life, for example. I'm sure that your eyes are not deceiving you. I am a *being* of further advancement, yet there were previous beings of further advancement than I. This is a place of poverty and limitation that is completely unnecessary with such abundance available to you, if you know how."

William and Edward looked at one another, not understanding what this person was trying to explain. It was something that their upbringing had ever contemplated. They stood there, remaining dumbfounded.

"You are born into a system. A bit like a sheep being born into a field. The sheep doesn't understand the value of money, nor does it understand why it is contained within a particular field, or pen, yet it accepts it as normal. They don't look beyond."

"How do you know how a sheep feels or thinks? I've seen incredible intelligence in their eyes. Some of them manage to escape, and boy do they run! They understand freedom. I am certain of it!" The stranger with concern for his mother was a hard-working farmer.

"Perhaps my analogy is not perfect, but you know that I am saying to look outwardly to possibilities. That crystal holds power that other civilisations hold dear to them. There are other civilisations. Now, please, let us take care of this dear lady and allow my generosity to cover the cost of your purchase, with a great amount on top for compensation for your obvious, priceless bond to it."

"I shall not, and I cannot! I shall make you a fair deal! You must lie the lady down nearer us, with great care, and step back. I shall heal the lady before our eyes... Following that, I may consider a fair exchange, but we shall sit at a table and write out a careful receipt for this deal. I believe these are fair conditions. It is also important that I receive a name and address of yours... I shall not be forced under such captive circumstances when a lady's life is used as bait! I am a fair man!"

Edward thought that this was actually quite a good set of words from his friend and felt that he could now support his actions.

"I am, in fact, a great leader of the land of this planet, and once you are aware of my dealings, you may give some deserved respect."

"If you wish to receive respect from us, you need to act with respect towards us, since we are the ones who *actually* own this land. We are the people. We are the farmers, the jewellers, the chimney sweeps, the service providers. We have the power to take it away from such forceful behaviours that you are currently displaying!" Edward was now supporting his friend verbally.

"We are reasonable people who can be approached with respectable behaviour. There are options to bargain without holding people's lives to ransom." William added.

The purple-shaded being looked surprised by the offered words and gently lowered the poor lady's body in front of himself. He stepped back by quite a few meters, actioning the others to move toward her at the same time to keep a similar distance apart. William was slightly annoyed about the control this person had, despite the suggestions given, but thought it was progress for now.

The three men moved cautiously forward. Everyone had intensity in their eyes! The poor lady groaned on the ground but sounded relatively calm.

Edward noticed the blue haze that aided their nerves was beginning to wear off, but he managed to retain his sanity, looking over briefly to note a greater hesitation in all of their paces. Edward's thoughts were that of *'how does the crystal always get them into ridiculous situations?'*

The stranger grew close to his mother and knelt down to give her instant comfort in words, trying to gain eye contact from her. She rolled onto her back, looking up, only a bit of blood around her nose. William took note and knelt down, holding onto the crystal like a man with a gun in his holster. He kept a keen eye on the intrusive being in the near distance, ensuring he'd allow the healing process to occur without interference.

Thankfully all went to plan at this point. William activated the crystal for the extreme brightness, causing all of them to cover their eyes. The lady instantly sat up with humour in her voice.

"Oh, my John! I had such a silly fall." She stood up with ease, despite her son's effort to lift her by the hand.

"Mother, I am so…"

John was about to express his gratitude for her newfound wellbeing, when in the corner of his eyes, he noticed the unusual being running swiftly towards them!

William threw an instinctive word in the air whilst holding the crystal tightly to his chest.

"Protection!"

Just as the word left his lips, a large, transparent bubble of light expanded instantly from the crystal, surrounding himself and their new friend, John, and his mother. It caused the purple being to grow angry and frustrated. He knew the capability of this power but wasn't aware that *they* knew anything of these abilities. William looked just as shocked as Edward did. This was all performed with panicked behaviour.

The deep and unusual set of eyes looked over at Edward now, completely aware that the two of them stood outside of the protective bubble of energy.

Edward felt extremely vulnerable and touched the extremities of this structure, not knowing how to gain access. William was looking down at the crystal in his hands, wondering if there was a set of various instructions he could use to adjust this situation. He was worried about undoing the protective ball that suddenly emerged, but he needed to save his best friend too! Thoughts rushed through his mind, wishing for further help to appear like magic.

Edward noted the deep eyes moving towards him, with hazes of colour moving all around the unusual, purple features. He felt the threat of the approach and lifted his fists in defence.

"Get away! I'm a good boxer around here!"

The being responded with a condescending chuckle.

"You have no idea what you are dealing with."

"Help us!" William shouted as loudly as he could.

Just as he *did* shout, a man from around the corner appeared, looking down the road at the chaos. Edward called out too, hoping for more people to appear.

At first, this fresh person looked around, encouraging some other onlookers to join in on this need to aid the local people.

Thankfully, the benefits of this new support of the local community gained strength in numbers, suddenly.

The purple being seemed to disperse into the atmosphere without a trace!

Edward felt a relief he'd never felt before in his young adulthood. His fists dropped, and his shoulders fell in behavioural unison. William's eyes rolled over to Edward and then down at the two family members who were continually consoling one another, then visualised a deactivation of all crystal effects, now holding new concerns of exposure.

Thankfully, everything seemed to suck into the size of the crystal itself, landing a scene of normal events.

Several men came running down towards them with preparation to aid in an unknown event.

The first, biggest gentleman, with a large black hat and heavy beard spoke initially. "Are you gentleman needing some assistance? You sounded very distraught."

"This lady fell, and we didn't know what to do!" William spoke swiftly.

"What? She looks as if she's just banged her nose a little bit. We could find a doctor if you are truly concerned." The gentleman couldn't understand the fuss, "come on everyone. It's a boy-who-cried-wolf scenario. You had us all worried out of our skin!"

His tone was pompous, but leading everyone away from what they assumed was a false alarm.

"We need to get out of this street, quickly!" Edward grabbed William's arm, forcing a swift move out of the vulnerable openness.

"Hello! Thank you good strangers for helping my mother!" John shouted with loud gratitude.

"It's fine!" William shouted back, moving away with a fast pace. John and his mother walked on in a different direction, looking back occasionally with gratitude.

Edward and William arrived back at the shop, to find everything still intact, much to Edward's relief. He twisted a sign to state a closure, hoping that people will assume a minor illness or suchlike.

"What was that?!" Edward was extremely stressed.

"That was me trying to do the right thing!"

"No, I mean what was that p-p-person?" He paced.

"I wish I could tell you, Edward. I think I have been familiarised with out-of-this-world strangeness, but I cannot explain it *all*."

"We are not safe with that crystal. You seriously need to bury it without question, and now!"

"They know I am in possession of it now, even if I bury it, they know to come after me!"

"Do you think that *John* was a set-up situation with his mother? Do you think there was a bribe to get that John to cry for help, knowing we would be able to?"

"I do not know Ed. I truly do not know."

"How did you know about the protective ball? Why did you not ensure *I* was within the ball?"

"This was the very first instance of the protective ball! This has all been very new to me too!" William felt he was fighting for the friendship now.

"I was so open to attack!"

"I know. I know!" William reached out to hold Edward's shoulder to comfort him. "Surely you could see that I was a lost soul in the circumstances. I wanted you to be just as safe. That is why I called for help!" William lowered his tone and tried to control his stress levels. He continued to reassure his friend, "Ed, you know you are my brother. Maybe not in blood, but in depth of friendship."

"I know Will, I know."

They both shook hands very formally, but with a grip that said something much more.

"Will, please bury the crystal with me. Let's do this now before it is too late."

"Ed, I need to tell you that my life purpose is genuinely to protect the crystal and to protect *you*."

"You say this, yet to bury the crystal will hide it for good. If this is away from us, then we shall be protecting both the crystal *and* I. Surely that is a logical suggestion."

William thought for a moment, recognising the logic of Edward's words.

"We need a deep hole if we do this. We need to ensure it is away from my home. We need to lose trace of all of this."

The final sentence of William's made Edward realise his need to get rid of all personal records of its' existence too.

Edward walked over to his work desk to retrieve his large book of notes. He opened it to the page he'd recently added information to.

"I have an idea. I'm going to add something just to sign it all off, then it will feel like some kind of conclusion for me… us - hopefully!"

He pulled his pen out of the holder and dabbed it in the ink nearby, scribing some words and a small drawing, stating that they will be the letters of closure.

"What are you going to do with that book? Perhaps we should burn all evidence."

"That is not a bad idea in-fact. Perhaps your idea is better."

"Well, what was *your* idea Ed?"

"I thought that I would conclude the notes, leaving some mystery, but perhaps it *is* safer burnt. I suppose I have some attachment to this book." Edward rubbed his chin and then remembered the location of some matches in his drawer, swiftly retrieving them and placing them in a pocket. "I did think about a potential place to hide the crystal. I could burn the book at the same location… Shall we go there *now* do you think? I believe I have a small shovel at the back." Edward grinned at the thought of their lives returning to some normality. He looked at William's expression of uncertainty, so continued, "I think we *should*. At least you are aware of the protective actions it has if we are threatened again on the way. If such things are ever witnessed we could put fear into many minds. The world is already a crazy place. I do feel the banishing of it is best. We have had enough difficulty with it ourselves. People finding out could cause mass chaos."

"I do still have some form of addiction to it. That strange addictive pull. I suppose similar to the feelings you have about your book." William looked sad at the visualised loss.

"Oh Will, we have such an amazing life ahead of us. We could move on, be with our ladies, and live happy, lavishing lives with the work we already do. The stress will be eliminated."

"My father said that there will be stress, always."

"Oh, at least we can remove *one* large issue from our lives and have a normal existence."

"I suppose I need to *concur*."

With reluctance, William followed Edward to the rear where a large cupboard held various tools. He picked up a small shovel that looked extremely sharp!

"I cannot believe what we have been through with this one special stone. In one way it has been an amazing adventure, but in others it has been extremely confusing."

"I know Will. I think we shall both miss the adventures, but it does appear to be getting dangerous, do you not think?"

Edward now held the shovel in one hand and the heavy book under his other arm.

William looked at Edward. "We're really going to do this?"

"It's what I *think* is right. Do you not agree?" Edward knew his friend didn't want to give the crystal up. He didn't want to force anything but did his best to encourage the action.

"I am truly unsure, but perhaps we should *try* to hide it and see if it brings us peace."

"Okay Will. Let's go before we are discovered for it again."

William walked behind Edward, noticing his struggles with the door and key.

"Let me carry one of these." William realised he wasn't thinking straight by allowing Edward to prepare everything. He thought it was right to take the shovel and pull the door open.

They both walked onto the street, checking for complete privacy before moving along.

They both walked relatively fast now, feeling vulnerable to attack or questioning of their behaviour.

"Hopefully you will agree on my location idea. If not, you can tell me otherwise." Edward offered a comfort in flexible options, hoping he wasn't being a bully on decision-making.
"I am sure I shall trust your judgement." William held the crystal tightly inside his trouser pocket, secretly hating the idea.
Edward guided them to the recent picnic area with the deep tunnel. They both moved with rushed legs, almost tripping over themselves.
There didn't appear to be anyone else around them at the time. Edward stopped them at the entrance of the large tunnel. There were train tracks that needed avoiding, but Edward's idea was to bury the crystal close to the tunnel, and the book somewhere near.
"What about this area?" Edward confirmed obviously.
"Well, I suppose it would be relatively secure." William wasn't clear of thought about *any* of it. His adrenaline obscured his view.
"Come on Will, I think it could be well disguised just here."
There was a nice turf that sat at the edge of a wall on one side of the tunnel, "this is the place I could see in my mind's eye. Hopefully you'll agree it's a good spot."
William didn't reply in word, but he demonstrated his response in action. He moved the shovel forward and began the dig. He took a top layer of grass out with a very tidy square, placing it individually on the side to re-place back on-top at the end, for the best element of disguise.
Edward looked on pleasingly, seeing the results of the plan unfolding well already. He kept an eye out for unusual approaches, feeling like a bodyguard.
William paused to rest his hands for a moment.
"How deep do you think we should go?"
Edward looked into his already-deep hole, impressed by his efforts.
"Wow! It looks satisfactory already."

"Perhaps a little deeper." William started actioning again, keeping the fresh soil tidily at the side.

They both decided the depth was prepared well enough, leaving William to carefully place the crystal in the centre of the hole, like a mini-tower facing them from their view above.
William felt like he was burying his best toy, or some kind of friend, as he initially used the shovel to cover it up. He used his hands to ensure the soil filled right to the top again. The square piece of grass covered the final patch of it all, making it look extremely tidy – almost untouched.
"I hope it will be okay there." William felt lost without it already!
"I'm sure all will be fine." Edward felt a huge relief.
William tried to push his emotions aside, now looking at Edward's book.
"I know." Edward offered, "Let's burn this somewhere safe.
As they both spoke, they caught sight of a few figures walking in the direction of the tunnel.
"Let's go!" William whispered as loudly as he could!
They both ran *into* the tunnel initially, peering their heads around the edge of the wall to see if they were definitely aiming for the same destination.
"Who are they?" Edward was the first to ask the question that they both couldn't answer quite yet.
They heard a familiar voice. That of John's! He shouted with pointing actions.
"There they are!"
"No! How did *he* find us?" William tried to keep his voice low.
"Come on, let's hide in the dark of the tunnel. Maybe run to the other side and then over the top or something."
"Good idea!" William agreed willingly, not knowing who John was bringing with him.
They both ran swiftly, hoping to reach the other side before the approaching people could gain the initial entrance. The book

weighed Edward down, but he held tightly to it, looking swiftly for a hiding place. William surprisingly managed to run relatively easily with the shovel in one hand.

The two of them were able to get to the opposite end of the section of tunnel in a reasonable time, but they could hear the echoes of the people at the entrance. They sounded keen to find the two of them.
"Come on!" Edward signalled for them to exit the tunnel and climb up the hill to the left, which gained access to the same level of height as the top of the tunnel.
They both got to the top of the hill and ran back in the reverse direction to fool their trackers.

Both William and Edward were swiftly reaching the original end of the tunnel, allowing a steep hill to decline at that end.
They cautiously clambered down to the track level again, looking through the tunnel to note several men's backs, as they walked through in an attempt to find them.
"Great trick." William whispered.
"Yeah. Let's run back to the shop!"
Edward didn't intend to fall into a leadership role, but they both ran in unison back to the streets that returned them to the shop. They both rustled their way into the front door and secured themselves indoors, catching their breath.
"John knows I work here." Edward said, in a heavy outward breath.
"I know." William responded briefly, still trying to regain calm, "What is he chasing us for? We helped him! He must have quickly placed his mum somewhere to be out with others so soon! Unless... Unless he wants the fortunes that strange *being* was offering."
"That makes some sense." Edward agreed. "How many people will be chasing us now?"

"Have we done the right thing Ed? Where can we hide?"
"I think we need to rest upstairs for a while and calculate our next actions."

Present Time

Tom and Rachel walked in through the front door, hearing some professional voices coming from the lounge area. They both looked at one another with suspicion, taking a slow walk to note two police officers talking calmly with Ethan.

Rachel walked into her lounge first, encouraging Tom to follow with a hand behind her, almost touching his. Ethan stood to greet Rachel, offering a natural kiss to her soft lips.
"Hey guys, the police have brought your phone back, Tom, saying the videos are too hazy, but the CCTV footage on our cameras show evidence of the lady being back in our garden." Ethan handed Tom his phone within a clear, plastic packet.
Tom held the phone and digested the words of Ethan swiftly but wondered why *his* footage would be hazy. Rachel gave Tom a glance that said *"weird,"* but then nothing was making sense at this time. They were *all* trying to put puzzles together.
The two police officers brought a comfort to the home. They both spoke calmly, offering an element of protection, saying that staff members plan to monitor things from a van that would sit in the street with surveillance cameras.
Rachel and Tom felt some tension leave their bodies in synchronistic timing. They both observed Ethan's improved mood from the morning.
There was a noise upstairs, with footsteps landing on the staircase, causing a stir in Tom and Rachel.
"Oh yes, I forgot to say that Tanya came back to give me some company shortly after you guys left."
Rachel frowned, surprised at the jealousy that filled her body. Tom noticed her emotions, wondering if complications would ever end! The police officers stood to depart, offering their cards out for contact if needed, reminding everyone of the surveillance van.

Ethan thanked them for their help and aided their departure with a polite walk to the door.
Rachel and Tom looked at one another, noting Tanya's entrance to the lounge to join them.
"Oh, hi both A-Ya." Tanya was chewing on some gum, looking quite at home.
Rachel breathed a heavy outward breath and decided to sit on the sofa with a tired slumping action. Tom went to sit quite close, tapping her on the thigh a couple of times for a gesture of comfort. Tanya looked on with a knowing smile.
Ethan came back into the lounge shortly after his escorting moves. He could feel an air of tension and tried to figure it out.
"So, what did you guys do while the police were analysing things with me?"
Rachel wasn't going to feel guilty, despite Ethan's obvious passive aggression. Tom spoke in a defensive manner, not intending to be transparent.
"We went for a walk to gain some sense of normality."
"It was a long walk." Tanya stirred.
Rachel stood and walked to gain distance of Tanya's ears.
"Can we have a chat?" She whispered.
"Sure honey."
The two ladies walked into the kitchen, leaving Tom to smooth things over with his brother.
"Hey, brother, we should have thought about staying here for the police. Sorry you dealt with them alone."
"Actually, it was good to do it solo. I could focus on the subject well. I didn't have to worry about Rachel's emotions."
"What's Tanya doing here though?" Tom didn't intend to sound intrusive, but he was always able to ask his brother anything.
"She's been so cool! It was like a neutral help. There was no stress that way. She's so tough, she's like a rock."
Tom looked at him with a questioning expression.

Ethan looked slightly guilty. "Okay, I do like her flirting too, but nothing happened. I love Rachel, man! Tanya is like a breath of fresh air in all of the crap that's going on. That's all."

"She lights the room up for you?" Tom smiled with a tease.

"Ah you know, if I was single she'd probably be a great laugh to hang out with. She seems to take all of my worries away. Rachel is so supportive, but in a sympathetic way. It seems to *feed* the worries. Tanya is like some strong force that takes that away. She was really cool today."

"You shouldn't feel guilty about needing a mother figure." Tom punched him on the arm in jest.

"Ah, come on!" Ethan was mildly insulted.

"So, what did you and Rachel get up to, truly? You both looked a bit unusual when you walked in. I sensed something."

"Well, we had a bit of a scare at the castle we decided to walk around. It was just a bit eerie." Tom thought swiftly on his feet.

"Oh okay. I'll badger Rachel later in bed." Ethan chuckled under his breath at the thought.

Tom stood after a short few minutes of sitting quietly with his brother.

"I think I need to head off back to my place. My plants must be missing me."

Ethan chuckled at his funny ideal. "You can stay longer if you need better company."

"I think I've already stolen your lady long enough today... and well, you could revel in the attention of two ladies for a while."

Ethan smiled and looked to the side, obviously imagining things he shouldn't!

Tom grinned knowingly and offered a high five as a funny goodbye action.

"I'll see you later." Tom walked out into the kitchen, giving Rachel a wink, whilst overhearing a snippet of their conversation. He got the impression of Rachel wanting to have some relaxation time with Ethan.

"Are you off then?" Tanya asked first.

"Yeah, heck, I could do with a hot shower."

"I'll follow you out." Tanya offered.

Rachel and Tom gave a mutual look that meant they were hoping for a private moment, but with Tanya in the mix, it seemed impossible.

Tanya and Tom left simultaneously now, with both of them stating that they'd visit again very soon.

Tom looked back, hoping to catch a glance of Rachel's eyes as he lowered his stance to get into his car.

The sun gave a disappointing glare from their house window, which encouraged him simply to drive off.

Tom found the drive automatic, with occasional glances over at the mysteriously huge leatherbound book that sat on the passenger seat on his return drive. It was a risk to leave it vulnerable during his brief stop at Ethan and Rachel's, but they'd assumed nobody would even contemplate any value if they looked into the car window. I mean who would leave a book of the eighteen hundreds on a passenger seat?!

Tom soon settled in at home. He sat at his dining room table, placing the book in front of him. He stared at it for a while, thinking Rachel should be there with him to witness the contents. He reached forward to open the leather cover, hearing the creaks of the age of it all. The envelope with the two rings sat just inside the cover. Tom couldn't believe the addiction Rachel had to them. It took a great encouragement and trust-building work to retrieve them from her fingers. Her resistance was so intense. Tom didn't think that she was the materialistic type. It was like a fixation she had no normal control over. Once they were secured in the envelope, she seemed to have her usual thoughts about her once again.

Tom grew concerned at the time and knew it was important to have control over the entire contents of the book for a thorough inspection, in private.

As he sat there, not knowing the reason of importance of this retrieval, he slowly inspected the entirety of the book. Initially, he placed the envelope of rings to the side and felt along the gold-rimmed edges of the pages. The vivid dream he had not too long ago filled his mind, allowing the same feelings to fill him. He felt anxious as he looked at the writing, hoping he wouldn't have words leave the page as in the dream! That would be too much to bear!

Thankfully as he turned the pages, normal black ink in cursive writing fell before him. He tried to read the odd sentence in a rush to get the gist of what the book was all about. Some of the writing was so cursive, making him feel honoured to read the words written with such skill.

He felt excited as he read some of the words. The author of the book was writing about some life experiences that were out of the ordinary.

Tom skimmed through masses of pages, noting the second half of this huge book were left blank. He scouted backwards to the last page of writing, finding a sketch that left him dumbfounded. Remembering his phone retrieval from the police, he took it out to switch it on, with intention to take some photos. This book needed hiding in his own home for now, for safety, until he could figure things out. The rings needed keeping out of sight from Rachel, for now. They couldn't risk any of this being found and questioned.

He took a photo of the last page and flipped some large content back to the initial pages once again, deciding to read large portions. As he read, he felt emotions fill him. He felt extreme love that he couldn't quite fathom out. The feelings were suddenly

drawn to Rachel. These emotions were so intense that it forced him to stand up and push himself back from the book, and the table. How could a book make him feel such a strong pull towards Rachel? He reached for the envelope of the rings again and dropped them into his hands. Guilt came forward over his feelings for Rachel, wondering if he was being warned somehow about interfering with the love between the two of them.
Tom needed to walk away from the book and the rings for a moment.
He took some calming breaths, walking to the lounge area.
His eyes caught a glimpse of the familiar golden haze developing in front of him.
"Oh no, not now!"

Trion and Bo

Trion stood on the top of a grassy bank, looking down on an empire that had been built by Bo and himself within a short space of time. He gloated at the small army he had built. The people here were easily manipulated once they knew of riches that could bring them a comfortable life. They all swore an oath of silence with a mark of a symbol which would be a secret code used to ensure the legitimate validity of their agreement. They all had a piece of the most powerful crystals created among them - crystals with energy that held immense manifestation power. They were all learning the capabilities of this and more, in regular meetings.

Large structures were built within a short time, with a large perimeter fence for protection of this mini-city in order to build a strong army that would overpower the planet for the possession of it.
Trion and Bo recognised that the people of this planet held a lot of sensitive emotion. This allowed them to manipulate their feelings with ease. They both knew that their emotions would be the driving force to manifest with the enhanced power of the crystals. They thought they had literally fallen on their feet with their arrival to this planetary location. This is where they could grow and spread, with luxuries and powers they'd never been able to enjoy on their previous, barren land. Trion wondered if it was meant to be, since it was a planet he mistakenly found and used to stash his "treasures."

The people were growing in confidence and abilities with practice within a short time, and Trion needed to ensure his leadership remained at the top of the pyramid. Occasionally he needed to remind the group of people of his *origin* to all that was literally brought to the table. The people mostly treated him as some type of deity.

Time appeared to have passed swiftly, and his growing empire impressed himself, with an occasional gloat of dominance.

As Trion grew to understand the life of this planet, he knew there were many people in various geographical locations. He zoned in on those who appeared to do successfully in life, encouraging them to join forces for so much more of the *magic*! He wished to ensure that the entire planet knew of his leadership. Kings and queens were forming over the land, much to his displeasure. He had enough power and protection to hold his own zone, knowing that the *others* were still of primitive mind, just seeking out brutal wars and murders. His plan was to retain pleasures and luxuries that the planet could offer, along with the source of power he brought along with him.

He had several pieces of the crystals pre-created and enhanced the size and power of every one of them, using the power of the people on the planet. The power allowed an abundance of creation. They built an empire on structures and systems that brought them so much food, water, and sensual massages to their skin. There were secret sexual acts among the people within certain private rooms. Trion and Bo stuck to their personal love for one another, retaining loyalty, allowing the pleasures of the people to occur if that is what they sought. At first, Trion thought it was a weakness of the people, but then realised that it was simply a need, just the same as food, water, and sleep. They analysed these people gradually to work on their needs and know how to manipulate their emotions for greed of power.

Trion walked through a grassy patch, leading to a thin path of dusty ground. His feet caught the path and followed it down to a very large building. He approached the empty door space and entered the door into a vast open-plan room of pure white. The glass windows were huge, allowing light to enter and warm the large space relatively well. Trion walked on to find a long corridor, approaching a smaller room that held a long, oval table with people sat confidently all around it. Bo was interacting, with pastel colours of light emanating the room from her body and head space.
The humans sat calmly and confidently, listening to her every word. Trion had only been away from the room for a short time, intending to return to the meeting.
The people looked at him with respect as he walked in, silencing themselves of any whisper or thought.
The meeting continued just as planned, and the people went about their ways just as they always did.

Trion and Bo met up to have a moment of privacy.
"I went to admire our little empire in the fresh air for a few moments. I am so proud of what we have done here." Trion looked content.
"Indeed! There is only a small concern though."
"What's that?" Trion asked, knowing of Bo's extra sensory abilities.
"As time is moving on, the people on the planet have been finding ways to get from one part of the land space to another part. They are beginning to conquer parts. I fear the population is increasing as well as evolving. We need to ensure our power remains within our space. They need to remain controlled and segregated."
"They will never find the mass, *buried* power. It is so deep within the land and well hidden. They are abandoned areas."

"Yes, but as the people spread, they will cover all areas. They could literally end up living on top of and around what we have hidden."

"What do you suggest we do?" Trion asked with concern.

"Perhaps ensure we have full control of the power. There mustn't be a weakness to our system."

"Do you think I should scour all parts when I know all are resting, to ensure all is still in place?"

"I think a fairly regular scouring of the land… If we could create a power that can monitor the planet without having to sneak through the atmosphere in the Sharp."

"Or we could build structures on top of the parts as a distraction maybe?"

"That is an amazing idea!" Bo was impressed by Trion's idea.

"It would take a little time, but the structures could be markers for us too."

They both smiled with excitement.

Bo wanted to add another slight concern after some thought…

"Then I worry that in time, their weapons may develop. We need to ensure they retain their primitive spears and suchlike." Bo was trying to prepare for the future, knowing how things can develop quickly with a biological brain and any evolving thoughts.

"Interesting thoughts today Bo. How can we monitor the people well?"

"Hmm. I'm not sure on that one just yet. Maybe one to ponder on for now."

"Maybe we can stop those concerned thoughts of yours for now and relax somewhere in peace, enjoying that ball of warmth and the ground of soft green." He grinned.

"Some lovely cuddles?" Bo's heart area grew in green hazes of light.

"And you say that the *people* are highly emotional. Maybe *you're* the emotional one. Or maybe your energy is rubbing off on *them*!"

Bo laughed, leaning into the chest area of Trion as they walked up into some soft green grassy parts to rest together in peace and harmony.

As the days moved into weeks and the weeks into months, the seasons passed, and the years moved by; Trion and Bo were building their empire well, retaining a select few under their wings. They managed to keep their main location a secret from the masses. They gradually managed to build structures over some of the areas of the buried crystals that retained the connection of power, through all of the crystals combined. These structures were like singular spires that pointed up to the sky.

While people were building in numbers, large crowds of people were travelling more by sea. Trion and Bo both witnessed the growth of transportation methods in the air, and on land. It became harder for them to retain their unique position.
Trion and Bo decided to create some underground roads and structures where they could hide a lot of the crystals. A larger space was developed deep within the planet, where they could hide the Sharp vehicle and all associations with it.
Trion noted the seasons and the changes of light, with shadows casting over different parts of the land. He tried to measure this with crystals cut into various shapes, hoping to monitor the portions of the day without needing to locate the area of the sun and shadows on the ground.
As he grew close to more successful measurements of the different processors on this planet, there grew a crowd of people who had travelled far by sea, seeking some rest for a few nights. These people spotted Trion's territory from the distance. In desperation they approached to beg for food in a hope to do some trade.

Trion noticed the people approaching on a beautiful, clear day. The figures were very tall, wearing shiny head garments and gradually gaining distance.
At first, Trion panicked about the exposure of their empire, but since they appeared *so* friendly and in great need, he felt some sympathy for their hardships. Upon welcoming them resistantly, he built a swift rapport.
He thanked his own intuition for the development of the secret underground passages and large spaces. There were only two secret doors to the underground spaces, that were camouflaged, appearing like large metal crates on huge concrete floors. These had high technology buttons that were extremely difficult to find. With it all in hidden locations, any unpredictable visitors would be non-the-wiser to such technologies.
These tall visitors brought interesting items in exchange for food. They declared that these shiny, golden objects were of high value, which Trion and Bo just accepted in politeness, not knowing what to do with them precisely. They already had everything they needed to live with.
Bo took good care of these people since they had much knowledge of the planet, with measurements of time and seasons. They kindly shared a lot of information about this planet within a short space of time. A bond built between them in the evenings, during food and drinking times together. Trion and Bo admitted that they came from beyond the stars and that they simply wished to live their remaining years in abundance in this beautiful place. The visitors were shocked to hear of their detail initially and found it difficult to accept, but their peaceful ways guided them to accept all possibilities. They also observed their self-sufficiency and structures, giving clear evidence of the truth they spoke of. They all accepted one another's differences since these particular people had travelled from an isolated part of the planet without interaction with others until they decided to take an adventure in order to understand life beyond their own lives. They explained

their discovery of sea travel having noted the way wood floated on water!

These visiting people left items of jewellery as gestures of payment as the days moved on but felt as if they were beginning to out-stay their welcome somewhat.
Bo sensed an end to their visit so began to supply large baskets of food for them to carry in their future journeys.
The further exchange of information made Trion and Bo feel grateful, but at the same time they worried about how conspicuous they were in their location.
One very early morning, they decided to take a discreet trip in their Sharp vehicle to inspect the population of all of the land space. It seemed important for them to update themselves in order to perhaps relocate to something a little more isolated. They moved in extreme speeds with hope of invisibility!
Trion noted the landmarks they had been creating across the vast space of the planet in order to locate the large chunks of crystals. He remembered that despite the visual markers, there was the small shard of crystal power that he buried deep within the ground. He had forgotten over time about this particular piece that felt very powerful in his hand. He remembered the location well so decided that they would land their vehicle to feel for the energy.
Trion stood directly over the location of this piece of crystal. Bo wondered what he was doing, but then felt the same power within her very core.
"Have you buried something underneath this part? It feels more powerful than all of the crystals we have known."
"It is the activator, I believe. I may have created it that way before I buried it, I'm not sure. It connected with me, so I chose this place. It is deep enough in the ground, I *think*!"
"Do we need to be sure?" Bo grew concerned.

Trion looked at how wonderful the green growth of grass was in every direction he looked.
"How could anyone disturb such nature?"
They both looked at one another, deciding to enjoy the splendorous view for a while. As they did, a strong wind encircled them, forming an interesting pattern in the ground. It looked like the formation of a few circles, with one large, outer one, like a ripple effect through the blades of grass. They looked at one another with interest.

After some time, they both moved swiftly within the Sharp vehicle, finding a very private location, untouched by any civilisation that they could note. They decided that they would relocate to this private space and leave the others to live luxuriously where they were. They could visit within minutes anyway to ensure all was continually happy.

It didn't take long for Trion and Bo to build a humble structure in order to form a home, with food growing abundantly enough to store and eat in every season.

The seasons did in-fact move on swiftly, making the two of them feel older, yet naïve to the world around them. Their visits to their previous empire grew less and less until they decided to hand it over to the people who loved it dearly. Trion and Bo became content in their isolated ways.

As time moved on swiftly, Trion was beginning to feel extremely weak. Bo looked on at his energy, not understanding the sudden changes. She stood, knowing that she needed to obtain some fresh food and energy for the two of them. The Sharp vehicle was rarely used now, but usually functioned extremely well all the same, until today - at a time of necessity. She could get it to function, but it seemed weak in action.

They didn't expect isolation to become their enemy! Bo still felt relatively well energised, so collected some of the crystal from the vehicle itself and manifested some further power with her mind and energy. She focussed on a piece of crystal energy in her hand and visualised it growing to a large size. It worked well, as always, growing to a size that made her drop it with the heaviness.
Despite the crystal growing in size, it didn't feel as energised as it *should* have felt.
Bo walked into their humble abode, looking a bit confused, making Trion feel useless.
"What is it?" Trion could see hopelessness in her face.
"The power doesn't feel the same. Not as energised."
"In what way?"
"Like there's nothing in it anymore."
Trion instantly thought about the activation crystal.
"Bo! Could you go back to retrieve the activation crystal? I buried it, but I'm very sure you can dig deep enough to get hold of it. Maybe I need to reactivate it."
Bo looked at Trion with sadness.
"Or maybe that particular crystal weakens when *you* grow weaker."
"You're not helping, thinking in that way Bo! Please try, for me!"
Bo felt guilt for her thoughtless words and stepped back.
"Sorry, I didn't think. I'll see if I can get the Sharp to work with more available energy."
She tried to power up the vehicle again, this time with hope. Trion sat back in their home, feeling his energy weakening, wondering if his life was coming to an end.
Bo managed to get the vehicle to move. It lifted her into the sky, moving along at a steady speed.
The transparent parts of the vehicle gave her a view of civilisation! There were homes and roads for transportation. She panicked about being spotted, so lifted herself higher. The Sharp took her to the location she directed it to. The area of the activation part had

been built upon! She couldn't believe her eyes! Had it truly been *that* long? Houses and dirty-looking streets were below her. The grassy sections were patches of green, but smoke bellowed into the air. She moved higher to gain a greater overall view. She noted boats that were interacting with the road vehicles. Items were transported to and frow. This was such a vast change. Bo realised how naïve the two of them had been, living in such peace without any interaction. The only other life they'd seen were the occasional wild animal and the plant life!

She took a bit of a vast trip, trying to understand the system that people had built. After a flight back to their original empire, she noted that they too had spread their wings in buildings and land. She decided to pay them a visit to discuss the changes.

When Bo had landed, she walked into the main grounds, not recognising anyone upon entry. Someone with a heavy metal helmet and sword came out to meet her, looking confused at her appearance.

"You are trespassing!" Was the strong voice from the man behind the helmet.

"I built this place!" Bo defended.

"You are deluded!" The man responded, threatening her with his sharp-edged sword.

"What have you done?"

"I do not know what you are talking about. Who are you?"

"Take me to your elders, please!"

The aggressive person grabbed Bo by the clothing on her shoulders and dragged her through the first, long corridor, and into a large meeting room.

"I built this room and created this empire from scratch!"

"Who are you?" An older man looked up from the far end of the table.

"I am Bo. Two of us came to settle on this planet and built these buildings."

The elderly man stood, taking a closer look at Bo.

"Leave us here to speak!" He spoke to the man with the helmet, who left once his command was given.

"We have needed to create leadership. I recognise you from many years ago. The others will not understand you. There has been a dictatorship for some time." The man directed his hand towards a chair, "please take a seat, I can explain."

"You do not know how to utilise the power that we brought to this planet. All energy will be wasted."

"We have found new forms of power upon the land. We have our buildings and use our riches to control the people."

Bo couldn't believe what she was hearing.

"What riches?"

"The riches of jewellery. Gold and silver. Those type of riches."

"We *already* created and encouraged those riches that you understand, but what do you use for the great sources of energy?"

"We do not find the use for such things. We use fire for warmth and the water for washing, growing, and drinking. There are trades of gold, silver, and all jewelleries. We make our clothes and have families..."

"You forget that we are the originators of this planet. We came to this planet as original dwellers, perhaps with a primitive human within the odd cave or two. We own the land, the waters, and the air. We hold the powers and secret technologies that can overthrow all who we have allowed to live here."

"You have left us for years to fend for ourselves. We needed to develop our ways of existing and build our own hierarchy. We have riches that others cannot have. We grow our food and have control over it. We have luxurious bathing and people who work for us in exchange for food and water, perhaps a little bit of shelter."

"You have forgotten about the power of technologies, and the energy supply to them?"

"What good is that to people when all we need are our foods and waters. Luxuries of our sensations is also here for us."

"You have forgotten about the secrets underground?"
The man paced, growing inpatient, wishing for Bo to leave, but attempting to retain his stature.
"What good are secrets?" He leant on the desk with a large frown on his face.
"We have intergalactic capabilities. Everything is energy; therefore, we can manifest great things. That is the bonus of such secrets."
"Even if we wish for this the people would not understand. We prefer it this way. It is simple and abundant."
"We are the ones of power. Your dictatorship is limited. We will take our place back."
"Well, you left us many years ago, leaving us to fend for ourselves. What were we to do? We needed to have some element of control. We needed to build our lives and create our own ways as I explained."
"Yet this is our structure. It belongs to us. It is theft."
"Not when you have abandoned it!" This person obviously grew angry, "I think you should leave straight away."
"You hold our items underground." Bo felt a slight frustration.
"Guards!" The man was now attracting his forces, who came into the room immediately as if hiding behind the walls.
Several men with the same helmets and swords came to grip the underarms of Bo and lift her out of the building.
Bo couldn't believe the way she was being treated. Her anger built and her energy shifted. Her body grew to a much taller state, with a harsher appearance in hair and facial features. The guards panicked and let go of her frame with fear and confusion, stepping away from the centre of her standing place.
"Keep your hands away from me! You will all suffer the consequences of this!"
Bo walked away with great strength. The guards watched on with relief for their own safety, realising their lack of understanding.

Bo realised the errors of her ways having left the people for too long to fend for themselves, creating their own version of life. In some ways she was impressed by their extremely strong independence, but she was surprised that they found other ways to trade with such dictatorship.

As she walked through the streets she wasn't used to, she noticed other people holding trade stands, trying to survive with the items they were growing or creating.

Things had changed so swiftly, much to her ignorance.

She knew that she needed to get back to Trion to explain her findings.

The Sharp was hidden behind huge rocks, allowing privacy.

She soon embarked on her journey in the vehicle back to the green land she appreciated so much. Bo and Trion were aware that people were building in numbers and forms of travel, but she didn't expect things to have evolved so swiftly and in the way that they had.

The Sharp moved speedily to the beautiful home they both had in isolation.

Trion was stood at the front, watching the landing and her walking-approach to his arms.

They both spoke, concerned for the prediction of what was to come. Bo explained her inability to locate the activation crystal for all of the distracting structures that had popped up within what seemed to be only short few years. Trion equally realised how isolated they had been for too long, and how naïve they had been. He needed to keep a better measurement of time on this planet.

"I think that we could utilise the people we have in our immediate vicinity and build our new army so that we can outweigh and conquer the space with the people, using the powers *we* have."

"Will we not be creating division and wars?"

"We could be teaching them how to utilise their great powers. We could do it in a clever way rather than a forceful way and have them all join forces."

"So, tricking their minds without physical battles?"
"Yes. That way everyone is on the same side, but the side we have chosen."
"How do we do that?"
"Let me begin the process. It could take some time, but it'll be worth it."

Seasons and years had passed yet again, with Trion and Bo yet again building in numbers of people and training them in their own ways. The people learnt how to use the great technologies, while Trion laughed about how he *still* needed a better way to measure the time-scale that the cycles of this planet had. Somehow, Trion rebuilt his own energy to a reasonable level enough to feel better-balanced. He knew he still needed to regain the activation crystal discreetly.

Once he felt confident in the number of people, and the amount of energy created through the manifestation of power, he would attempt to sweep into the location of the activation crystal.

He felt he needed to reconquer a vast area of land. If he could move in on the spaces that were once his own (in his head), then he could re-establish everything.

He would dictate to his own people, to state that the land was theirs and that they needed to spread themselves out and take it back in a mind-manipulating manner.

Time was moving swiftly again. Bo came to him one day to talk after she noticed his energy was depleting yet again!

"People are making families on top of families, and time is swiftly moving on." Bo demonstrated concern. "People have died over poor conditions without us even needing to intervene with our plan."

"Well, that is good, as then the offspring know no different to their parents and so forth. It will appear normal to them."

"They don't live as long as we do, I noticed. It is important to take advantage of the situation when our power peeks."

"Okay, Bo. I have been observant to that."

"We have developed so much of the power source that we can move in *now*. Your energy is concerning at times, so we need to be selfish. We need that activation crystal."

"I know you are concerned, but as you say, we live much longer than these people. We have plenty of time. Look at the numbers we have built. We can conquer the entire planet, I am certain."

"We are growing lazy again Trion! We get too comfortable and then your energy depletes. Haven't you noticed the recent depletion of your energy again? I think we can make the most of this if we move in now. Enough of the time wasting. I don't want it to become so serious that you end up crawling on the floor or lying in your bed indefinitely."

"Bo, you need to relax. We have control of this planet already. Look at the numbers of our advanced people. We have trained them up so well that we have some generation time on our side now. If you feel we truly need to wipe some of the old out and bring our new in order to take hold, then let's make our move."

"I definitely feel it is time! We need to locate the activation crystal *now*! You should see your state the way I am seeing you. For some reason I sense the activation crystal really affects your energy on this planet. We need it to *keep* the power of this planet. Someone may have found it, not knowing what to do with it."

"We wanted a peaceful life here. Maybe we could relocate to yet another planet once we locate that crystal again. Start fresh with an abundance of power."

"Trion, are you thinking straight? The effort of training people to stay on our side is now immense. We need to take action very soon."

"You're always right, Bo."

"I am." Bo grinned, "When shall we begin?"

"How about we do a trip together initially. I know a great location by figures, so I am certain I can find it."

"The planet has changed so much Trion, you will be very surprised. The location for your idea of an escape may have been swallowed up already." She wanted to prepare him. "The people have evolved. They aren't as primitive as we initially found."

"It *does* sound as if we do need to gain control of these people then, particularly if they are having a pattern of evolution. We don't want them to out-intelligence us!"
"Control indeed, along with your energy fix. Something has changed."
Trion agreed with a nod and prepared himself for a trip in the vehicle to see for himself. Bo ensured they would travel together.

As they both hovered above the skies in their Sharp craft - too high to be spotted - they viewed through a screen of advanced camera footage - clear scenes of the ground space. The Sharp had amazing hovering capabilities that allowed them to remain relatively still for a few hours in order to monitor the land. They noticed the behaviours of people walking to and from the doors of various buildings. Smoke bellowed from internal fireplaces into the sky space.
"It doesn't feel as if the crystal is in *this* area anymore. I can feel a funny pull over that vast space of water to the opposite section of land." Trion wondered how someone was able to locate the crystal in the ground and transport it to a completely different area.
"I told you the people have changed. I hear *mining* is something of an event these days. Gold, silver, and items that they create decoratively as jewellery seems to be something of riches to them now."
"Do you think the crystal has become a *jewellery* to the people now? It could be broken into separate pieces. Then what do we do?"
They both looked at one another without spoken word.
The Sharp moved over a vast space of water by deliberate control, moving over to a new section of land. Trion felt it was nearby now, driving him to move the vehicle over another similar-looking inhabitancy.

"People have erected so many houses now. Such strange structures."

An extremely bright light occurred once or twice, indicating the use of the crystal, much to Trion's excitement! There was now no need to dig into any ground space, only to locate the person using it without any knowledge of the connection or ability. At least that was Trion's assumption.
"Did you see that? The crystals can only create that kind of brightness when activated."
"There's hope. How amazingly timed!"
They now needed to land somewhere secretively and monitor the movements of the person in possession of the crystal. Trion grew excited about the prospects of regaining his power.
They were able to land their vehicle within a couple of seconds, on top of a hill, but within a large area of trees and bush space for camouflage.
Trion exited the craft and moved his legs now at such a surprisingly good-speed, finding the location of a gentlemen and a lady who looked in need, and lying upon the ground. Bo slowly tracked behind, ensuring there were no witnesses of their presence.
Trion lifted the lady with one arm and looked ahead to witness *three* men now, looking startled.
He felt the energy of the crystal that one of the men held, which prompted Trion to request for it to be returned to him. Trion attempted to explain that they didn't understand the purpose of the crystal. He tried to explain in his own way, looking on at the concerned individuals.
With observations of their stress levels, Trion decided to throw a ball of energy that would calm his peculiar conversances. The blue haze had a wonderful impact on them, but they still didn't take kindly to his demands for the return of the crystal. The strangers claimed to have purchased the item, which made Trion wondered

what travels the activation crystal had been through, as well as in who's *hands*.

Trion felt an explanation of who he was, was needed in order to enhance their lack of understanding. He noted how intellectual they actually were, which made him realise how condescending he may have been in error.

They appeared to have calculated some of the crystal's benefits with the activation of the ball of protection as well as the intention of healing the lady who appeared to be injured and dazed. With Trion's energy reductions in the recent times, he was unable to face the crowd of people who had appeared once help was called for! Trion was concerned yet impressed by the ways in which these people had dealt with things. He needed to break loose from the situation, so slipped back behind a corner and out of sight, where Bo was approaching, in case of the need of assistance.

Bo sensed an urgency to aid Trion back to the Sharp vehicle in order to disguise themselves yet again. She gave an unusual frequency call from her own energy – a noise that omitted from her enough that Trion could sense his need to retreat. He crept swiftly back in Bo's direction, finding the vehicle a safe escape. They both rested inside their transportation, keeping an eye on their screens for any approach.

"They are quite advanced in their ways. We may need to forcefully retrieve the power." Trion grew in frustration.

"We could use our advanced abilities otherwise, Trion. I could transfigure to one of their feminine beings and mingle for a while until I am able to retrieve it. That would be discreet and cunning without harming anyone." Bo offered willingly.

"I'm starting to think we need a more forceful plan. Perhaps if we rest at home to think for a while." Trion looked tired and frustrated.

"How much is your own energy depleting? I feel there is a tight deadline."

"I will be fine for a long time yet. It would be *nice* to rebuild my energy, but it can wait."

They both arrived home, attempting to connect to the energy of the large crystals deep within the land, but it seemed difficult. They couldn't quite grasp the concept of the reasons for this sudden change, when everything functioned extremely well for so long. They wondered if the person who holds the activation crystal is the holder of *all* of the power. Trion knew that the level of power wouldn't be understood by someone who held the limitation of just the *one* crystal.
He wanted so desperately to reclaim the power.
"I think your idea of transfiguration may just work, if you can mix with this group of humans for a while. Maybe we didn't need all of them people trained up after all."
"It seems nice to have our own army though, don't you think?"

15th December 1860

Edward was sat in his lounge space above his shop floor.
He managed to retain his journal, and decided he needed to add more information to it before he finally removed it from his own possession. William hadn't brought the subject up about the thoughts of burning it, so he thought he had more time to decide what to do with it.
There were quite a few days of peace following a time of caution and awareness of possibly being hunted down for the crystal. Edward had hoped that with the approach to Christmas that most would be in the joyous spirit of family affairs.
He sat with his inked pen, writing calmly with mention of the chase for the crystal and the dangers they felt at the time. He felt the information would be useful to an authority figure one day, but didn't know how this situation would come about.
As it was a Saturday, Edward craved a peaceful moment or two in his own company. He heard knocking at the front door of his shop, but by the tone of the knock, he knew it wasn't one of urgency or desperation. In fact, it sounded like a polite attempt of hope that he *may* approach the door if he was anywhere indoors. Either way he decided to completely ignore the intrusion with his decision to rest.
After completing his notes, he felt it was relatively important to hide the book. He sat back, pondering over a safe place for it, picking up one of his pencils from a nearby pot, followed by his sharpening knife. He sharpened his pencil with the penknife, thinking about potential hiding places for such a large size of book. He looked down at the penknife that was used *specifically* for sharpening his pencils and thought it could be a useful defence tool. Visualising a returned trip to the tunnel, he saw himself finding loose ground to lift, retaining safety with his boxing confidence, and the enhancing weapon just in case!

He wasn't sure if he was trying to play some invented hero in his head or if he was a bit fearful of the idea.

After a day of lazing around, playing thoughts around his mind, he looked through his window upstairs, noting the appearance of the sunset. He grabbed the book and decided to take his chances with a trip to the tunnel, hoping to avoid any attention. His eyes were adjusting to the dimming light anyway, so he felt confidence in the timing, even in a darkened tunnel!

A swift run to the tunnel, with eyes in all directions - Edward ran inside. Darkness hit his eyes with intensity. It instantly feared him, making him consider a retreat. His hairs stood on end, and his instincts were screaming at him.
He continued to walk despite the atmospheric warnings.
Luckily, his hearing was always acute, so he switched his mind to awareness of advanced warnings by noise. The tunnel seemed endless, as well as his decision of distance! He walked in, seeing the small exit light at the other side of this long tunnel. A moment of loss of footing made him fall onto his elbows, book still in arms. When he stood, he felt the ground, noting a large piece of rock on the ground having tripped him up. Thankfully his young bones swiftly recovered.
"Argh." He grumbled to himself.
Thoughts of simply getting to the exit part of the tunnel seemed more important now. He questioned his decision to attempt this on his own, and in the dark.
After regaining his standing position, he noticed he could see a bit more detail. His eyes seemed better adjusted now. He could see the coarseness of the structured tunnel. Looking down at the piece he'd tripped over, he noted it was part of the structure that had fallen to the ground. Looking at the tunnel wall, it was clear as to where it had fallen from. When he looked back down, he noted two large pieces of the rock.

There was a very dark patch within the structure of the tunnel, making Edward realise the depth of the hole it had created inside. He reached into the hole with bravery, hoping that a rat family hadn't settled in there! His imagination was now working overtime. His hand felt a deep hole, with great width to it. He measured the book by prising it into the gap, and strangely it went in well, with about a handspan-space back from the edge. Feeling contented, he ensured the book was in a steady setting by patting it into a steady, flat position. His eyes adjusted even more, obtaining more detail of the book shape within the hole. He reached down now to see if he could get at least one of the large, perfectly shaped rocks to fit the entry point. It was an extremely heavy lift, straining his shoulders and back with surprise! He couldn't get it to fit well, so he dropped that particular rock, and tried the second one that sat just as closely. With a huge effort and slight cuts to a couple of his fingers, he managed to fit this rock into the outer layer that blended with the rest of the structure. He felt entirely satisfied, testing with presses and prods, ensuring it wouldn't fall out again. He knew it must've taken some extreme force or gradual erosion over much time, to have these two heavy slabs of rock fall to the ground. Contemplating how they would have fallen, he thought he heard a noise in the distance in the direction of the entry point. He gasped and spun his head around in extreme fear. Edward pulled his penknife from his pocket, preparing for a reluctant set of defensive events. Standing still for a few minutes - there were no further noises or situations. With much relief, he was about to place the knife back into his pocket with hope not to catch his skin at any point - when he thought about leaving some form of marking on the rock for identification. He scraped his name almost-blindly into the rock, not quite knowing how it would look, but he felt it was enough should he need to relocate it for some reason. After this, he recognised his attachment for his book. In such a vast space it would go unseen anyway, unless severely hunted for! He reached

down to collect the remaining piece of rock to move it away. It seemed important to hide any evidence of a missing piece when there didn't appear to be any gaps.
Another similar noise of intrusion hit his ears while he moved swiftly with this extra piece of heavy rock! He tried to run with the intense weight, becoming heavy in his breath, and noisy with his foot-slamming. He looked back to note no bodies approaching, so decided to slow his pace. This was intense exercise that reminded him of his missed boxing lessons and football games of recent times with all of the distractions.

The end of the tunnel finally arrived, large enough to form the long-awaited exit in front of Edward's eyes. He dropped the rock at the end of the wall space so that it held no recognition to being an internal part. He bent forward to stretch his back out and dangle his arms for muscle recovery.
"It's done!" He whispered loudly to himself with much relief! Only *he* would know where his book sat should he need to have evidence of events.
He started a relatively swift walk back home, hoping that nobody had caught sight of him at all.
It grew dark with a dry-cold air that expressed his hot expelling of breath in front of his eyes. He picked up his pace to arrive home, assumingly without any witnesses. He ran up the stairs to a much-relieving sense of relaxation on the settee. His thoughts were that a new chapter of *calm* would embellish their lives. The intensity of weirdness was a bit too much, becoming overwhelming for him. He hoped now that they would have a chance to heal from the shocking events, even if they couldn't fully explain them.

That night he fell asleep on his settee, in the comfort of the warmth of a thick blanket. Dreams filled him, making him wake up more often than he'd usually prefer. Just before sunrise he fell into the most interesting dream. It was so vivid that when he woke, it took him a while to figure out what reality he was in! It felt real that someone had pinned him up against the tunnel wall right next to the place he'd hidden his journal, asking him to reveal the location of the book. In the dream the location of his book was still confidential, even though the enemy attempting to locate it was so close!

Edward woke with a sweat, believing he needed to double-check his hiding-efforts. He dressed swiftly and combed his hair back, checking in a nearby mirror for confirmation of his "keeping up of appearances." Once satisfied, he fumbled his weary legs down the staircase and to the front door. He unhooked his front door key and took himself out onto the street, locking the premises behind him.

It was a fresh, sunny morning. The birds kindly distracted him from his strange night and carried him into the present reality.

He paced himself to enjoy a pleasant walk back to the tunnel, wishing to ease his mind with a better view of his efforts.

The approach to the tunnel made him feel nervous, reviewing the plot of space in the ground that hid the crystal extremely well. The walk into the tunnel now made him hurry his pace, hoping he could locate the wall space swiftly since it was so vast!

Edward found the brick swiftly, noting the sloppy markings of his name with his penknife after having the poor lighting times as a hindrance. He felt happy about the solidity of the large brick and gave it a few prods to ensure its' security.

He could now confirm his good job as complete, and that the dream was simply a doubtful thought of anxiety.

His walk back gained a worthwhile stroke of luck! Ann had spotted his features from a distance and approached him with a wonderful smile. She brought such a beaming light to his morning. Ann ran over to give him a surprisingly loving hug!

"Good morning dear Edward! I have attended church with my father this fine morning, which gave a kind nature enough for him to suggest I pay you a visit! The subject at church was finding the love within ourselves so that we may love others. I think it gave him consideration of my feelings."
"Oh, well then I am *grateful* for your morning ventures!"
Edward beamed a tremendous smile and welcomed her to his home to see if he could offer a generous form of breakfast. Ann couldn't stop cuddling Edward, which made him feel amazingly appreciated at last, given the history of her father. He carefully prepared a nice hot drink and plenty of food for Ann to enjoy next to him at the same table. The two of them felt wonderful at the thought of freedom at last. This wonderful surprise took Edward's previous concerns away from his mind, bringing relaxation.
The two of them sat comfortably on the settee once they'd finished their abundant breakfast.
"I could do this for the rest of my life." Ann cuddled into Edward's chest.
"How did such a beautiful person inside and out, fall into my arms the way that you have?"
"Sometimes I feel that an instant attraction is a way of finding your soul partner."
"You are quite a deep thinker then. What about the thoughts of beauty being deep within?"
"Well, dear Edward, this is simply my belief, but I think that when one person is attracted to another it is like the saying of beauty lying in the eye of the beholder. Their eyes are meant to match up. I am a believer in matching with the eyes first. The rest matches up perfectly, just as we are falling into place so naturally this morning. Many say that the eyes are the window to the soul, so I believe our souls have matched."
"I suppose there could be some truth in that, but what of that with the visually impaired? It could be a chemistry that we *feel*

more so, like a feeling that is magnified somehow. An *excitement* of sorts."
"I like that concept too. Oh, we are deep thinkers. You see? We have already found an interesting subject between us."
Edward smiled and moved in for a brave kiss with an equally accepting pair of lips.
They both relaxed and hugged for quite a time, bonding nicely.

Present Time

Tom felt nervous about the familiar golden haze that stood before him. He knew that this usually meant an unusual character was going to appear. Just as he had the expectancy, the figure manifested in front of his eyes once again. This pale person stood before him, golden energy encircling him.
"Okay, okay! What do you want from me? From us? This is already too crazy for any human being to deal with! Is this all about this *book* you wanted us to find? What do you want me to do with it? Take it if that is what you want! Please take it and let me have my normal life back."
The pale figure tilted their head to the side in sympathy.
"I am incredibly sorry for involving you in this situation. I never believed that interfering with human life would cause such emotions right from the start. Do you think you can have the courage to do one more thing?"
Tom stepped forward, trying to study what he was seeing and hearing.
"I am using a holographic version of myself. I'm not actually on your Earth. I used to visit your planet and use humans for their gifts. Many beings from other planets have always been jealous of *your* planet and wanted the powers for themselves. They wish to see your powers stolen or controlled. Some think that they could do better with the same powers, but it is easy to judge without fully understanding. We all grow at various rates within our Universes... Over time I realised I couldn't hide amongst humans, so I can only visit in *this* form. That is why I need your help!"
Tom reached forward, noting his hand could move through the golden haze.
"Like I said, I'm not actually physically stood before you."
Tom felt a huge sense of relief at the explanation that made sense for the first time – although this was still beyond him!"

"So, after all of the risk we took finding this bazaar book, you want another favour?" Tom spoke with courage, feeling a slight anger at all of the commotion these strange events were causing.

The being appeared to stand tall yet retaining a peaceful response. "What you have done and hopefully agree to do - will actually be to the benefit of your entire planet. Other planets are trying to consume your planet and eradicate the human species."

"What good would that do? And how can finding an old book benefit the entire planet?"

"You will know if you can find a place in your heart to help us just one more time. At the end of the day, humans hold the power to work with their heart-centre if they are willing to."

Tom softened slightly but held a frown of confusion.

"We promise that this is the last we will ask anything of you. We ask you, as we know you have the ability. It is important for us to know that you are capable, and that we aren't asking beyond *that*."

"How do you know I am capable? I've been crapping myself ever since…"

"Ever since the first event in your car. The light and the vision I presented to you."

"That was you?" Tom looked directly into the hologram.

"That was another hologram, but only under controlled methods. I knew you wouldn't be harmed. I kept you safe at all times. I've been drip-feeding you information so that your mind can gradually understand the situation that I'll unfold for your understanding."

"You have no idea what you've been putting me through!"

"Oh, I do, Tom. You will be greatly rewarded once this final task is complete. Everything will make sense to you, even your life will make sense soon."

Tom found a chair not too far behind and sat on it for stability.

"What did you want me to do *now* then?" Tom gritted his teeth with the thought of another risky situation.

"There is a group of people who are fighting over a type of power that controls what can happen to your planet. They have built quite a bit of a following."
"A type of power? We always seem to be fighting over fuel or money or suchlike."
"This is something much greater. There is a battle over technology and control over the masses. Have you not seen it unfolding?"
"I must be oblivious."
"Without going into huge detail, you're monitored in absolutely everything you do."
"Well, we all know we are being watched through our phones and our gadgets."
"...And more than you even know. While you are being monitored and controlled, there is a huge battle over a source of power. This power needs to be in the right hands. At the moment, the central source of the power is out of sight, as it was cleverly hidden by someone many years ago. I don't want to confuse you too much, but you have already seen the signs of *who* that person was. You've felt something within you every single time you come across the same name."
Tom thought for a moment. "Do you mean the name of the person who has written this journal? The same name that I keep seeing in various places such as a graveyard, and on the side of a monument?"
"Indeed! You are correct. This was a clever person who knew to hide it for the safety of many."
"Why does someone need to hide a book though?"
"If you look to the rear of the book – not the empty pages, but the final written pages, you will see a design."
Tom carefully moved chunks of pages over to seek the final page of written word and found an unusual drawing.
"This is the vital part of the book…"
Tom felt a weird sensation work through his body – a cold chill that was comfortable and familiar, but also confusing.

"You never knew what was finally written in this book, but you have known about this book since the time it was written."
"What on earth are you talking about?"
"This may surprise you, but you know the person who wrote this book."
"What? This book looks so old! How can I possibly know who put this journal together?"
"You can feel the familiarity though. Am I right?"
"I can feel *something*, but the book could just literally be giving me chills."
"It is more than that. You made a strong bond with the person who put this book together. You worked together."
"You are living in cloud la-la land my friend."
Tom pushed the book away from him and turned away but caught sight of himself in a mirror ahead. His appearance changed slightly, making him stare deeply. Old fashioned clothes covered his frame, and words whispered into the back of his head! He froze, wondering if he would die on the spot! He held a vision of a fight he was involved in with a vague view of others in the room. The others had similar clothing, but there was someone on the ground that needed help. Tom reached down to note that this person was of female nature and had been seriously injured. He somehow knew to reach into his pocket and reveal an object. His instincts told him to place this object of a shiny, smooth, bright appearance – on to the body of the lady. As he did, the brightest light made him cover his eyes, but just as he refocussed he caught a fresh sight of this lady sitting upright with a smile. This jolted him back into the present view of himself looking into the mirror!
The whispers behind his head confused him further, telling him that his life was important, and that he needed to protect the item.
Tom gasped and tried to regain his normal mind.
The being's hologram within the golden haze still stood, now behind him, offering comfort.

"Please do not be alarmed. This is something you needed to see. I only created the doorway for this to occur so that you could understand things better."
Tom spun swiftly, looking on at the pale being, wondering if his *own* skin was just as pale from the shock.
"I am even more confused now! I feel like I understand, but my mind is spinning!"
"I have opened the gateway to different dimensions. You have just witnessed one of your previous lives."
"It felt like me, but it isn't me!"
"It *is* you, in a different mind and body. Your real, internal-self is always *you*, but with the physical bodies you're in a three-part, connected frequency."
"What?" Tom felt dizzy.
The dizziness started to find a black view ahead, causing him to find the floor in a progressive faint.

25th December 1860

It was wonderful to feel the unity of so many people at this time. Edward and William sat in the vast space of this lounge, along with Eleanor and Ann within the confines of Ann's dad's home!
Dinner was lavish, with candles flickering a calm light, creating the wonderful atmosphere. The light bounced along the roof of the huge ceilings and walls. It was a bright day outside, but the browns and golds of the room mixed with the candlelight created a nice atmosphere.
Everyone laughed together and felt extremely privileged.
Ann's father, Francis, had gradually accepted the two young men and made an effort to make them feel welcome and supported in ways that he knew how.
After much self-indulgence, the five of them had decided to walk the cold, cobbled streets to see if they could offer food and drinks to less privileged families. They gathered plates, cutlery, and bottles of alcohol into a couple of wheelbarrows, and walked to hunt for those they could help. It felt a joyful, compassionate charity with many accepting humble amounts to ensure plenty to go around.
Every person that passed them shouted "Merry Christmas," adding to the spirit of the day. People were wrapped up from the cold, with the occasional person looking a bit disgruntled. William pushed one of the wheelbarrows and offered drinks to the least-happy looking of people. Edward seemed to take on the role of handing out food to those who looked hungry. Ann and Eleanor chuckled amongst themselves, seemingly discussing their partners.
Ann's father pushed one of the wheelbarrows, and occasionally made conversations with those who wished to stop for a few moments.

The food and drink moved swiftly, leaving them with empty wheelbarrows. They continued the walking however, leaving the wheelbarrows on a side pavement. They walked to soak up the last few moments of daylight in the early-darkening hours of the winter nights.

A recognisable face came into Edward's view.

"Will! I can see that *John* gentleman just over there." He pointed to a tall person in the distance.

"Ah! Hopefully he won't see us. He looks busy chatting with some others."

"It's been a while. I wonder where he's been. I thought he'd come back to haunt us or at least ask about what happened. Surely he would feel relatively vexed or uncertain about that particular day and wish for more answers."

"I suppose you would expect such a response."

Edward kept an eye on John's actions as they all walked on through the streets. When they grew closer, Edward had spotted his head movement and his eyes locking onto the two of them!

"Oh no! He has his eyes focussed directly on us." Edward was nervous.

"There are more of us, together. It is Christmas! Relax and enjoy the day!" William attempted, despite feeling nervous himself.

Edward felt a bit foolish with his concern, so attempted to relax, and continue on in his little, happy crowd.

John didn't look relaxed however, and came over to them with a fast, aggressive walk. William was the first to notice the change in motion before them.

"Hey! I have been wishing to speak with you for some time now! I work too much to have time to come hunting for you. I knew that I would bump into you soon enough though!" John expressed loudly upon his approach.

Edward felt the hairs rise on his neck and adrenaline pump through his veins, especially with threatening words such as "hunting!"

"Merry Christmas!" William offered, trying to convert the energy.
"Erm, yes. A Merry Christmas to you too. Now, as I was saying, I wish to speak with you both."
Ann surprisingly moved to the front of their group.
"Excuse me young Sir, it is Christmas, and we wish for no business talk on such a day. Have some respect!"
John hushed himself, pulling his chin back toward his neck. He removed his hat, "I am sorry Ma'am. I shall choose another time."
Everyone turned to fixate their stares at Ann, surprised at her bravery. John walked away, occasionally looking back in astonishment.
"Wow Ann!" Her father was proud. He took his smoking pipe from an inside pocket of his jacket and struck a match after two failed attempts. He lit his pipe with a few little mouth puffs, followed by a satisfactory, calming breath.
Edward gripped Ann's hand and looked deep into her eyes with further pride.
William monitored John's actions, noting that he returned to a group of young men who all looked a bit dubious. They talked amongst themselves and looked back at William and Edward, making it obvious that they were talking about them.
William was the only one keeping an eye on the crowd ahead.
"I think we should return homeward now my beautiful people." Ann's Dad offered kindly.
William felt relieved at the decision, but hoped it wasn't sending John and his fellow friends a signal of retreat following the heated words.
As they spun in the opposite direction, William noticed John's observations, but thankfully he turned to have ongoing discussions with his group.

The five of them didn't take long to sit comfortably on the seats, back in Ann's Dad's home. Everyone slumped into the back of the seated arrangements. The skies darkened and the candlelight flickered vibrantly, recreating the fresh, calming atmosphere. William was the only one with a buzzing mind, worrying about any tracing back to the house or a future plan to discuss what went on back at the time of John's Mum's incident. He tried to reassure his own mind by asking 'what John could possibly do.' He was probably only wanting answers to a puzzling time.

Everyone seemed to have a sleep, or an almost-dosing time with heavy eyelids. Ann's Dad, Francis, dropped his pipe-smoking hand onto a tall table next to his seat, causing some flicker of lit tobacco to twinkle a redness in the light. William was the last person to drift into a relaxed state enough to fall into a light nap.
It only seemed a few seconds later that Ann was screaming in hysteria! Everyone woke with a startled expression, wondering what all of the stress was about.
"Ed! It's Dad! I cannot wake him! He looks as if he is not breathing!"
Edward stood in shock, walking over in hope of a simple explanation, but she was correct! His face was turning blue, and his lips were almost purple at this time!
William felt numb and uncertain of the required actions. He touched his pocket, remembering his inaccessibility to the crystal and feeling hopeless as a result.
"I'll fetch for the doctor!" Eleanor ran out of the house swiftly, hoping the doctor may be accessible on Christmas Day. It was dark outside at this wintery time of the year, but not too late in the day.
Edward looked at William, obviously thinking the same thing. They both felt helpless, but both wondered if it was possible to retrieve the crystal. Edward looked at Francis, knowing they were all out of their depth, but also that they couldn't leave Ann on her own in such a desperate time!

William stepped back from the scene and was about to turn to run with an aim to collect a shovel and perform a desperate dig!
"No!" Edward shouted, "there's no time now!"
William looked side-to-side and paced a bit in frustration.
Edward appeared to hold more concern for his friend than Ann's dying father.
William decided that he needed to take action, ignoring Edwards' warning.
Running now, out of the house, into the darkness, William opened the large access-gates, leaving one side open in haste! He ran up through the streets, gaining distance to his own home. There was no time to *think* about his own breath! His running was intense, and his breathing was extremely heavy. The thought briefly crossed his mind that he may even keel over with extreme exertion. Thankfully, he managed to run into his front door and rummage through a small out-house in his rear garden, quickly enough to grab a shovel. It seemed easy to run with the weight in his hand, like a baton in a relay, propelling him forward. He ran swiftly over to the sight of the buried crystal. He had no idea how the darkness would inhibit his desperation during the run to the grounds, but at the time he didn't care. The space of grass was re-traced by the edges of the tunnel wall, and his rush to dig brought haste of creating a large mess of turf. His breathing was laboured, but his adrenaline still pumped hard, giving him the super-charged-energy he needed to unravel his desperate healing-treasure. As he dug, he wondered why they would need to take such measures to hide such a literal healing-gem, when such situations occurred. He also realised that a normal life *without* such things would allow non-interference with the only nature their minds knew. It was most certainly a conflict of thoughts in a brief space of time.
The shovel was no longer needed as the soil was soft under his fingers enough to dig with his hands. He called out in a light whimper as his fingers touched the item, creating the familiar

bright light! The light blasted through the soil just as if there wasn't a restricting barrier. William felt relief as he felt the solidity of the crystal and was able to feel around to retrieve the entire shape of it!

He rubbed the crystal on his trouser leg, cleaning it best he could. "I'm so sorry we buried you!" He felt a warming connection, followed by the reminder of the urgency to return to Francis!

He took some deep breaths, deactivating the light of the crystal, and ran swiftly back towards the house, dropping his shoving on his front lawn. He had no care for what people's opinions were at this point.

As he ran through the streets again, he witnessed John and his group following him with their eyes. It was clear to them that William was extremely distressed. He ran with legs that were becoming a bit wobbly with urgency, looking as if they could tangle themselves up if he didn't keep the momentum going.

He found the large gates of the home and then panicked for a few seconds about the scene he may find upon re-entry.

His adrenaline was still pumping wildly, edging him on despite his fears. The door he'd left through was still accessible, allowing him a swift return into the huge lounge. Ann was now sobbing on the floor, sat with her knees tucked up to her chest, with Edward kneeling with her, with his arms wrapped around her upper body. At this time Eleanor was still somewhere hoping to gain access to the local doctor.

Edward looked up at William, impressed at the time it had taken to retrieve the crystal despite the obvious labour it would have required. He couldn't disagree with the decision to try this healing potential now.

William took a few calming breaths and activated the crystal, making Ann look outwardly.

"Is my Dad going to the angels?" She asked so innocently.

There weren't any replies, with fear that the healing may not work. It would be the first attempt at healing someone who had allegedly passed over!

William placed the crystal on Francis's chest.

After a few seconds of expectancy, nothing appeared to occur! This panicked William despite the spectacle of the bright light surrounding all of them. During the brief wait, William also realised the holding of his own breath. He took a deep breath and tried to focus somehow.

"Will!" Edward shouted over, recognising a familiar feeling.

As William looked over to respond, he noticed the particles of himself drawing toward the crystal.

"Oh no!" William wasn't sure what to do on this occasion. He just watched open-mouthed as Edward's body disintegrated into the small space of the crystal.

Thankfully, Ann was crying into her folded arms that held her knees up to her chest. When she noticed Edward's lack of physical touch, she looked up to seek his presence.

"He'll be back in a few moments." William tried to comfort, as they both squinted in the blinding light!

William moved the crystal up to the top of Francis's head now, wondering if another form of action was required.

A familiar cough came through, followed by some gasps of gulping air breathed by Ann's father! Ann looked up, uncertain of the reality of his return to life! A few pieces of tobacco left his mouth, revealing that he had quite a large amount of it in his mouth. He then coughed out a chunk of chewing gum.

William deactivated the light of the crystal swiftly.

"You were chewing too much tobacco!" Ann shouted, lunging in for the greatest hug of her father.

"Chewing gum and tobacco?" William looked at the contents to the front of Francis.

"We thought you were dead!" Ann shouted in distress.

"Oh, my sweet darling. I do not think I could leave you if I tried. Is it still Christmas?"
William and Ann looked at one another with humoured relief.
Eleanor ran through the large entry space, expelling heavy breath, "I cannot find the doctor for the life of anyone!"
Before anyone had responded, she noted the joy and relief in the room.
"Oh, thank goodness!" Eleanor reached to hug William for her own comfort and gave a relieving whimper.

They all gathered around the warmth of a log-filled fire, trying to calm from the events. Thankfully, no questions were asked over the strangeness of the extreme light.
William knew that there was an overwhelming sense of relief in the room, which was enough of a distraction.
"You all rest up here and I shall see to the whereabouts of Edward." William stood, knowing that he needed somewhere private to *attempt* to "retrieve" Edward!

William went outside into the main pathway that brought him to the access gates of the property. He felt uneasy when there was a rustle of voices around the outskirts of the property boundaries, making him feel wary. He reminded himself of the protective properties that the crystal had, with only one command, which comforted him now. For a few seconds he was tempted to experiment with other potential commands but reminded himself of the urgency to bring Edward back into the physical world that he knew.

William hid in the shadows and did his best to scuffle around the large grounds of the house gardens instead of moving into public space. He felt safer, hoping he wouldn't need to give his position away with any crystal activation. He found an outhouse with the door wide open, so crept inside and crouched down to prepare his retrieval attempts.

"Ed! Ed, please come back through to *this* side. I know you can hear me! You usually come back! I need you!"
Without hesitation, the formation of cellular retrieval poured from the crystal and reformed the figure of Edward in front of William's eyes! His relief of the ease of this action filled him with intensity. As usual, Edward took a while for his consciousness to return to his body. This was the only way William understood the process, without understanding it in any academic form.
They both stood now, facing one another, with William staring directly into Edward's lifeless eyes at this point.
"Ugh!" Edward suddenly became "active," and got a huge fright from the stern stare received for his welcome!
"Oh, sorry Ed! I was waiting for you to return in full form!"
"I'm back, but I do not know my position!"
"Oh, you are standing in an outhouse to Francis's property. I needed a private space."
"Ann's Dad!" Panic filled Edward's face.
"Ed, he's okay! He has been healed with the crystal!"
Edward looked about with thoughts racing.
"The crystal can bring people back to life! It can transport me to another life place too! I wish you could find a way to go through this space too! I feel as if I have received some information since this present visit!"
"What kind of information?" William was interested and concerned at the same time.
"Will, there is a whole civilisation over there. I remember much more this time. Someone spoke with me... I just need to recall who it was and what was said. The transportation back seems to make it all appear like a distant dream once again."
"Try to remember Ed. What can you remember?"

"I'm certainly trying Will. Everything is fading. I am back here, in this time, now."

"Were you in a different time?"

"I believe I moved to a more advanced time with the ability to move *through* time."

"Well, that is something I would not be able to comprehend my friend."

"I am wondering the same. Once I knew, I knew, but now it is as if I do not know! It was so vast but now it is so vague once again. One moment I understood everything, but now I feel limited once again."

"That sounds a bit like a riddle."

"I can see why it would." Edward looked quite mischievous in his expression now.

"Are you ready to return to Ann now? We still have Christmas evening to enjoy after the scare!"

A sudden realisation hit Edward.

"You saved Francis! For him to have passed away on such a day would have truly ruined Ann's life!"

"It was the crystal that saved him. Somehow."

"I think it is a combination of your purpose and the crystal's existence."

"You are truly speaking with some complication Ed. Are you sure you are ready to return to the household?"

"We do need to return to normality and attempt to enjoy the celebration again, hopefully eradicating the trauma we have just witnessed."

"I think we can make the most of the evening with the company of our ladies."

"Without making Francis feel left out, my friend."

"Indeed." William offered an arm around Edward's shoulder and encouraged the walking direction.

Everyone sat to enjoy the evening once again. Francis took to drinking spirits to calm his own nerves, whilst everyone else played a card game and nibbled at an abundance of nuts on a side table.

Edward sat for a moment, relaxing his head back. William studied him briefly, remembering some drawbacks to his energy levels after the unexplainable journeys.

"I think it is simply us ladies then!" William expressed with humour.

Ann looked to notice Edward's chin drop with him falling into a deep sleep. She smiled at his change of appearance.

After approximately thirty minutes of sleep however, Edward woke with an immediate start.

"I know!" Edward shouted, causing everyone to spin their heads in surprise.

Edward realised his sudden return to his present reality, feeling embarrassed.

"Sorry everyone. Did I shout in my waking?"

"You certainly did!" Eleanor had a light-hearted tone in her voice.

"I need to head home." Edward stood with a look of action.

"Right at this moment?" William glanced at his wristwatch.

"There is something that I must do."

Edward didn't behave with pleasant departure and simply walked away, aiming to leave swiftly.

"Let me see to him." William expressed to the rest of them as he stood to follow him.

William ran to find his friend already jogging out of the main gates of the property. Edward didn't even think to close the home door behind him, leaving William to pick up the trail of securing all of the doors and gates as he attempted to catch up with him.

"Ed! Where are you going?"

Edward didn't reply, leaving William following behind in a jog, feeling his legs tighten up after his previous sprint to retrieve the crystal from the ground.

Edward continued to move swiftly, running for quite some time, leaving William trailing behind attempting to keep him within his sights, feeling tired and confused.

"Ed!" He attempted again, "where are you headed?"

Edward ran continually, looking almost mechanical with an upright posture, keeping his eyes focussed forward.

William limped and cursed, continuing to keep up.

They both ran for quite some time. William was about to give-up, feeling like his chest was about to burst.

Edward slowed to a swift walking pace, still facing robotically forward.

"Thank you Ed for slowing down. Perhaps you could talk to me to explain what we are doing, and how we intend to return once we are completely exhausted from all of this!" He tried to throw his voice.

William couldn't help but see the situation as madness, yet with a little hint of humour in the strangeness.

"Follow me William. All will be revealed!"

Finally! William thought! An answer that helped connect to some form of sane decision making! He didn't feel a desperate need to stop or save his friend so much now. This was more of a trusting action he decided to give a chance to instead, despite the aching muscles from so much running.

William looked at his wristwatch again, noting they had been out in the cold, dark winter's night walking and running for about forty minutes.

"How much further do you intend to go Ed? It'll take all night to get back!"

"Things are different now Will, you will see!"

They started walking swiftly off the beaten track now, and over some soft grass.

"How on earth do you know where you are headed?" William started to fill with doubt yet again.

"Trust me Will. I have seen this route."

William frowned with a puzzle over his response, but knew he needed to be with him on this journey.

Edward stopped suddenly, reaching his hands forwards.

"Bring the crystal here Will."

William felt some elevated emotion knowing his help was part of this journey.

He walked up to Edward's side and looked at his side profile, waiting for his next set of instructions.

"Remove the crystal from your pocket and reach it out in front of you."

William acted without question yet with uncertainty.

Without any hesitation, the air in front of them hit a huge, sparkly, kaleidoscope pattern, making William step back with slight fear, trying his best to keep his one arm forward to keep the momentum.

"It is fine Will. Trust this process."

William frowned again, wondering if someone had taken on Edward's brain function.

They both looked forward to notice that the light formed a wall made up of sparkling, transparent features. This was vast in size, leaving a dark cave-like entrance in the centre of this large wall of transparent crystal formations.

"We need to walk through this Will."

"What happens when we *do*?"

"Trust the process." Edward repeated himself.

William was now convinced that Edward was in some kind of trance-state.

"Are you actually in there somewhere Ed?"

"I am good my friend. I am simply focussed and do not wish to lose the vision I am following."

"Vision?"

"I feel all will be explained. Come, let us walk forward."

They both walked through what seemed to be an arch-shaped tunnel of crystal light.

When they walked slowly into this "light," they both "whooshed" through a great distance, weightlessly, at a great speed, and fell at the other side of what seemed to be a very long tunnel!

William fell forward and rolled on the grass in an attempt to stop the movement. Edward seemed to compose his body with a few fast steps that brought him to a halt.

They both stood together to study their new environment. It was still dark, with surrounding green hills and large trees. Some structures were in view, and with a closer inspection they confirmed that these were large stones that obviously weighed several tonnes in weight! They seemed orderly placed.

"Where are we Ed?" William felt a bit overwhelmed by the scene.

"We entered a gateway that brought us here. This area will bring a portal to us."

"What are you talking about?"

"Wait a few moments." Edward held his elbows slightly bent but pushed his palms forward as if he was reaching to feel for something that couldn't be seen.

William felt a strange pressure of air from above, forcing him to look upwards. A large circle of light with crystal edges made its way down very steadily. It felt inviting, but William still wanted to know more, understandably.

"Ed! What are we getting into here?" His voice was panicked.

"We shall literally be getting into it in just a moment and then you will be amazed."

William noticed another strange movement in the corner of his eyes and felt the hairs stand at the back of his neck.

"Ed, are we meant to be in company?"

Edward looked to see the same figure of Trion, walk toward them with others behind him, moving in unison like a small army.

Edward faced them, knowing they were traced with the use of such futuristic technologies of uncertainties. He knew he was truly out of his depth.

"What are we messing with here, Ed? How did they trace our whereabouts?"

The crowd walked steadily with aggressive-looking intention.

"Will, I had this dream at Ann's after the exhaustion of the crystal event, and I am simply following the vivid dream I had. I do not in-fact know what this is leading toward."

"At least you are more coherent now, Ed. I thought the crystal may have done something strange to you, the way you were behaving… What do we do now? Shall I request the crystal's protective circle? Did you see this interruptive group in your vivid dream?"

"I think that perhaps we should only allow them a certain closeness to us before we resort to the crystal protection. See if they say anything of explanation first."

Edward and Will stood solid, the huge circle of light still descending, gradually nearing, encouraging both of them to occasionally look up. With Trion and his group walking directly towards them, they mostly kept their eyes forward, not knowing what to expect from the events above *or* ahead!

Within voice-hearing range, Trion spoke clearly.

"I knew the activation would lead me to you. Give me the crystal *now*! It is rightfully mine. You do not know what you are dealing with!"

Another voice clearly spoke to the back of William's head now, frightening him more-so than Trion's words!

"Please do not give the crystal to Trion. His intentions are not of good in this world. His intention is to ensure an army of dictatorship, to treat people like cattle, containing and entrapping them. This will be the future if you allow him to receive the crystal. Protect it with your life. It is your purpose."

William didn't want to turn his head to the voice, in fear.

The tone was powerful and deep! It sounded like the voice of himself from the other dimension, yet extremely stern with the severity of the situation.

William just stood rigid, wondering how he was surviving the severe stress of the evening!

"Did you hear that?" William asked Edward, still noting the timing of the descending light and the approaching gang!

"Trion cannot have the crystal." Edward responded, leaving William feeling grateful for the mutual agreement, however still not sure as to whether Edward had heard the voice behind his head.

Trion approached, standing a slight distance before them now.

"I insist that you return the crystal to me. It belongs to me! This entire *planet* belongs to me!"

"How can you claim a planet for yourself?" William bravely offered.

"I discovered it long before you people came along, but then you crept up from somewhere and began to multiply. I have the power that keeps the planet alive. You hold the final piece that is needed to keep the planet entirely whole! Without that piece, you are simply messing with the lives of all of us!"

"It hasn't changed anything since we have had possession of it other than healing those in desperate need and protecting us from *you*!" William spoke in bravery.

"What has made you so bold to hold onto something you have no idea about? The energy source and connections will crumble without your understanding of this crystal."

"I know what I am doing." Offered Edward on this occasion, "I have been shown what to do to *save* this planet!"

"You are deluded! Leave the crystal on the ground and move backward before I *forcefully* remove it from your possession."

William looked above, noting the slow movement of the descending light, wondering if it would save them when it *finally* reached their level! If so, it needed to speed up considerably! Trion moved forward, making William hold the crystal with intent - beginning to contemplate an activation by commanding it for protection.

Trion moved faster than the two defensive men could ever have predicted, followed by an army of people behind him, all jumping in to aid the claim of the item.

There was a big fight that drew them to the ground. Some rough wrestling began, with William clutching the crystal with one tight grip, wondering what command to give since they were all too close to one another now! He gripped with his other hand too, overlapping the hands for extra strength.

He gasped, feeling as if he was in some huge nightmare. His lifeline went through his mind, wondering how it ever emerged to such present circumstances. He then focussed on the physical defence strategy. Edward was attempting to pull people away. He lifted them and threw adrenaline-filled punches to the jawline, extremely accurately, knowing that they would drop unconsciously to the ground from his years of training. William noticed the number of attackers reducing swiftly, but there were three people scuffling around him, attempting to pull his arms out, and unclasp his hands.

Edward was desperately moving in and out, still boxing with adrenaline pumping wildly through him. William felt helpless, not knowing how to save the crystal other than keeping the hands gripped as tightly and as closely to his body as possible.

Trion was very powerful indeed, and pulled William's arms away from his body, slowly undoing one finger at a time, making William feel weak and defeated! Edward noticed the urgency to leave his current fight, so gave one swift uppercut to knock his opponent back and onto the ground, hurting his hand on the base of the jawbone. For a split second he cared about the receiver of such impact.

He ran over to Trion and kicked his side, hoping the weight behind his kick was enough to topple him over. Thankfully he was successful in this plan! He felt the bones of Trion crunch even through his shoe, which surprised him. Both Edward and William held fear over Trion's appearance with not understanding his abilities, but this sensation of some vulnerability gave Edward a form of comfort.

William regained his grip over the crystal and quickly rose to his feet, hoping this would achieve advantage. Edward watched Trion lean on one hand to push himself back up, but obviously felt pain now.

In the corner of William's eye, he noted a tall, incredibly speedy figure running towards them! The two men braced themselves for further battle, with another injured party recovering from the ground to attempt to support the opposition. Trion looked pained but willing to continue with a gritted jaw through anger or frustration. William and Edward looked at one another, knowing each other well enough to say words without speaking! They stood only a meter apart, readying themselves for battle. William was grabbed by this new, tall person and dragged like a piece of pray across the ground! He felt his adrenaline heighten like never before, expecting an enormous sense of loss. He hoped he was wrong, but his life felt at threat, along with the safety of the crystal. He almost gave up within the first few seconds with the force of this person!

"William!" Edward shouted in distress, wishing to help his friend, but recognising the superhuman abilities of this new enemy. William heard Edward's call but looked up to see this very tall person's face, clearly portraying feminine features. Deep colours mixing with red seemed to emanate from them. William sensed a huge anger from this person. Their impatience was obvious. She grabbed one of William's hands, pulling it away from the joint grip. He looked up in a panic.

"No, please don't!" He tried to keep his remaining gripped hand out of range, but knew he had no chance with the strength of this person.

The tall being stood tall and held out their hand, giving William an opportunity to simply hand it to them with submission. William sat up slightly, taking a glance at Edward in the near distance feeling defeated and appearing sorrowful at his moment of failure. He knew his enemy was too powerful for him to override.

"Okay. You have me." William offered.

The person still held their hand out in expectancy, looking extremely impatient now in their definitively final offer of receiving the crystal without force.

William leant back slightly – and then with a forceful thrust forward, he threw the crystal as hard as he could in Edward's direction!

The person was shocked at the foolish decision, looking at the direction of the throw, and then back at William in disgust!

In the meantime, Edward only needed to move approximately one meter to the left of himself to obtain the very-accurately thrown crystal! As he repositioned his upright stance, he noticed that the gradually descending and consuming *light* was now at a level that was covering his head! He knew this was a fantastic thing from the dream he recalled again suddenly, as the same action played out! The crystal in his hand threw an amazingly bright beam up to the centre of this descending form of light, which completed the shape of this structure. Edward looked around to see a better definition of the construct now consuming him well! He saw three walls of strong light meeting to a point, creating a huge pyramid of light, with shimmering crystal features defining the lines of the edges, and a triangle form that was now landing at his feet!

"How could you let them find the portal?" The very tall person shouted towards Trion.

They all gazed at Edward who appeared to fade out from his solid, physical form into an almost-invisible person. The onlookers could see Edward's outline enough to make him out. Everyone looking in Edward's direction could see that he was now standing in a very large pyramid shaped vessel that was full of amazing, magical light. This light had descended so gradually for anyone who was preparing to embark upon this vessel. Edward was so grateful to have been the one to be consumed by it, knowing that it would somehow aid the entire situation.

The tall person now looked back at William and lifted him by his shirt collars with great force. He panicked at her intentions, wondering how this person could be so immensely strong! Trion looked over at Edward, making a fresh threat now.

"William will be destroyed if you do not reverse the portal process and return the crystal!"

"No! Stay there Edward!" William felt the consequences of any compliance to the enemy.

Edward was about to walk out of the pyramid of light, but there was a new ground that had formed to this surrounding structure that began to lift him. He was now standing on a clear platform of light, a crystal formation of solid ground. The three of them watched on as Edward looked at his feet and all around himself. As the structure ascended now, Edward knew he was elevating in some form of transport, but he felt out of control with this new ascension!

William attempted to stand and run, but Trion and his friend pushed him down, stopping him.

Edward tried to push against the side of this construct, noticing it had also become solid, leaving him unable to escape.

Edward looked up to see a large ring of light above the pyramid structure. The light of the ring was so bright that he covered his eyes with his forearm.

William looked up to notice the bright beam, forcing all three of them on the ground to shield their eyes.

Another member of the "Trion army" managed to recover themselves from the knockout he'd received from Edward. He ran over to William with slightly wobbly legs, and thumped him in the chest, extremely hard!
William took a gasp at the sharp pain, knowing his time was most likely over with the force of people around him. He felt a warmth with the pain of the strike, looking down to notice the thick, red liquid leaving his body. What he thought was *just* a punch, must-have been a stabbing.

There he lay now, knowing that the blood was creeping out faster than there was any time for any last word or action. There he was, knowing his time would be up in less than a few minutes. At first he was worried about the future of things falling into the wrong hands, but a bigger picture was forming. The mind was fading, and a new view of light was forming in front of his eyes. Was this the afterlife? He guessed he was about to find out.

Present Time

Tom was in a deep state, seeing his hands working at an old desk. He rubbed the desk and felt the smoothness of it. It was very real, and he was truly there. He looked into a packet and noticed some beautiful crystals of various colours, shapes, and sizes. He offered most of these to a friend who was sat in front of him, moulding and shaping silver into rings. He looked to his left to note that his friend had made a homemade envelope and placed two beautiful rings inside. In his heart he felt happy that a good job was done. He knew that a beautiful task had been completed. He watched as his friend knew he needed to get the rings to a place of safe-keeping and observed him, automatically standing to walk in hard leather shoes that looked unusual. He knew this person was his very close friend.
They began walking together. Their clothes were firm and extremely well ironed, or so it seemed since there wasn't a crease in sight. They took the envelope and followed one another with the intention to take it to a place they knew of. As they walked on this glorious, blue-skied day, the occasional passer-byer waved in their direction. He knew that they knew these people but couldn't quite recall their names in this different mind. He sensed that their work had so many acquaintances and sale networkers.
The ground was cobbled and uneven, but their ankles and feet were used-to every single dip and angle. He knew he was this person at *this* time, and that he was with his closest, most trusted friend, but he sensed something unusual. As they walked, they came to an offbeat track and found a path up toward a beautiful green patch, with an old tunnel ahead, and a castle within eye's recognition. People were working within the grounds, building, and restructuring parts. He noticed how much hard labour there was in the neighbourhood and observed everyone's dirty clothes. Their walk took them to a tunnel of which they walked through. The direction of the walk was a magnetic pull toward a very large

brick within the tunnel walls. They came to an engraved brick that they knew they'd marked out with a firm and repetitive scraping action.
They needed to remove this heavy rock of a brick! Tom, within this *other* person's body, pulled it steadily from the secure setting of the deep hole and reached in to pull out the leather-bound book. His friend knew that the rings would form a crease in the pages, but inside the hard cover, it was the only safe place that made sense. It was important that the rings would be found later when things settled down at this present time in life. They both felt the tension of knowing that there were hunting enemies, so the safest of hiding places could be no better than behind a tunnel wall!
They managed to tuck the envelope of rings inside the book, and the book back behind the re-placed, huge brick with the obvious weight to it. Tom's arms were strong and rugged in this view of himself, with a very clean and precise type of professional clothing that fitted so snugly. His assumed profession didn't quite look fitting to the body-type, as it looked labour-induced. He couldn't understand how this was *his* body and mind right now.
He walked back through the beautiful green place with his close friend, back through the area of people working very hard, toward the cobbled, uneven road and found the front door of his friend's workplace once again.
Working themselves back behind the desk space, they comforted themselves back into their usual positions, expecting some of his friend's regular customers. At least – this *felt* like the regular routine for them!

Himself within himself fell asleep into another depth of darkness.

Another brief view came to his mind, and some heavy breathing came to his ears. His extra rugged arms came back to view, with a second set of arms equally helping somehow. The four arms were digging desperately, trying to hide another item of great importance. The *area* of digging was of extreme necessity! It needed to be exact to the centre of several, very large rocks. The marking was of absolute importance to his mind. This would be an area that would hold great value to the future of mankind. He knew he was with a bonded brother, not that of blood, but that of decision through a tight and lifelong friendship. They were full of gratitude for this moment, filled with huge relief, but with more purpose than they could ever imagine.

The digging was extremely deep, but they knew it needed to *be*. When the digging was deep enough, and the veins were pulsating in his forearms, he looked at his dirty hands, knowing they were his, but it confused him, as they still weren't his *current* arms. He tried to get a view of the person helping him dig, but it was a bit hazy. He knew that the task at literal-hand was the most important focus at this very moment – a task that couldn't be witnessed by *anyone* else other than them two.

He now reached into his pocket and studied the item they were attempting to bury, as if it was the last time he'd see a much-loved treasure. Monitoring it, this was a beautiful clear crystal, with an amazing blend of a royal and slightly paler blue. This blended crystal glimmered intensely with a feeling of immense power. He held it, and a vibration of strength, purity and connection somehow filled both of them, and the entire space they were in. He felt that he literally had-to say goodbye to the crystal and then place it into the depth of the hole, completely centralised as planned, with the tip of it facing upward.

They both filled the hole swiftly and solidified the ground on the top layer of soil with a unified stamping of feet. They both behaved in twin-like action, knowing one another's thoughts so well.

Within the depths of Tom's mind, he now stood in a *new* background of a *clinical* scene! He looked to the same close friend opposite him, trying to get a clearer view, but there were words exchanged instead. His friend made a promise in a strong, deep voice.

"We promise to return at the time of need once again, as true brothers, in order to retain the power for the greater good of mankind."

He offered his pinky-finger, where the both of them made a childish pinky-promise.

"What is this?..."

Tom had an extremely bright light directly in his eyes as he came to his present state in a shocked waking! At first, he thought he'd fallen into some vivid dreams, coming back to the room he'd fainted in, but then realised it was something of a set of visions! His experience, although vivid to his mind, wasn't his present reality. He waved his arms, trying to gain focus on what was causing so much light.

"I am sorry that you needed to be unconscious to understand a previous time." Spreckley was stood in a swirl of gold before him, trying to revive his mind to the current situation.

Tom sat up, covering his eyes with the palm of one of his hands.

"What just happened? You are confusing the crap out of me!"

"What you just saw was given to you to show you a previous act from a timeline you once existed in."

"Can you turn the bloody bright light out and explain things in plain English, please!"

A smile came to the unusual being's face, making Tom feel very nervous once again.

"I am Spreckley, your friend. You can relax. Let me help you." The being placed his hands on the ground and allowed a blue haze to rise up through the air.

Tom felt an instant calming sensation.

"Wow." Tom enjoyed the wonder.

"Can you recall what you experienced?"

Tom heard the question, but his mind grew a little hazy for a few moments. The visions returned.

"A stone... I was burying a stone of importance with a brotherly figure."

"Well done, Tom. This was in a different timeline, but you knew the importance of this event. You and a great friend had a strong purpose, back many decades ago. You saved an important piece of power. All of the signs that I have gently guided you to, whether you were aware or not, have been to coax you to relocate the crystal power that you saw in your visions since your brother moved to a house over the land that held a large chunk of crystal... Many decades ago, there were secret portions of large crystals buried deep within the ground. One large piece was buried deep within a space of a mass of trees; another was buried deep within hills; another was buried deep within a very sandy area and the final one was hidden deep within a cave space near a large space of sea water. There was one piece that acted as the *activator* of all of these large chunks of crystal, and the person who held this, had control over the *will* of the energy of this entire planet. With the power over the energy of the planet, it can be within ruins and control, or it can be in the opposite energy of peace, joy, and abundance!"

"So, hold on... We buried this... activation crystal many years ago in...? Did we bury it to save it from getting into the wrong hands?"

"You are understanding well. The person who initially used the activator had very little power without it and grew extremely weak. His partner – a very strong feminine-being, has been trying to locate the very large crystals as well as attempting to figure out the clues to find the activation crystal. She has been very aggressive about it lately. One of the larger crystals lies below your brothers garden and house space, but when you and your brother knew to reincarnate at just the right time, it was pre-decided that one of you would protect the largest crystal by moving near it, and that one of you would re-locate the activation crystal."

"So, we have past lives? I thought that was all here-say or conspiracy wacky theoretical stuff."

"Surely you know that you are completely sane, yet you have been having all of these extremely unusual circumstances, and here *I* stand as a *being* you find familiar, yet not of *your* kind, and you still doubt any so-called-mysterious possibilities?"

Tom stood with a deep stare at the person in front of him, studying his features, trying to recall any memories from a past lifetime despite thinking that he must be from some future time! Although he was confused at this point, he knew the person who stood in front of him *felt* like an old friend.

Spreckley looked into Tom's eyes, recognising a glimmer of recollection.

"So, do we need to find all of these crystals?"

"They are all marked somehow for locating, by the use of landmarks such as the monument, but you and your brother once had an experience that gave you both a view of every single crystal's location, therefore, there is a subconscious knowing of their location that can be retrieved. Either that, or you can locate the activation crystal and re-experience your bird's eye view once again, living out a wonderful past life experience that will make you realise the power that can be uncovered!"

Tom looked down at his hands and arms, somehow disappointed not to see the strong, gritty arms and hands, but simultaneously grateful to recognise his own structure that he realised he always loved.

"I sensed the importance of saving that crystal, but now that I'm in the here and now, I don't quite understand the battle."

"There has always been a light vs dark conflict, but this planet's nature was interfered with by a couple of what you call "alien-beings." All was good and peaceful with a will not always understood by humans. There are some universal laws that this couple broke, and then they inhabited and mixed energies of different natures. They then created their own powers of control and used their advanced technologies to suppress the building populations to retain the greed of their own power. As time moved along, some travelling people unravelled diamonds, gold, and then equally discovered different types of crystals that were all dug from the depths of the Earth. These were all used variably for value, riches, and power. People generally didn't understand the power of the crystals but traded with them or sold them on. Gold was limited in availability, so held more value, as decided by humans. Food and water has become a commodity despite it being naturally available.

Money became an idea by a select few in order to keep the masses enslaved to trading with it despite it being unlimited at the top. Having said that, money is simply an energy just the same as everything is on this planet. It is a powerful planet for energy manipulation in whichever direction it's chosen. Everything is energy and energy can create whatever you choose, just as decisions can bring about what holds value. You can *be* and *have* anything from the seed of a thought and the words expressed. I used-to teach many people the power of manifestation through visualisation, intention, and action with belief. I admit that I broke the laws but to the benefit of *all* by discretely using the human power of manifestation, but it was in desperation to build free energy for much greater reasons. Humans don't understand the power of the energy within and without the crystals. There's more value in them than the gold and money as it's a huge power source."

"We've mixed with alien life form and been unaware?"

"We are all intergalactic. It's all in the name. Then there are interdimensional lives. There's intergalactic trade too, behind the scenes."

"How can we perceive such elaborate complications?"

"There is a lot you can't understand without seeing it, experiencing it, or feeling it. The part of the brain that is said as unused is actually *used*! It stores *so* much that it can explain so much if unlocked."

"Oh shit! I don't know how to take all of this in. I've heard about different frequencies and stuff, but never needed to look into it. All of the latest events are unravelling *some* mysteries for me I guess."

"It's something that happens over a long period of time – a growth within you. Awakenings of truth that gradually unfold can be helpful, but growing needs either great challenges or frequent, and deliberate connection to the true self within each person."

"Have many have awakened to deep truth like this?"

"Some have. They're usually labelled as crazy or wacky. Some wouldn't be able to cope when all they know is what they sense with their eyes, ears, nose, mouth, and touch connection through their nervous system."

"I think the next question is: how the heck do I explain this to my brother?"

"He has secretly known in a deep way more than he realises. He's had dreams, and he knew to move to the area he lives in now in order to be in the correct location for all of the preparation. Everything has been intentional and mapped out. It may take a few days for things to sink in, but although things are growing desperate, there is still time for both of your minds to adjust."

"Are you needing me to tell my brother the same way you're telling me?"

"I think the best method with your brother is to explain the importance of obtaining the activation crystal and that it does in-fact activate the energy of many that lie within the Earth. You can show him the book and declare that you read it and that it makes sense. There's a map of everything right at the back. It explains everything anyway. His dreams will match up with all of it. His dreams have been drip-feeding him with information. Trust me."

Tom felt a little calmer over knowing that information has already perhaps been drip-fed into Ethan's mind. He now worried about how he felt about Rachel, however.
"I can read people's thoughts well, Tom. Everything with Rachel will *also* act out as it should."
"Wow."
"Just trust me and go with the flow of it all."
Spreckley reached for the floor again to generate a colour of oranges and yellows, with smear of reds.
"What is this?" Tom felt less calm but more energised.
"That should give you extra vitality, ambition and joy."
Tom felt the shift of energy within him and wanted to get on with the major task at hand.
"That's better now. Let us work through this. Whenever you need me, just call my name. Remember my name of Spreckley. I will hear you!"
"That certainly aids in comfort. Thanks!"
"Just one more thing…" Spreckley walked over to the old book that was left on the table Tom had been studying it at.
He placed his hand over the cover and allowed a golden swirl to spin above it. Tom stared as Spreckley seemed to encourage the swirl with his first finger. A holographic image moved upward, forming an image.
"You will understand the three dimensional image of the map you need to complete the purposeful task you have ahead of yourself."
Tom looked on to recognise huge rocks above a space of land. Below these rocks seemed to be similar to that of an iceberg, where a larger chunk of rock sat below. Within the centre of a circle of these huge rocks was a piece of softer turf. Looking about three or four meters down, there sat a beautiful, glimmering stone! Tom recognised this stone from his vision and from previous visions!
"Is that the activation stone? The one we buried?"

Spreckley smiled. "The challenge is to keep it safe now that you know where it is."
Tom sensed humour from Spreckley for the first time.
"You underestimate my strength!"
"That is the perfect, confident response."
There was a pause in the entire conversation and situation as Tom registered a few things.
Spreckley suddenly disappeared like a genie – into nothingness! No goodbyes – just a slipping away!
Tom gasped but retained his new level of confidence. He walked over to the book to get a closer view of everything.
A mild worry hit his mind as he brushed his hand over the cover of the book, causing the golden image to disappear. He wondered what his *exact* actions were meant to be with this new knowledge. He almost wanted a manual to follow!
He wondered if he should call for Spreckley for further questioning but felt the urgency to take the book and rings to join forces with his brother and Rachel.

Tom pulled up to the front of Ethan and Rachel's property.
He noticed Ethan's observations of his unexpected arrival by a head turn and eyes locking on. Ethan walked to the front door of the house, wondering about the intention of this unpredicted visit. Tom walked up to greet him, book, and rings in hand.
"Brother, what's up?"
"I need to tell you some important stuff."
Ethan was welcoming, thankfully, making the initial move easier than planned. Tom grew nervous of the next selection of words, however.
"Can I grab you a drink?" Ethan always had a good house of drink offerings.
"Oh yeah! You will probably need a calming drink too!"
"Eh? What's going on?" Ethan pulled a couple of large glasses from a cupboard while inspecting Tom's eyes.

"We'll need to sit down." Tom placed the heavy book on the nearest kitchen worktop.
"Do you suspect something?" Ethan looked a tad guilty.
"Have you *been* up to something?" Tom smiled with a calming effect for the two of them.
"Only if you're asking." Ethan retained secrecy.
Tanya then casually walked into the kitchen, wearing a thin, white satin dressing gown, holding onto clothes she was about to dress into.
"Oh, Bro." Tom's tone dropped downward with a little disappointment.
"Don't worry, it didn't happen without a change of circumstances first.
"What do you mean?
"Rachel assumed I was having an affair, but at the time I *wasn't*, actually. We had an argument, she stormed off, and then Tanya popped over and…"
"Yep, yep. I get the picture."
"We probably shouldn't have, but…" Tanya interjected.
Tom picked the book up again, "perhaps I should come back at another time."
"No, no!" Tanya insisted as she collected her shoes from the entrance to the room. I was genuinely about to leave, wasn't I honey?"
Ethan nodded with a thin, embarrassed smile.
"I need to get to a night shift, so I'll just get myself together and I'll be out-a your hair." Tanya added, creeping back out of the room.
"I still think I should come back another time." Tom felt uncomfortable.
"No, please. We had a lot of rest-time so I'm fresh in energy. Tanya genuinely needs to leave."
"Do you feel no shame?" Tom asked with a gentle toned probe at his morals. As soon as the words left his mouth, he recognised the same guilt within, but even worse, given his brother's partner.

"It was all in the heat of the moment." His head dropped.
"I think we have bigger problems, but I need your mind to focus on what I need to tell you." He wanted to move away from the subject for obvious reasons.
"Let's just wait for the front door to confirm our privacy. We need to sit and drink - by the feel of it."
"Can you focus with all of the emotional drama though?"
"I can. Rachel has gone to her Mum's. Tanya was a comfort, and now you're here, so I feel in good company. I'll focus on your issue and sort my other crap out later."
They both moved with their drinks to a comfortable position on the sofa.
"Ethan, this is deadly serious. It could literally be deadly."
Ethan's jaw dropped with fresh concern.
"Okay, well I guess I need to focus!"
"This book." Tom patted the cover at it sat on his lap, "it's really old."
Ethan looked over and felt a familiar chill work through him.
"What *is* that book?"
"It holds a historical event that we need to sort through. It involves *us*... Without a lie."
Ethan touched the book and felt the thickness of the cover.
"What on earth are you talking about?" Ethan took a few sips of his drink as if he had a huge thirst.
"Are you sure you're up to this? It's pretty serious."
"I am. It helps to have the drink in me." Ethan smiled politely.
"Hold on... What are you and Rachel going to do *now*?" He needed to know before tucking in.
"Oh, Tanya leaves her lipstick smears all over the place. We have flirted many times. I do think she's hot, but I don't think she's relationship material. Rachel spotted some lipstick on my shirt collar yesterday. It was just a flirty kiss once, that shouldn't have happened. She flipped and said she was leaving. She packed a bag and went to her mum's. She said she *might* be in touch."

"Ah man. I'm so sorry. So, if Tanya caused the issue, why did you invite her to do what you've done?"

"She comforted me with a random visit. Bloody weird timing, and we just started kissing. Before we knew it, we did what Rachel suspected we'd done. I guess I've really done it now huh." Ethan looked down at his drink.

"Hey, I can talk about the book stuff another time. Maybe you need to get your head sorted first. This info is pretty heavy."

"Honestly Bro, I'm cool. Rachel and I are always up and down. We just keep our issues out of sight, out of ego I guess. Maybe we need to move on. In fact, I always thought she was with the wrong brother. You two get on so well."

Tom was shocked at the hearing of his thoughts.

"Oh wow! Well, Rachel is amazing, but you guys could sort this out I'm sure." Tom felt the hypocrite again.

"Maybe. Anyway, please tell me what this visit is truly about. I could do with a big distraction."

"Well, it would be a *big* distraction, so I need you to be strong if we go ahead with this." Tom felt repetitive but needed to ensure he was truly ready.

"It's a history book though huh?" Ethan prompted the continuation.

"It's more than that, but I don't know how much you'll believe." Ethan stared at the book with intrigue, then lifted it to place on his *own* lap after carefully placing his drink on a small side table.

"Boy it's heavy huh?" Ethan took respectful care of the book, taking intriguing note of the introduction of the name and title, "E.Taylor... Interesting."

Tom looked for any form of reaction, hoping he wouldn't need to say as much as he had planned in his mind.

Ethan moved through the pages, seemingly speed reading. "It seems to be a diary full of intriguing events."

"Keep going." Tom encouraged.

Ethan turned the pages, each one sounding thickly set with age and original quality.

"This would take me some time to read..." Ethan was reading intently with interest, appearing to speed up with excitement. Tom watched for any reactions, noting enough interest to keep the momentum going. The pages continued to turn, with many a word digested.

"This is amazing!" Ethan interjected after some time.

"A personal journey." Tom added, not knowing the written content as such.

"I feel like I can relate to this person's character so much. His concerns and thoughts... but he is quite tough. He's a boxer. There's a stone that holds some magical healing powers.

Tom realised that he *should* perhaps have read *some* detail of the book!

"Oh wow! These two guys have been through so much but couldn't say anything. A huge secret to keep, but with such tough decisions to make!" Ethan continued to speed read.

"A secret?" Tom encouraged.

"This powerful, blue and clear crystal holding such powers they couldn't speak of in their time."

"You've already gathered that information?"

"I feel like I've already read it! Like I've read it... Like I've even..." Ethan paused and stared at one page! "I feel like I've even *written* it! I can relate to it without knowing it! I don't even know what I'm saying right now!"

"You can relate to it?" Tom held his shoulder to comfort him.

"There were some gruesome fights. Some really bloody noses and fights over this damned stone. I feel it! I can feel it in my hands. They're *my* hands! I had to fight so much! This book is ... E.Taylor... Those are *my* initials... They were my hands... They *are* my hands... These are *my* thoughts... This is *my* brain!" Ethan stood, allowing the book to slip to the floor.

"How can this be?" Ethan paced up and down, clutching his forehead.
Tom wondered if he was right about it being too much. He knew this was a crazy idea. He gathered the book and placed it on his lap, feeling the weight.
"Wait, wait! This all makes sense now. The dreams I had... I buried this crystal. This is another lifetime! The therapist was right! Oh my... The therapist was right! I thought *she* was the crazy one!"
"What do you mean? You've seen a therapist?"
"I needed some help to analyse my dreams. You know how much they were impacting me! She helped me and gave me some regression therapy. She said we can have past lives stored within our subconscious – a part of the brain we are told we don't use, but we do! We apparently come back time and time again. We choose to keep coming back – here to take on certain experiences. If we don't fulfil the things we chose to do, we come back, but we keep coming back because it's so wonderful. We forget the gift of this life until we remember, by losing this character and going back to our true ethereal selves. That's where we recentre and decide on our next move with our team. We all have a team."
"That's a lot to take in!" Tom was happy to hear him talk the situation through.
"She – well – *we* - said that the dreams were a recollection of a previous time and that you and I decided to come here again when times were vital. A time of great awakening and revolution."
"Wow! That's amazing!"
"We were bonded brothers in a previous life, but we knew we needed to return at this time, when there would be a peak in a battle between the darkness and light, but the light always wins, because no matter how dark a room is, a candle flame can still light the room!"
Ethan was pacing now, holding onto his lips, pulling them forward, "My therapist does Hypnotherapy, Past Life Regression, and is a councillor. A good mix of viewpoints."

He continued, "I dreamt of rings that I made for my decided brother. He was preparing for a marriage. I made jewellery... and boxed... a lot! Some for training and some to defend us. They were hard times back then. We were hardcore men. Not as we are today. Today many of us live like kings and queens. Our freedom is slowly being coaxed away though, but in very subtle ways. There are inter-Galactic beings trying to help... What?...I'm pausing now because I think I sound crazy Tom."

"It does sound crazy, but if you're crazy then so am I, as you're making sense of what *I've* been experiencing."

"What? Have you had matching dreams somehow?"

"Well, some dreams... some visions, and some bloody weird visits by beings that aren't human, that's for sure!"

Ethan sat next to Tom, staring into his eyes out of concern.

"You went through all of that without saying anything? I've seen a therapist, I had Rachel by my side, I've been taking time out and trying hard to digest this stuff... but you... you've dealt with this on your own?"

"Well, I've been... guided... in a sense."

"So, you *haven't* gone through it on your own?"

"Erm, well, yes, and no. I have a lot of explaining to do." Tom felt his brother needed to speak his thoughts outwardly first.

"Well come out with it then! Come on, interject. I need to hear this more than you know!"

"Okay, well, it'll sound bonkers."

"I'm spilling my bonker-ness! Please spill *yours*! I need to feel some logic here!"

Tom grinned, "Well, I've seen this... crystal you described, in visions. I've been chased by this crazy person – the same one who dug the garden up. You have been experiencing this crazy person - as you know... Then there's been this alien being communicating with me, asking me to gather this information. He told me we chose to come back to this planet at this heightened moment of energies to save the crystal from getting into the wrong hands."

"Wow!" Ethan was just staring at Tom's face, digesting every word with such intrigue, "This all matches up Tom! We need to work together now! This makes me feel wonderful, like a completeness. This feels like a true purpose to my life, at last!"
Tom beamed with a huge smile.
"I'm so glad you said that. I was terrified of telling you this. I was instructed to tell you all of this."
"Okay, so we are here!" Ethan stood in excitement, "We are here at this amazing time, completely aware of a past life we had! What an amazing discovery for both of us! What an amazing purpose and power we have!"
"I'm glad you see it that way." Tom looked at *his* facial expressions now.
"Where do we begin with this crystal thing then?"
"I'm glad you asked…"

The Evening of Christmas Day 1860

Edward looked up to see that he was ascending into the huge circle of extreme brightness in an immense pyramid-shaped transportation vehicle with edges of sparkling crystal! Although he was aware of the ascending transportation, he was desperate to help William. He could see that Trion and two others were looking up at him, leaving his friend to bleed out on the ground. Edward bashed the side of his fists on the transparent wall in frustration, just wishing he could swap places with Trion and his crew. He would give this strange discovery up in an instant for the safety of his friend.
Trion looked angry and frustrated, watching on with a squint through the extremely bright light.

Edward shielded his eyes as the transportation met up with the bright circle. He had no idea what was about to occur (of course) but hoped that this discovery would be a heartful experience, and perhaps a very temporary one so that he could aid his best friend as swiftly as possible. He tried to look into the light and then attempted to look back down at the horrendous scene on the ground.
A huge burst of light hit Edward's eyes, making him cover them completely with the palms of his hands.
From the ground, the burst of light looked like a star-shaped explosion that hit the entire space of sky and filtered over the land like an overspill of white liquid!
Everyone looking upward were now crouching on all fours, worried about the effects of this explosion of extreme light.
Edward appeared to have disappeared literally into thin air! The sky cleared to leave the usual darkness of a wintery evening.
Trion and his friends looked down at William, assuming his life would disappear from him, if not already. They walked away,

rubbing their eyes, and feeling a sense of empty victory. Trion decided to ponder over his next move to resolve things for his own benefit, but with the expected death of William coupled with the escapism of Edward, he decided that he needed to lay low for a while. Everyone moved, occasionally looking back at the limp body of William's.

William was shallow breathing but had slipped into an unconscious state. It wouldn't be long before every system would fail. Time ticked to no imminent rescue, leaving his body destitute. Trion and his team were now nowhere to be seen. They all managed to recover enough to return to their place of dwelling, to rest.

A long, cylindrical tunnel of light now reached down from the outer realms of the Earth's atmosphere! A powerful beam of light that would have been labelled as an "unidentified tube" (to any onlookers) beamed down, creating a circle of light all around William's body, encompassing him and beginning to draw him up like some powerful suction tool! His body lifted with the base of this tube like a transparent lift! He was elevated into the highest part of the darkness and appeared to disappear into the brightest star of the sky!

...

"Will he be okay?" Edward asked.

"We have Med Beds here. He will be fine." Shayze stood calmly, encouraging others to come to their aid.

Edward watched on as two ladies moved along on two huge flat-shaped stones – at least that is what they appeared to be. The stones hovered along smoothly, allowing easy transportation to tend to William's body that currently led lifeless on a pure white bed. Edward felt extremely worried but almost equally relieved by the fact that he was comforted by the technology of such advancement, for the good of mankind, all of which was beyond him!

The ladies seemed to magnetise another bed towards them with some gadget which sat in one of their hands. A modern, pure-white stretcher-bed hovered over to William's body. Another intentional action by the gadget in the hand, caused a very thin sheet of something to gather underneath William and lift him, like magic, up onto the modern stretcher! Edward watched on with amazement, wondering what else they could do. There he stood in his heavy 1800's clothing, watching on to see other humans with advanced knowledge.

"Don't worry, your friend will be fine within minutes. Do you want to travel with us to see?" One of the ladies offered space on her travelling device by moving to one side. Edward willingly climbed onto the hovering stone, at first with a test of balance, but then with amazement.

"I'm Jess, and this is Sue. We'll take you to the medical space." They all hovered slowly and comfortably through smooth, white pathways that were mapped out in this huge circular, gridded globe that Ethan knew he'd been to before!

The three of them arrived at a large white wall, that separated into two parts, like two large walls, creating an entrance to a room larger than any open space Edward had seen. He looked back to notice William's stretcher had been moving along with them, as if magnetised to the transportation devices.

"Don't worry, he'll be fine." Jess offered.

"He looks as if he's already *gone*." Edward spoke his fearful thoughts.

"He's still with us. We can feel his life force." Sue spoke with confidence.

They all stopped on their devices, and Jess pressed something on her handheld gadget to move the stretcher bed to lie on top of a transparent-looking bed. William lay lifeless on top of this strange, transparent bed, which produced an extra transparent lid, which came from one of the wide ends and wrapped itself over the top of William like a giant covering!

Once William was covered within this cocoon-like super-bed, a strip of light ran through the entirety of the base of the lid, like a line of a super bright wire, and moved up and over the whole of William's body. The light moved back and forth, with the view of William looking peaceful.

"He'll be fine very soon. It'll just be like a very deep sleep for him." Edward suddenly started to panic about where he was and looked around with big, bold eyes trying to fathom out his position in the world.

"We remember that feeling." Jess offered, "We have been here for a very long time. Initially we were taken from Earth without *will*, but then grew to prefer it, so requested that we stayed."

"You jest. You prefer it in this place? There's no amazing nature or birds flying in the air. Do you no longer see butterflies or perfect, emerald, green grass? What of the beautiful lakes and fresh wind that blows about?"

Sue looked at Jess, noting his extremely valid points.

"Since you put it that way, I guess you're starting to sell it to me again." Jess looked saddened.

"I already miss it with the fear of remaining in this cold and lifeless place." Edward added.

Sue and Jess looked more panicked at this point and questioned their reasons for staying.

In deep justification, Jess took a deep breath and offered a valid reason, "We have helped here for so long, helping to keep many planets and some universes energised. In this space we can be healed just as instantly as your friend is about to be healed. In your time of the eighteen hundreds, there was innocent survival and hardship, but everyone stood together to keep one another in units of family and friendships, but in later generations the food became scarce, and so much of it was mass produced. Many crops were messed with chemically, so the natural health of humans wasn't as good. People were becoming addicted to clever gadgets that made them less dependable on one another. Addictions that weren't so natural were formed... so when we were gathered here to help, we felt safer here and part of a team of people who are now our family."

Edward had listened intensely with a concerned expression. "Are you all from the future? Where is this place?"

Jess felt as if his compassion was lacking after her heartfelt explanation. Her expression demonstrated disappointment, but upon studying Edward's face, she realised he was in some form of shock.

"Can you comprehend how your planet's future may have looked? It was getting close to how it looks here, on this globe."

Edward looked around, still bulging eyes, trying to take it all in. "You try to save other planets by working within this large centre?"

"We do. It works. We try to keep peace and harmony whilst providing a particular energy source."

"Have I been here before somehow?"

Jess looked at Sue with a large smile. "Are you starting to recognise something?"

"I believe I transported here a few times but cannot quite recollect all of this detail. The familiarity is uncanny."

"You have visited, but briefly each time. You transported to us through a very powerful source of power, but you were always called back by your wonderful friend."

A loud buzzing noise came from the futuristic bed that William led in, shocking Edward. He looked over with panic.

"It's okay, your friend is now cured of his injuries. We can see him now." Sue offered the direction with her hand.

The three of them walked over to his bedside just as the transparent lid seemed to reverse the action and tuck itself back into the side of the bed, exposing William on the flat bed. Edward looked down at his friend's face with concern, noticing the blood stains on the body of his clothing.

William slowly opened his eyes, recognising his friend's face and feeling excited about his own revival!

"Ed! How did I make it? I was left for dead! Did you retrieve the crystal?"

The two ladies chuckled innocently in the background.

William reached out to cuddle Edward with heavy slapping on one another's backs.

"How do you feel?" Edward was surprised at the instant recovery.

"I feel amazing! How did you do it?" William asked as he looked about at the clinical setting.

"That will take some explanation, but everything is very much alright."

William sat with his legs dangling over the edge of the futuristic bed.

He touched his chest, checking for any fresh blood, but knowing he felt absolutely fine anyway.

Edward looked over at the two ladies with a questionable expression. "What is it that we do *now*?"

Sue and Jess looked at one another, knowing what they needed to say but held back for a few seconds.

Sue started with the explanation, "you came through a portal with transportation that was created by beings from a different planet, who have infrequent access to your planet. Some humans calculated something unusual around that particular area, but it's not usually seen, because it works at a different frequency. That area was marked out by the use of huge stones that made up a circle with a leading path. Spreckley wanted you to find that particular zone to access the portal, combined with the energy of the crystal. The pyramid ship sits above the Earth's atmosphere, which is pulled down when requested by the power source of the crystal. Spreckley was able to send a gateway for access to *our* planet, hence the circular connection to the pyramid. The pyramid isn't usually seen by the naked eye with it being of a different frequency… Spreckley had full control over all activations, but the crystal was needed to fuel the power of the entire event, as it activates larger crystals by all of them connecting on your planet. We aren't meant to gain access to your planet for risk of being seen and interfering with the purpose of human life. Trion broke the laws by entering with a form of transportation and settling to a new life. Fortunately, he hasn't mingled much with the mass of the general public but has his own select army of people who are sworn to secrecy. Some people found his activation crystal amongst other crystals and transported it in order to sell or trade with, innocently."

Edward looked at William, understanding the trade of crystals for his wood.

"Where am I?" William's observations were now waking him *fully* to the present moment.

"It will all make sense in a while. Just rest for a moment." Jess tapped him on one of his knees.

"Are the crystals not meant to be on our planet at all?" Edward continued.

"There are crystals of your planet, but there are also crystals that Trion took from our place to hide within your place. That is why you must have had many unusual experiences with that particular one. The main activation one is very small by comparison to the others he stole." Sue explained.

"Can you get us back? Now that things are the way they are, will everything be safe for us?"

"They are safe at the moment, as he thinks you have gone, and that William has passed away. Trion is growing weaker by the day however, so he is expected to attempt to return to his home planet for a while to rejuvenate. Spreckley does his best to read his thoughts and keep an eye on his actions. Trion simply wishes to keep your planet under his control, but your planet is self-contained and easy to live freely on, in reality. People can trade a skill for food or one type of food for another type of food, dependant on what grows where. Making up a value with coins and paper can buy things outright, but it encourages greed and the wrong kind of focus. There is battle for fuel and other sources in the meantime. This started quite some time ago but certainly gets worse. People have forgotten this because a money system began for trade. Abundance is good, but control is bad."

"How do you understand our future?" William was catching up.
Time is complicated, but there are different timelines and dimensions. We can see these, where on your planet you're still in your early evolutionary years, which is quite heavy and dense. It will be exciting though as energy changes all of the time where you learn and grow. Your abilities will evolve over time, and it will all make sense on a gradual level. It needs to be gradual. *We* have advanced through Spreckley's teachings and with what we have been developing."

"Spreckley can read Trion's mind?" Edward focussed on that part.
"Spreckley can read the thoughts of humans, he can communicate with them too, through dreams, visions, and holographic methods."

"Holow-graphic?" Edward asked.

"A way of reflecting ourselves in our image, but a distance from where we actually are physically, or like playing a real-looking movie directly into the air, in front of your eyes."

"What?" William interjected.

"You're not ready for this information yet. It's okay. You were guided here by a long process, for good reason. The crystal needed to be retained by good people, for the power to be with those who will use it for the good of all of mankind. Trion is a thief who has interfered with your planet and trying to change it for the will of his own power and influence. He gets clever at escaping the clutches of potential imprisonment, but when we have an opportunity once again, he'll be captured and retained until we are no longer fooled.

The powers of the human have been suppressed in the meantime, as they have forgotten their own power. We need to influence and inspire as much as possible to have people remember their power so that they push back and regain the power of their own planet."

"How can you inspire our humble people from here?" Edward quite rightly asked.

"The beings such as Spreckley and Shayze, and many other of the good ones, have influential power from a different frequency that can communicate gently through people's minds without them fully understanding why they have certain thoughts."

"So, they can speak to people's minds, and they think that they are thinking their thoughts themselves?"

"That is correct. There is so much to teach you, but you need to decide some important things first.

We need to know if you wish to return to your normal life and live it out, or if you prefer to stay here and live a life like ours."

Edward spoke without hesitation. "I would like to return to the beautiful planet that I was born into."

"So would I!" William was only certain that he wanted to be with his best friend.

"Should you return, you will live your life out, but you may have enhanced abilities through hidden memories."

"That sounds good to me." William was sold on the idea.

"When the time comes that humans discover their power, the beings here will need enlightened ones such as yourselves to help to re-engage all of the crystals, as that will be the time that everyone will awaken to the full power of *their* power, mixed with the amazing energy of these crystals."

"Are you asking for our help?" William asked, feeling disappointed in the lack of reward despite the suffering and confusion.

Sue looked at Jess with a smile. Jess explained further.

"Your gift is immense growth in your mind and body for evolution beyond your imagination. If you help us, you will be able to create easily on your planet where others will still be trying to figure out your successes."

"I am still confused." William responded with a low tone, "We have been through so much, where I nearly died, and you're going to send us back to our normal lives with extra ability? Then you want us to help you when a particular time comes?"

"Only if you are willing. In each lifetime you will forget the one before and start a-fresh. Everything is freedom of choice in each and every life however." Jess offered gently.

"Will we still be able to work together? Ed is my brother in life. I can only do it with him." He looked over for a response.

"I would only do it with William." The confirmation came.

The two men offered one another an agreement with the link of their two little fingers.

"When the time comes, in a few lives ahead of now, your agreement between the two of you will have you both born into the same family as brothers. That way it is a gift in life with strength in numbers and abilities."

"Real brothers?" William grinned broadly.

"Indeed. True, brothers in blood and love." Sue offered this time.

"It is a deal then." Edward agreed for the two of them, "Although, how do you have the power to do so much? How can one make that happen?"

"It isn't *us* that decides. *You* decide with your intention. It is strong enough now that you will have enhanced ability to manifest from one life to another. This will make more sense when all humans evolve to a great awakening anyway, some faster than others with this."

"That is all too much for us to comprehend. Our brains need to evolve to even have any understanding of what you have just said."

"You can learn in time, don't worry, in other lifetimes. You will remember this adventure for a short while in this lifetime, unlike many who come here only to return without *any* memory of this place." Jess offered gently.

Sue and Jess knew of their lifetime, but also knew that they would understand from great teachers who had already walked the Earth if they were willing to look into it.

There was a moment of silence where they all looked at one another's expressions of confirmation.

"That only leaves one thing then." Jess broke the silence, "We need to get you two back to your home planet."

The two men grinned in joy at the thought.

"Spreckley may give you a set of instructions for your safety in the meantime, but everything should return to normal with a keen eye over you from here, just in case.

We just want to install a view of where the crystals lie in the Earth, so that it sits in your minds for time to come."

Jess set up some very technical machine, that looked like a transparent bed with lots of lines made up of light.

"This is a map of your planet. There are huge crystals of power that have been buried very deep within the Earth by Trion, as we explained. One is here, another is here, here, and here, with the activation one just within this circle of marked stones." Jess

pointed to different parts of the Earth that had drawings made up of light, mapping out the locations of the crystals.
"How are we meant to remember such parts when all we know is of our hometown?"
"Please do not worry. This will be in your subconscious for your entire lives from this moment forth."
"That is difficult to comprehend." Edward scrunched his facial features up in confusion.
"This is what we would expect at this time. You being here with witness to what you see, will be remembered, at the right time. Your planet will have more technology by then for you to locate them, but you won't need to. You will just have a *knowing*!"
"This is all too strange. We just need to believe you." William offered with politeness.
"That is a completely correct viewpoint to have. Well done." Sue comforted.
"So, what occurs now?" William felt uncertain of *all* action.

William stood, testing the strength of his legs, with much relief to witness a great feeling.
"Wow, I am well and truly healed!"
Edward was happy to see his friend back to full strength.
"Let us begin the process of getting you home." Sue offered.
Spreckley walked over to the group of four, offering a timely hello.
"Hello! Now, I know we look peculiar to you, and we know you need to remain calm, which I believe you have already adapted to really well, given all of the events you've both been through. Your planet and all of existence will be grateful to you in time. It will all make sense to you when you go through the circle of life. Right now, we need to get you both home safely. I have been monitoring Trion, and he seems to be getting rather weak. This means he should remain in hiding for some time with possibility of his return to his home planet. It should give you chance to settle back in and adapt once again."

William and Edward just stared at the features of Spreckley, wondering how they were managing to stay stable on foot. Spreckley knew they were calmed with an energy they wouldn't fully understand, so continued.

"When we return you home, you will remember some of your experience, but some parts you will naturally forget. You should be able to live your lives out without any further interruption. The crystal is safely in the ground, but I need to explain that you are both selected for the function of the crystal. This may be a little hard to understand." Spreckley looked over at William, "William, you are the activator of the crystal, as the crystal holds a particular energy and is drawn to you." Spreckley now looked over at Edward, really looking into his eyes. "Edward, you are the only one who has been accepted to move between the two worlds once you have intention to!"

"This we know, but it is wonderful that the confusion of it all is in fact real!" Edward confirmed, looking a bit nervous with his hands.

"Trion activated this crystal initially. In other words, he made it come to life. After leaving it alone for so long, he left it to fade out in power – or energy. This crystal needs energy interaction in order to continue to build a connection. Trion is mostly powerless with the crystal now, hence his weakening state. He needs the connection with *that* and *all* of the crystals, which has been lost. He will need to figure out a way to regenerate his own energy and the energy of the crystal. If the activation crystal is retrieved from the ground it will remain loyal to you both, only, but being in *his* hands will bring about a weakening to the power of the other crystals, and eventually a large source of energy will be taken from the Earth, leaving all intellectual life to remain at the same level of intellect and ability. This is okay, but the future of humans is all about evolution! *Evolution* means positive change and growth! You need to evolve for the greater purpose of the planet and for the recognition of your own power."

"I do not understand." William offered.

"How can I help you to understand?"
"Well, if the crystals were placed there by Trion, then without him having placed them there, humans would not have changed or grown anyway. When we change and grow will we get bigger and stranger?"
"There are already crystals within the ground of the planet, but Trion brought an alien source of crystal, which benefitted himself, but also interferes with the rest of the crystal life within your planet. He has messed about with your natural balance. To change and grow is to benefit from learning from within yourselves. It is about becoming aware of your powers and using them to the advantage of better ways of living and producing. I think this is the best way to make sense of it perhaps. The crystals are going to be *enhancing* all that you do."
"So, we had a natural balance of this so-called *energy*, with our *own* crystals, but Trion interfered with *extra* crystals that could cause us to either lose our erm, ev-olu-tion or enhance it. Do I understand this correctly?"
"That is a good understanding. For now, I have placed an invisible forcefield of protection over the *activation* crystal, with the intention to keep a regular eye on the area. Humans can walk through without even noticing, but the ones who are sensitive may feel *something*. Trion may attempt to retrieve the crystal, but his weakness won't mix well with the energy of the forcefield."
"I remain more confused than you may choose to believe." William stated, rubbing his eyes.
"All that you need to know is that we will be returning you, with the agreement that you return decades later, in another life, as brothers, in order to allow the height of a great awareness and recognition of power when the time is vital. For now, however, you deserve a life of great abundance back on your planet, which you shall receive."
"Perfect." Edward wanted to confirm his agreement.

"Just to clarify one final time in a slightly different way... There will be a heightened time of growth in energy, and a *knowing* of this, by the humans. Trion and his friends will try to stop humans from gaining their new power, with the use of fear-mongering. Trion will equally be afraid of potentially losing his control over the planet. This is when you will both be needed, as the powerful force of brotherhood mixed with an underlying understanding. I will communicate with you in ways that you will understand too, when the right time comes. That's why we need you to return later in decades to come. This is a future prediction based on what we can see is building over a period of many years. Humans will want their power, and their planet back once and for all!" William and Edward looked at one another in a puzzle but sticking to their agreement to help.

"Right! I have explained best I can for now. Let's send you back! I just need to warn you that you will have a few moments to prepare anything you choose before your minds will forget most of these pressured events. Choose your actions wisely before your memories return to how they *should* remember things."

"We shall forget this?" Edward didn't want to forget any of it.

"Your subconscious mind will have memories stored, but your conscious mind will not remember *everything*. There will be a short time given to remember for any future preparation you feel necessary." Spreckley winked at William, hoping to help him understand with some telepathy.

Present Time

"So, let me clarify all of this simply so that my startled brain is in line with *your* startled brain." Tom offered, "We were *kind* of brothers before, and we saved a crystal from getting in the wrong hands."
"Yup. You came across the crystal in a trade and discovered the healing abilities of it, and we had all of these crazy adventures." Tom and Ethan were studying the book in great detail now over an expanse of table space in Ethan's house.
"So, I was told about this map at the back, but that unusual person somehow made a holographic version of it too in front of my eyes. I know where the crystal is hidden! Are you brave enough to find a time to dig it up with me?" Tom pointed to the strange drawing at the very back of the book.
"Who is this strange being that told you about a map I would have drawn in the eighteen sixties? How are we even experiencing such weird things? I have a vague recollection of one of my dreams where I was actually putting this map together." Ethan then went into deep thought with his eyes closed.
"This is something that's turned my world upside down. I guess that must be how *you* feel too."
Ethan was responding with noises as he tried to recall a memory.
"I have it! I have it! I remember the dream! Hold on!" Ethan stood and ran from the table and up the stairs. Tom could hear his heavy footsteps and clambering around.
Tom wondered if they had both slipped into yet another weird time space where they were both kids stuck in adult bodies. They were on a new adventure now, bringing about memories of their imaginary childhood.
Ethan ran back to the table, standing with placement of a large notepad in front of Tom's eyes.

"Look!" He pointed, "I drew that very same image in this scrap book of dreams I was told to keep. The therapist suggested I keep a diary of dreams no matter how messy it gets."
Tom looked down to see an almost-identical drawing to the one in the ancient journal.
It was fun for the two of them to compare a modern scrap book drawing with a cheap ink pen – to an extremely old, thick piece of paper and smudged ink from a calligraphy pen. "I know where this map leads us to. I heard we're meant to protect this *crystal* that keeps being mentioned, but I don't know *how*."
"I feel the time is near with the dreams I've been having, coupled with that strange, tall lady hunting for the same things we need to protect. I feel she is connecting the crystals together somehow, since you told me about that person's description of how some have been hidden. It all makes sense with her request for the thing she was initially demanding at our door. She must know who we are!"
"Do you mean we've been in danger all along?" Tom sounded panicky.
"Don't worry! I have a sense we need to get to this place on the map very soon and the answers will come to us." Ethan seemed very confident, and somehow connected to some imagery in his mind.
"What's going on in your head brother?" Tom wanted some more detail.
"I can tell this lady is *buzzing* things up. I don't know what other word to use, but it's so that they can take the power of this planet and make it their own. I can sense her urgency."
"How are you getting this feeling and this knowing?"
"I think it's having read this book! It's bringing my dreams and the writing together. The book is reminding me of the events we had back in this previous time, and how there's been a battle between the human life and this other form of life, who brought this unusual power source here to control the planet."

"This is the kind of thing that *strange being* has been trying to say. We are in some kind of literal power struggle."

"That's it! You know that we need to keep this source of power in the right hands."

"This source of power was stolen from the person who has been guiding me. It's not meant to be on... or *in* the Earth."

"That's true, but different beings have been to the Earth and other planets interactively. Humans have been lied to for too long."

"How are we collating such strange information in such a short space of time? It's such a lot to take in from having such a normal life, to suddenly seeing things so differently."

"It's exciting! At least we have an amazing purpose that nobody else could ever have. Just picture it! We know things that nobody else knows. Well, as far as we know." Ethan chuckled.

"I guess. So shall we head on over to the area of the map today do you think?"

"There is an urgency, but how about we have a good night sleep first? I might get another telling dream, and we can prepare better. Watch-a think?"

"I don't know if I'll sleep knowing all of this is going on behind the scenes. I think we'll *both* need therapy after all of this. It's a lot to take in."

"So, you want to head out tonight and see what we can do?"

"Come on, it's got to be worth an adventure, even if we just get a good sense of the location of this thing."

"Alright brother. Buckle up. Let's head on out. I'll take my car but let me just get something more appropriate on. Help yourself to a drink for a minute." He moved away with his words, growing out of earshot.

Tom grinned with a huge sense of excitement and apprehension all bubbling up inside, still flicking through the old book, heavy-page by heavy-page. He then felt the two rings in his pocket and pulled them out, removing them from the envelope. He placed them carefully on the table, admiring their beauty. The silver was so old with such density. The gems, or crystals inside, glimmered in the light. They were both chunky rings from the time created. Tom knew they were for him and Rachel. He hoped the subject would arise, and the agreement on what was meant to be, wouldn't cause any issues between them. He wasn't assuming any action on relationships at this immediate time, however. It was simply putting some old pieces together in his mind, as if something needed completing from the past.

"I remember them rings!" Ethan spoke from the distance, "I remember making them! They were for you and your lady back in our *past* lives! I feel crazy saying that!"

Tom spun, not expecting his brother to get changed so quickly! He didn't hear his approach!

"I'm so sorry Ethan. I know we need to talk about these. They were comfortably inside the book when found. I don't know what to do for the best."

Ethan stood, looking on with a long stare.

"If I made them for you and your bride-to-be, then I am certain you are meant to keep them."

"It feels like some kind of closure on something unfinished." Tom offered with hope that he wasn't speaking out of term.

The rings caused a few moments of distraction for what they were actively setting themselves out to do.

Tom noticed the continual stare. "Perhaps if we leave these here with the book for now. We can look at that later."

Ethan stared on. "I can see myself making them with love for my best friend. I think I have this ability to focus on these snippets of views, like small reels of a movie in my mind's eye somehow. They come with feeling. It's quite distracting."

Tom stood now, trying to get Edward's eyes to focus on the world he currently existed in.

"Come on brother, let's go and find this area and see if we can unravel this strange crystal. It'll hopefully put a few things to bed so we can get back to some form of normality sooner rather than later."

"Do you think we could ever go back to normality after all of this?"

"Well, you need to get back to having fun with Tanya or sorting things out with Rachel. That'll bring you back down to reality."

Tom grinned with a cheeky mind.

Ethan gave a light-hearted chuckle, appreciating the thought of aid for focus.

They both slowly walked to the front door and found their way into Ethan's car.

His smaller, silver car had food wrappers and drink containers in all available slots and gaps that were unavoidable with Tom's feet and arms settling in.

Without word, the car moved swiftly through the streets, reaching the large area of green tourism space they were aiming for. Ethan parked up on a quiet side street that wasn't really agreeable with the local homeowners, but his thoughts were that it was after hours, without need for disagreement.

They both pushed their legs out to stand and quietly close the doors. Ethan led the pair of them over to the large tonne of rocks that formed a walkway, leading to the huge marking out of ancient stones.

"We're definitely in the right place." Tom whispered, looking up with hope of some continual light from the dawn sky.

They both walked on the uneven grass, preserving their ankles with the caution.

Ethan stopped abruptly, holding onto his chest in discomfort.

"What is it?" Tom felt instant concern.

"There was a lot of injury and harm in this area. I'm not sure this is a good idea. This could be a warning."

"If you think it's better to head back then I'll go with your feelings."

"Wait, wait. It's passing. I think I can ignore it."

"Maybe it's just stress." Tom offered without truly understanding.

"I feel like a tonne of understanding is entering my mind. It's so odd! Like a download of information from the past."

"You must have some kind of extra sensory ability, I'm certain."

"I'm thinking you're right. I'm not sure it's entirely pleasant though!" Ethan still looked slightly pained but ventured on.

They both felt some kind of magnetism in the air.

"Can you feel that?" Tom now offered, "like a change of atmosphere."

"I can certainly feel *something*."

Ethan went down on all fours suddenly as they neared the centre of the large circle of huge stones.

"Ethan, are you okay?"

"I feel a strong pull toward the ground. Hold on a moment…"

Tom watched on as Ethan attempted to crawl. He hoped this would be a moment they could laugh at later in time, since it was so peculiar.

"What are you doing?"

"I feel like the thing we need is directly below my position right now."

"It looks weird from here." Tom attempted to joke.

A strange noise came from only a few meters away, given their sensory perception, forcing the two of them to look ahead.

"Don't speak for a moment." Ethan whispered, noting a large, shiny object emerging from a huge grass mound.

In the slight distance, a very tall, thin person formed, looking like an eerie shadow. Just to the side of this person there was a hovering item, holding someone of weaker ability. As the two of them grew nearer, Tom and Ethan noted the familiar, frightening tall lady, with an unusual purple-shaded *being* sat in a hovering device that looked like a very advanced mobility scooter.

"Stay where you are!" Ethan shouted very bravely, instantly surprising Tom!

"You know that the item belongs to us! It is extremely advisable for you to finally submit it to us. You do not know the features or dangers of it." The tall lady offered, still looking as strong and as threatening as ever.

The shorter, less-abled *being* remained in the futuristic mobility aid, sitting silently, appearing relatively vulnerable.

"Have we known one another for many decades?" Tom asked with a tremendous amount of fear but curiosity.

"You know we have been intending on locating this power source for some time, but that you have been keeping it from us. It is time to hand it over so that we can replenish the Earth once again."

"It doesn't look un-plenished to us, so I'm not sure what difference it'll make." Tom felt very daring and cheeky given the threat.

The two characters in the distance held their threatening positions.

A rush of gold and silver swirls came crashing through the skies above, with a formation of Spreckley, appearing in a central position.

"Trion, you need to leave with your bodyguard and allow the Earth to evolve in the way that it's meant to. Just as evolution is set to become." Spreckley spoke just as he seemed to *land*, as if already rehearsed!

"There is no set result, as you know Spreckley. Choices are made, and paths in directions are changed all of the time."

"You and Bo came here without permission, interfering with humanity and all natural life here. You must now leave or once again be arrested, which I'm sure at your time of life, you would prefer against."

"Oh Spreckley, you know that I can replenish should your forcefield disperse as it should, and I regain what is rightfully mine. I'm not the criminal here."

Ethan took mental note of the *forcefield* word, realising the distance the two shady figures had retained wasn't of choice.

"In fact, the item isn't rightfully yours. It was taken from *me!* From *us!*" Spreckley confirmed some truths, "Another useful fact to know is that the crystal has since been programmed by these young men. That means *they* have the connection to the activation... and the power."

"They don't have a clue what they are doing! Just look at them!" Trion pointed, "Besides, what does it matter to you that I consume this very dense world? You know it isn't of any considerable significance to what *we* already know!"

"You are wrong Trion! This has an immense value to all of life no matter what the frequency. They have the ability to remember their true power after so many years of only knowing one way. What an amazing growth for them, and advancement of all *universal* growth. You've kept all of humanity in fear and weakness, not knowing of their true power."

Tom was stood with an open mouth at the scene before him, taking in the names, and picking up the summary of information. Ethan remained on all fours, looking directly at the soft grass, feeling a magnetic pulse in the ground, wondering how to obtain the source that appeared to be connecting with him.

Tom then looked at Spreckley, wondering if he was visiting as his holographic-self or if he had actually transported himself through somehow.

"Trion, why do you wish to stay on this planet when it sucks you dry to a point of lifelessness?"

"Because, despite it being so dense in the life forms, it's a planet we all want. It still holds nature and beauty, where others have been controlled by technology to the point of synthetic-ness. It has beauty of seasons and running waters, with animals of all sizes."

"Yet it is important not to mess with the process of the evolution of humanity, as beautiful as it is, we didn't pick this planet initially. We need to stick with the laws otherwise we are interfering with what was intended here."

"Save me the babble Spreckley. I'm tired of the useless discussions. We may change some form of evolution, but we may be creating another with this situation right now! Besides, Bo and I love it here. It's our life now."
Spreckley paused, obviously uncertain of the impact of his select cautionary words.
"The power of these crystals don't belong in your hands. They are part of the Earth now, as they integrate with the energy here, but they are no longer yours."
"In that case, they are no longer *yours* either, Spreckley! Why are you trying to control the outcome? What business is it of yours?"
"Our intentions are good, whereas your intentions are all about manipulation and control. We encourage peace and freedom, where you're driving people to become imprisoned."
"They don't *know* that."
"The universe knows *that*."
"So then why isn't the entire universe here to stop us?"
"Because they don't interfere."
"Whereas you do!"
"Oh Trion, this is going around in circles. You were the initial one who interfered by entering this planet unlawfully. You need to return to your planet, where your health matches your land; and at the same time, the right level of energy and equality returns to *this* planet, allowing *their* natural rights."
"I've had enough of this. Gather them all!" Trion instructed a few people hiding in the darkness, behind the hills, to do his dirty work for him."
The surprising new numbers outweighed Tom and Ethan, forcing Spreckley's image to move up through a transparent cylinder, up into the skies above, and out of view yet again.
Tom and Ethan were gripped by strong men, forcing them into uncomfortable positions with their arms wrapped behind their backs, as if arrested forcefully.

Another few strong-looking people came along with tools to dig the ground, forcefully digging into the Earth-space that Ethan was hovering over for the duration of the strange conversations. Ethan leant forward in anger of the action, feeling helpless, wondering why the forcefield wasn't repelling the people.
Another few people gathered, looking official to the tourist ground.
"What's going on here? This is meant to be a sacred place!"
The officials were also dragged away by this new army before they could speak another word.
Ethan and Tom were held in the same position as if it was intended that they witness the event first hand.
It didn't seem to take long for one of them to reach in and pull out an obvious crystal that glimmered in the palm of their one hand, with the now-moon-light bringing a greater spectacle.
Ethan and Tom were thrown to the ground, face first, as the crowd walked away, confidently moving back toward Trion and Bo.
"Thank you boys for your hard efforts!" Bo shouted as they all turned their backs on them, walking back into the shadows of the night.
"What?" Ethan grumbled under his breath.
Tom stood, looking wobbly, holding onto Ethan's shoulder.
They both walked over to the hole in the ground to witness the space they'd fathomed out.
"Maybe it's just meant to be. At least we can forget about it now. Whatever will be will be. We have the rings. That's an amazing gift." Tom offered.
"And the book!" Ethan added through gasping breath.
"The book! That's the evidence to our ownership, surely!" Tom proposed.
"Ah, let's not bring it all up again. Maybe it is just best to move on." Ethan concurred.

"We unravelled quite a bit. We had quite an adventure, right?" Tom smiled, hoping to comfort the two of them.
"I guess."

Ethan and Tom were shaking with adrenaline after a risky drive home. They both took to strong drink to calm their nerves, hoping to get themselves into an unconscious sleep-state. They both tried their hardest to swipe their minds of the events that were beyond anything *normal*.

Tom was the first to awaken from some form of unconsciousness, let alone a drunkenly-deep-sleep. He sat himself up, recognising the space not to be of his own home. He clutched his head with one hand, surprised that he didn't feel as bad as he thought he should have. He heard a similar whirl of action in the next bedroom.
Tom walked down to Ethan's kitchen, helping himself to a large glass of water. Upon lowering the glass, his brother walked into the room.
"I don't feel too bad, considering." Ethan offered first.
"Strangely, neither do I." Tom was surprised again by the two of them feeling relatively well rested.
"Tanya taught me how to make really good pancakes, I'll put some together for us. The sugar may do us good."
"That sounds like an amazing treat."
Tom walked over to the dining area which sat parallel to the kitchen. He closed his eyes momentarily at the bright light coming in from outside.
"I guess it'll be a sunny day today just for our sensitive eyes." Tom rubbed his eyes for comfort.
"It does seem bright this morning. What time is it?"
Tom looked at a clock on a nearby wall.
"It's only nine. We didn't disappear for that long."

"What time did we start drinking?" Ethan seemed to want some answers for their time in bed.

"I can't remember." Tom knew about as much as him.

Tom squinted his eyes and looked at the view through the window. It seemed a lot brighter than usual.

"Hey, Ethan, come and look over here!"

Ethan looked over at Tom, not understanding the interest he had, so walked over to the dining room table to look in the same direction.

"Wha'?"

They both stared at an amazingly bright aura coming from the garden.

"What is going on?" Tom asked in amazement.

Ethan unlocked his backdoor to get a clearer view, noting that the hole created for the pond seemed to allow penetration of extreme light from a deeper area of the ground.

They both stepped out, squinting their eyes at the brightness. Ethan started to pull the sand away from the edges of the plastic-moulded pond shape, allowing even more light to shine through. Looking at one another with the same thought, they both stripped the entire area of soil and the large plastic mould, eventually unravelling the top of a huge, clear, expanse of transparent crystal!

They both stared back and forth at one another's reaction as well as the site of the crystal.

"This all matches up with what Spreckley told me." Offered Tom.

"Heck, this matches up with *everything*!" Ethan unintentionally competed.

"Do you realise it's since Trion has potentially activated the little crystal?" Tom guessed it was the possible cause.

Ethan's thoughts were flying about, wondering what a potential threat this could be to their safety.

"Do we need to cover this up do you think?" He asked concerningly.

Tom looked up at other houses, wondering if they had caught sight of this immense light, or if they were also still immerging from their beds, assuming it was an extremely sunny day.
Tom started to act for the two of them and offered a fair coverage of soil over the clear crystal, doing his best to dim the unusual light as quickly as possible. Ethan joined in, hoping it was the best action to take, considering their new fears.
Tom caught sight of another bright light from the house and turned to investigate it.
"Ethan!"
"What now?"
"Look inside!"
Ethan turned his head to note yet another bright light coming from inside the house. They both ran indoors to note the light coming from the inside cover of the old leather-bound book!
Tom looked at Ethan before slowly unwrapping the cover to note the two rings gleaming brightly from the envelope – enough to make up for the one very large crystal!
"What's happening?" Ethan sounded uncomfortable.
"Please tell me you've got a dream that answers that question, because I don't know what this part is all about."
"Maybe all of the crystals are connecting somehow."
"So amazing!" Tom picked one of the rings up and placed it on his finger just out of admiration. Just as he did, he had a vision right before his eyes!
He noticed his arms as the strong, muscular forearms again, leaning over a large desk, watching a friend make the very ring that he placed on his current finger.
He watched as his friend gently tapped the silver into a wonderfully accurate shape, sitting next to a sign about a Lapidary poster of some type. He watched the work of his friend as he gently lifted an already-chiselled piece of crystal with a pair of tweezers and placed it into a concaved part of the ring created for it to sit within. He admired how his friend knew exactly what he

was doing, as his mind and fingers had completed this task many times before. There were now gripping parts of silver that he needed to place over the crystal to keep it in place.

He then watched on as his friend picked up another already-prepared silver ring and filled that with an already-chiselled blue crystal, completing the setting with small, silver gripping parts around the edges.

He looked at the two rings that were handed to him for approval. Feeling overwhelmingly grateful of the beauty of them, he felt excited about keeping one for himself and the other for his beautiful lady.

A faded calling of a voice filled his ear, jolting him back to the present moment.

"Tom! Where are you, man?" His brother's words came with a gripping of his shoulder.

"Oh! Sorry, but I think this ring told me something!"

Tom's eyes looked a little jaded.

"What do you mean?"

"Please don't think I'm crazy. I get a few of these weird moments that I don't understand."

"Bro, why would I call you crazy when my multiple dreams make some crazy sense?"

"True, true. Okay, time to be more open with things. We have kept things from one another for way too long!"

"So, the ring spoke to you?"

"Ha! I used the wrong words I think. I had a vision when I put the ring on! I've had some visions where I'm someone else with these really strong forearms. Like Popeye!"

Ethan chuckled slightly through the strange moment, feeling a sense of relief with the humour. This encouraged a bit of giggling time between the two of them, which helped them both to relax a lot more.

"Okay then, you had a vision?" Ethan encouraged.

"I sure did! I was that person with the Popeye arms again, and I was watching my best friend making these rings. I was really pleased with the results. They were made for two of us – my newly found lady and for... me!"

"So, the rings are meant for you and a lady?"

"Could you see anyone else in your vision?"

"I, I could see my friend's hands working so nimbly, so amazingly." Tom looked over at Ethan's hands and stood in shock.

"What's wrong?"

"You have the same hands *now*! I think my visions are of you and *me*! I can definitely confirm that *you* made the rings!"

"I'm a ring maker?"

"It all makes sense!" Everything came to Tom as if he was living in both worlds, feeling himself as he was presently, and feeling similar, but dressed differently, holding different circumstances in a previous time.

"So, the crystal in the ring seems to shine with the large crystal for some weird reason too." Ethan reminded the two of them despite the huge amount of information they were trying to uncover already.

"These crystals in the ring... they are a shard of the activation crystal! There's some kind of connection with it all!" Tom was recognising it all now.

"So, the rings have some kind of power over the big crystal in the garden?"

"Seems bonkers doesn't it?" Tom confirmed, "I realise I've seen this so-called activation crystal in a previous vision. The clear and the blue mixed together looks the same as these two rings if we put them together."

"But then what are we meant to do with this? What's the next move? I'm confused." Ethan was pacing between the dining room and kitchen now.

"I'm not sure! Maybe we could head back to the place we just came from."

"The circle of stones?"

"We could at least try."

"Should we have a big breakfast first do you think?" Ethan always wanted to prepare with food.

"I suppose we should have energy inside." Tom smiled.

They both ate breakfast with such speed as if they hadn't eaten for days.

Ethan and Tom left the house swiftly, and drove to the ancient stones of Avebury, aiming back to the main circle of structural stones, finding a small trace of the hole that the crystal was stolen from.

Tom held the envelope of rings with intention, allowing their location to gain distance.

"Here we are!" Ethan shouted, noting the lack of tourists for a change.

"Okay, here we go then. Worth a shot right?" Tom opened the envelope and placed a ring on his finger, offering the remainder to his brother, who copied the action on his own hand.

They both moved directly to the centre, noting an immediate humming sound building.

"What is that?" The hairs began to stand on Tom's arms.

"I don't know, but I hope it makes some kind of sense."

"Sense? When has any of this made sense?" Tom's tone was humorous with an attempt to keep both of them calmer than he knew they were feeling.

A rush of hums felt as if they were spinning around them. Bright lights came into their view, making them look down to note their rings had activated again somehow!

The hums spun in a circle, within the circle of huge rocks! Tom could actually see similarity to a weak wind spinning around them. The rocks of Avebury appeared to keep the momentum going! The view was similar to a tornado encircling them as they stood well, in the centre!

Tom felt a magnetic pull from the ring finger, guiding him to place his ring on top of the other ring, on Ethan's hand! As the two rings connected, a huge light surged downward into the ground, and then upwards into the highest viewed part of the sky! The word "frequency" came to Tom's mind. This confirmed that the energy was creating the right frequency, as it hummed around the stones, keeping the tornado-like view spinning powerfully, not impacting the two of them, amazingly! Tom and Ethan stood with their mouths open, uncertain of what to do, hoping the *nature* of this will continue to occur.

A familiar figure suddenly appeared at the external circumference, looking in at them. This was indeed - Trion!
He stood, looking in anger and frustration.
"What are you doing? You are interfering in the safety of your planet!" He spoke, looking powerful compared to the weakness he had previously endured.
Both Ethan and Tom stood strong, now staring at Trion, hoping they were safe within the strange circle of the spinning wind!
As they all stared at one another, the ground carried a bright, golden light upward, filling Ethan and Tom with an empowered feeling. An instant later, another golden light came from the highest part of the skies above, filling them with yet another powerful sensation. Tom and Ethan looked at one another to confirm the same feelings. Their rings felt vibrational, confusing them slightly.
"Stop messing with what you do not understand!" Trion shouted again from the external parts of the safe, encircling wind.
Tom and Ethan trusted their instincts, knowing somehow that they held amazing intuition. They both knew that Trion was now expressing extreme fear for the loss of his power, and just with that, the activation crystal that Trion must have had in his possession as he stood there – was powerfully magnetised into the centre part of the circle, joining forces with Tom and Ethan.

The activation crystal hovered in the air in front of Tom and Ethan's eyes! This felt perfectly right for their purpose.
An amazing view of all of their past lives flew into their minds at this point! Ethan saw himself as Edward, writing his journal and attempting to keep the secret close to his heart. He was strong and rugged with the same personality he felt he was as Ethan!
In the meantime, Tom saw himself (as he had recently experienced) with his strong arms. This time he could see and feel *everything* about himself, and although his clothing and skin looked different, he felt the same in his mind, with a lot less understanding of the current technologies of course. He knew that at this point, he was known as William!
They both went through the stages of the life they shared as good friends in the eighteen hundreds – the promise of brotherhood; the fun drinking times; the relationships they had, and the parties they went to. They witnessed the jobs they had, and how the crystals came to be in their possession in the first place.
The engraving of clues were now in their foresight, with every question answered within a few seconds!
Trion watched on, knowing that they had both woken to the truth of their lives. He stood angrily at the crystals connecting and creating a better energy.
Ethan and Tom felt the love of brotherhood and the love of their previous and current partners, bringing about them a powerful energy that spun within the wind around them! They suddenly understood the crystals and knew the successive action they needed to take. They both looked down at their rings, brightly shining, to the point of them squinting. The tiny metal grips that held the crystals in the concave space of the rings slowly unfolded, magnetising toward the activation crystal that was still centrally hovering! The two crystals that were secured within the rings were now magnetised toward the main activation crystal. The magnification was so intense that their fingers were pulled toward the main crystal now. The two crystals flew off the two rings and

immediately stuck to the central, activation crystal. Ethan and Tom dropped their arms and looked down to notice the rings were simply silver bands now, with sharp pieces sticking outwardly from the force of the gripping parts, having been pulled apart to relieve the crystals.

They all watched as the activation crystal hovered between them, in the air, becoming brighter and brighter!

The wind around them, along with the unusual frequency of humming slowed, making them realise that they needed to reach out to catch this activation crystal.

They were both correct, as this crystal fell into the two pairs of cupped hands.

The wind still whirled around them, with the momentum created by the rock energies.

Images of people in ancient clothing slowly unfolded before their eyes, as if those of the previous ages, from robe-wearing - to ceremonial wear, came to witness the great revelation of freedom! Some of them held wooden staffs, with others wearing interestingly heavy jewellery around their necks. Some of them had head dressings of various forms, with one of them wearing brown cloth and a side power of a strong sword, like a lone warrior. Another person looked like a native American Indian. Tom and Ethan felt something wonderful of the power of humanity regaining their freedom and power. These beings appeared to show themselves, in order to form a strength of support and wisdom.

Trion clearly began to lose his strength and power. He crumbled over in weakness now, leaning down on all fours suddenly. Tom couldn't help but feel sorry for him.

An image then came to Tom's mind. As William (his past self), he felt the pounding hits to his body, knowing that enemies were pummelling into him. They attacked him in order to attempt to end his life, drawing his blood, and leaving him to waste on the grounds, not too far from their current position. Tom now realised

that this was all about justice for himself after many decades of passing, with the newfound freedom and peace now remaining for the rest of humanity. This was all in favour of humanity literally reclaiming their planet.
The crystal glimmered with yet *another* unusual event.
A symbol was now forming on the crystal, as if being etched with a golden laser beam from the sun!
A circle spiralled inside itself, suddenly glowing, with a huge golden brightness. As the crystal remained hovering between the two brothers, they observed with open mouths.
The sun beam calmed after a few minutes, leaving a symbol on the crystal, that appeared to represent the sun itself.

The grass beneath their feet seemed to rustle and stimulate their feet now, making them both look downwards. A glow of colour filled their feet and lower legs, creating a rising haze of emerald green.
Tom was first to notice that another symbol formed on the crystal from this new, rising, green haze. This symbol sat at the base of the crystal and looked similar to rows of lines wriggling downward. Tom started to catch on with the event, seemingly creating an acknowledgement of the crystal - being accepted by both the universe and the Earth. If he was correct, this was being performed in a very spectacular fashion.
As the green calmed on the ground, as well as on the crystal, yet *another* symbol activated swiftly. A triangle *within* a triangle formed the shape of a basic star! This third symbol came to shine in an extremely bright, silver colour. As soon as the two brothers noticed this, a dark cloud covered the sun, creating a mild darkness. This seemed similar to the darkness of a full eclipse. This allowed an unusual view of two very bright stars beaming a strong, silver ray that hit the crystal with such force! A large blast of light caused everyone in the vicinity to cover their eyes swiftly.

As the light settled and the clouds moved along to permit normal daylight, everyone slowly revealed their eyes to a calmer scene.
Tom looked at Ethan briefly to monitor his expression.
They both looked bemused at the sight in front of them.
The crystal beamed with all of the symbols in unison now, omitting a calmer, beautiful spectacle of mixed colours of light.
Tom tried to study the lights and symbols and all surrounds, noting the entire ground around them was now glimmering brightly. He looked over at the surrounding view to see that some parts of the land held *extreme* brightness.
Within a few seconds this crystal gradually lowered itself to sit gently on the grass, with all lights now diminished.
Tom looked down and around to recognise a return to normal circumstances, with the only unusual sight being a bent-over *Trion*, on the outside of the circle of rocks.
Ethan decided to trial the touching of the crystal to see if it was safe to handle after the dramatic scene. He managed to pick it up and hold it in the palm of his hands. Tom, remembering his old self as William, reached over to touch the crystal to see if he could activate it, but it remained in the same state, much to his surprise.
"I think it's all over." Ethan offered the first sentence.
"I think so too." Tom sounded slightly deflated.
"Maybe our lives will return to some sort of normality now."
"It just seems to be the end of some kind of long era." Tom looked at the crystal, sitting in Ethan's palm, noticing the etching of the symbols, all within and around one another. He admired both the clear parts, and blue parts of this beautiful crystal.

Another familiar figure came into their peripheral vision.
Spreckley formed his image, not too far from the bent-over lump of Trion's body.
"The Inter-Galactic beings have witnessed this momentous event! I'm visiting in holographic form again in order to congratulate you. You figured out the final pieces in which to create the Earth in the

new frequency it deserves! This planet will now open up to the awakening of many minds, with peace, and immense abundance of all natural life. The crystals from our world have integrated with the crystals of the Earth in order to balance one another out for the benefit of *all* life here. We only have one final piece of action to fulfil."

Tom and Ethan looked at one another in concern, having assumed the drama had ended.

"Do not worry, the crystal will keep you safe now. The symbols represent the sun, Earth, and stars... all integrating and reforming through the power of the crystal energy."

"So, are we meant to just hide the crystal again?" Tom offered.

"We would love for that one final task, but you may find it an interesting challenge. Bo, Trion's partner, is still in great force, and will feel the change of energy across the land. She will no doubt aid Trion shortly and attempt to re-energise him by transportation to their original planet, but she will be a threat to the future balance of these lands if she is able to steal the crystal again. The crystal is vulnerable here with it being a known location, and we also need to hide the portal access, so there is an unpredictable point that I need you to place it within. Your phones today can provide the satellite navigation. I need you to place it in this *exact* location."

Spreckley allowed a connection somehow to activate Tom's phone that sat just inside his pocket.

Tom pulled his phone out to note his navigation application had been opened, and a location already, literally mapped out.

"Just follow it partly by car and by foot. If you need protection at all, the crystal still uses the command words just the same as you remember from your past lives. No doubt you're dazed and confused at this time, but you'll soon have time to allow the soaking in of information once this final task has been completed. It'll never be found again by any other, and we trust that you will both move forward without any revisit to this powerful object. It will lie in a place of calm with a perfect balance of energy output in the location I've given."

Tom and Ethan gave one another body language communication once again and acknowledged their task, hoping that they won't witness any further issues.

"Go well and you will prosper, literally. Within this new *frequency* on Earth, you will find things attract to you easily, so be careful of your thoughts and words." With that, Spreckley diminished from their eyes.

Trion left some weak mutters under his breath while Ethan and Tom watched his space, feeling no threat.

They both looked at one another to confirm their need to move swiftly.

Running back toward their car, they followed the linked satellite navigation screen, to discover that the location was within a busy, local town!

"Is this right do you think?" Tom offered.

"I guess we just need to trust it." Ethan stared, hoping they could get the location extremely accurate.

"This shows where to go, but not the exact location of where to *place* the crystal."

"I suppose we just need to go with the flow and see."

They pulled up at the nearest roadside to allow a walking distance. They walked nervously through some side streets toward this town, wondering where the location was by view. A large blue and white building appeared to be the place that was marked-up, but they didn't know where exactly the crystal needed to go.

"There!" Ethan spotted a beam of light from the greatest heights, fall down onto a piece of ground in the distance.

The light of the day started to fade already, making them realise how late it was becoming. Thankfully, the area seemed clear of people and crowds.

An unusual craft moved through the nearby sky.

"Oh gawd, look!" Tom pointed to a ship that had a very aerodynamic shape, such as a metal form of a long, thin triangle, with a small, raised shape to the rear for the navigator. The sharp point of the ship spun to face the two brothers, making their adrenaline pump so hard that they began to run toward the nearest building in order to hide!
They ran into the gap of a large basement car park and attempted to hide.
"What the hell was that?" Ethan whispered loudly as they crouched behind some wall space.
"I guess that must be the Bo character we were warned of."
"Unless it's a friendly ship and we're hiding for nothing!"
"What if it's spotted by the locals? That way we're kind of exposed!"
Tom spied between some barriers of a gap to note no view of anything in the sky now.
"Shall we creep back out to see?" He suggested with a nervous shake in his voice.
"I guess we can't stay here forever."
Just as they began their cautious walk, an obvious security officer walked out from a rear door, and into the basement car park area, shining a torch to the ground. He was tall, with a strong frame and very short, dark hair. There was no getting away from the fact that they were spotted.
"Do you realise you are trespassing here?" His deep voice matched his image.
They both shivered with the idea of his potential physical force.
"Our safety felt threatened, we do apologise for hiding here but we mean no harm. In fact, we were just about to leave now that we feel safer."
"What do you feel at threat of? I watch camera footage most of the day and just spotted the two of you running down here. If you're here to create issues you can think again."

"We're just leaving!" Tom shouted, wondering what threat they could possibly be to this person.
Tom grabbed Ethan and began walking purposely and determined to escape yet another threat. They looked ahead, then behind to ensure there wasn't a follow. When they spun to look ahead again, they came to the open air, clearing to witness the vehicle hovering just slightly above, with the threatening point of the triangle facing *them*, directly! They spun to run back in toward the less threatening security officer, who was keeping an eye on their departure whilst gradually re-entering the basement door to the building! He stopped in surprise to see the two men running back in his direction.
"Look up there! That's the threat!" Tom managed as they ran back into the deeper parts of the basement.
The security officer was halfway in the door when he stood in stiffness at the two men running towards him.
Tom ran past the security officer with Ethan in toe, not thinking of the consequences of entering a business centre without authority.
"Hey! You can't just come in here!" The deep, authoritarian voice didn't seem such a threat at this point.
The stairwell had a decorative glass side to it, making them feel exposed yet again, as Tom and Ethan aimed for higher ground within this large building. As they ran up the staircase, they felt vulnerable to being spotted, which was rightly so, as the same vehicle moved swiftly to point directly at them! Tom and Ethan took great gasps, trying to allow some form of breathing in order to climb to the nearest level in order to take a run into the internal parts of the building. The vehicle seemed to move so swiftly that they felt extremely exposed and weak to the super technology! A beam of weaponry, similar to that from a sci-fi movie ripped through a glass panel, penetrating the glass like a hot knife through butter, leaving such an accurate hole shape, both in the glass, and in the wall that fell within the same target line.

The two brothers curled up in the corner of a landing space between two sets of stairwells, feeling like two terrified and huddled mice who were about to be captured by a huge cat! They both breathed with great labour and felt their adrenaline pumping.

After a few moments, they both wondered if they could make a race for it, hoping to get to the next level, but knowing the speed of the vehicle had the advantage and expectation of movement.

"Maybe..." Tom gasped, "we could trick them by running down the layer of steps we just came from, and head back into the basement area for a while."

Ethan breathed heavily, attempting to reply, but needing a few more cycles of breath.

"What if one of us... runs up... and the other runs down." He managed.

"Oh gawd, isn't it better to stick together?" Tom was too frightened to part ways.

"Why do we have-to do such a dangerous favour? This is bloody ridiculous. I mean look at us, crouching down in the corner." Tom was growing angry and frustrated, beginning to build some warrior spirit.

Ethan felt the frustration build in his brother, making him fear for a reckless decision that Spreckley promised would be safe to do!

They both continued to crouch in the corner for some time when Tom went off tangent with his words.

"Did you witness your past life with me when we were at Avebury?"

Ethan grinned slightly, "I did. I was your great friend. Isn't it really cool, but weird?"

"Yeah. I still love the chunky arms I had." Tom attempted to encourage a bit of humour.

"When you think about it, our lives truly do make a difference for the next potential life we might choose, don't you think?" Ethan grew deep in thought.

"Sure, not only *that* but it makes me realise we can leave this one, and suddenly end up in another. Death doesn't seem to exist."
"Confusing, but…"
Another beam of attack came through a windowpane, striking a wall only a few inches away from their heads, stopping Ethan in mid-sentence! They both gasped with a slight call in terror, forcing them both to make an immediate run for it! They both stood and ran with all of their might to the next floor layer, managing to make it before the ship changed direction of view. Tom and Ethan gasped, looking back at their amazing escaping achievements!
"Let's run to the end of this floor to the fire exit and run down and back towards the car! It'll be the last thing they expect!" Tom offered as they moved through an open-planned office place. Thankfully there were only two late workers fixing their eyes on the brothers running through the main corridor. They seemed completely oblivious to any unusual noise or events. Tom realised their assumption of building security.
They both managed to run through to the rear fire escape and find their way back into another angle of the basement car park. Tom grabbed Ethan's arm to encourage him to a spotted fire exit gate, both knowing that they needed to depend on their *silent* body language. They both constantly looked at their surroundings for safety, managing to hide from their pursuer at this point.

The security guard to the building managed to gain distance to the room of security cameras, attempting to find the two intruders somewhere within the building, but all of the screens held a strong interference, confusing him. He ran up the nearest staircase, noticing the unusual damage to both glass and walls.
He called his contractual client to attempt to explain the strange occurrences.

Tom pointed to the beam of light in the distance, once they gained the external areas once again, assumingly remaining as their guide for the hiding location of the crystal.

They both crept behind a wall, pondering over the next plan, knowing that they needed to speak.

"How are we going to...?" Tom whispered.

"I don't know." Ethan interrupted.

They both scanned the terrain before the destination ahead.

"The beam appears to be over solid ground, just next to a wall that holds some garden design." Ethan was zoning in the best he could.

"Is it shining over some water drain cover or something?" Tom grew concerned about needing tools.

"I guess we need to get closer." Ethan looked up as he spoke, wondering how they would get there without literally being murdered.

"I don't think we can stay here all night. Do you think we could create a diversion? I wonder why we're led here if we were likely to be attacked. Surely the beam is seen by anyone looking, which is a huge give-away to any highly evolved being."

"Where's that Spreckley bloke when we need him?" Ethan looked up to the sky.

"I'm just going to make a run for it." Tom stood, holding a sprinter-starter pose.

Ethan held his arm back. "What if...?"

"I have a feeling I'll be fine."

Tom ran before Ethan could say anything else. His run was extremely swift, jumping from wall heights with ease, leaving Ethan looking about the skies in great panic.

Tom ran until he stood directly under the beam! He stood with his arms almost praising the light he stood within and below. He looked extremely comfortable with a look of tremendous achievement, breathing heavily with his chest movements. Ethan looked on wondering if he should run to the same location, but his fear superseded him.

Tom held the crystal, wondering where the *exact* location needed to be. Ethan observed his brother looking along the floor, looking confused. He decided to take a large gulp of air and run just as deliberately, to his brother, feeling like an animal of prey!

1st January 1861

Edward and William gradually came through a foggy mind, lying near one another on a grassy patch of land that sat not too far from their remembered homes.

They both emerged from vague memories, uncertain of how long they'd been lying there.

"Ed! What were we doing last night?" William asked, moving his head and eyes about, attempting to shake his mind of heavy-feeling cobwebs.

"Oh, this feels heavy." Edward responded, unsure of his whereabouts just the same.

They both rubbed their faces and readdressed their hair strands with their fingers, looking about in disbelief.

"Did we drink one of your weird concoctions again?" Edward was convinced they'd had a heavy drinking session.

"No, I don't remember... Wait, I do remember something." William's eyes grew large.

"Oh my, so do I!" Edward stood swiftly, shaking anything away from his trousers and jacket, "Did we have the same dream?"

"Was it a dream? If it was, why would we have shared such a thing?"

"Did we bury that shiny crystal?" Edward was recalling the stressful moments.

"I remember Spreckley saying that we would have several moments of remembering events before our mind would return to *not* remembering events. We need to hurry!"

"Hurry to do what? Edward wasn't sure of any tasks they needed to complete, and assumed everything had been completed.

"I feel it is important to make markers." William offered.

"What do you mean?" Edward was still rubbing his fingers through his hair.

"We need to go back to your place, quickly!"

"What is the mad rush my dear friend?"
"Trust me!"
William grabbed Edward's arm and pulled his sleeve in order to encourage movement.
They both ran, with Edward remaining slightly dazed trying to keep up, eventually reaching the shop front.
Edward found his door key within an inside pocket of his jacket out of usual habit, thankfully, given his current state.
They both went indoors, with William encouraging them both to have a drink of strong drink of tea.
"Now then," William appeared to take some form of control, "We need to attempt to leave some form of memory behind with the marking of things."
"I still do not understand."
"Let us begin with the book."
"What about the book?"
"You kept a strong diary of events."
Edward panicked, remembering the book in the hidden rock within the tunnel walls.
"I did. I hid it within the tunnel."
"That is good. What now of the rings with a small section of the crystal?"
"The rings sit in a safely made envelope."
"How do we remember where these items belong and the meaning of them?"
"I am certain you will remember the rings, and that I would remember my own journal."
"Well, I recall that our memories shall be cleared up to a point. We need to ensure all is memorable somehow."
"You are right! I need to document the latest map and the safety of the rings! Perhaps we could retrieve the book and update everything so that it is in current order."

"Now you are coming together Edward." William was pleased to note his friend's forming of consciousness, reminding of his times of returning from his *"crystal trips."*
"If I may take you to the place of the book and bring it back here, we could agree on what is required."
William was satisfied, as they both sipped their teas swiftly with a plan to rush to the tunnel, to regain access to the book and rearrange everything to their agreed desire.
Within a few minutes they could both tell that they were ready for their immediate adventure.
The two of them walked swiftly over to the green area that gained access to the tunnels within the area of the castle construction parts.
Edward guided the two of them to the marked stonework, pulling the heavy part away to access the hole which was a wrist-length grip away to obtain the book.
William was obviously impressed by Edward's efforts to hide the book, giving words of genius action!
They both carried the heavy book back to the shop to make the next set of plans.
The book sat heavily on the table now with the two men gazing and working through their ideas.

"The crystals within the rings may have some form of connection, with it being part of our crystal, so we need to keep them as safe as possible. Do you think?" William suggested as he took a fresh look at the rings in his palms.
"Yes, that is a possibility. We also need to form a clear map of what we were shown. The location of the stone formation that had the portal area – as they called it. Also, the location of the large crystals that we saw. Can we remember all of that? It feels fairly fresh to my mind to me." Edward answered his own question and began work with his calligraphy pen.

William leant over on his elbows, feeling the strong wood of Edward's worktable, observing his writing efforts and drawings. Edward finalised the drawings and felt successful with his complete design. He placed his pen in the ink pot and thought for a moment.

"I shall sit the rings within the envelope I made and place them inside the book."

"Good effort. Could you leave a marking somewhere otherwise to remind us of the location of the book itself? I was very impressed with the marking you carved within the tunnel."

"Do you hold any ideas as to what I could scribe, and where?"

"I have considered already, two squares together to form the appearance of a book. Perhaps your name above the drawing of these two squares that make the shape of the book."

They both rubbed and held their chins in thought.

"A marking ideally needs to be in a place we are likely to visit time and time again. Then we could leave the markings that are on the crystal to match things up to make sense if we can find both items."

"We don't want to make things too confusing, but that's all a good idea somehow. Finding a place for markings is the tricky bit. This building or your home appears to be the most likely option for relocating things."

"How long do you think we will retain our memories?"

"I think we need to focus on doing what we need to, in this very moment, before we even attempt to fathom our time of remembering."

They both agreed with their eye-locking and thin smiles, continuing to plan to leave marked messages to keep the memories alive.

Edward wrote some detailed messages inside his journal about how everything came to *be* up to that very moment.

He finalised his actions by placing the rings that he created into his homemade envelope, and then sat them inside the cover of the book.
"Do you think that will be sufficient for the book?" Edward wanted reassurance and agreement.
"Absolutely perfect!" William was very pleased.
They both stood in preparation to return the book now.
"I just need my penknife if we need to scrape anything into rock." Edward remembered the useful tool.
William looked in agreement and encouraged their needed movement.

They both gained the same distance to the tunnel once again and carefully placed everything back in the same location with the disguising rock that formed the construction of the tunnel anyway. Edward enhanced his markings on the heavy rock to finalise this part of their plan.
"Now to leave some markings to find *this* location." William confirmed.
"Shall we scrape some words on that large rock that leans upon your entrance at your *house*?" Edward viewed a rock in his mind that sat to the side of William's front door.
"Good idea! I shall view that upon entry every single day."
"We need to get there swiftly."
And swiftly they marched to reach William's home, focussing on the path that led to the rock sitting at the side of his entrance. Edward removed his penknife, reaching down to sharpen the edges on another small rock nearby.
"That is a fantastic tool." William observed the length of the blade to be of great use.
Edward thought for a moment before cutting deep marks into the shape of a book, scraping in two rectangles right next to one another. They both admired the simple symbol, about to create something else.

"How about the two of our names?" William offered.
Edward moved in again to scrape the names of "Edward and William."
"I think we need a hammer and chisel in order to get a deeper engraving." Edward suggested.
William unlocked his front door to gain access, shortly returning with a hammer and chisel.
This allowed a much deeper engraving, to the pleasure of Edward's results.
Edward added some more details, looking up occasionally for William's approval, which was instantly given with every single glance. They needed something to direct them to the tunnel area.

Edward stood in admiration of his own work and then moved to glance across the view of some hills in the distance. Across many green fields and rising to steep hills, sat a monument, apparently in memory of a historical figure.
"How about another engraving around the base of that monument in the distance?" He stared in the direction he was suggesting, giving William some mutual inspiration.
"If you think it is a good idea? Do you believe it will add strength?"
"Perhaps, if we need to leave clues for another beyond our lifetime."
William grinned in instant agreement.
They both walked swiftly through a long, old Roman pathway that led them to the top of some beautiful green hills. At the peak point sat the monument.
Edward found a useful spot to create some useful markings with the heavy hammer and chisel that he trekked with. He created the book drawing and marking of his name. Afterwards, they both admired the amazing view of hills and shades of green.
"We live in a beautiful world, don't we." Edward gave more of a statement rather than a question.
"We are extremely fortunate."

They both took a slow walk back down to the main cobbled streets and back into their local locations, looking a bit cold with the warm air leaving their breath.
"Shall we stick together for now?" William wasn't sure how their minds would be and wondered if they needed company for one another.
"You are more than welcome to sleep on my comfortable sofa." Edward preferred to offer first.
"I do wonder how we shall feel after one night of sleep."
"Do you think we have done enough to recall our circumstances?"
"I certainly hope so."

The two of them walked casually over to Edward's premises attempting to relax with a fresh brew of tea.
The day grew dusk, and they both fell into a deep sleep.

Present Time

They both stood together now, feeling as bright as the beam they were within. Their chests expanded and contracted with the large gulps of breath, partly through running-recovery and partly through fear! Somehow they both felt extremely safe within this large silver beam of light that seemed to appear from heights they could never understand, despite all of the so-called Sci-Fi movies they'd ever seen!
They both looked continually up and down, trying to figure out the next move.
A tone hit both of their ears, like a strong frequency that spun around them. The crystal's symbols shone brightly in their unique mix of colours.
The two brothers looked at one another feeling a sense of déjà vu. The familiar craft moved swiftly to meet the location they were in but appeared powerless as it hovered in observation.
The brothers looked down at the crystal that sat in Tom's hand, and occasionally back at the aircraft to keep tabs on the behaviours.
Tom and Ethan both observed that the ground below them had a water drain cover that was slightly loose.
Ethan decided to crouch down and lift the cover with surprising-ease, which created a vibration in the crystal that remained in Tom's hand. They both looked at one another in confusion.
A wind grew around them and mutually around the crystal. A levitation of the crystal occurred, seemingly making a decision for itself. It rose to eye level and then slowly lowered itself into the drain. The crystal went very deep into the hole, becoming a smaller beam of light with the distance. Tom and Ethan were both staring at the strangeness of this location. When the light of the crystal became a single dot, the cover of the drain dropped and sealed itself completely. The drain appeared to melt itself into

another form of metal which blended with the pavement surrounding this section. They both looked down to note a beaming light from the entire ground, meeting with the beam of light that came from above. The light spread across the ground. It shone so brightly, filling the entire space around them, and beyond.

Everything was so white that they could only see one another, but they both looked extremely glowing. They looked at their own hands and feet, noting star-like beams coming from themselves!

It took a few minutes before the glow calmed, followed by *bubbles* of light which seemed to drop from the sky.

The two brothers looked about now, wondering what this fresh view of life was before their eyes. Everything looked amazingly different! The plant life literally glowed with life, the sky seemed a more vibrant blue, the air felt lighter and fresher, and the birds flew freely, with fresh songs.

Tom watched a larger-than-usual butterfly move past his eyes. "What just happened?" Tom managed to speak for the first time in a while.

"I don't know, but everything seems so fresh and alive!" Ethan's voice sounded slightly whispered.

"The sky is clear of all planes and that *weird* aircraft." Tom checked in all directions with his mouth open at the amazement.

A few people walked out of the surrounding buildings, looking up to the sky and around at the plant life that was originally sparce, given that it was in-fact a fairly built-up town space. Plants appeared in abundance, but within the beds of soil that were created between the buildings and surrounding deliberate pathways.

Everyone looked bemused, watching on in amazement at the immediate transformation!

Tom caught sight of Spreckley's hologram, moving towards them from a distance.

"Look! It's Spreckley! Perhaps he will explain what's just happened."
Ethan's eyes grew, hoping for an explanation, despite feeling carefree and joyous!
Spreckley grew close now and spoke without hesitation. He appeared not to worry about any other observations of his presence.
"Well done to both of you! You have brought about you a New Earth! That of which all of humankind and nature deserves! It was all for the greater good, where the crystals could all connect in the *correct* energy, with the power of the *love* of two great brothers! The old Earth has now gone and all of those who were instigators of a slow death of all natural systems have been left behind in a frequency that can't be seen by those who are within this newer, brighter, more vibrant, and loving energy! You are all safe now, with love and harmony until the end of time."
Tom and Ethan stood open-mouthed at the words.
"Do you mean good has conquered the bad somehow?" Ethan managed.
"People have different terms for it. Some would say the Matrix has been lifted or released. Some would say there has been an intervention that couldn't be comprehended. Others would say that there are different frequencies that we have brought about through ultimate manifestation. It all depends on a person's perception."
"I feel lighter." Tom offered.
"You are lighter bodies, with an abundance of fresh, living plant life and the freshest, purest air and water. You are away from the density of the other frequency that Trion and his army had control of with intention of conquer and control."
"How will others understand what we understand now?" Tom asked, still amazed at the surroundings.
"Observe and you will see! Have fun! All you need to know is that things are very different. Things are easier to create and grow. You

will hear and see things from one another without having to speak. In this frequency you will see yourself and one another as lighter beings. You will be able to use energy and communicate in so many ways! Have fun and *rediscover* yourselves!"

"Is this what we came back to this time for? I remember everything about my past lives." Tom felt this was an important question.

"This is exactly what your purpose was. The New Earth thanks you with her beating heart. You will see!"

And with that, Spreckley's hologram dispersed, making Tom and Ethan feel a form of completion.

A familiar figure moved toward them from a distance. Tom recognised Rachel, raising a hand to encourage Tanya to follow her from a short meter away. The brothers were confused at their sudden arrival!

Ethan expected to feel a sense of guilt for recent events with the approach of the two ladies, but he felt tears of love fall down his face. Rachel and Tanya both ran to Ethan together to give him an equal hug, and then looked to Tom to give him an equally unconditional, loving hug.

"We understand things now. Our previous lives have been shown to us, along with everyone we have come into contact with on our way to find you both."

"You've seen your past lives?" Tom asked with surprise, thinking they were the only ones aware of such things.

"People are calling it a great awakening, as if something big has fallen and allowed the truth to come through." Rachel offered.

"That's a lovely representation of it all." Ethan felt an intense sense of joy fill him.

Tom looked at Ethan and then back at the two ladies, with everyone understanding his thoughts on their past, knowing of one another in a deeper sense.

They instantly understood their love for one another and simply loved unconditionally without judgement. Their understanding of human nature was greater than they ever could have imagined.

"There's something that I need to say now that we realise what we *currently* realise." Tom wrapped an arm around Rachel's shoulders before continuing, "We all depended on our past lives in order to get this far, and our future lives depend on our present lives in order to evolve."
"Wow!" Ethan responded, "Our lives *are* dependent on ourselves and one another."
"No matter what we believe, we are all love, and we are all one." Rachel offered.
"How have we suddenly come to know this?" Tanya asked in slight confusion.
"I truly do not know, but this is an exciting time for all of us to discover. Perhaps for what is *yet* to come!" Tom smiled with a knowing that everything will work out to be perfectly fine and that everyone will navigate their way through this new world with a fresh excitement!
Joke conversations began between them.
"So, I was William, and you were my Eleanor." Tom confirmed with Rachel, "I was meant to receive commitment rings made by Edward, who is my brother, now Ethan!"
"And yeah, I was Ethan who was with an Ann, who I remember very clearly."
"I was Ann, but I look very different now!" Tanya offered.
"So, what do we do now?" Tom asked.
"Who says we have-to do *anything*?" Ethan offered, "We are free without commitment!"
They all chuckled with genuine joy without the feeling of confines or ownership of one another, knowing they were all light beings set simply to enjoy the abundance of this new life!

"You know, there is something I recall from the past that wasn't completed, when we were all together in the eighteen hundreds." Tanya added after a mutual time of contemplation.

"...And what was that?" Tom asked.

"We didn't finish our Christmas celebrations!"

They all recalled the drama, and splitting of circumstances, causing some light chuckles within the group.

"Well then, let's start our new lives with *that*!" Ethan added.

"Merry Christmas!" Ann shouted, grabbing the nearest hand to encourage a walk in a fresh direction.

The End.

EJT

"I hope you enjoyed this adventurous book!"
- Emma Jayne Taylor

Other Books by Emma Jayne Taylor: -

Fiction: -
The Teenage Defender.
An Alien Poked Me.
The Spiritual Prophecy.
Eternal Love and Protection.
Autobiography of a Vampire.

<u>Non-Fiction: -</u>
-Positive Programming:
The Secret Key to Releasing Anxiety and Finding Internal Happiness.
-Positive Programming, The Power of Thought.

www.ejtbooks.com

Emma Jayne Taylor has been an established author since her first publication in 2009!

Emma began writing to use her imagination productively, as she always had a quirky way of expressing this in cartoon drawings, and bed-time stories, provided to her siblings when growing up.
Writing books seemed a natural progression!

She is qualified in Holistic Therapies, Fitness Instruction, Foot Care, Adult Teaching and Management.
Emma is also a second degree Black Belt in Martial Arts, a Meditation Teacher, and a Reiki Master.

Emma has a natural talent for writing. Her imagination coupled with her life experience, has an amazing impact on her chosen subjects.

"I am writing, and writing is me!"

EJT

If I am a light *being* just experiencing this manifested body, then I am free wherever I be!

Printed in Great Britain
by Amazon